SEARCH

SEARCH

A NOVEL OF FORBIDDEN HISTORY

JUDITH & GARFIELD REEVES-STEVENS

THOMAS DUNNE BOOKS

ST. MARTIN'S PRESS ⚏ NEW YORK

This is a work of fiction. All of the characters, organizations, and events portrayed in this novel are either products of the authors' imaginations or are used fictitiously.

THOMAS DUNNE BOOKS.
An imprint of St. Martin's Press.

Book design by Jonathan Bennett

Library of Congress Cataloging-in-Publication Data

Reeves-Stevens, Judith.
    Search : a novel of forbidden history / Judith and Garfield Reeves-Stevens.—1st ed.
        p. cm.
    ISBN 978-0-312-37744-1 (alk. paper)
    1. Human beings—Origin—Fiction.   2. Geneticists—Fiction.   3. DNA—Research—Fiction.   4. Conspiracies—Fiction.   5. Secrecy—Fiction.   I. Reeves-Stevens, Garfield, 1953–   II. Title.
    PR9199.3.R428S43 2010
    813'.54—dc22

                                                                                2010020607

First Edition: August 2010

10 9 8 7 6 5 4 3 2 1

For John Bullicz
and for the treasures he left behind—
Adam, Justin, and Robin

What we call the beginning is often the end
And to make an end is to make a beginning.

The end is where we start from.

—T. S. ELIOT

SEARCH

CORNWALL 7,312 YEARS B.C.E.

When it was known that the last of the shadowmen had sailed from their stronghold at Kassiterithes, the people of the oak began their attack, and even the innermost walls of stone were breached by dusk of that first day.

Fields of wheat blazed beyond the wooden stockades that formed the outer walls. The flames sent thick ropes of black smoke to dim the setting sun, bringing on night too quickly and too soon.

The bronze swords and battering rams of the oak people smashed through interior doors never meant for defense. Their torches set fire to the blasphemous tapestries torn from the walls. The library of scrolls and sewn parchments and map rubbings from the Hall of the Navigators itself became ash.

The shadowmen's followers scattered, rushing through supply tunnels built into the cliffs to avoid the winter snows. Some escaped that way. Some did not. Unarmed, those that were captured were savagely cut down. Their heads were carried on spear points, and there was no reason for it but hatred and fear.

By the time the stars shone weakly through the pall of dying smoke, the slaughter was over. Blood slicked the cobbled passageways, and desperate handprints smeared smooth stone walls, each block so perfectly aligned. Sword and axe scored intricate frescoes, erasing the story record of those who had built this place and how they had come here. Braziers in the great halls were overturned, and the intricate plumbing of clay channels and pipes shattered, so that fire-lit water spilled freely from common baths and latrines as if the crashing sea outside were already returning to reclaim its own.

In the end, after mutilated bodies had been heaped on burning pyres, only one last thing remained to be done—find the treasure that all men knew was hidden here.

The leader of the oak people, chieftain by blood and by combat, began the search, his sword sheath still dripping red. His full russet beard was braided with the knucklebones of adversaries he had killed in earlier battles. His pale cheeks were daubed with ocher mud. His leggings, foot wraps, and stiffened chest plate were made of deer and bear hides. The bark-and-tinder torch he carried high, wrapped in cedar cord, sputtered loudly, sending hissing droplets of rendered fat to sizzle on his scarred forearm without his notice. All he could think of was uncovering the secret trove that would enrich his power and ensure it would pass down to his sons, and to theirs.

At the farthest point in the deepest passageway, he found the carved pair of doors he searched for. As the stories had told, they were bound by iron bands and were themselves made from thick oak planks carved with oak leaves, colored green and red.

That the defilers of his land had dared to conjure the essence of the sacred tree enraged the chieftain. The oak was painted on his chest plate in deer's blood and charcoal, identifying his line and his kin. It had no place here.

He kicked at the doors, and they sprang open. All the stories said that the shadowmen's greatest treasure would be found here, but even this vault was undefended. What fools the masters of this place had been.

As he stepped into the arch of the doorway, the chieftain saw the pale amber flicker of an oil lamp. Instantly, he drew his sword, eager to kill again.

But only a follower waited within, head bowed, hands clutched to her chest in subservience. Her hair was the color of dried grass, and her skin was as pale as his own. Her telltale white tunic, hemmed in thin strips of purple cloth with strands of purple string at each corner, was the mark of one of their concubines. Once, she'd been a child from his own village or another nearby, given in trade years ago. Despoiled, she was worthy now only of death. He stepped forward to dispatch her.

Then he hesitated, awed by this room.

His eyes fixed on the domed ceiling, more than twice his sword's reach above him. In the light of his torch and the concubine's lamp, he saw the gleam of hundreds of small disks of silver, their arrangement matching some of the patterns of the stars at night. The circular, plastered wall beneath was overlaid with other patterns: swaths of brown and green against blue, cut by black lines that arced across the blue from point to point. Why anyone would do this made no sense.

Contemptuous of what he couldn't understand, the chieftain scraped his sword across the wall nearest him, destroying the profane art, then thrust his torch at the silent woman. She retreated, seeking refuge behind a round stone table set in the center of the vault.

The chieftain's interest quickened: The table's twelve inscribed wedges each held an object. He slashed his torch across the table, spraying fat and burning sparks of tinder, then growled in sharp frustration. Only one of the objects looked valuable—a square of gold a hand-stretch across and three fingers thick, with the death's-head face of a shadowman embossed upon it. The other objects were common: a lump of pitted rock, a long wood dowel jacketed in tin and fitted with a slender haft, a coiled and knotted rope; craftsmen's tools, nothing more.

With his torch he backhanded the tin-wrapped wooden dowel, and from the sound it made when it hit the floor, it was hollow, weak—useless. With his free hand, he took the gold square, at once realizing by its lack of weight that it wasn't even solid. Instead, it was a pile of gold sheets, held together on one side by cords of sinew.

Growing anger sweeping through him, he flipped roughly through the thin layers of gold, finding only a different, meaningless pattern on each, some like the ceiling stars, others like the pointless shapes on the painted wall, and almost all bordered by rows of small symbols of no meaning to him.

"Where's the rest of their treasure?" he demanded.

The woman's voice was steady, but her eyes showed fear as she answered in the language of his own people. "This is their treasure."

The chieftain let his rage explode. He slammed the worthless stack of golden sheets on the table and shouted at her. "The shadowmen had a ship. My sons watched them load it. They took no treasure with them. Where did they hide it?"

"This is all there ever was." She dared meet his eyes again. "All that's needed."

"Liar." At least he'd found gold here, as paltry an amount as it was. The concubine might know of other vaults. He edged around the table, slowly swaying his sword and his torch, each a snake poised to strike.

The woman backed away from him, her hand grasping at something that hung from her neck on a leather cord.

It was the hated symbol of the shadowmen—a cross formed by a circle above a diamond sail. They painted it on the sails of their ships. In their temples and circles of quarried rocks, they carved it out of stone. The woman's cross was silver, though, and could be melted and reworked into a proper symbol worthy of sacrifice to the spirits of the green.

"Give me that! I'll make it serve the true gods."

"Not my gods." The woman's back was against the wall.

The chieftain stepped closer. "You serve theirs?"

"They have none."

Fearless as he was in battle, the chieftain felt a thrill of unease in the presence of her sacrilege. "Then there's none to save you or them." He raised his sword, and only then did he hear the faint rasp of a foot on stone and turn his head to the open doors just as the spear flew at him.

It struck his unprotected side beneath his uplifted arm, and he grunted, dropping his sword, his chest pierced by a thunderbolt of icy cold.

Sword arm useless, he toppled sideways against the curved wall, his torch sparking against the floor. With his other arm he strained to reach around and yank the spear free. Because of his girth and his chest plate, his trembling hand closed on nothing.

In the failing light of the torch and the glow of the oil lamp, the chieftain could just make out the two figures who now stood over him. The woman and—a youth. The spear-thrower. A stripling not yet grown had felled a chieftain.

Even worse, his killer was one of them: shadow-dark skin like no man of oak, black eyes narrowed by lowered lids, hollow cheeks and flattened nose.

"I saw you leave," the chieftain wheezed, each breath an agony. "All of you . . ."

"They returned to their home," the woman said. "To the White Island."

3

Uncomprehending, the chieftain watched as she pulled apart the circle and the sail to reveal a slender silver blade. "Then who is . . ."

"My son." She put the blade against his throat. "The shadowmen have no gods, because they are gods. And they gave us their bond they will come back to save us."

"My sons . . . their sons . . . will avenge me," the chieftain gasped as he felt the bite of the blade, then nothing else as the false stars spiraled into darkness and he died thinking only of his sons, their sons, and vengeance.

But his body was never found, nor was the treasure understood.

Until the day the gods returned . . .

ONE

"Is that human?"

David Weir was dying, and the reason was on his computer, even though he didn't understand it. His finger moved reflexively to strike the key that would blank the screen, but he stopped himself. *Too late.*

"Sorry, ma'am. I didn't know anyone was still here." He turned, covering his surprise. It was almost ten on a Friday night. Last time he'd looked, all the workstations in the lab's open office space were empty, computer screens dark. He'd been so lost in his search, he hadn't heard approaching footsteps—unusual for him. His mother used to say he had better ears than a dog. As a child, he'd been able to detect his father's pickup make the turn onto their street five blocks away.

"Budget hell." Colonel Miriam Kowinski hefted the thick green binder she carried. From his one year's experience as a civilian technician in the Armed Forces DNA Identification Laboratory, David knew those two words were as much of an explanation as his boss would be giving him.

The colonel leaned forward to peer more closely at his screen, then frowned. "Mitochondrial DNA. But some of the markers are wrong."

"It's a reference sample." The lie came easily.

"Chimp?"

To the untrained eye, the electrophoresis patterns on his screen would resemble smeared, ghostly photographs of banded worms lined up side by side, some sections dark, some light, with a scattering of small numbers and letters running to either side, spelling out gibberish. Kowinski, though, wasn't just another army bureaucrat. She was a trained forensic biologist. It would be foolish to underestimate her.

"Closer to human. Neandertal." David held his breath, gambling that the colonel's expertise didn't stretch to extinct hominins.

"Really."

"Yeah. A twenty-nine-thousand-year-old Neandertal baby. From the Mezmaiskaya fossil."

"Is this a personal project?"

David knew why she asked. The lab's primary mission was to identify the remains of American military personnel through DNA analysis, not just for present conflicts, but for wars past. Beyond that, if resources and personnel were available, the lab could use its expertise to aid outside researchers in cases of scientific or historic interest. It could also help other government and law-enforcement agencies carry out drug tests, develop forensic evidence, even determine parentage in child custody cases.

However, "personal projects" were just that—personal and unauthorized. Illegal.

"No, ma'am. It's part of that new quality assurance protocol I'm developing."

Colonel Kowinski regarded him impassively. She'd folded her arms over her budget binder, holding it close. Despite the late hour, her olive drab jacket was still buttoned and crisp. Her sleek salt-and-pepper chignon might as well have been molded from plastic, not a hair escaping.

"Go on."

David couldn't tell if his supervisor wanted to hear more because she was interested or because she sensed, correctly, that he was lying. Either way, he felt ready. The old saying was true: Imminent death did have a way of concentrating the mind.

"The lab's been collecting DNA from every recruit since 1992. That's just over three million samples."

Kowinski tapped her budget binder with a short, polish-free nail. "I'm aware of the statistics."

"Well, statistically, there's always an error rate in sequencing DNA samples to create a genetic profile."

The colonel said nothing, and David continued. "Out of three million samples, we can estimate a few thousand of our profiles will be incorrect. Since it's expensive to repeat the sequencing of all three million to look for just a few flawed results, I'm hoping a mathematical analysis of the profiles in our database will find the errors instead."

"The Neandertal connection, Mr. Weir. It's late."

David pushed on. "We know the mitochondrial DNA in every cell of every human in almost all cases passes directly from mother to child, without sexual recombination with the father's DNA. So, technically, every person on Earth today can trace their genealogical descent back to a single female who lived in Africa about a hundred and fifty thousand years ago and—"

"Mitochondrial Eve." Kowinski interrupted to remind him he wasn't shining a visiting politician.

David instantly jumped ahead to details he hoped would distract her even more from what was actually on his screen. "Okay, so when we compare nine hundred and ninety-four key mtDNA sequences from people around the world, the average number of those sequences that differ between any two people is eight, and the maximum is twenty-four. That's how closely related every person is—less than a three percent difference.

"MtDNA from Neandertals, though—that differs from modern humans by twenty-two to thirty-six sequences, with an average of twenty-seven."

He touched the screen's incriminating image with one finger to draw her attention where he absolutely needed it. At the same time, he tapped the function key that expanded that image, to force the codes beneath it off the screen and out of sight.

He shot a glance at Kowinski, wondering if she'd caught his manipulation of the image.

"That difference indicates the last common ancestor we and the Neandertals shared dates back to maybe four hundred and fifty to five hundred thousand years ago."

"This helps quality assurance how?"

"It gives us a baseline for identifying improperly processed samples in our database. So I set up a simple comparison program— strictly using the lab's idle computer time—comparing our samples with this one."

Kowinski's expression was unreadable. "Couldn't you use a set of standardized human sequences just as easily?"

"Oh, I'm using that technique, too. My program compares our samples with a range of ten different datasets. It's a statistical study more than anything else. The Neandertal sequences just add another range of values to make comparisons with. After a couple of hundred thousand runs, I should be able to cut it down to the two or three sets that consistently give the best results in identifying erroneous results."

"And you're only using idle computer time."

"Yes, ma'am. For now it's strictly a background program that runs as an adjunct to the lab's standard quality checks."

Kowinski's clear eyes studied him. David tensed, unsure what he'd do if the verdict went against him.

"I don't suppose you've found any Neandertals among our recruits."

"Only in the marines, ma'am."

The colonel's smile was brief but humanizing. "Carry on, Mr. Weir."

"Yes, ma'am."

David waited until he had seen the main doors of the lab offices swing closed behind her before he restored the full image on the screen, complete with the identifying codes that ran along the bottom.

If Kowinski had been able to read those codes, and understand them, she'd have realized the DNA they described did not come from *Homo sapiens neanderthalensis*. She'd have realized why he was working late and alone, and why he'd felt the need to lie to her.

Because the DNA sequence that was on the screen, that carried the genetic markers of something other than human, was his own. Working swiftly, David copied the eight personnel files from his computer to the small flash drive he had hidden in a U.S. Army promotional key fob. Then he wiped his work history from his hard drive, so that no investigator could ever recover any trace of what he'd done. Or discovered.

Thirty minutes after the colonel, he signed out of the drab, utilitarian armed forces facility. As usual, the guards gave his backpack only a cursory inspection.

In the parking lot, beneath the impersonal gaze of the lab's exterior security cameras, David walked unhurriedly to his beat-up Jeep and tossed his pack onto the passenger seat, handling his ring of keys casually, as if they weren't keeping company with a flash drive of files worth at least another ten thousand dollars to him. Just like the last two sets.

He waved to the parking lot guards at the gate and sat back as they shone their flashlights into the Jeep, then opened the barricades for him.

Focused on survival, David pushed the speed limit all the way to Washington, D.C., and his meeting with his buyer that might save his life.

Tonight, using a computer program roughly similar to the one he'd described to Kowinski, he'd succeeded in identifying a cluster of eight more individuals among the lab's database of more than three million—proof that there were others like him. So far, though, he'd failed to find the exception to the rule. Those who shared his nonhuman DNA markers had one thing in common: They were younger than twenty-seven or they were dead.

David Weir was twenty-six.

TWO

Nathaniel Merrit was a killer, and underwater he found it easy to practice his craft. His contoured silicone mask kept his vision focused only on what was directly ahead, no distractions. The rhythmic rush of each exhaled breath from the regulator in his mouth reminded him of his daily meditation. Each slow and deliberate kick of his fins made him think of the kata he performed every morning: a ritual ballet of unarmed combat. His arms floated loose at his sides. His knife was sheathed—but not for long.

On the fifth day of this expedition, his two-man crew had found what he searched for, exactly where they had been sent to look on the small southern comma of this barren atoll. Now it was his job to make the retrieval—if there was anything to retrieve.

The water was warm, crystal clear, visibility near sixty meters. Merrit had no trouble seeing Krause and Renault. Dappled by sunlight, marked by silver threads of air bubbles, they were holding their positions by the opening in the steep coral bed twenty meters down. Their scuba tanks were fluorescent yellow. Even their dive knives had bright yellow stripes, all for better visibility.

Merrit's twin tanks were unpainted, bare aluminum alloy. His buoyancy compensator vest, weight belt, equipment, and titanium-thread wetsuit—all were black. For some of his assignments, visibility could be counterproductive.

At the ragged opening, Merrit first engaged his crew in a showing of their wrist dive computers. Krause and Renault had been down twice this morning to set the explosive charges and then check the results. They were good for at least another forty minutes at this depth, longer if Merrit could lower fresh tanks to them so they could take more time ascending to avoid the bends. Merrit gave them the okay sign to let them know they didn't have to worry about their return to the surface today—he'd be taking care of them.

He next began his examination of the edges of the opening for structural integrity. The chunks of drab, dead coral that had been blasted free had tumbled down the sloping bank of the atoll. Another twenty meters deeper, they lay amid the almost imperceptible mounds of stone blocks that once made up the rest of the structure built when this atoll was an island. As for who those builders were and when they had toiled here, Merrit had no opinion. The fewer questions he entertained, the simpler his work.

Satisfied the opening wouldn't collapse in the next hour, Merrit unclipped the pistol-grip LED spotlight from his vest and shone it into the waiting darkness. The turbidity from the explosions had settled, and the water in the revealed passageway was clear.

Merrit swam in first, barely moving his fins to avoid kicking up the thick layer of silt that covered the passageway's floor. After ten meters, the rough textures of coral and barnacles ran out to reveal the passageway's bare walls and arched ceiling.

He checked over his shoulder. Krause and Renault swam after him, but clumsily. Behind them, billows of silt rose up in their wake to obscure the route back to the open sea and sunlight. The reduced visibility would make it easier to do what Merrit had planned.

He swam on, locating the chamber entrance at fifty meters, exactly where the coordinate map had placed it.

His employer's briefing had described this particular section of the site as originally protected deep below the structure's central core, and the open passageway he floated before as sealed by a pair of thick wooden doors bound by iron. Once the ocean had swallowed the island, either through a gradual rise in sea level or the violence of the volcanic explosion that had formed the atoll, the ocean's woodborers had come and consumed the doors within decades. After another century or two, the ocean's own oxygen had transformed the iron bands to rust, long since swept away.

Merrit signaled to his divers to wait in the entranceway, then swam ahead into what his employer called the treasure chamber. This was the third expedition on which he'd seen such rooms. The first had been three years ago in the Ghaggar-Hakra dry river valley of India. A second had been high in the Peruvian Andes just three months ago.

This chamber, like the others, was circular, with a diameter a little less than eight meters, and the height of the encircling wall just over two. Its curved ceiling was a perfect hemisphere.

In the Andean chamber, the wall and ceiling had still retained traces of a type of plaster on which markings of some kind had been made. Merrit's employer had been disappointed that not enough plaster remained to permit reconstruction of what those markings might have been. Here, underwater, Merrit saw no remnant of any wall covering that had survived the sea's corrosive chemistry.

However, something else familiar had—a circular stone disk mounted on a central stone pedestal. Like those in the Indian and Andean sites, the structure resembled a round table about two and a half meters across and a meter high, though the buildup of sediment on the chamber floor made the pedestal's height seem less.

Only the stone disk interested Merrit.

With Krause and Renault watching from the open entryway, Merrit drew his knife and delicately probed the disk's surface layer of sediment as if searching for land mines. In a few weeks, his employer would dispatch a full archaeological team, and they would use vacuum hoses to meticulously expose the site and the other rooms it contained. But Merrit's employer had made it clear that only Merrit was to retrieve the artifacts from the treasure chamber.

On his fifth attempt, his knife made contact with an object. Merrit waved in his crew to assist him with their lights. Then, using his free hand to scoop away the silt, he located the outer edges of the object. Recognizing it by touch, he didn't reveal it further. Instead, he continued methodically probing the rest of the table-stone. If it was identical to the others, then on its surface would be twelve incised wedges radiating from the center. Each wedge would have a uniquely shaped, carved indentation designed to hold a different object. On his two previous expeditions, the treasure chambers had been looted sometime in the past. In only one—in the Andes—had one of the twelve artifacts been recovered. Merrit's employer had hopes that this long-lost chamber would be different.

Again and again, Merrit slid his knife into the sediment, each time hitting only stone. When he was certain there were no other artifacts to recover, he paused and made a show of patting his buoyancy vest, looking for something not found. Then he signaled Krause and mimed using a camera, indicating the diver should retrieve one from the equipment cache netted against the coral slope outside.

Krause signaled "okay" and swam off.

Merrit waved for Renault to enter the room, then pointed to the top of the curved ceiling where a mercurial pool of light shimmered—the captured air from his regulator.

Directing his attention to the ceiling, where reflections from his dive light flashed rippling streaks of silver across the chamber's walls, Renault was unaware of danger slipping into place behind him until he felt the tug as Merrit slashed his air hose.

Merrit watched from behind as Renault wasted a few of the last seconds of his life flailing blindly for the thrashing hose behind him. By the time Renault remembered to reach for the emergency air bottle on his vest, it was too late. Merrit had grabbed both of his forearms from behind and now held on as the diver kicked and writhed and sent them both on a twisting trajectory across the chamber. Merrit's metal tanks clanged against the wall of stone.

Abruptly Renault went limp, but Merrit didn't relax his hold. He and his victim had worked this site for five days, trading stories. Renault had enjoyed displaying the jagged crescent of scars on his thigh where a shark had pulled him under years ago—a shark he'd fought off with his knife and fists. Men like that don't die easily. Merrit maintained his grip. He was in no hurry.

Ten seconds later, Renault jerked violently as he fought in vain to escape.

He failed. This time when the diver's body sagged, it was due to loss of consciousness.

Merrit twisted the handwheel on Renault's tank regulator to stop the flow of air, then unhooked the diver's weight belt so he'd float faceup to the undulating bubble of silvery air, reuniting with his last breaths.

Merrit recovered Renault's dive light, switched it off. He took a position above the entryway, extinguished his own light, and waited in the warm darkness of the still water for the second diver to return.

It took longer than anticipated.

Merrit was tempted to drop down and look back along the passageway. His eyes were dark-adapted now, and he was certain he'd be able to see Krause silhouetted against the faint blue glow of the opening, but to leave his position was to risk losing the advantage of surprise. So he stayed in place, breathing slowly, not once thinking of the body floating a few meters above him.

Until he felt a current flow past him, as of someone swimming in darkness.

Merrit instantly stopped breathing, listening for the sound of another regulator. Why would Krause swim back without using his dive light? Did he suspect what was planned for him?

Hearing nothing, Merrit consciously took another breath. Unconsciously, he looked up into the darkness above him. What if Renault had outwitted him, held his breath just a few seconds longer—enough for Merrit to release him, look away? Did the diver get to his emergency bottle of air?

Merrit felt the water move around him. There *was* someone else in the chamber. He reached for his knife.

Another hand was faster, ripping the quick-release sheath from his leg. Now *two* hands grabbed each of his forearms, dragged him down.

Merrit took a deep breath, bracing for his own air hose to be cut.

Instead he was blinded by a disorienting flash of light.

In the instant before his vision whited-out completely, Merrit saw two divers with sleek rebreathers that released no air, and impenetrable obsidian lenses that glinted on their full-face masks.

They'd used infrared to hunt him.

Their next move was unavoidable. It was what he'd do in their place.

Kill the enemy.

THREE

No one looked twice at David Weir as he entered the busy lobby of the Hay-Adams Hotel. Late on a Friday night, even speeding when he could, the drive from Rockville, Maryland, to the center of D.C. had taken him just over an hour, most of that spent bumper-to-bumper on the George Washington Memorial Parkway. He'd had no opportunity to change from the clothes he wore at work—jeans, Nikes, a creased white shirt with his one concession to the lab's dress policy: a narrow black tie.

Tonight, a majority of the people in the dark-wood-paneled, amber-lit lobby were clad in Beltway power suits, the exception being a few women in dramatic evening wear. It was that kind of place. Still, since the historic old hotel was located directly across from the White House and attracted clientele from international diplomatic circles, a mix of dress and ethnicities was also to be expected. Neither he nor his jeans would cause notice. Politics ran this town, not fashion.

He stood in the doorway to the lobby bar, backpack in hand. With its small square tables, soft lights, high upholstered chairs, and a multitude of hushed discussions, it was called Off the Record for a reason. Its sound had a complex, layered ambience that on another occasion David would be recording for his collection.

He glanced around the room, looking for the contact he had met the last two times—a tall, blank-faced man with a shaved head. Instead, a different figure approached, built like a powerlifter, with a full head of bristling brown-black hair, spiked with gel. The hairstyle was ten years too young for the beefy face beneath it, and the dark banker's suit with chalk white pinstripes was a good twenty years too old. The whole effect was of a bad disguise.

"Weir, right?"

David was very aware he was risking his freedom, and his life, by what he was prepared to do, and had done before. In these circumstances, he wasn't about to talk to a stranger.

"I'm waiting for a friend."

"Merrit's not here. I'm taking the meeting."

"Where is he?"

There was a faint trace of Texas in Pinstripe's husky voice. "On that island you sent him to."

David's suspicion grew. "How'd he know which one to go to?" It had only been five weeks since he'd sold Merrit the second set of files outlining a possible common geographic origin for the nonhuman DNA he shared with a few unlucky others. "I only tracked the second cluster to Polynesia—that's more than a hundred major islands."

Pinstripe's only response was to tap his suit jacket, where something in the inner pocket made a bulge. "I've got your money."

David weighed the odds: his need to understand the bomb ticking in his own genetic structure against the risk of being entrapped. If Pinstripe was working for the FBI or Army Criminal Investigation Division, David knew he'd be arrested, guaranteeing he'd die in detention before he ever got to trial. On the other hand, if Pinstripe was a source of new information that could help him—

"Okay."

Pinstripe led him to a corner table with two chairs. There was an empty glass and a Heineken bottle on the white linen cloth. All the cashews had been picked out of the bowl of nuts. Pinstripe had been waiting.

David sat down, backpack between his feet. A white-jacketed waiter arrived to take his drink order. David chose water. Pinstripe looked at his empty glass, clearly wanting another beer, but he ordered a club soda instead. His left foot thumped against his chair leg, restless.

The waiter left.

"Give me the files."

David suddenly saw a chance to accelerate his search. Whoever Merrit and Pinstripe were working for, they had the capability—and the cash—to launch field expeditions halfway around the world on only a few weeks' notice. Maybe they could help him more directly.

"I want to change our arrangement."

Pinstripe leaned forward, threatening. "Ten grand. That's it."

"It's not the money."

Pinstripe hesitated, confused.

"You know how I'm getting my information. It's risky."

"So? You're getting paid." Pinstripe half turned away, touched his ear, and for the first time David noticed he had a small device in it.

David tried to recapture his attention. "Look. It takes weeks to run simple searches without being detected. Searches that a dedicated lab could do in a day or two."

Pinstripe was already pushing away from the table, getting to his feet.

David saw his sale evaporating; he retrenched immediately. "Okay, okay. Forget I said anything. I'll do it your way." He shoved a hand into his pocket to dig for his keys but stopped as Pinstripe's next words changed everything.

"You got an invite upstairs. He doesn't like to be kept waiting."

It seemed redundant to have a presidential suite in a hotel within sight of the White House. Then again, other countries had presidents whose visits required similar accommodations. Tonight, the figure sprawled on the yellow brocade sofa beside a woodburning fireplace was anything but a public official, though he was often a target of their investigations.

He was oversized himself, six foot five, three hundred pounds, and instantly recognizable from near constant exposure in the news.

David revised his speculation about potential access to resources. Holden Stennis Ironwood had been on the *Forbes* billionaire list for more than a decade, hovering easily in the top ten even in the throes of global recession. He owned telecom companies, bought and sold entire news organizations, cornered strategic metals, and was building his own orbital tourist rocket in Nevada. This man could buy the world.

Ironwood held out his hand without getting up. The man's heavy grip was crushing, and from his predatory smile, he knew it.

"Now you know who you're dealing with, you're thinking you should've been charging more." As familiar as his face, Ironwood's voice was a raspy baritone with a down-home southern twang, the same as Pinstripe's.

"Pretty much."

"That's what I like." With a grunt, Ironwood swung his bare feet onto the thick Persian rug and sat up. Piles of newspapers and magazines, in many languages, were scattered on the floor around him. "You stay honest, we can do business." He nodded to Pinstripe, who swept David with a metal-detector wand. "You *are* honest, right?"

"I'm selling you restricted data from army files that technically I don't have access to." The wand squealed as Pinstripe moved it over the backpack. David handed it over without being asked.

Ironwood's expression was the look of command, just like Kowinski's. The billionaire's good ol' boy routine was exactly that: a routine. David had no doubt that the mind behind it was as sharp as the creases on the colonel's uniform.

"Honest with *me*," Ironwood said. "The army's corrupt, just like the government. Stick it to those fools, I say." He stood up, towering over David, as formidable physically as he was financially. "But you try and stick it to me . . . Well, you're a smart guy. You can figure it out." He looked over at Pinstripe. "J.R.—everything aboveboard?"

J.R. had sorted the contents of David's backpack on the table in the dining alcove: gym clothes in one pile, two old paperbacks, a small black iPod tangled in earbuds, an even smaller digital recorder, and a phone.

"So far." He removed the batteries from David's phone and recorder, then shoved everything, including the iPod, into a lead-foil bag intended to protect film from X-rays.

Ironwood padded over to another alcove, this one with a well-appointed kitchen. "Who's got the files?"

David held up his keys and drew the end off his army key fob to reveal the flashdrive. "I'll need a computer."

Ironwood opened the refrigerator, waving a hand at J.R., who took the keys from David. J.R.'s attitude said he didn't like being waved at. "So you have a proposal for me." Ironwood pulled out a bottle of generic diet cola, filled a cut-glass tumbler, and drained it. "Go."

In the few minutes it took David to lay out his idea, Ironwood was back on the sofa, feet up, eyes closed.

"So what's it going to cost me?"

"The computers and peripherals would be the most, maybe a hundred thousand. Another fifty for lab equipment and supplies."

"What about millions of DNA samples? Collection costs? Personnel?"

"All that work's been done for us. The Genographic Project. Six or seven private genealogical companies. Another dozen universities. The information already exists. We just need to sort through it."

Ironwood rubbed his nose, eyes still closed. "Those companies and universities, they just *give* us access to their data?"

"The universities, yeah, and we—you—can buy most of the rest of it. Everyone trades in information. Last month, I downloaded the published mitochondrial DNA sequence of a Neandertal for free."

Ironwood opened one eye to look at him. "I thought it was 'Neander-*thal*.'"

"Six of one. The first specimen was found in 1856 in a valley in Germany, the Neander Thal—spelled *t-h-a-l*. In German, you say *th* like *t*, like thyme in English, but before long, scientists anglicized the pronunciation of the name. Meanwhile, around 1900, the Germans changed a bunch of spelling rules, and *t-h-a-l* became *t-a-l*. Now you see 'Neandertal' spelled both ways, but the fashion's to go back to the German pronunciation."

"The fashion." Ironwood sat up, fully awake. "You ever hear of Charles Fort?"

David hadn't, but whatever Ironwood wanted to talk about was fine with him. No one else was going to help him find someone with his markers who lived beyond a twenty-seventh birthday. When, not if, the army discovered his misuse of its resources, the inevitable investigation and delay would literally be fatal for him. It'd be months before anyone took him seriously and even planned to repeat his research.

Ironwood warmed to his lecture. "Fort was a great man. A scholar. Died in '32, but he was one of the first to blow the whistle on the scientific establishment. You know the way they gather evidence to support their pet theories, then disregard any findings that contradict those theories. I'm sure you've seen that in action, right?"

David needed this man's help, but that didn't mean he had to agree with everything he said. "Sometimes you make a bad measurement, so you want to exclude that from your research." He shrugged. "Though sometimes the exception does prove the rule."

"Exactly!" Ironwood aimed a finger at David as if he held a gun. "How about Richard Feynman? You heard of him?"

"Sure. Manhattan Project. Quantum physics. Probably one of the top scientists of the twentieth century."

"No 'probably' about it. He said the same thing about exceptions to the rules."

"And that is?"

"If the rule has an exception that can be proved by observation, then the rule's wrong." Ironwood stared hard at David. "These clusters you've been selling to my man, you ever think it passing strange that a junior tech in a government lab is the first to come across something as big as this—I mean, *nonhuman* DNA?"

"Not really." David had checked the literature, asking himself the same question. "Lots of other workers noted the results, but they—"

Ironwood didn't let him finish. "They call the results a processing mistake, or a contamination error, and the greatest discovery of all time is flushed down the crapper! You've looked at the data and the clusters. Do *you* know what you're seeing, Dave? Because I surely do." He heaved himself off the sofa and stood up in all his immensity. "What you've found is absolute scientific proof—*proof*—of what the government has always known, and always hidden from us. But you—I believe you have stumbled on the smoking gun."

David didn't understand.

Ironwood gave his shoulders a painful squeeze. "Welcome aboard, Dave. You're gonna help me put our lying government out of business, and we are gonna turn this world upside down."

With that, David realized Ironwood was giving him his funding and his lab, but he still had no idea why. Nor did he care.

But others did, and their infrared laser measuring the vibrations of the suite's windows recorded every word.

FOUR

Nathaniel Merrit was still alive.

An hour after his capture, his shaved scalp beaded with sweat in the tropical sun, he was tied up on the teak deck of his own chartered dive boat—a fourteen-meter Azimut hired out of Tahiti, a three-day trip from the atoll. Partly covered by a blue nylon tarp, a body lay under the bench on the port side of the deck. Renault.

Then someone familiar slid open the teak door of the forward cabin and stepped onto the deck.

Florian MacClary.

Over the three years they had been in opposition, they had never met, though Merrit had read her dossier often enough. There was little doubt her people had an equal file on him.

He revised the picture he'd built of his sixty-year-old adversary. In person, she was more imposing. Her hair had fewer dark streaks. Her steel gray wetsuit was zipped open to reveal a well-toned body in a black bathing suit. Against the dark fabric, a large, ornate silver cross hung from a thin silver chain—an unusual item to wear while diving.

She gestured to a large cooler on the deck between them. Earlier the blue plastic container had held cans of Coca-Cola, water bottles, and a few Hinano beers. Now it protected the artifact from the underwater treasure chamber. Immersion in saltwater was the standard procedure for preserving anything retrieved from long submersion.

"We finally beat you to one, Merrit."

He stayed silent, testing the tightness of the yellow nylon rope that secured his hands behind his back. At the same time, he checked for any sign of the two divers who had captured him.

He spotted them, anchored astern on their own dive boat—a sleek, fifteen-meter catamaran, sails furled, twin hulls gleaming white against the jewel blue waves. A crew of three could easily handle her, so it was probable the two divers were MacClary's only crew. He liked the odds.

In the forward cabin of his own boat, Merrit caught sight of Krause at the wheel. Krause glared back at him with open hatred.

Merrit looked up at his captor. "Krause gave you some inside help."

Florian MacClary, looking suddenly fatigued, sat on the Azimut's side bench, steadying herself with one hand though the ocean swells were gentle.

"Tell me about the help *you* had. Finding this place."

Merrit seized on his advantage. "You didn't know this site was here. You followed me."

The slight flicker of her pale green eyes told him he was right.

Whatever she had planned to say next, Merrit sensed that she changed her mind. Instead, she knelt on the deck and reached into the cooler, carefully removing the irregularly shaped, football-sized artifact.

It was similar to the one he'd recovered in the Andes, smoothly pitted and cratered everywhere but on its one flat, polished side. The pattern engraved there, as far as he could tell, was the same. From the reverent way MacClary handled it, the object had special meaning to her.

"I need to know," she said. "Do you have any idea what this is?"

Merrit had some idea what the object meant to his employer, but there was nothing to be gained by sharing that information. He made a show of studying the artifact more closely, wondering if she would share information with him. As long as they were talking, he still had options.

"It's a meteorite. Nickel-iron. Someone told me most of them are formed in a star, just before it explodes. That one landed here a long time ago. Someone found it, cut it in half—more or less—polished the cut surface, and carved that pattern into it."

"Not a pattern. A map. Of the solar system." MacClary's fingers lightly traced the almost invisible lines cut into the smooth metal surface. "On the boundary, this band of stars, and then the sun, here in the center. Six planets circling it. Mercury. Venus. Earth with its moon. Then Mars, Jupiter with its four major moons, and a ringed Saturn." MacClary shifted her attention back to him. "Is any of that significant to you?"

Merrit changed the subject. "What happens now?"

Krause hadn't moved from the wheel. It wasn't hard to guess what he wanted to happen next. Renault's body was still in its wetsuit. The air tank had been removed, but Merrit could see the outline of the buoyancy vest under the tarp. That could mean the rest of the diver's equipment was in place, as well.

But it seemed MacClary hadn't finished her interrogation. She cradled the meteorite as if it were as fragile as a newborn. "Do you know when this map was carved?"

Merrit shook his head. Sweat stung his eyes. It was late afternoon, and the flybridge deck overhead provided no shade from the sun.

"Nine thousand years ago," she said.

Merrit thought he had heard this before, but it was just a number, no different from millions or billions.

"Nine thousand years," MacClary repeated softly. "When historians tell us our ancestors were just beginning to settle in the first villages, just beginning to learn about agriculture." She gazed at the incised meteorite. "The heliocentric solar system in this map—with the sun in the center— doesn't even show up in ancient writings until Aristarchus of Samos—270 B.C. Almost seven thousand years *after* this was carved. Even then, the idea wasn't generally accepted until Copernicus proposed it seventeen hundred years later. And Jupiter's four major moons, Saturn's rings—you can't see those with the naked eye. They don't turn up again in the astronomical records until Galileo recorded his own observations through his first telescope in 1610. So how is this map possible?"

MacClary was speaking as if she were alone, as if she weren't on a slowly rocking dive boat under a blazing sun in the middle of nowhere.

"Can I move into the shade?" Merrit asked. He made himself sound exhausted, unthreatening.

MacClary gave no indication that she'd even heard him, still lost in contemplation of the artifact, so he acted. "Right. I'm sitting in the shade." He dropped to his knees and awkwardly shifted his body until he was sitting against Renault's body. "Okay." He began working his hands behind his back.

Taking no apparent notice of his movement, MacClary gently replaced the artifact in the cooler, then stood to face him, answering the question she'd just asked herself. "There's only one explanation, Merrit. You must know it as well as we, or you couldn't be finding our sites before we do."

Merrit kept his silence.

"You won't tell me, will you?" MacClary fingered her pendant cross as if drawing strength from it; she seemed to make a decision. "May the gods forgive you your desecration." She spoke with a strange mixture of pity and contempt. "Because I won't." She raised her hand, signaling the white catamaran to come alongside the boat.

Merrit heard the catamaran's engine growl to life, and when Mac-Clary's dive boat bumped into his, he was rocked forward, away from Renault's body. But that no longer mattered.

One of Florian's divers jumped from the catamaran onto the deck of Merrit's Azimut. The diver was tall and black, in a loose white linen shirt and trousers. MacClary spoke to him in French, instructing him to take the recovered artifact onto her dive boat.

The diver hefted the water-filled cooler and its contents as if they weighed nothing. He asked MacClary what they should do about *le captif*.

"*Rien,*" she answered. She glanced back at Krause. Merrit understood. He was not her problem anymore.

MacClary's diver nodded, turned, and stepped up on the Azimut's side bench, heavy cooler in both hands, timing the swell of the waves for the perfect moment to leap from boat to boat.

Merrit timed the waves as well.

Just as the diver tensed to make his move, Merrit sprang from the deck, trailing nylon rope from his wrists, Renault's yellow-striped knife in hand. With the same sure motions he practiced every day, with the same sense of calm he felt while diving, he swept out one leg, throwing the man off balance, the attack enhanced by the sloshing water in the cooler.

"*Florian!*" The cry came from MacClary's dive boat—her second diver.

Merrit's momentum didn't falter as the white-clad man fell back onto the deck and Merrit slashed once, deeply, across his throat. The man's groping hands couldn't stem the fountain of blood that spurted with each heartbeat of his dying body.

Before Krause could even make it halfway through the forward cabin of the Azimut, Merrit had wheeled to face a startled MacClary and smoothly grabbed her and twisted so he stood with his back to the bulkhead, one arm around her chest, Renault's knife at her throat.

MacClary instantly resisted, attempting to drive her heel into his instep, but Merrit countered swiftly, slamming the knife haft into her temple.

"Try that again, you're dead. Understand?"

Her body shuddered with fear or shock. Merrit didn't care which. He shouted the question again, violently shaking her as he did. "Understand?"

"Yes!"

"Then tell them!"

Krause was in the doorway to the cabin, transfixed by the sight of the knife at MacClary's throat. The second of MacClary's divers stood on the catamaran, struggling to keep an Uzi submachine gun trained on Merrit despite the rocking of both decks.

"Stay where you are," MacClary called out.

"Throw the Uzi in the water," Merrit ordered.

The gunman hesitated.

Merrit put pressure on the blade and felt MacClary stiffen as she tried to pull away. "Do it!" she cried.

The diver's face twisted in anger, but he pitched the weapon overboard.

"Now both of you," Merrit ordered him and Krause. "Into the water. Swim for the rocks."

Neither one moved.

"After I've left, you can swim back to the cat. I only want the artifact." He put his lips close to MacClary's ear. "You've read my file. You know I can kill all three of you if I want."

"Go!" Florian said.

Her diver leapt into the water. Merrit inched forward to see the man resurface, shake his head free of water, then strike out for the barren atoll one hundred meters distant.

In the doorway, Krause slowly shifted position.

"Don't even think about it," Merrit said. "Think about him." He jerked MacClary's head toward the body on the deck.

The dead man's neck wound gaped like a second mouth, his white shirt sodden with blood. The meteorite gleamed on the deck beside him, a shimmering black island in a sea of red.

"Last chance," Merrit said. "I don't count to three."

Krause sprinted for the side of the boat and dove into the waves.

"If you're just in this for the money," MacClary said, "I can pay you more than you're getting now."

"I doubt that." Her diver had reached the atoll and was now standing on the rocks, shading his eyes to look back at the two dive boats. Krause was still in the water, swimming.

"One million? Two?"

Merrit pushed MacClary away. "Your turn. Into the water." The moment Krause made it to the atoll, Merrit would set a fire on the catamaran that would reach its diesel bunkers before either diver could swim back.

MacClary stood by the meteorite, facing him, eyes strangely bright. She'd brought both hands to her cross, saying something that sounded like a prayer. It wasn't any language Merrit recognized.

"Asking God to strike me down?" he asked.

"Something like that." Then she flung herself at him with unexpected speed, a small silver blade flashing in her hand, sweeping toward his unprotected face.

Merrit, however, was a killer, and without the need for conscious thought he anticipated her again, driving Renault's knife up through the soft flesh beneath her jaw, on through the roof of her mouth and into her brain. Impassive, he held MacClary's body as she arched in spasm, then sank to the deck, dead before she reached it.

Impressed by its workmanship and by the way it had been hidden, Merrit retrieved her blade. Taking the other half of the cross from around her neck, he slid the blade back inside, then slipped it into his open wet-suit before throwing her body overboard, followed by the first of her divers, and then Renault.

Krause and the other diver were already in the water, swimming for their dive boat.

Merrit didn't care, knew how it would play out. The catamaran would be blazing before they reached it, and with all the blood in the water now, the sharks would soon complete his work for him.

As usual in matters such as these, he was right.

FIVE

Jess MacClary zipped up her red Gore-Tex parka, snapped the high collar closed, and stepped from her flapping tent into the Arctic wind.

It streamed strands of long red hair across her face, bringing an immediate flush to pale cheeks, making her smile. The low sun was bright, the sky brilliant blue, and the gentle hills of stunted grass and peat stretched endlessly around her, broken only by the handful of other tents that made up the camp, and the far-off red and yellow jackets of the dig team, working the site a half kilometer away.

She pushed her gloved hands deep in her pockets, inhaled the freshest air on the planet, and was as happy and content as she could ever remember. Doubly so today because the word had just come from Charlie Ujarak, the Inuit elder overseeing her work: She'd been right. Again. The burial ground had been found exactly where she had told the oilmen to look for it.

By the cook's tent, Charlie was waiting for her, a mix of the Canadian Arctic's past and present. He wore the latest mirrored Ray-Bans, but his traditional sealskin parka had been made by one of his grandmothers from seals Charlie had harpooned himself. Its design and construction hadn't changed for centuries, probably longer. He wore it open to reveal a red T-shirt with a faded white logo for York University. For him, August north of the Arctic Circle wasn't cold.

"Hey, Jess, Mr. Kurtz is waiting for you." Charlie sounded as pleased as she felt.

"I'll bet."

She did without her morning tea—the constant wind was a bracing enough wake-up tonic. They set out across the springy, yielding ground toward the dig.

"Did he say anything?" Jess asked.

"Nothing to say. The old settlement was right where you told them it would be. They found the first remains this morning. Article Twelve of the UN declaration takes over now."

"The remains were a burial, right? Not just a body."

"Definitely a burial. The skeleton's in a fetal position, and there're still bits of grass and deerhide wrapping it."

"Good. It was a big village, maybe a hundred people or so. There'll be more remains."

Charlie took on a more serious tone. "Then it'll take a lot of praying to keep them at rest."

Jess understood. What was paleogeology to her, with a smattering of anthropology and archaeology mixed in, was to the Inuit elder his living culture and religion. She envied him his freedom to speak so openly of his beliefs—a freedom she didn't have and likely never would. "Better that than seeing them dug up by machines for a pipeline, right?"

"A lot of praying," Charlie said.

At the site, most of the workers stood around a dented metal table with steaming mugs of coffee or tea, waiting for an official verdict from their foreman. Another field table had laminated topo maps held down by heavy metal clips and a bulky gray laptop computer hooked to a GPS tracker.

Lionel Kurtz, the foreman, greeted Jess with a wry smile, his blue-black skin, close-cropped hair, and flat, midwestern speech all seriously out of place in the Barrens, yet sure signs of the twenty-first century and mass globalization. His red jacket sported the corporate patch of Haldron Oil, the energy company that was going to regret it had hired Jess to examine the planned route of its multibillion-dollar pipeline.

"You here to gloat?" Kurtz asked.

Jess knew he didn't take what she had done personally—it wasn't his money the company was spending here.

"Like I said," she told him, "the land tells a story. Every hill, every hollow, every rock." She pointed to a small rise where yellow gridlines of plastic ribbon had been strung, crisscrossing from a perimeter of thin metal stakes that marked the area for digging. "A couple of centuries ago, there was a river here, and that's the perfect place for a village on its banks."

There was a hint of admiration in Kurtz's tone. "You called it, all right. Charlie says we shouldn't rebury what we've found until the shaman gets here, so you want to check it out?"

Jess turned to Charlie. "Would that be all right?"

"Just don't touch anything more." For Kurtz, he added, "And you should tell your team not to use their knives or any cutting tools until the grave is closed."

"Because?"

"Now that the burial ground has been disturbed, the shades of the dead could be anywhere. If your people accidentally cut one of them with a knife, then they'll become angry and could cause all sorts of trouble for you. Sickness, bad luck, polar bears . . . or your next seal hunt might not go too well."

Jess could see Kurtz was trying to decide whether or not Charlie was being serious. Fortunately, he made the right choice. "No knives. I'll let 'em know."

"Thank you."

The three of them walked up the rise to the gridded area. Kurtz whispered to Jess, "He knows I don't hunt seals, right?"

"A metaphor. Maybe the shades would make it so you'd have a hard time finding a new route for your pipeline to skirt this place."

"Fair enough." Kurtz didn't sound convinced. "As long as he didn't mean it about the bears. Once was enough."

When they stood by the open grave that revealed the skeletal remains—bones burnished dark brown by time and decay, webbed by shriveled tendons and shreds of hide—Charlie softly chanted a mournful dirge in his language. Kurtz bowed his head respectfully, and Jess realized she'd made a terrible mistake.

She waited until Charlie had finished, then said, "This isn't Inuit."

The grave was just over two meters deep, and Jess pointed to the exposed side of the excavation. "Look at the layers of sediment. About halfway up, see the river gravel?"

A thin layer of small, light pebbles stood out in a distinct line, sandwiched between other bands of darker soil.

"Give me more," Kurtz said. Jess could tell she had his interest. As for Charlie, she could see his expression harden—he knew what she was about to say.

"Modern Inuit moved into this area about a thousand years ago. Any Inuit burial that took place here since that time should be above the river gravel, when the river shore had receded." She pointed a hundred meters to the west, to the slight dip in elevation she had noted three days ago that marked the vanished river's course five to six hundred years earlier.

"My ancestors could have dug a deep grave," Charlie said.

"Not through permafrost. Sorry. Permanently frozen ground puts a limit on how deep a modern-era grave would be." Jess looked around at the terrain, reading it, staring back in time. "For this area to have been low enough for the river to run over it, then rebound with the release of ice and snow . . . I'm thinking three, maybe four thousand years ago. That's when this burial would have taken place. I'll need to check the aerial surveys again, climate records . . ." She looked at Charlie apologetically. "The company will carbon-date the remains, and that'll tell the story, too."

Charlie shook his head. "My people won't go for that. We didn't come from anyplace else. Raven created this land and created the people in it. We've always been here."

Jess could see that Kurtz was caught between trying to be respectful and doing his job. If this burial mound wasn't Inuit, then the company's archaeologists could dig it up in a month, send what they found to museums, and the pipeline's path wouldn't have to be altered.

"If not Inuit, then who?" Kurtz asked.

Jess didn't know. "That's out of my area. In this region, Pre-Dorset culture, for sure. The company'll need to examine any artifacts with the remains, maybe pull genetic material from the bones."

"Please," Charlie said. "You can't disturb them."

"Pre-Dorset," Kurtz repeated. "Any living descendants?"

"Descendants? Sure. All through the aboriginal populations of North America. But there's nothing of their culture or their religion remaining."

Charlie's voice was tight. "You can't know that for certain."

"Again, I'm sorry, but, yes, I can." Jess pointed to the ancient bones below them. "These people aren't your people. Geology doesn't lie."

"It's subject to interpretation."

"Like I said, carbon-date the remains, check the artifacts—but I know I'm right."

"And I know the history of this land as my father told it to me and his father to him, all the way back to when Raven told it to all the people." Charlie jabbed a finger at Kurtz. "This is my family business. Don't touch my ancestor, don't dig, and for your own sake, don't use any cutting tools until the shaman gets here to make this right." He walked away, as if not trusting himself to say anything more.

Kurtz watched him stalk off. "Any idea when that shaman will get here?"

Before Jess could say she didn't know, they both looked up as they heard the distant thrumming of a helicopter.

"Is this my lucky day?" Kurtz asked.

"He couldn't get here this fast. Especially not from Inuvik." The helicopter was coming from the east, and Inuvik was the closest airport in that direction. By air, it was three hours away.

Kurtz squinted as the helicopter closed. "It's not a company helo." He sounded hopeful.

Jess saw he was right. Haldron helicopters were painted a distinctive green. This one was white with red bands. "Canadian Air Force?"

JUDITH & GARFIELD REEVES-STEVENS

The helicopter began its descent between the camp and the dig site, close enough for Jess to see it wasn't a military helicopter but a private company's. She could make out the word SIGHTSEEING on the tail.

Kurtz patted her shoulder with a smile. "C'mon. Let's see who's crazy enough to be a tourist out here. Ten to one it's the shaman—or more elders."

Jess didn't take the bet but fell into step beside Kurtz, joined soon by the rest of the dig team. Anything that broke routine in the isolation of the tundra was worthy of attention. Jess saw Charlie standing alone, keeping his distance. Whoever was arriving, it was no one he was expecting.

The helicopter settled slowly, the pilot obviously taking great care that the landing site was solid so the skids wouldn't be fouled. Surprisingly, he kept the rotor spinning slowly instead of shutting down the engine.

"Guess he's not expecting to stay," Kurtz said. He and Jess and the rest of the team stood a safe distance from the aircraft, waiting.

The passenger door opened, and a man stepped out, dressed in an open green parka, jeans, and tall rubber boots. He wore black aviator glasses, no gloves.

He ducked as he walked out from beneath the rotor, looked at the twenty people waiting for him, cupped his hands, and shouted to her, "Jessica MacClary!"

Kurtz looked at Jess. "You know him?"

Only one thought came to her, one explanation. "Something's happened . . ."

"What?" Kurt asked.

Jess took a breath. "I might have to go." She started for the man.

"Go? Where?" Kurtz kept pace with her. "I'm going to need a written report."

"I'll explain to the company," Jess said. Her heart was pounding. She had always known that something like this would happen but expected it to be years away. Then her heart stopped.

The man from the helicopter had pulled a short black gun from his open parka and aimed it toward her.

From instinct, from training, Jess slammed into Kurtz. *"Down!"*

They hit the peat together as a ripple of soft popping sounds filled the air, mixed with the foreman's sharp gasp of pain.

She felt him tense, saw red blossoms dot both legs. "Play dead . . . don't move . . ." She turned her head to see him staring at her, dark eyes blank with shock.

Half the dig team had scattered. A few others held position, startled, uncertain of what they had witnessed. Two now started running toward her. One after the other they jerked grotesquely as the gun fired again and dropped them.

Still on her stomach, Jess eased away from Kurtz's rigid body, stripped off her gloves, tore at the neck of her parka with shaking hands, heard the wet sounds of boots approaching. She reached inside her parka, fingers seeking the heavy silver cross she wore. If she died here, she'd take one of *them* with her.

"On your knees," the man ordered.

He stood out of knife range, his weapon leveled at her. Jess recognized it as a Heckler & Koch MP5K—an easily concealable, short submachine gun. She'd been trained to use them.

She palmed her cross and pushed herself up.

"This won't stop us," she said.

The man gave a half-grin. "It'll stop you." He took aim. "They told me you'd want to say a prayer."

Jess's fingers slid the blade from her cross. She pictured bringing her hands up to pray and throwing it at the same time. He'd kill her, of course. She wasn't faster than bullets. Still, with luck and his unprotected neck, she'd—

The man's green parka puffed out on one side, and he registered surprise. Only when his temple erupted in a bloody explosion did Jess recognize the sound of rifle shots.

She instantly dropped beside Kurtz again, looked back.

Charlie Ujarak was striding purposely forward with his Remington— the one the camp kept for polar bears. She saw a flash from the long-barreled rifle's muzzle and heard a metallic ping. Now he was firing at the helicopter.

Jess wanted to see it start to rev up for takeoff. Instead, as she'd feared, she saw the pilot roll out of the far door, putting the aircraft between him and Charlie. The pilot would have his own H&K. The enemy was always prepared.

Jess shouted back at Charlie to hit the ground, then scrambled forward, slipping on the wet turf, to dive at the dead shooter and get his weapon.

The pilot saw what she was doing and fired a burst that stitched across the shooter's body.

Charlie fired the Remington again, and one of the helicopter's forward windows cracked.

The pilot fired back at Charlie. Jess popped up and fired at the pilot, shattering side windows.

The pilot ducked back behind cover, and Jess guessed he was changing magazines. She saw Charlie, prone but unhurt, aiming his rifle like a sniper.

This time, Jess stayed down, clawing through the dead man's parka for his spare clips.

Then she heard a stutter of hard impacts, braced for bullets to tear into her, and instead felt a blast of heat and a thunderclap of air as the helicopter *exploded.*

Flaming wreckage wheeled across the tundra. Jess rose to her feet in amazement. The aircraft's tail had blown off where the auxiliary fuel tanks had detonated. The pilot's body was pinned by the blazing cabin, unmoving and in flames. But how?

She looked back at Charlie. He pointed to the sky.

A second helicopter was landing. Unmarked.

Jess dropped the spent magazine from the shooter's submachine gun, slapped in a new one.

Charlie hurried to her side and pushed down the stubby barrel of the weapon. "No, Jess, they've got to be friends of yours. They shot up the first helo."

Jess watched the second craft set down. Its side panel was open, and a man with a rifle much larger than a hunter's Remington was sitting in the open hatchway.

Two more men in red parkas without insignia jumped out, running, arms open to show they carried no weapons.

Jess stayed where she was, H&K held ready but pointed down. Charlie stood beside her.

The first man to reach them turned his hand to display to Jess a dark metal disk not much larger than a silver dollar. Twelve segments were inscribed on it, a different symbol in each.

She let the H&K drop to the ground.

Then the two messengers knelt before her and spoke as one. "Defender."

Jess could feel Charlie stare at her, but, as tradition demanded, she held her left hand out, palm down, and each man, in turn, held it briefly to his lips.

"She's dead," Jess said.

The two men nodded.

"How?"

Both messengers glanced at Charlie. "You're summoned home at once," one said.

Jess knew better than to press the point. She nodded, and only then did the two men stand.

"Who are you?" Charlie asked her quietly.

Jess also knew better than to answer. "Charlie, thank you for saving my life. I'm sorry, but I've got to go with these men now."

"Why?"

"Family business of my own." Then, as she had always known she must, Jessica MacClary turned her back on her life in the world, to assume the mantle of her birth, and her gods.

CORNWALL 7,322 YEARS B.C.E.

When the sentinels with their distant eyes had first sighted the painted sail of Torhi-ram's bridge ship, the signal flags they raised on the watchtowers were old and faded. Still, to see the purple cloth streaming against the gathering storm clouds sent a charge of anticipation through the scholars of the outpost.

It had been twenty years since those flags had last flown. Twenty long years since the people of Kassiterithes had been visited by a ship from home.

Hamilkir, Master of the Star Paths since his mother's death, waited at the docks with his apprentices, on the largest wooden pier. A crew of oak people used ropes and poles to reposition the trading barge already moored there, making space for the un-expected visitor. The tide was high, the water choppy, and the first gusts of rain from the darkening skies swirled in with the sea spray. Yet Hamilkir and the others like him—whom the people of the oak called shadowmen—felt no discomfort. The oldest among them had memories stretching back two decades and more, and had known weather far worse, while the youngest had heard the stories of home. The raging thun-derstorms of this region, one day to be known as Cornwall, were minor distractions to the shadowmen, especially now.

Even as anticipation of hearing news from home kept Hamilkir strengthened against the storm, he realized the visitors were not what he had hoped.

The massive wooden vessel, its triangular mainsail bright yellow and marked with the cobalt blue cross of the Navigators, had anchored two stadii offshore, as if its pilot couldn't read the floating markers showing safe passage to the docks. Instead, a land-ing boat was launched, and even at this distance through rain and spray, Hamilkir could see that seven of the boat's eight rowers were ahkwila, small and light-skinned like the people of the oak. Only one rower was khai—a true person.

As a crew, though, the rowers were sure and strong, and the helmsman, also khai and female, brought the landing boat to the pier with skill. The oak people threw ropes to lash the boat in place by the floating gangway, and, true to tradition, the helmsman was the first to debark, carrying her wayfinder's chest.

In the brief glimpse he had of it, Hamilkir admired the workmanship of the rounded and polished wooden case, as long as an adult's arm and twice as thick. He would tell from the intricacies of its silver panels that it was from home, marked with the star paths in the old way, with no text engraved to aid in memorization as his apprentices preferred. It was the chest of a star path master, perhaps one who had studied in the Navigators' Hall itself.

Hamilkir and his apprentices stood aside without speaking as the helmsman carried her burden along the dock to solid land and secured it in the storage cairn. Only when the chest was safe from loss at sea, when its distant eye and timekeepers and horizon boards were secure, could she—or any wayfinder—attend to other business. Such was the importance of navigation. Such were their traditions.

In less time than the passage from ship to shore had taken, Hamilkir had dispatched an apprentice to return on the landing boat and serve as pilot to guide the anchored ship through the shoals to the pier. The apprentice took the female's place as helmsman, while one of the oak people replaced the male khai *on the oar.*

The visitors had misgivings at seeing a single khai *on a boat with eight* ahkwila.

"Have you tamed them?" the female Master asked. Her name was Rutheme. She stood as tall as Hamilkir, a full head above the tallest of the oak people. Her skin was as black as the spans between the stars and, in the custom of the travelers, her scalp was shaved and oiled. Few of the khai *at this outpost maintained their appearance in the old way, and Hamilkir found it unexpectedly alluring.*

"They don't need taming," Hamilkir answered. "They need to be fed."

The khai *spoke in their own language, whose clicks and harsh consonants defied the understanding of most of the people of the oak, and the* ahkwila *remaining on the dock made no effort to listen to what the two shadowmen said. They only stared at Rutheme. There were few females of her kind at Kassiterithes. Such was the price of children—a price not paid by the oak people, who bred more easily, with many fewer deaths in childbirth.*

"At Ehschay, teaching them farming isn't enough."

Hamilkir knew of that outpost, slightly closer to the world's middle circle than Kassiterithes, but almost twenty thousand stadii across the dark sea before him. "Is that where you've sailed from?"

Rutheme clicked her agreement. "Seventy-two days."

"Before that?"

Rutheme understood the intent of his question. "I was born at Ehschay. I've never been home." She pulled her fur-lined cloak closer as the wind kicked up. Wolf fur, Hamilkir recognized, but of a species not found here. Fifty years ago, his grandparents had told him, trade had not been limited to barges traveling up and down the coast. Bridge ships from other outposts had made regular arrivals at Kassiterithes, bringing goods from all the world's lands.

"And my outpost has not been visited," Rutheme continued, "for almost thirty years."

"Thirty . . ." Hamilkir looked away. The storm-tossed horizon was hidden in the gray mist of driving rain, moving onshore, almost here. "Has it happened, then?"

"I think it's up to us to find out."

Hamilkir turned his attention to the bridge ship at anchor. The launch boat had reached it and was being hoisted on board. "We have no more ships that can make the voyage. Can yours?"

"We can cross the sea, but not to the White Island."

Hamilkir knew what his next question had to be. "Then we're to build new ones that can?"

"We must. I've brought the knowledge."

"We have it here as well." The knowledge of the bridge ships was safely preserved on the stone altar in the outpost's Chamber of Heaven, along with the eleven other gifts.

"Do you have the workers?"

"Yes. And the forests."

Rutheme clicked again. On her ship, both rows of oars were being set in motion to maneuver it to port. The wind was too strong to risk the sails, and they'd been struck.

Hamilkir saw beyond the reason for her questions. "You no longer have those resources at Ehschay."

"We've had to turn the library into a fortress." Rutheme wrinkled her forehead in confusion. "We've given them everything. Yet they attack us. Do they not do that here?"

"A few ambushes out past the farmlands. It's more a question of differences between the hunters in the forests and those we've taught to farm." Hamilkir knew there would likely be more ambushes in the time to come as logging operations expanded for the new ships suited for the voyage home. The ahkwila here believed the oak forests held special properties that Hamilkir had not seen demonstrated, and so could not accept. For, if an unseen force could produce no consistent effect, in the way that channeled lighting could always attract certain metals, then the force wasn't simply unseen, it wasn't real. The people of the oak, however, had yet to grasp that basic understanding of the world and its workings: that a thing was a known fact, or it was not.

Rutheme glanced at the ahkwila standing together, waiting for her ship to reach the dock so they could moor it. She dropped her voice as if she feared that one among them might understand her language. "Do you feel safe here?"

"I do. We're making a difference. The oak people honor the library."

"Then they're different here. Different from all the others."

All the others. Hamilkir was afraid to ask her what she knew about the other outposts. Though, in time, he knew he must.

That night, the storm raged and lightning flashed. This time, though, it wasn't captured in the rods of iron to be stored in glass jars and slurries of iron filings. Instead, the scholars and apprentices of Kassiterithes gathered in the great hall for the *evening meal. Not for companionship—the* khai *had little need of that—but to hear the story of the crossing of the dark sea.*

It had been uneventful. For three days of the crossing, the winds had slowed, so the rowers had toiled: Bridge ships were never becalmed. Most importantly, the star paths remained true. When land had been sighted on the seventy-second day, the watchtowers of Hamilkir's outpost had been easily seen through the lenses of the distant eye. Rutheme's wayfinding had been that precise, even on a voyage that she, and her khai *rower, Torhiram, had never made before.*

After the formal stories had been told and reports given, the visitors mixed among their fellow scholars to ask and answer questions. Rutheme and Torhiram shared Hamilkir's table, but the conversation was strained.

Hamilkir was puzzled when he realized the cause of the unusual tension: the presence of his ahkwila *concubine, Brighid. True, at first sight, she could seem alarmingly pale, the straw color of her braided hair indicative of disease had she been* khai. *Even so, he had learned that, like all creatures, different* ahkwila *took on forms and coloration specific to their different regions. This was a known fact, and easily adjusted to.*

Instead of her appearance, then, Hamilkir wondered if it might be his concubine's knowledge that caused his guests' concern. He had seen the flicker of surprise in both Rutheme and Torhiram as Brighid had greeted them in their own tongue. Yet why would anyone be troubled by evidence of knowledge shared?

Finally, he thought he saw the answer in Rutheme's eyes. The way she stared at Brighid's belly when the concubine's purple-trimmed white shift pulled across her. A child grew there. His.

Then Rutheme, noticing that her host had registered her distaste and disapproval, spoke as if Brighid were not capable of understanding.

"Are there others?"

Hamilkir knew she meant children born of oak and shadow. "Twenty-two."

Whatever Rutheme and Torhiram thought of that answer, they shared their reactions only in a glance between them.

"Are there not similar children in Ehschay?" Hamilkir asked.

"There were," Torhiram answered.

Hamilkir could see his concubine's concern at Torhiram's use of the past tense.

"Where did they go?" Brighid asked. She slipped her hand into his and squeezed it. As mysterious as the gesture was, Hamilkir had learned the ahkwila *took comfort from it.*

"They were not khai," *Rutheme said. "They were not* ahkwila. *Where could they go? Accepted by no one."*

Hamilkir squeezed his concubine's hand as she had taught him. "We accept them."

"So did we," Rutheme replied, "until the attacks began."

"I told you," Hamilkir said, "there's no fighting here."

"There's always fighting."

Hamilkir refused to accept that pronouncement.

"Two wolves in a cage," Torhiram said. "There can be only one. So, in time, there is only one."

"We're not animals."

"No," Rutheme agreed. She stared at Brighid. "But they are."

Tears trickled down Brighid's cheeks, pale no longer but splotched with red. Hamilkir had been with her long enough to know the tears did not mean his concubine was in physical pain—instead, some thought had caused her an internal, unseen discomfort.

He spoke more sharply than he meant to. "That's not a known fact."

Neither of his guests responded to his unintended insult.

"Sometimes," Rutheme said, "I believe that the ahkwila are what the Navigators warned us against."

"They warned us of the ocean."

Rutheme gestured at the pregnant ahkwila. "Which one? The ocean of water? Or the ocean of flesh? Both can swallow us."

"Unless," Torhiram added, "we take action against them."

Hamilkir stood. He found the conversation unpleasant. "I'll take no action against the people of the oak."

"Someone must," Rutheme said. "Or else the Navigators will be proved true twice over. Once for the fate of our home, and once for our own."

"Tell me you're going to arrest David Weir."

Jack Lyle's response was a snort of amusement. Twelve years in the air force, another sixteen as an agent in the Air Force Office of Special Investigations, and he knew Colonel Miriam Kowinski's type. One detail out of place, one comma missing, and she'd bring down the wrath of heaven on the hapless fool responsible. A quality he could admire, if not emulate.

"Eventually," he said.

As if preventing herself from saying anything she'd regret, the colonel shifted her attention to Lyle's specialist working on David Weir's computer. It was midnight on a Monday, and the rest of the office area in the lab was deserted.

"He was stealing DoD data," the colonel said.

"I understand."

"We've known about it since the first day he tried to cover his tracks."

"Colonel, your lab's security is outstanding."

"So why isn't Army CID in charge of this investigation?"

"Because the Air Force OSI is in charge, per General Capuzzi's direct order."

Lyle saw Kowinski's spine straighten at his not too subtle reminder that in this affair, he, a civilian agent of the air force, had authority over her, an army colonel.

Before she could protest again, his specialist said, "Gotcha."

She was Roz Marano, delectably freckled with short brown hair and, like most of the agents in Lyle's detachment, all of fourteen. Sometime around age fifty, Lyle had begun to notice how everyone else he worked with was growing younger.

Roz, who was actually twenty-nine, sat back in Weir's chair and cracked her knuckles. "I've extracted the core roots from the protected files and set it to write to disk." She turned her head to look innocently at her boss. "Want that in English?"

Lyle shook his head. Two months earlier, when this investigation had led him to Weir, Roz had slipped a program into the lab's network that recorded every keystroke Weir made, and whenever he deleted a file, it made a copy where he couldn't find it. Lyle was content not knowing more than that. In his life, machines that required anything beyond an ON and OFF switch rarely stuck around long enough to become good friends.

"How about an ETA?" he asked.

Roz checked Weir's computer screen. Lyle couldn't tell what she saw there that could give her a time estimate. "Five minutes."

He turned to Kowinski. "Then the computer's all yours."

"It's always been mine."

"Colonel, I don't like getting my toes stepped on, either, but sometimes we have to let the little fish go so we can get the big ones."

"Mr. Lyle," Kowinski said, emphasizing his civilian title, "I get that Weir is selling the data he's stealing to someone you think is more important than his sorry ass. But the only reason this lab accomplishes its mission is the trust the men and women in uniform have for it. Maybe stealing someone's genetic profile isn't as big a crime as whatever you're gunning for—but multiply that small crime by three million people feeling they've had their privacy rights trampled. Then add all the people who, because of that betrayal, decide not to cooperate with us in the future. To this lab, and to me, that's irreparable harm."

Lyle thought that over, though he knew he didn't have to. Three million service members having their feelings hurt and future recruits being hesitant to add their DNA to the armed forces registry was an easier challenge to deal with than America's enemies being able to pinpoint every secret underground command post and continuity-of-government facility in the country, and every hidden U.S. sub pen around the world. How Weir was linked to the person responsible for that very real threat, Lyle didn't know, but he was determined to follow any lead that would result in achieving his mission to bring Holden Ironwood to justice.

Of course, he could say none of that to the colonel. "I understand your concern."

Kowinski folded her arms, apparently realizing that if he couldn't give her even the slightest indication of the stakes he was playing for, then those stakes must be huge. Lyle felt bad for her, but relieved.

While the two women watched whatever there was to watch on the computer, Lyle ran his eyes over the featureless office cubicle, noting how little had changed in Weir's absence. When the suspect had resigned this morning, a security guard had watched as the kid boxed up his personal items, not that there had been many to begin with. Two months earlier, the first time Lyle had searched the office, he'd been struck by the impersonal feel of it.

Almost everyone else in this section of the lab had a personal coffee mug with slogans or pictures. Almost everyone had photos of family and friends on the bulletin boards and on the walls boxing in their desks. At least a third of the cubicles had artwork by children. David Weir's was different.

On his cubicle's bulletin board, he had lab schedules and memos, all current and neatly arranged. The only other item on the board had been one personal photo: a three-by-five color print of a forested landscape, completely nondescript.

Roz had copied the photo with one of her handheld gadgets and sent the file to OSI forensics for analysis. She'd also noted that it was an actual photograph, not something produced on a home printer. The code on the back of the print revealed it had been made twenty-one years ago at a large film-processing lab that, in the predigital age, served more than two hundred supermarkets, drugstores, and camera and gift shops in Los Angeles. After all that time, there was no way to determine where the original roll of film had come from, or who had submitted it for processing.

However, OSI had forwarded the image to the National Geospatial-Intelligence Agency. By measuring the angle of shadows in the photo and the terrain elevations in the landscape, and, for all Lyle knew or cared, doing something that involved chicken bones and chanting at midnight, the image analysts had determined the exact place and date the photo had been taken: twenty-one years ago near Big Bear Lake, California, on July 2, at 14:24 hours, local time.

Alice Weir had spent that July Fourth weekend at a local lodge. David, listed on the hotel registry as "and son," had been five. Nothing indicated that the date had any special significance to either, except for its proximity to the holiday weekend.

Lyle had had Roz make him a copy of the photo for his own office crime board. He was still trying to understand why the suspect had hung on to this specific image. Maybe it would explain a kid brazen enough to steal from the U.S. military for a traitorous billionaire who believed in wild government conspiracies straight from the tabloids.

The only additional personal effects in Weir's work cubicle had been the non-work-related reading material on his bookshelf—mostly assorted car and motorcycle magazines, continually changing—and, like all his co-workers, the kid had his own coffee mug. White ceramic, with a drawing Roz identified as an X-Man named James Howlett, now called Logan and known as Wolverine. Apparently Wolverine was one of the most popular superheroes these days, had a bad temper, and wanted to know where he had come from.

"Don't we all," Lyle had said.

The end result of their search of the office cubicle was that Weir remained a complete cipher. That was informative in itself. In Lyle's business, people who were ciphers were usually that way for one specific reason: They were deliberately hiding something.

"Last file," Roz announced.

Colonel Kowinski looked over Roz's shoulder. "Those are the files he was working with Friday night. He stayed late."

"We know." Lyle had been in the car that followed Weir to the Hay-Adams Hotel. He'd heard every word spoken in the bar, and in Ironwood's suite.

Kowinski peered more closely at the screen. "Yes, that's everything. Even his nonhuman data's there."

"His what data?" Lyle ignored the instant interest on his junior agent's face.

"Nonhuman. He was doing comparison testing for a quality control program. At least, that's what he said he was doing."

"Define 'nonhuman.'"

Roz's grin widened. Lyle shook his head at her.

The colonel paused before answering, as if she sensed there was more to his question than just an investigator's curiosity. There was, but he wasn't telling. It was one thing for Ironwood to gab on about evidence of non-human DNA in Weir's stolen files, but for a rational army colonel to say the same—that was worrisome.

"Neandertal DNA."

Lyle remembered the kid telling Ironwood that he had downloaded that genetic information. "As in caveman?"

"We all lived in caves once upon a time."

Lyle thought about Weir's basement apartment, also thoroughly searched, also devoid of personal details. "Some still do."

Roz hit the keyboard. "Heads up, boss. Here're the files he copied to his magic keychain."

This time, Lyle took a closer look at the screen data. These files were the evidence that would give him the leverage to have Weir choose between going to federal prison or becoming an informant against Holden Stennis Ironwood.

A drawer slid open on a piece of equipment under the desk. Roz removed a silver disk, signed and dated it with a marker, then put the disk into an evidence bag. "That's everything."

Kowinski gave Lyle a half-smile. "You know the Neandertal data can't be evidence."

Lyle understood. "Right. He got it from a public source, so it's not government property."

"And if he really was preparing a comparison program, there's a chance none of the other files he was working with that night are government, either."

Lyle realized the colonel was offering a warning. David Weir had given these files directly to Ironwood, perfectly ensnaring the billionaire in a conspiracy to steal government property. On the other hand, if the files the kid sold that night *weren't* government files . . .

"Roz, can you still check the files Weir put onto his keychain Friday night?"

Roz battered away at the keyboard. "Here you go." As simple as that.

Lyle looked to Kowinski. "Colonel?"

Kowinski reached past Roz to tap a few keys of her own. "This is exactly what he did with the other files he stole. He extracted family history, place-of-birth data, and genomes from personnel files."

Lyle relaxed. He'd never been in danger of losing his case, but knowing Ironwood had taken possession of stolen property after all was going to make his life much easier.

Then Kowinski said, "That's odd."

"What?" In Lyle's experience, nothing good ever resulted from those words.

"The Neandertal genome isn't in any of those file names."

Roz tapped at some keys, and eight files were highlighted. "Those are the ones he put onto the flash drive." She looked to Kowinski. "Want to open them? In case he renamed them?"

Lyle stood back, and Roz did what she did best as he and Kowinski watched the screen change to show what looked to Lyle like X-rays of earthworms.

On the eighth file, Kowinski said, "There it is. That's the one he told me was Neandertal. Definitely nonhuman mitochondria." She pointed to some numbers off to the side of one of the earthworms. Then she frowned, sounding startled. "This was sequenced at this lab. That's an employee-identifier code."

"Have you worked with Neandertal DNA here?" Lyle asked.

"I'd love to, but the answer's no."

"Maybe Weir slipped a sample through without telling anyone?"

"You can't do a cheek swab on a Neandertal. Just extracting DNA from a twenty-nine-thousand-year-old piece of bone is a painstaking process. The chances of contamination are—"

Lyle wasn't interested in anything except his case. "Is it Neandertal, Colonel?"

Kowinski's answer was anything but reassuring. "I can't be sure exactly what species it is, but I am sure it's not human. Close, but . . . not." She leaned down to hit a few more keys. "The employee's name should be right . . . Hmm." She straightened up, lips pursed. "There isn't one."

Lyle definitely didn't like the level of concern he was reading in her. "Is that important?"

"Leaving aside the issue of why Weir lied to me about the origin of the sample, it's important because to do this, he circumvented *all* our collection protocols, and our privacy safeguards. It's a significant breach of our operational standards."

"Why would he—or anyone else, for that matter—do that?"

Kowinski looked at him for a long moment, obviously engaged in some inner debate. "Let me ask you a question instead."

Lyle sighed. This was not turning into a good night.

"Why is the air force so interested in a petty espionage case that involves nonhuman DNA?" Before Lyle could even attempt to reply, the colonel continued, very seriously. "I can think of some answers for that, but I don't like them. And I think whatever you're investigating is way above my pay grade. Way above."

Lyle savored the silence that followed. It made it easier for him to concentrate as he worked out the percentages of what to do next. *Strength in numbers,* he finally decided.

"Colonel, I find myself in need of a specialist in genetics. Rather than break operational security on my investigation by going to a third party, I'm inclined to ask you to serve as a consultant to my team."

Kowinski's lips thinned. "Just so we're agreed. I will not allow the reputation of this lab to be sullied by having it involved in research that could be considered fringe, speculative, or . . . or laughable."

"Agreed. You accept?"

"Do you have the authority to give me the necessary clearance?"

"I do."

"Then I'm in. Now what the hell is this all about?"

"What do you know about Holden Stennis Ironwood?"

Lyle was gratified to see that the colonel was thrown off guard by the unexpected question. "Wealthy. Very wealthy. Outspoken. I know he's been in the news for government investigations. Something to do with buying newspapers and television stations. Oh, and he's building a private rocket for tourist—" She stopped. Lyle guessed her mind had finally dragged up the one piece of information she had hoped wouldn't be involved in this matter. "He believes in flying saucers."

"Big-time," Roz added, not helping.

Kowinski waved a hand at the screen, her shoulders not nearly as square as they had been. "Is that what that's supposed to be? *Alien* DNA?"

"No," Lyle said, doing his best to sound reassuring. "Ironwood is the focus of this investigation, but it has nothing to do with his various . . . let's call them hobbies."

"If it's not alien DNA, and it's not human DNA, then what is it?" Kowinski demanded. "And what is its connection to David Weir?"

"All very good questions," Lyle said. "The exact ones I need your help to answer."

SEVEN

Ironwood said something, but Merrit's attention was elsewhere.

He was watching the lights of the Los Angeles skyline brighten against a twilight orange sky, but in his mind's eye, he was picturing the sun-sparkled waters of the South Pacific, himself cutting easily through those warm turquoise waters, sharks slicing past on all sides, silent, effortless. It was where he'd been five days ago. Where he'd prefer to be. Now, however, in the confines of the lounge of a private observation rail car, Ironwood's words merged with the rhythmic clack of steel wheels on steel tracks, disturbing Merrit's perfect moment.

He turned from the window. "Sorry. A gift from what?"

Ironwood, in linen pants and a vintage silk Hawaiian shirt, cradled the Polynesian meteorite Merrit had retrieved for him.

"A gift from the Nommo." Ironwood said the odd name with satisfaction. He held the meteorite up to the light as if it were fine crystal and not an eight-kilo lump of metal.

Merrit replayed that last word in his mind. Outside, the surprisingly small cluster of the city's tall downtown buildings slid past the chrome-framed window as the train picked up speed, leaving Union Station. Merrit wasn't looking forward to spending three days crossing the country. He didn't understand why someone as rich as Ironwood wasted so much time, no matter how much he hated flying.

Ironwood was on the other side of the lounge, on a long green divan designed for much smaller frames. Each side of the mohair-wool-upholstered bench sported Streamline Moderne curves of pale blond wood striped in thin flashings of brushed nickel. A round glass and chrome table to the left held a polished steel lamp shaped like a cobra head. It cast a warm glow on the man and his newest treasure.

"Nommo. The aliens who gave us civilization. Probably jump-started our evolution, too."

Merrit normally avoided discussing his employer's crazy-ass beliefs. What did it matter where civilization had come from a billion or whatever years ago? What did it matter if aliens had been here if they weren't around now?

Billionaires, however, enjoyed the luxury of indulging their obsessions and, as jet-lagged as Merrit was after his flight from Tahiti to Los Angeles, he knew from experience he'd be expected to take part in the conversation. Ironwood lived in his own private time zone, and that meant everyone in his employ did as well. No one slept until the top man did.

"The aliens have a name?" Merrit asked. Who knew?

"Nommo. 'Course, that's probably not their real name, but that's what the Dogon tribe call the amphibious beings who taught them astronomy. See here?" He motioned for Merrit to come closer.

Merrit took a moment to find the rhythm of the train, then crossed the lounge with a rolling gait. Two or three years ago, someone had told him how much it had cost to rebuild this car. A staggering amount, in the millions. And for what? It was still just an old train car, even if it was clad in gleaming sheets of fluted steel and had an upper deck with an observation dome that looked like something from a World War II bomber. The damn thing still rattled and bucked like a mine train. He dragged a low-slung armchair into position beside the sleek divan.

Ironwood held up the meteorite to show its engraved map of the solar system. "Just consider the knowledge this image represents." He shook his head. "It's got all the planets circling the sun. Jupiter with four moons. Saturn with a ring. Details that folks on this planet shouldn't be able to know without some sophisticated math and some fine telescopes. But the Dogon knew all of it, and even more, thousands of years ago. *Thousands.*"

Merrit wouldn't have cared if the Dogon had known all of it millions of years ago. Besides, he'd already heard this lecture from the MacClary woman.

"So you're asking yourself . . . who are the Dogon?" Ironwood gave Merrit a sly grin, knowing full well he couldn't care less about the Dogon. Not that that stopped him. It never did. "African tribe. Their territory's a few hundred klicks south of Timbuktu. Real end-of-the-earth sort of place."

Merrit suppressed the sudden and overwhelming desire to yawn. "Good place for aliens to land, then. Nobody to spot them."

"Oh, I doubt they landed there. It's more than likely the Dogon's ancestors started out up to the Mediterranean. That's where the Nommo—or whatever they really called themselves—landed and seeded the cultures that became Egyptian, Phoenician, Harappan, you name it. Then, when things went south—global flood, pole shift, whatever the heck happened to knock the stuffing out of the first civilizations—the Dogon migrated down into Africa, set up shop there." He paused, as if in his enthusiasm he'd said more than he planned to. "Something like that."

Merrit nodded as if any of this mattered to him. It didn't. He did wonder, though, if his employer knew all this, why did no one else? The way Merrit looked at things, either there was evidence or there wasn't. If the map on the meteorite was as important as Florian MacClary and Ironwood said, then why didn't either side try to show it to the professors or scientists or whoever it was who decided such things? Merrit knew those weren't questions to ask Ironwood. All that would get him would be another hour-long lecture on conspiracy theory and the evils of big government.

Ironwood regarded Merrit with open amusement. "Here's something I guarantee won't bore you."

Merrit doubted that, but before he could reply, a young steward in a green corporate blazer approached with a black champagne bucket. Inside, packed in ice, was a large bottle of diet cola. She poured a glass for Ironwood, offered to pour another for Merrit. He asked for coffee instead.

Ironwood waited for the steward to return to the kitchen. He kept his hands on the meteorite still sitting on his ample lap. "You remember the boy from the army lab?"

Merrit shrugged. "Weir, David. Sure."

"I hired him."

It took Merrit a few seconds to process that. Weir was already on the payroll, so to speak. He brought Ironwood information from military records, and Ironwood paid him. Or, at least, Merrit did, acting as go-between. He decided Ironwood could mean only one thing.

"Full-time?"

"Dave tells me he can use other genetic databases to get me what I need, and he can work faster if he's not trying to squirrel into government computers."

Merrit didn't care what Weir could or couldn't do, but he was concerned by what Ironwood had just implied. "He told you? You spoke to him in person?"

"Some reason I shouldn't have?"

"Your security is what you hire me for. Weir's a mark I found on the Internet. He's not supposed to know you're the end buyer of what he's selling. You can't trust him."

"The boy's come through for me. Besides, I looked him in the eye. He's not a problem."

Merrit persisted. "The *boy's* breaking federal, state, and military law stealing files from a military computer system. When the CID catch him at it, and they're going to, they'll offer him immunity *and* a huge reward if they think he can lead them to you."

"Then it's a good thing the *boy* isn't working for the military anymore, isn't it?"

Merrit glanced at the meteorite in Ironwood's lap. "You also hired me to keep you isolated from anything anyone might call . . . illegal."

Ironwood's eyes narrowed. "You telling me you did something you shouldn't have? Something to do with this?" He held up the meteorite.

Merrit was taken by surprise. *Where did* that *come from?* "I told you I didn't have permits for the dig site. And, technically, I should've reported anything that I took from it to the French authorities. But none of that's—"

"You know I don't give a rat's backside about paperwork. Especially *French* paperwork. I'm asking if you ran into any trouble out there that you didn't bother to tell me about."

Merrit told the truth as he knew it. "Not for me."

Ironwood didn't look convinced. "Didn't cross paths with any Mac-Cleirighs, say?"

"Way ahead of them."

Ironwood appeared to think that over. "Okay," he said at last. The rich scent of fresh coffee filled the lounge as the steward returned. "Enjoy your coffee."

Merrit sat back as the steward pushed down the mesh disk in the pot of café filtre on the side table. A new concern slippped into his mind. The moment the steward retreated to the kitchen, he voiced it.

"When you spoke to Weir, did he sell you another set of files?"

"Sure did."

"Did those files pinpoint a new site?"

"Not this time."

Shit, Merrit thought. The files were fakes. Exactly what he'd expect if the CID had flipped Weir to help snare Ironwood. There could be army investigators serving warrants on Ironwood's offices across the country right now. And when Ironwood went down, Merrit knew, he wouldn't go alone.

"Weir set you up. We need to get off the train." Merrit got to his feet. Ironwood had long had a Plan B in case any of his ongoing battles with the government appeared to be leading to prison.

His employer waved his hand. "Sit down, sit down. I'm way ahead of you. It wasn't a setup. The new files—the new genetic cluster—it was for Ganganagar. India. Ring a bell?"

The name was familiar. Merrit sat down. "That's where we found the first outpost. Three years ago."

Ironwood nodded, looking smug.

Merrit found the expression irritating. "What good is that? We've already been there."

"But Weir didn't know that, did he?"

"So?"

"So what it does is confirm his technique: Find a concentration of folks with alien DNA, and somewhere nearby there'll be one of the outposts the aliens built. So my boy Dave is three for three, and now he's going for four. Not bad."

"And he's not working at the army lab anymore?"

"No he is not. He's mine."

"Army CID can still nail him for what he did while he was working there, and then turn him against you."

"He won't turn against me."

"He's a crook selling what he steals. He's a proven liar."

"So? Everyone lies. *All* the time. Especially to me. Always telling me what they think I want to hear so maybe I'll fart money on them or something." Ironwood tapped a finger to his ear. "You know what else I hear?"

Merrit didn't.

"That boy doesn't like what he's doing," Ironwood said. "Stealing from Uncle Sam."

"Right. He's afraid of being caught."

"Oh, it's more than that. You see, as much as I want the genetic cluster information Dave can get me, Dave wants that same information even more. Something bad's driving that boy." Ironwood fingered the meteorite, which hadn't left his possession all this time. "Me, now, I'm as safe as a crow in a gutter. If it comes down to a choice between lying to the Army CID or lying to me, that boy's going to lie his pants off to the army, because I'm the only one who can give him what he wants."

Another possibility occurred suddenly to Merrit. "Does Weir believe in . . ."

"Aliens?" Ironwood drained the last of his diet cola. "Not a chance. He's one of those *Skeptical Inquirer* types. Wouldn't believe in aliens if Predator bit him on the backside."

"Then why's he after the same genetic information you are?"

"About that, I admit, I do not have clue one. But I'm gonna find out." Ironwood grinned a big predator grin of his own. "Interesting, isn't it?"

Merrit understood what had to happen now.

Desperate men did desperate things, and if Weir was as driven as Ironwood believed, then Ironwood could not interact with him again.

The tech was a loaded gun, and Merrit was not about to take that bullet, not even for a billionaire.

EIGHT

Three days from the Barrens, in the backseat of a sound-silenced May-bach limousine, Jess MacClary turned her head to watch the streets of Zurich slip past the smoke-tinted window. Between school years in Boston, this ancient city had been where her real studies had taken place: her Family education. Every twist and turn, each transition from cobblestone to smooth pavement, was as familiar to her as the thoroughfares of earlier times had been to her ancestors. The Family's presence here stretched back before the Romans to the Celts, when little more than muddy paths ran through a thatched-hut village.

As a child, she'd taken this route every summer, though never, as today, accompanied by helicopter-borne snipers, ready to protect her from any new attack.

Jess adjusted the Maybach's reclining seat until its position was almost fully horizontal. She stretched back, weary from the long trip across the Atlantic, the turmoil of conflicting emotions. Here, in the financial capital of Europe, it was midafternoon, and the armored, bombproof limousine moved slowly along Bahnhofstrasse, now approaching Paradeplatz. Elsewhere in the city, shadowed by other helos, Jess had been told, two other armored Maybachs were following different routes to the same destination—decoys.

To either side of her vehicle, the city's stone buildings now gave way to steel and glass monoliths, soaring upward to a cool gray sky. Seen through the car's passenger skylight, those towers appeared to crest like dark waves in a storm-tossed sea, frozen in the instant before they could crash down on her.

Jess had never liked this part of Zurich. She missed the openness of the tundra. Vanished now, along with her separate life, into the past.

The past.

History was what defined the Family—the history it had witnessed, the history it preserved, and the history it would someday make. All children in the Family learned that each generation might be *the* generation: the one that would change all of history on the day when they'd be rewarded for their service through the ages.

Now it was her turn to share leadership of her generation. Her grandfather had been Defender of the Line MacClary, and Florian had been his first child. Her father, Florian's only sibling, was his last. By right and tradition, Florian's own first child, male or female, should have been next in line, but Florian had been childless when Jess's parents had died so senselessly. So the aunt had taken in her orphaned niece, age twelve, and at age sixteen Jess had been formally acknowledged as the Line MacClary heir.

Fresh tears filled her eyes. She touched the control on the center console, to change the limousine's skylight from clear to opaque. A few more minutes and the car would arrive at one of Zurich's most modern structures and the home of humanity's oldest secret. It still seemed unreal to her that within days, if not hours, she, like her aunt and grandfather before her, would be admitted to the highest level of the Family's faith, and at last learn the Secret that its twelve defenders guarded.

That was the nature of succession by bloodline. The new advanced only when the old died.

There was no sign on the dark blue glass tower. Those who had dealings with the MacCleirigh Foundation knew where it was housed. Those who didn't had no need to know.

Around the world, though, academics and scholars and even governments knew of the MacCleirigh Foundation and its work: in Italy, the laboriously computed tomography scans and virtual reconstructions of carbonized scrolls from Herculaneum so fragile they could never be unrolled; in Guatemala, the delicate work of stabilizing Mayan frescoes in ruins scattered deep throughout impenetrable rain forests; in South Africa, the Balkans, and New Mexico, programs to record and document ancient languages before the last of their speakers died.

The Foundation supported historical research and restoration projects on every continent but Antarctica, and had done so for centuries. It was so renowned for its efforts that researchers rarely questioned where the Foundation's funds came from, or thought about who might have been the original MacCleirigh for whom it was named. To most historians and ethnologists and archaeologists who relied on its grants, the Foundation had always been there, always doing what it did to preserve and protect knowledge of humanity's past. And they were right.

Compared to every other human institution on Earth, the MacCleirigh Foundation *had* always been there.

Always.

In a well-protected inner courtyard, Jess remained in the limousine until the armed chauffeur opened the passenger door for her. She got out and looked up to see what she knew would be there: rooftop spotters in position. Another sign of how her life had changed. She would never truly be alone again.

She headed directly for the massive glass doors that led into the main lobby. She wasted no thoughts on wondering how the Family would deal with the open attack on her in the Barrens, the deaths, Kurtz's wounding, the destroyed helicopter, and her abrupt departure from the Haldron project site. She only knew they would.

The building's pristine white entrance hall, seldom busy, was empty. Jess heard the main doors lock behind her, saw the security cameras automatically tracking her. She kept walking toward the only opening between the lobby and the bank of elevators: a metal-detector frame.

A man waited on the lobby's other, secure side. He was old, frail, the worn collar of his expensively tailored white shirt two sizes too large for his wizened neck, his black-framed glasses thick.

Jess stepped through the metal detector. The old man bowed his head deferentially. "Jessica." His accent was full German, and not the soft blend of German and Swiss that arose from the city's unique *Zürichdeutsch* dialect. A frondlike wisp of white hair floated above his age-spotted scalp. "I am glad to see you well. Sad that you must be here."

"Herr Reims," Jess said formally, but her smile of greeting was affectionate. The old man had been her personal retainer at the Foundation since she was sixteen. She offered her hand to him. He did not take it.

Everything was different now.

Reims bowed his head again and gestured toward the elevators. "That one, please." Hands clasped together, he nodded to the only car that could reach the top level. Jess spread her fingers against the spotless glass of the biometric scanner.

The elevator door glided open.

Jess walked in, and Herr Reims disappeared from view as the door closed. The car ascended smoothly. An eye-level panel displayed the passing floor numbers, then the words PRIVATER FUßBODEN. The car stopped. The door opened.

Jess stepped into the hallway, and her scuffed hiking boots sank into thick slate-gray wool carpet. The sudden softness underfoot triggered memories of all the times her aunt had brought her here. Her gaze went automatically to the priceless relics displayed against the fabric-covered walls. Each treasure glowed in subdued pools of light cast from tiny spotlights in the hall's low ceiling.

On one wall ranged a set of portraits of men and women that spanned hundreds of years and distinct, diverse styles of art and clothing. The other wall bore a faded parchment, a silver-bladed cross, an Egyptian death mask, a small black leather-bound book barely a century old. Only the twelve family lines that made up the MacCleirighs would understand this collection's unifying principle. Each relic told a story of past defenders and their fabled exploits.

Jess paused by the leather-bound book—a King James Bible published in San Francisco in 1897. Florian had loved telling her the story that went with this one—how the little Bible had come to have a bullet hole that passed only halfway through.

Jess wondered to whom *she* would tell the story.

Her reverie was broken by a familiar voice.

"Cousin."

"Su-Lin," Jess said, even before she turned to see her older relative approaching. "Cousin" was the Family's honorific that merely indicated a member of the Family, not necessarily a close relation.

Su-Lin Rodrigues y Machado was a short, slight woman of middle years. Her skin was pale coffee in color, her eyes almond-shaped and gray, and her still-lustrous black hair was loosely twisted in a tress that hung down her back, just as she always wore it. Today, however, though Jess had never seen Su-Lin in anything but severe business attire, the older woman was dressed in classic black trousers, an immaculate white blouse, and intricately woven leather flats. Jess herself was still in the same dusty, wrinkled jeans and ExOfficio travel shirt she'd put on three days ago.

"You're early," Su-Lin said—an observation, nothing more.

"Ten years, at least," Jess agreed. Then, reflexively, she dropped to one knee and reached out to take Su-Lin's left hand. "Defender."

Su-Lin motioned her to stand. "No, we're the same now. The Twelve Restored."

Jess responded to the phrase as automatically as she had knelt. "The Secret kept."

"Until the Promise is fulfilled."

The catechism said, Su-Lin reached up to embrace Jess, who bent down, feeling awkward, so much taller. Her cousin was defender of the Rodrigues family, a MacCleirigh line originally based in Lisbon at the height of Portugal's golden age of exploration. When the British Empire achieved ascendancy, Su-Lin's branch had relocated to São Paulo, Brazil, to become the inner heart of South America's financial and political future.

The moment the older woman released her, Jess impulsively blurted out the question that had tormented her since the Barrens. "How did she die? I need to know."

Su-Lin's gray eyes revealed nothing of her own emotions. "The others are waiting."

The penthouse hallway ended in a pair of tall oak doors that shielded the most secure room in the Foundation building, where the Family's trustees and officers met to set investment and funding strategies for tens of billions of dollars in MacCleirigh assets. The sanctum's other function, however, had less to do with material concerns.

Su-Lin gave Jess a frank look of assessment. "Are you ready?"

Jess was. Su-Lin swung open the heavy doors and led the way into the Chamber of Heaven.

There were twelve other rooms like it in the world, one in each city in which a line of the Family was based. Like all the other rooms, this one was round, eight meters in diameter. Its ceiling was domed and painted with a midnight blue sky against which gold stars traced the constellations of the zodiac. In the center of the floor was a circular oak table. Its polished tabletop was bare, revealing darker woods inlaid in pale wood, creating a radial pattern of twelve equal segments. Each segment bore the stylized depiction of a flower or a mountain or an eye or another symbol—twelve in all.

Around the table, positioned one to each segment, were twelve oak chairs with an almost rustic, handmade quality jarring compared to the refined luxury of the rest of the Foundation building.

A casual observer might guess that the chamber's round table was inspired, in part, by the legends of King Arthur. In fact, even the Family's children, brought here in tour groups for their lessons every summer, knew that the Arthurian legends were inspired by the stories of Arturus Uther Brae, a defender who'd lived in the second century of the Common Era.

Su-Lin drew out one of the chairs and sat at the table. After a moment's hesitation, Jess took the seat beside her. They were alone in the room.

"Jessica," Su-Lin said as she folded her hands on the table, "you know everyone."

Without any apparent trigger, the chamber's curved wall panels moved up and out of sight to reveal ten large video screens. Above each was a separate display that identified a city and a local time, from London to Canberra and all points between.

Ten familiar faces looked out at Jess.

Of the Twelve now restored, five were female, she herself the youngest, Su-Lin the next. The other three were in their fifties, their Lines based in Athens, Buenos Aires, and Canberra.

Of the seven men, Andrew McCleary of New York was senior. His Line had been the first of the Family's to be successfully established in North America. Andrew was a distinguished figure, nearing eighty yet unbowed by age; tall, whip-thin, with thick white hair brushed back. His suit was Savile Row, marine navy. His clear blue eyes intelligent, measuring. Jess recalled there had been tension between Andrew and her aunt, but Florian had never said why.

Andrew, as eldest of the Twelve, spoke first, but with no words of condolence. "Jessica, at the moment of Florian's death, by our traditions, you became Defender of Line MacClary. Is it your choice to continue in that role?"

Jess looked from screen to screen and found one face not quite as stern as the others—Willem of Macao, closest of them all to Florian, a fellow archaeologist and Defender of Line Tasman. When she was much younger, Jess had told Willem that he looked like a pirate with his shaved head and warm brown skin, and he'd sent her a photo from Belize in which he had an eye patch and an iridescent green and yellow parrot on his shoulder. Her aunt had been beside him, her bright face caught midlaugh. On the occasion of Jess's confirmation as her heir, Florian had confided that Willem was why she had never married.

Defenders had few rules, but the most important was that no defender could marry another. The First Gods had created the Twelve Lines by scattering the Family on the Twelve Winds, and those Lines were kept distinct. The names of the Lines might change over the generations, reflecting marriages and changes in locale and customs, but the Family's genealogists worked hard to chart the lines of descent, and to ensure that at no time would more than 144 individuals know that their direct family could be traced unbroken to the time of the First Gods. In that way it was easier to ensure the Family's origins remained unknown to the outside world.

Now Willem, whose readout indicated he was in Reykjavik, Iceland, and not Macao, seemed to give her a signal, a barely perceptible nod of encouragement, as if telling her there'd be time for the two of them to talk, later.

"It is my choice," Jess said.

"Have you been told how the Defender of Line MacClary died?" Andrew was a lawyer. He spoke crisply, as if he were leading her through a deposition.

"The messengers who came for me, they didn't know. No one's told me anything."

"Emil," Andrew said.

Jess looked to the screen marked ROME, where Emil Greco's character-istic hard-eyed expression marked the man whose role it was to think of the worst possible thing that might happen to the Family, and then protect against it. He was solidly built with a thick mustache and goatee. He had trained her personally in small arms and hand-to-hand combat.

"Florian radioed in just before it happened." Emil's voice was decep-tively gentle, his lilting Neapolitan accent making his words almost musi-cal. "She was at the site of a new temple, Jessica."

Jess blinked. *Another one?* Her aunt hadn't told her of a new find.

"It was Ironwood." Andrew offered the information matter-of-factly. "Apparently, he's developed some method of locating them that we're unaware of."

Everyone in the Family knew Florian loathed Holden Ironwood and his rapacious plundering of historical sites to support his theories of aliens as mentors of humankind. She'd despised him even more for not publish-ing his finds. Jess had found that somewhat ironic since the MacCleirigh Foundation was also selective in the information it released about its own discoveries. If something had relevance for the Family's history, outside scholars never heard of it.

"Did she enter the temple before . . ." Jess was unable to continue.

It was Willem who answered. Willem who understood. "Flo saw it, Jess. There *was* a Chamber of Heaven. An original. The temple's under-water, so it's not intact. But she did see it before she died."

Jess silently thanked him for that small comfort.

Until the incredible revelation that actual Family temples had been found, the only MacCleirigh legacy of the earliest days, when the First Gods lived and worked among humans, had been the *Book of Traditions:* the MacCleirighs' written memories that were taught as scripture to every gen-eration of each Family line.

The *Traditions* described the Temples of the First Gods supposedly con-structed by the Twelve Lines of the original Family, whom their gods had scattered throughout the world.

Until three years ago, the accepted interpretation of the *Traditions* was to view the twelve temples as mythical, not real, part of an allegorical story explaining how the First Gods had chosen the Family to work at their side to establish humanity's first farms and schools and cities.

That scholarly interpretation had changed literally overnight with an Ironwood-funded team's unearthing of an unusual structure near the Indo-Pakistani border. The ruins lay in what had been the heart of the advanced Harappan civilization, dating to 2500 B.C.E. They matched the temple descriptions in the *Traditions*, and they held an actual Chamber of Heaven.

It took more than a year for the Family's archaeologists to learn of and take control of the site. When they did, the ancient stones confirmed their hopes—the temple ruins predated even nearby Harappan cities by an additional four thousand years.

If Ironwood had publicized his find, and he did not, the ruins in India would have been classified as a "historical anomaly." They would have joined hundreds of other atypical finds that appear to fall outside the generally accepted timeline of history, without providing enough information to suggest that another timeline should be considered.

To the Family, though, the ruins were *proof* that their traditions were the literal truth. The original temples were myths no more.

Florian had drawn Jess into the feverish excitement of those early days, the renewed sense of purpose that reenergized every line of the Family. The new mantra became *If Ironwood can find them* . . .

Then, less than two years later, another Ironwood expedition reached a second temple in the Andes. The Peruvian discovery had rocked the MacCleirigh Foundation: How could Ironwood's information be so much better than the Family's?

Now, Florian had been at the site of a *third* temple, again found by the Family's old rival, within months of the second . . . and, somehow, her being there had led to her death.

Jess couldn't restrain herself any longer. "What's going on? What does Ironwood know that we don't?"

Victoria Claridge, heavily tanned with permanent smile lines creasing her face, answered from Canberra. "That's exactly what everyone at the Shop is working on, dear. We're beginning a new translation of the *Traditions,* starting with cuneiform."

Jess had been to the Shop. It was a vast, climate-controlled cavern in Australia where the Family had relocated its most precious artifacts during the Cold War scare of the 1950s. Under the administration of Line Claridge, it was now the Family's key research facility.

Andrew interrupted. "If I may, this isn't the time to discuss Ironwood's technique."

Jess felt all eyes on her, the intensity of the moment palpable even through the vast distances bridged by the screens before her.

Andrew glanced down at a sheet of paper on the table before him and began to read aloud.

"Jessica Bronwyn Ruth Tamar Elizabeth Miriam Ann, child of MacCleirigh, Line of MacClary . . ."

Jess heard the words, felt the enormity of what they meant.

". . . as was the first of our Family chosen by the gods, so now are you chosen. Stand please."

Jess stood as ordered. She heard Andrew's next words as if through thick and dampening fog.

"You will go with Su-Lin to the Source of our faith, and there you will learn what only defenders can know." Andrew looked across the miles and into Jess's eyes. "We'll talk again tomorrow."

One by one, the ten screens switched to black, then disappeared from view as the curved wall panels slid down to hide them.

Jess and Su-Lin were alone once more. Jess's throat felt dry.

"What's the Source?" she asked Su-Lin.

"You must see it for yourself."

"Why? Where is it?"

"Right here. Where it's always been. Ever since our ancestors first arrived in Turus."

"Turus," Jess repeated, feeling uncharacteristically stupid and confused. "That's what the Celts called Zurich."

"That's what *we* called Zurich."

Jess thought that correction over as they walked down the hallway and into the elevator.

The car descended past every numbered floor, past the lobby, and kept going.

"Our family came here two thousand years ago, Jessica. It's the one city we've never left."

Jess felt a slight shake in the floor as the car slowed, then stopped.

A sudden gust of cool air lifted the hair on her neck, and she wheeled to face a glaring light. The back wall of the elevator was opening.

Su-Lin regarded her with a steady gaze. "We've all been through that door," she said. "This is your time."

NINE

One step out of the elevator, Jess was engulfed in sensory overload. The dazzling brilliance of unnatural light . . . hot. The hollow, uneven clang of her boots . . . some type of metal grid. A pungent damp fragrance . . . rich and earthy. She closed her eyes. The smell was familiar, unmistakable. She opened her eyes, and her vision cleared, adjusting to the full-on illumination from a circle of floodlights.

She was on a metal catwalk, suspended above an open excavation cut into living earth.

At the railing, she stared down three stories at—

"A church?" she asked. "How old?"

"You tell me," Su-Lin said.

The primitive, cross-shaped edifice below was stained with age. Scaffolding supported the three stone-block walls she could see, but Jess could still read pages of their story.

"Fifteen hundred years. Plus or minus . . . two hundred."

Though metal beams and heavy planks of wood shored up the sides of the excavation, she could see the stratigraphy of the soil in the wide gaps between supports. The top twenty feet or so was uniform. That suggested it had been added deliberately, probably when modern construction had begun on this site and the builders needed greater stability. Other than that, the lower strata of soil deposition looked natural to her—a few signs of flooding over the years, and three narrow black bands signifying at least three major fires.

"If I could carbon-date samples from that fire layer about a foot up from the lowest point, I could refine it to within fifty years, plus or minus."

Beside her at the railing, her fellow defender gave an approving nod. "No need. The building dates to 524 of the Common Era."

"You said we were here for two thousand years."

"We have been. This *building* dates to 524. Before that, we built a Roman temple here, dedicated to Apollo. Before that, a sanctified grove for Celtic rites. This site has always been ours."

Su-Lin took the lead as she moved past Jess to a steep metal staircase that clung to the bare walls of the excavation. Jess felt flutters in her stomach. Su-Lin had just said the Family had *always* been here, in *this* place. Andrew had said Su-Lin was to take her to the Source of their faith, where she would learn . . . Jess stumbled, then recovered quickly. *Could the Secret be here? In the church?*

With each step, she tried to steady herself by remembering the reasons the MacCleirigh lines had survived over centuries. Scholarship, of course, was primary. There was nothing more important than ensuring that history was recorded and passed on as an unbroken tradition. Accumulated wealth was another. Being free of want allowed the pursuit of scholarship.

However, the most important reason to account for the MacCleirighs surviving longer than any other human institution, whether nation or bloodline, was the Family's ability to remain unnoticed.

Jess, like all children of the Family, had been taught that past generations of MacCleirighs, before they had even taken that name, had worshipped with druids in the forests of England and made sacrifices to Zeus and Hera in Rome. They had wandered Europe as Jews, settled in Africa as Muslims, established universities as Catholics, funded schools as Hindus and Buddhists. In region after region, time after time, whichever set of religious or cultural beliefs offered the most security to the Family, those were the beliefs with which MacCleirighs cloaked themselves.

Thus the MacCleirighs who built the ancient structure below in the sixth century C.E. had disguised it as a Christian church because the Zurich of that time was a Christian principality.

Jess did not believe hypocrisy was involved in this strategy. The First Gods chose the Family to keep their knowledge safe until they returned. For the knowledge to be safe, the Family had to be safe. If history had taught the MacCleirighs anything, it was that proselytizing was dangerous. And so, they kept their actual beliefs to themselves, knowing they'd have ample time to convince the rest of the world of the truth of the First Gods when those gods returned. Until then, the Family was content to be background noise to the pageant of history. Unseen. Unknown. Safe.

Jess stepped from the staircase to a wood-plank walkway. It led to the entrance marked by intricate carved pillars and decorative panels that framed age-worn main doors.

"You understand?" Su-Lin asked her.

Jess did. The Family had constructed this to hide in plain sight. "At first glance, early Christian iconography."

"But what do *you* see?"

Jess didn't think her scholarship was in doubt. It was more as if she were being tested, as if Su-Lin had begun some kind of ritual that Florian had never spoken of. A ritual that led to revelation.

Composing herself, determined to succeed, Jess carefully studied the entrance to the shrine. "First, as a geologist, the stones appear to be limestone. Common for the area, easily obtained. When the shrine—the church—was first built, it would have been pure white. A beacon in a sea of mud and wooden huts. Impressive."

"What about the carvings?"

Jess looked to the left of the main doors, where a robed female figure had been carved from a stone pillar. "Starting with her, that figure has attributes of Mary, mother of Jesus. She holds a radiant cross to her heart, a circle of light above the transept. Around her head, obviously the glow of a halo."

"Obviously."

"Behind the female's right shoulder, looking on, a male figure." Jess assessed the carving for a moment. It was badly weathered, more so than the female figure, which she found odd. The man's hands and fingers appeared unnaturally long, even for the primitive style of the carvings. They had lost definition, but his thumb and forefinger were touching to form a circle, with the remaining fingers each curved to a different degree. "Not a lot of detail left, but he's giving a blessing, so it could be Joseph. Maybe even John the Baptist. Definitely a male secondary to Mary."

She pointed to the figure's other shoulder. The weathering wasn't as bad in that section. "That sun with twelve rays of light coming from the center, no question but that's the Holy Spirit."

"Now tell me what you really see."

Jess nodded. She looked past the veil in which her ancestors had wrapped this building: to the world, a Christian church, but to the Family, a shrine to different, older gods.

"That's not Mary," she began, "and that's our cross, not theirs."

The Family knew that the bladed cross the female figure carried owed nothing to Christianity. In the outside world, though, some historians recognized it as a Tuareg cross. The best-known example was *la croix d'Agadès*—the Cross of Agadez—symbol of the ancient trading city in central Niger. There were many variants of that early symbol, and they reflected many other nomadic communities throughout Saharan Africa.

In modern times, the bladed cross was often seen as a symbol of Islam, though there was some thought that it might have originated as a Christian symbol prior to 700 C.E. Still other historians suspected the cross's circle-and-diamond motif reached back a thousand years earlier, to the cult of Tanis, goddess of Carthage and wife of Baal.

Only the Family knew the true history of the bladed cross. Its origins went even further back than the Phoenicians, to the time of the First Gods, whose symbol it truly was. Why that should be so, not even the Family's scholars knew, but to this day, each member of the Twelve Lines continued to wear the distinctive symbol of their faith, whenever and wherever it would not draw undue attention.

Florian's cross . . . she'd wanted me to have it . . . Jess wrenched her mind away from that dark thought. Her aunt's body had not been found. Her cross was lost forever.

"The male figure," she continued, "his hand—that's not a divine blessing. It's our sign, of the Hidden Scroll, the traditions we follow." Even now, with certain phrases, that sign was used to identify one MacCleirigh cousin to another.

"And that sun," Jess added, "is not the sun. It has twelve rays of light, the table of the defenders."

She paused, realizing that the familiar symbolism now had meaning for her *personally*. She would be written into the *Traditions* as an individual, for future Family lessons. She wondered if there'd ever be a keepsake and a story from her life to add to the wall of defenders.

Her gaze shifted to a second pillar to the right of the doorway, to a figure of a robed male. The stones on that entire side, like the small section on the female's side, were also more heavily weathered, and the figure's nose was long missing, its remaining facial features worn to an eerie, almost skeletal appearance. A swaddled baby floated behind the male figure's right shoulder. Behind his left shoulder stood a shining cross on a distant hill. As with the female on the facing pillar, Jess saw grooves to indicate a glow surrounding the male figure's head as well.

The only significant Family symbology missing from the male figure was the sign of the Twelve Restored. However, the figure's hand was broken off. There was no way to know for certain, but it might once have held an inscribed disk, like the present-day Family's identifying medallions. The two messengers who'd rescued her in the Barrens had each shown her theirs.

Jess was ready to state her conclusions. "Both figures in the pillars, male and female, they're defenders."

"What does that tell you?"

"There's something inside worth defending."

Su-Lin fixed her gaze on Jess. *"An deiseoil air?"*

Jess inhaled deeply. It was the ancient question she'd heard for the first time on her sixteenth birthday, when Florian began preparing her for her turn. The question asked of each defender since the first was chosen by the First Gods. *Are you ready?*

She spoke the ancient answer.

"'seadh."

I am.

"Then the doors are yours to open, paid in blood."

Blood, Jess thought. *The price of succession by bloodline.* She walked forward, put both hands on the heavy iron latch that held the church doors closed, pushed up, and—

Pain.

The underside of the latch was studded with twelve sharpened, X-shaped blades.

Jess jerked her hands free. She stared, shocked, at her blood-smeared palms and fingers. Florian had said nothing of this.

Sweat pricked her face, and she looked at her cousin.

Su-Lin was unmoved. "You said you were ready."

It took a long moment, but Jess finally understood. *Not Florian's blood—my own.* She turned back to the door, put her hands on the latch, pushed up with all her will.

The blades cut again, but this time she was the chosen.

The doors gave way.

Inside. Cool and timeless silence. Jess trembled, senses heightened by adrenaline and pain. A soft amber glow drew her eyes upward to see—

Electric lightbulbs, tripod-mounted, high along the walls to her right and left.

Jess heard Su-Lin's voice now. It was as if she were speaking to her from some great distance, and not from right beside her.

"Those were installed fifty years ago. The soot from torches was damaging the stonework."

Su-Lin took her to a battered wooden chest against the stone-block wall.

Draped over the chest were three separate garments. A simple white linen shift. A long white linen cape, sleeveless, with purple edging and braided purple threads. An ornate vest, also sleeveless, near-rigid with glittering metallic embroidery of oak leaves, red and green and gold.

Religious clothing.

The long sleeveless outergarment was like the cope worn by certain priests in Christian ceremonies, and the decorated vest, though embroidered with leaves, not crosses, was an *amphibalus,* similar to the chasuble worn by Catholic priests when celebrating Mass or Holy Communion. Like most priestly garb, their design was an echo of druidic times.

Jess's wounded fingers were clumsy to obey her as she struggled out of boots, then jeans, then travel shirt and underwear. She shivered, naked in this ancient, hallowed place.

Jess turned to see Su-Lin by a stone basin on the far right wall. She held out a natural sponge.

The basin held cool water. Jess plunged both hands in to rinse them, then dabbed them with the sponge. She winced as each cut stung.

"Alum," her cousin said. "To stop the bleeding."

When Jess had finished, she held out her hands, and Su-Lin bound them in scarlet strips of cotton.

Only then did she help Jess don her shift, the *amphibalus,* and finally the cape.

Su-Lin stepped back, assessing her. Then she beckoned Jess to follow her into the long central hall of the cross-shaped shrine.

Still barefoot, Jess walked on smooth limestone tiles worn with two distinct trails. How many generations of defenders had followed this path before her?

Ahead, where an ordinary church would have had its altar, the long aisle ended in another wall, unornamented. Centered in that wall was a pair of doors, oak again, bound by iron. There was no latch to seal them.

Su-Lin put her hands on the doors and looked back. "Jessica, you will follow as others have before you." Again, the words sounded ceremonial. "You will arrive by a way you know not. You will be led in paths you have not traveled. Darkness will be made light before you, and what is broken will be mended. These things will you do for our Family, and you will not forsake it."

The Secret. Jess nodded, ready for her turn. Her burden.

The inner doors swung open.

"The Chamber of Heaven . . ."

Jess breathed those words, barely audible, as she turned slowly in a circle, awed, reverent.

Each modern replica of this room that she'd seen before—whether here in Zurich or Hong Kong, Rome, everywhere—had resembled this one: circular, its walls plain stone, its ceiling midnight blue, a painted hemisphere of stars and constellations. In its center, a round table ringed by twelve chairs, signifying the equality of those who would sit there.

But this ancient inner sanctum . . . this chamber . . . almost a millennium and a half older than any of the others . . . it was that much closer in time to the real Chamber of Heaven in which the First Gods had made their Promise to the Family.

Her gaze traveled up to the dome high above the chamber's curved walls of stained limestone blocks. The ceiling's plaster was cracked in places, the vivid colors of its sky and stars faded in the dim electric light. She looked down to a floor black with age.

Jess's chest tightened with emotions she could barely contain. It was an incredible reaffirmation of her faith. To see that the Family of today had preserved the knowledge of this site so precisely over the centuries. Such respect for continuity of knowledge. Direct evidence that made it so much easier to believe that the rest of the Family's traditions from the time of the First Gods had also survived their passage through the ages.

"Over all that time . . ." Jess marveled. "Nothing's changed."

Su-Lin took Jess's arm. "Not quite." She guided Jess to the room's central table and positioned her behind the high-backed, carved oak chair marked with the symbol of Jess's Family Line. "Look closer."

Jess put her bandaged hand on the chair before her. Not fifteen hundred years old, but what piece of furniture could last that long and still be in use? The chairs, she decided, had been replaced over the centuries, but they were still oak.

She turned her attention to the table, to check if that wood had also been—

Her eyes widened.

"The table," she said. "It's stone."

"Look closer," Su-Lin said again.

Jess moved the chair aside and touched the table's surface with two of her uncut fingertips. The cool stone felt smooth, honed. "Granite . . . fine grain . . . this green cast's common to Switzerland, so I'd say it's local. But why would it not be—"

Her fingertips stopped as they reached one of the twelve lines that radiated from the table's center, dividing it into twelve wedges. All the lines she'd seen before on the oak tables in the Family's replica chambers were either painted on or made of inlaid wood or metal strips.

Jess turned to her cousin. "The lines are engraved. Is that what you meant?"

Su-Lin said nothing.

Jess turned back to the old stone table. A moment later, she caught her breath in surprise. She'd missed something else. Something significant.

In every modern Chamber of Heaven, the oak tables had been identical. Each of the twelve sections of the table bore a different symbol—a representation of the constellations. Not those of the common zodiac but those of the Family; to this day Family astronomers still argued over where the twelve celestial patterns fit among the stars.

"The constellation silhouettes, they're not—"

"They're not constellations."

Jess stared at her cousin, shocked. She'd just contradicted a basic fact of Family history that Jess had been taught since childhood. "But . . ."

"Look closer, Jessica."

Bewildered, Jess looked again at the table's surface, then, after a moment's thought, chose the concave design on the segment closest to her. It was the Blossom constellation—a large circle atop a small circle atop a horizontal bar. What else could it be?

She bit her lip in frustration. It was clear she was still being tested, but she had no idea what was expected of her.

After a moment, Su-Lin pulled one of the chairs away from the table, revealing a purple-cloth-wrapped package, the size of a small shoebox. She picked up the package and carried it to another segment of the table whose indentation Jess had been taught was the constellation of the Archer's Bow.

Reverently unfolding the richly colored cloth, Su-Lin uncovered a pitted black metal object, which she placed in the indented symbol. It fit perfectly.

She looked at Jess inquiringly.

"Is it a meteorite?" Jess asked.

Su-Lin's only response was a repetition of that maddening instruction. "Look closer."

Her professional knowledge challenged, Jess walked around the table and picked up the object. It was surprisingly heavy, but she was relieved to discover that it *was* a meteorite, and it had an endcut. The fact that the dark stone was cut made it a "half individual" in the parlance of her field. She studied the diagram inscribed on its flat surface, recognized it.

"It's a heliocentric solar system, so it dates around . . . third century B.C.E."

Her cousin shook her head.

Jess felt a flash of annoyance. "I can't date it precisely without a lab. How much older?"

"Nine thousand years."

The impact of those words struck the sound-hushed chamber like rolling thunder after lightning. "It's not possible."

"Even so." Su-Lin waved a hand at the other segments of the table. "It's our belief that the so-called constellation silhouettes painted or inlaid on our wooden tables are, in reality, two-dimensional outlines of three-dimensional hollows designed to hold twelve different objects. One of these twelve objects is that meteorite."

"Our belief?" Jess's grip tightened on the meteorite. Was Su-Lin saying the defenders didn't *know* what the twelve symbols really were? Or what they really meant?

Then, at last, like countless others before her, she assumed her burden as she learned the truth.

"The Secret's lost," Su-Lin said, "and not even the defenders know where to find it."

TEN

Ironwood stepped through the airlock of the alien spacecraft.

Someday, he thought. *Someday . . .* Then his casino's tidal wave of sound slammed into him and the illusion was destroyed.

Bells chimed, electronic tones warbled up and down the scales, sirens screamed, and, woven through it all, was the omnipresent rush of what pros called the sound of rain—the raucous dance of coins against coins as they tumbled from slot machine hoppers into hard metal payout trays. Of course, these days, only a handful of the slots on the casino's main floor operated with coins. The majority of them used player cards, electronically deducting dollars and cents in small and regular amounts, occasionally adding back large sums, but invariably according to finely tuned gaming equations that guaranteed slightly more deductions than additions, except for the lucky few.

Because of those player cards, the sound of money that filled the air surrounding Ironwood—the sound of wealth and luck and dreams come true—was itself a recording, an illusion, no different from the green-skinned alien drink hostesses in their silver miniskirts, his dealers and croupiers in their Space Service uniforms, and his personal favorite: the soaring Syd Mead architectural flourishes evoking the inside of a fantastical otherworldly vehicle.

"Welcome back, sir!"

And so it begins. Ironwood nodded to Osman Mirza, manager of his Atlantic City Encounters Casino & Resort. The slim young man in a sober black suit had charged on the double through a throng of tourists. In his wake fluttered two executive assistants in narrow pencil skirts and steep stilettos never meant for running. All were slightly out of breath. As they ought to be.

As a matter of personal policy, Ironwood never gave his employees advance notice of impromptu visits to his properties. They had to be prepared to see and welcome him at any time.

"No one broke the bank yet, Ozzie?"

Mirza gestured out at the sea of flashing lights and noisy electronic misdirection. "No, sir. Statistical analysis shows we're dead-on our rate of—"

Ironwood thumped Mirza's narrow shoulder. "Don't mind me, son. You're doing a fine job."

"Thank you, sir," Mirza said, relieved. "Your suite is ready."

"I know it is. But I'm going to the Red Room first. Tell J.R. when he comes in."

Mirza blinked, and the two executive assistants shared a sudden furtive glance.

"Your son is here?"

"Junior's watching them park the bus." Limousines were too small for Ironwood's liking, so he kept his offices in a fleet of buses. "Like a rock star on tour," the *Wall Street Journal* had said in a recent profile. "Tell him where I'll be. And tell him I said he's to get his backside in there ASAP. No side trips."

"As you wish, Mr. Ironwood."

Ironwood walked on, oblivious to the noisy groups of dreamers who enriched him with their gambling, dreaming his own dream. *Someday . . .*

Officially, the Red Room was the smallest of Encounters' six main gaming areas. It was located off a corridor that did nothing but loop around a set of upscale shops, and as such it seemed to be an afterthought in the meticulously designed resort complex. As a result, the New Jersey Casino Control Commission accepted without question that the Red Room wasn't utilized as a full-time gaming area but was instead what Ironwood's management team called a research facility. A place where new games and technologies were tested. Naturally, that use required safeguards, falling within the same security procedures protecting the casino's counting rooms.

Thus, the Red Room was unsecured by electronic systems or biometric hand scanners, retinal readers or numbered keypads. Entrance was granted only by personal recognition by three guards posted outside its doors. Sometimes the simplest precautions were the strictest in the world of high security.

As Ironwood approached the Red Room, he noted with approval three former marines, all of a type, attentive-eyed, solid with muscles. There was no attempt to hide the bulge of the weapons they carried under their smart hotel-staff blazers.

Two of the guards simultaneously turned their keys at wall-mounted stations sited far enough apart that one person could not operate both at the same time. The third opened the heavy door. Its Kevlar-reinforced ceramic core—bullet- and blast-proof—was discreetly masked by pale oak veneer.

Ironwood nodded at the guards as he passed into the Red Room. "Thank you, gentlemen." Respect was earned, and these men had his.

High overhead, the Red Room's ceiling was a frozen sea of curved, reflective panels studded with bright lights. The deliberate visual chaos was designed to hide overhead remote-controlled cameras that could move ceaselessly and undetectably from table to table on their search for cheaters—if the room were ever restored to its original purpose.

Now it contained all of the trappings expected of a research facility for new gambling technology. A traditional carousel placement of video slot machines was oriented toward the main door, each machine with its covering console removed to expose electronic workings, while their screens flashed with seductive displays.

The rest of the visible space was occupied by banks of computer equipment, also in constant operation. A conference table against a featureless beige back wall was littered with file folders, empty coffee cups and soft drink cans, and crumpled candy wrappers.

The air was cold. The background hum of industrial air-conditioning was noticeable; the murmured conversation of eight technicians, barely audible.

Whenever the representatives of the New Jersey Casino Control Commission wanted to check for unauthorized, private high-roller playing of unsanctioned games, they were welcome. The Red Room was exactly what everyone expected it to be.

Except that it wasn't. Because of what lay behind the featureless beige side wall, through the single cylindrical darkroom door, installed not to keep light out but to maintain the temperature on the other unseen side.

The eight technicians were also not what they seemed. Unofficially, each made five times the salary of Osman Mirza, who was, as Encounters' manager, the highest-paid member of the resort's staff. At least on the resort's official books.

"Hey, boss." Keisha Harrill led Ironwood's Red Room team. She wore a blue T-shirt with a large Union Jack above the word GREECE, which Ironwood found comical for someone whose expertise involved mapping. Just twenty-eight, Keisha was already set for a comfortable retirement due to the seven-figure bonus he'd paid her to reject Google's latest offer.

A few of the other technicians looked up from their workstations for a moment, curious about what new challenge he might be bringing them. Of the eight people on his handpicked team of specialists, four men and one woman were close to Keisha's age, young and eager and brilliant, as innovative mathematicians are apt to be. The other two were veteran engineers, both in their fifties. When it came to building custom computers from scratch, experience counted as much as innovation.

"What can we do for you?" Keisha asked.

"I had an idea. Something to try while we're waiting for a fourth set of search coordinates."

Ironwood was pleased to see that with those words he had her complete attention. The work the team did in this room on his behalf was not something he could ever discuss by e-mail or by phone. If the government ever learned what went on here, they wouldn't call him to the Hill for testimony—they'd lock him up and vaporize the key.

"What if we compare the first three sites, you know, come up with all their points of similarities? If we find some other locations that have the same ones, we'd have ourselves some new target spots to check."

Keisha fingered her long, beaded dreadlocks as she considered the request. "That's cool. In fact, Frank's been working on that since we got the hit on that third set of coordinates." She called over to a member of her team. "Frank? You mind coming over here?"

Frank Beyoun reluctantly wandered over to join Keisha and Ironwood. He was short and bearded, wearing tattered jeans, sandals, and an untucked green and brown flannel shirt. If Frank's outfit ever changed, Ironwood had never seen it.

"Any luck?"

"Haven't cracked it."

Keisha gave the glum mathematician an encouraging look. "Explain to the man, Frank."

"The thing is the first site, in India, it's in a river valley. Inland, low altitude, reachable by boat back when it was built. The second's in the Andes. But high altitude. Way inland. Unreachable by boat. Third's in the South Pacific. Originally above sea level. On an island. Boats all the time." Frank looked away as if he were embarrassed by his failure. "So far we found nothing else to link them. Other than the three outposts have identical designs."

"Okay, Frank, that's all we needed," Keisha said. "Back to it."

Frank nodded and shuffled off toward his station.

Ironwood had deliberately held back a few details from the team, though he'd shared the important ones they needed to do their work. Now he reminded Keisha of one of those details. "Don't forget we found identical designs *and* similar artifacts in all three outposts."

The carved stone tables in the outposts in India and Peru were virtually the same. Merrit had reported there was a similar-sized table in the underwater outpost in Polynesia. Then there were the two black mete-orites, from India and Polynesia. Each was inscribed with an identical diagram of the solar system.

Keisha looked thoughtful. "I don't think there's any question the outposts were built by the same people, what with the ones in India and Peru con-structed within a few hundred years of each other. My guess is the one in Polynesia will turn out to have similar dating, too. That said, it's no big shock the artifacts in them are the same." Her smile was playful, ques-tioning. "You ever going to tell us what the artifacts really are?"

Ironwood winked, letting her know there was no chance in hell of that. "Just what I told you before. Furniture and carvings."

Keisha properly didn't press the matter. "Anyway, the point is—"

A warning chime sounded, and she broke off. The main door was about to open.

"Keep going," Ironwood said. "It's just J.R."

"Okay, well, the point is, we've yet to identify a common factor that accounts for why the outposts were built where they were built."

"What about the one in Peru? It's not too far from Machu Picchu. That's a sacred site. Maybe some ley lines nearby? Earth energy? Any chance there're some of those lines at the India and South Pacific finds?"

Though it made sense to him, Ironwood didn't expect his suggestion to go down well with this particular brain trust. He was right.

"If there *were* such a thing as mystical ley lines," Keisha said, "you can be sure geologists and physicists would be happily engaged in rewriting the laws of nature at Sedona and Glastonbury and Rosslyn and who knows where else. And I personally would be checking to see if they ran any-where close to the outposts."

"But there's no such thing, is what you're saying," J.R. interrupted as he entered and joined their conversation. Ironwood smelled the reason for his son's tardiness and attitude—he'd stopped at a bar or, more probably, lifted someone's drink order from one of the hostesses' trays.

"What I'm saying," Keisha said pleasantly but firmly, "is, if phenomena like ley lines or Earth energy lines are real, their existence has yet to be demonstrated with appropriate scientific rigor. Bring me the evidence, and I'll change my mind."

Ironwood smiled. That intellectual openness was why he'd chosen Keisha to lead his team. His only point of disagreement with her was on what constituted appropriate evidence.

His son, however, was a different matter. No choice there.

"J.R., they're waiting for you in security. Novak's going to put you on rotation. Pick up some coffee on the way."

Ironwood could see the resentment in his son's eyes—his usual reaction to parental orders—but J.R. wisely moved toward the door and left without further comment.

"Hey, boss," Keisha suddenly added, "if you've got the time, we can show you something new we're trying. No results yet, but you never know."

Ironwood brightened. He loved new things. "What've you got?"

Keisha led him to the room's biggest display, nine feet on the diagonal, turned so it couldn't be viewed by anyone coming through the main door. She picked up a remote control with a large touch screen and tapped it several times. "Remember I mentioned Glastonbury before?"

Ironwood nodded, intrigued. Glastonbury was a small English town in the county of Somerset, and of particular interest to him. Among the many legends associated with the place, some maintained it was where Joseph of Arimithea had traveled about thirty years after the death of Jesus, and where he'd built the first church in Great Britain as a secure fortress in which to hide the Holy Grail.

A series of place names materialized on the giant display.

Keisha moved her finger across the remote, and a highlight bar flashed down the list until it reached GLASTONBURY/SOMERSET/ENG 51.09N 02.43W. "Here we go." She tapped again. At once, an aerial image appeared of a small town with a distinctive triangular layout surrounded by multihued farm fields.

The aerial perspective zoomed in.

"Glastonbury Abbey," Keisha said. "World's oldest Christian church. At least, probably the oldest one originally constructed aboveground. Built around A.D. 60, more or less."

The zoom stopped.

In a green field, the white outline of a building was visible—the ruins of the abbey. Ironwood knew he was looking at stones that had been put into place almost two thousand years ago. Moments like these always filled him with awe. How long humans had lived on this small world—and after all that time, how little they knew.

"So," Keisha said, "this is one of those places we thought we'd search on a hunch. See if there had ever been an outpost here."

"You already told me you didn't find one."

"No outpost, but under that hill—"

"It's called a tor," Ironwood corrected. "Glastonbury Tor."

"Right. Under that tor, then, there's a structure that's not in the textbooks. Take a look."

Ironwood watched the screen, hooked as always, as his illegal $20 million investment came to the fore.

Keisha tapped the remote, and all the colors on the screen shifted, becoming wild and garish. "False colors," she'd explained to him once, arbitrarily assigned shades chosen to heighten the differences between various materials. On the screen, the tree leaves were now white. The grass beneath them, orange. The white stones of the ruins were bright red. The cars parked in the nearby lot were black.

"Switching to SARGE," Keisha said. She hit a key, and the parking lot they'd just been looking at suddenly disappeared. Apparently, it hadn't been built back in 2005, the creation date of the particular version of the SARGE database he'd acquired. "Now we take a one-meter slice to eliminate surface structures . . . following the topo contours . . ."

The trees disappeared, and the bright red stones of the abbey ruins shifted slightly as only the foundation material remained visible. All the other surface detail disappeared as well. Instead, a spidery set of black and green lines appeared against a multicolored mottled background.

"Pipes?" Ironwood asked.

"Drainpipes, for the most part. There're lots more at two meters. But we'll go straight to five meters below ground . . ."

The image shifted again. Now a smaller rectangle of red stones appeared where the abbey ruins had been. Ironwood knew that meant that sixteen feet or so under the abbey, another, older structure had once stood. Likely a Roman temple. It was common practice for early Christian churches to be constructed on the sites of pagan temples.

"Five meters is where we start to look for the outposts in this kind of soil. Want to try?" Keisha held out the remote.

Ironwood couldn't resist playing with his toys. He tapped the control.

On-screen, a bright blue in-scale floor plan appeared of what he'd taken to calling an alien outpost. A moment later, that floor plan began flickering over the screen, angled one way, then another, back and forth, appearing and disappearing so quickly he could only see it as an afterimage. It was how the computer program was attempting to find any pattern in the high-contrast mottling of the site's soil and stone matching the layout of an outpost.

The same technique was used by the military to analyze surveillance photos. While a human eye might be unable to notice the camouflaged silhouette of an enemy tank, a computer could apply that outline to every possible point in a photo, at every possible angle. The pattern search was time-consuming. It was also virtually infallible.

After half a minute, the flickering stopped and a message appeared: NO MATCH.

"Now," Keisha said, "in an actual search, we'd be covering a square kilometer at a time, and we'd go down in half-meter increments. It took us three days to do the full search of that tor."

She tapped the control again. "Here, let me take you to the fun stuff right away."

Ironwood watched the screen intently, anticipating it would soon reveal the familiar outline of a megalithic burial chamber beneath the abbey. The hills of Great Britain were riddled with them.

Then the screen refreshed and he blinked, surprised. The structure hidden far below the abbey was five times bigger than any megalithic burial chamber he had ever seen; moreover, its walls were remarkably straight, and all its angles were at ninety degrees.

"How deep is that?" Unconsciously, he held his breath as he waited for the answer.

"Twenty meters. Guess what it is yet?"

Ironwood thought quickly. *Twenty meters. It's got to be thousands of years old. But the construction is so perfect. As if it were built recently and*—Then he had it. "It's a bomb shelter."

He regarded the buried structure with real interest, not regret. The data that Keisha had just used to flush it out was the reason why the security in this room was so tight. SARGE. Or, as the U.S. Air Force called it, the Synthetic Aperture Radar Global Environment database.

SARGE was his newly adopted $20-million child born of unprecedented air force remote-sensing technology, first tested on two space shuttle flights in the 1980s. After those flights, the technology had evolved in two forms— one public and the other very private.

Publicly, SARGE was being used in global scientific efforts to create topographic maps and monitor sea levels and earthquake movements from space. Privately, the massive database was being used by the United States to create a classified satellite surveillance network: EMPIRE, a network of free-flying constellations of multiparameter imaging-radar satellites. Those satellites could not only produce images of the Earth's surface at night and through cloud cover at unprecedented resolutions but could also look past the surface for buried installations, or anything else that might be hidden a few meters underground—and many more meters beyond that, too, if the right techniques were used to mine the data.

SARGE was perhaps the greatest trove of intelligence information ever developed.

A version of it now belonged to him.

"Most likely from the fifties," Ironwood said about the shelter, "built to protect local government in the event of atomic war."

"Optimists," Keisha said. "Anyway, here's the 3-D model we assembled from ten-centimeter slices."

Ironwood watched, fascinated, as the outline of the bomb shelter appeared to lift off from the screen and rotate, revealing a three-dimensional reconstruction that showed its curved roof, and even the blurred shapes of the bunks, desks, and room dividers inside.

It was a deceptively simple demonstration of capability that came with complex significance. Using the massive collection of information in the stolen SARGE database, it would be possible to create similar images of every hidden U.S. Navy sub base, every secret U.S. Air Force missile silo, every secure and undisclosed location built to protect elected officials and preserve the continuity of government in case of war or disaster. All it would take was someone—or some country—who could afford the computer system to go looking for them, and who also had access to the algorithm that allowed unprecedented detail to be extracted from what most analysts would call static or noise.

Ironwood wasn't thinking of the legal and moral consequences of his acquisition, though. He knew the air force was aware a copy of the SARGE database had been illegally made, and he didn't doubt there was a high-level investigation already under way. Nor did he have false hopes of evading that investigation forever.

He was in a race, and the only way he would avoid a life of exile or imprisonment was to find the proof that he'd need to discredit the government before the government found the proof they needed to arrest him.

How long that race would last, he didn't know. For the moment, in the sanctuary of his Red Room with his team, he didn't care. Instead, once again he dreamed.

Someday, Ironwood told himself, he'd see to it the whole world could look through the government's lies to the real truth they were concealing. After all, what was the good of great wealth if it couldn't leave this world a better place? A world without secrets.

ELEVEN

Four days later, Jess MacClary's hands still hurt.

The palm of her right hand was shielded by a rubberized strip of bright green bandage. Five sutures. Her left hand was immobilized in thick white dressings from which only her thumb and fingertips emerged. Nine sutures. Even so, Jess's real pain was spiritual, and she wasn't sure how to deal with that.

She'd returned to the highest floor of the MacCleirigh Foundation building, the same secure level where ten defenders had welcomed her via satellite screen links. But there was little sign of such technology in the Foundation's library.

As evidence, three computer terminals, concealed behind the rolltops of antique desks in one secluded alcove, provided the Family's researchers with instant access to the digitized MacCleirigh archives in Australia. That concession to the twenty-first century was unobtrusive, though, as if computers were only a passing fancy.

For the rest of the library, double-height bookcases and cabinets that could be reached only by wheeled ladder were the order of the day. As were the antique brass lights with green glass shades, somber wall hangings, massive walnut reading tables, and high-back green leather chairs. Over all drifted the thick, musty scent of ancient paper and oiled wood. Without question, a place for scholarship, not relaxation.

Jess was not in the mood for either pursuit. She sat alone at a long table, a single book before her, as yet unopened.

As a defender, she now could access all locked shelves reserved only for the Twelve. Yet with centuries of journals and secret writings available to her, including her aunt's archaeological field journals, the volume she'd taken from the shelves today was one she'd read before, when she was in her teens: *The Lost Constellations and Zodiacal Traditions of the Family, Their Lore and Meaning, by Percival Lowell, Director of the Observatory at Flagstaff, Arizona; Non-resident Professor of Astronomy at the Massachusetts Institute of Technology; Membre de la Société Astronomique de France; etc., etc.*

Lowell's efforts were legendary. Not only did the renowned American astronomer further the scholarly goals of the MacCleirighs, he did so while diverting mainstream academics to safer pursuits not in conflict with the Family's. At the turn of the last century, he'd been third in succession to be defender of his line but had never been called to serve. His scholarship, however, was such that he had been admitted to the 144 who knew the truth of the First Gods and their Promise to return.

"I see you've gone back to the classics."

Her cousin stood beside her.

"May I?" Su-Lin gestured to the chair across the table, sitting only when Jess nodded her assent. "We're all troubled at first, you know. It's unsettling to discover the thing we've waited all our lives to defend doesn't exist."

"But it does."

Su-Lin looked surprised. "Sorry?"

"The Secret existed once, didn't it? The First Gods gave it to our ancestors, or at least put our ancestors in charge of defending it."

"As it is our tradition." Su-Lin's reply was another meaningful phrase to those within the Family.

"So the only thing that's happened is . . . we screwed up. *Lost* the Secret. But it's still out there. Which means it can be found."

Su-Lin regarded Jess like a wise parent who's heard her offspring spin a foolish, wishful chain of logic. "We looked for thousands of years, Jessica. The Secret's gone."

Jess ran the fingers of her right hand over the worn leather of the Lowell book. It had been privately published, as all Family books and pamphlets were. This one in New York, 1908. A Tuareg cross was embossed upon the cover. "The temples were also lost to us for thousands of years." She looked up at Su-Lin and caught her cousin in a frown that swiftly disappeared. "And *they* were found again."

"To what end?" Su-Lin asked. "The temples in India and Peru were looted long before Ironwood's arrival. Now that you're at the table, I can tell you that Florian recovered a second sun map in the Polynesian temple, the engraving on it identical to the one in the Shrine. But that was all she found. Presumably Ironwood has it now. The one I showed you has been in our possession for as long as we've had written records." Su-Lin's expression was sympathetic but firm. "Whatever clues those ruins once held, they're gone now. The Family must move on."

"We've failed our sacred trust with the First Gods and we should just 'move on?' To *what*?"

"That's something you have to decide for yourself. Reread our *Traditions*." Su-Lin tapped the old book between them. "This one, too. There're different ways to view what they say. Some of us believe the Secret the

First Gods gave us was not a goal but a process, a way of life. So we honor them by living that life as we were directed—in the pursuit and preservation of knowledge." Su-Lin sat back, her expression expectant of compliance. "That's how I've moved on."

Jess still felt bewildered, even angered, but dutifully she opened Lowell's book and flipped through to a page she knew well. On it, a simple silhouette, the symbol of her line: the Branch.

It was one of twelve symbols inlaid or painted on every round table in every modern reconstruction of a Chamber of Heaven. Jess had been taught since childhood that it represented a constellation—but after Su-Lin's revelation in the Shrine of Turus, it seemed the Branch had no connection with the First Gods' ancient skies. It was merely the *outline* of an object the gods of her faith had entrusted to the Family. To revere, protect, and *defend*.

An object the MacCleirighs had lost.

The Branch itself was only one of twelve symbols—the twelve constellations in the Family zodiac. Jess at age three could recite them by heart, could draw them blindfolded.

Three were symbols from the Earth—those things that were inanimate: the Diamond, the River, and the Mountain. Three were symbols from the Green—those things that brought life from the Earth: the Seed, the Blossom, and the Branch. Three were symbols from the Hand—those things that humans made to give them power over the Green and the Earth: the Blade, the Archer's Bow, and the Chain. The final three were symbols from the Blood—those things that gave movement to the Hand: the Skull, the Eye, and the Heart.

The lesson-stories of Jess's childhood had taught her that the gods of her faith themselves had drawn these symbols' shapes among the stars on their maps. They'd recorded them as constellations so the knowledge they contained would always be there, for all who looked to the sky. She now knew that those stories, the same ones Lowell the astronomer had secretly relayed, which had guided her education as an adult, were incomplete.

It wasn't merely *knowledge* that had been given to her family—it was actual, physical artifacts. Twelve literal gifts from the gods that had fit within the hollows on the carved stone table.

Jess turned the page, to the symbol she knew as the Archer's Bow. Its story had once made so much sense. The bow and arrow were a powerful piece of technology, extending the reach of hunters a dozen times. That made food-gathering faster, more efficient. When a small team of hunters could provide food for a village, other members of that village were freed to pursue other specialties. To the Family, the bow and arrow marked the birth of scholarship.

Now she knew that the object that fit within the silhouette of the Archer's Bow had nothing to do with hunting. It was a meteorite with an impossibly ancient map of the solar system.

Under her cousin's watchful gaze, Jess turned page after delicate page of the old book, trying her best to look anew at each illustrated silhouette—the symbols of her faith. What object could possibly fit within the Branch? The Skull? The Blossom? What had been their purpose? And why had the dimensions of the Chamber of Heaven remained unchanged over millennia while the secret of its contents vanished?

Jess felt her heart pound. Her fingers pulsed painfully with the same urgent rhythm. What she believed and what she knew had never been in conflict before.

What if *everything* she'd been taught was a lie?

"What are you thinking?" Su-Lin asked.

Jess wasn't ready to share the depth of her fears. Instead, she offered a question of her own. "Why keep this from the rest of the Family?"

"Jessica, really. You know the answer to that."

"I don't."

Su-Lin replied as if she were stating the most self-evident truth. "Because the Family would fall apart. As defenders, we can't permit that. The Secret is what unites us. Not just the Twelve. Not just the 144. All of us. We've almost a thousand in the direct lines. Without a unifying purpose, the Family would have no reason to continue. Nine thousand years of unbroken history would come to an end."

Jess closed Lowell's book, thinking of the locked cabinet in this library, filled with writings only a handful of people had ever read, even over millennia.

"Has any defender ever lost faith? When they've learned the truth?"

A momentary shadow seemed to cross Su-Lin's calm face. "None that the *Traditions* record."

"Then how can you say what the rest of the Family would do? If everyone knew what we've lost, I believe they'd work tirelessly to rediscover it. A thousand scholars can do considerably more work than just the twelve of us."

Her cousin's voice cooled. "A word of caution. If I, or any defender, has reason to think you're going to betray our knowledge, you'll be replaced . . ."

Jess already knew about the two other "cousins" who would remain in reserve until she had children of her own: a twelve-year-old boy in Athens and a nine-year-old girl in Barcelona.

". . . or confined," Su-Lin added.

Confined? I've never heard of that . . . Jess felt the stirring of unease. "Has that ever happened before?"

"As often as required."

Jess closed the book and spoke carefully, truthfully. "I'd never betray the Family."

"That's right. You won't."

The ensuing awkward silence was broken by Su-Lin. "Do you feel ready to go back into the world?"

"Yes." Jess had slept for almost twenty hours after the revelations in the shrine and her subsequent trip to the building's infirmary. The three full days since then, spent shuttling between the Foundation's residential quarters and the library, were more than enough time spent in limbo.

Su-Lin slid a stiff brown envelope across the reading table. "Good. Your first assignment."

Jess opened the envelope. There was a large color photograph inside, apparently a blow-up from a driver's license. It showed a young man, good-looking, somewhere in his twenties, rather long dark hair, unusual eyes. Caucasian, but his features suggested a mixed background of some kind: Native American, Chinese . . . Jess couldn't tell. "Who's this?"

"His name's David Weir. He works in a lab that does genetic analysis for the U.S. Armed Forces. On the side, he works for Holden Ironwood."

"Doing what?"

"That's what you're going to find out."

There was only one reason Jess could think of that would explain why Su-Lin was giving her this assignment. "Did he have anything to do with Florian's murder?"

"It's possible." Su-Lin passed over two sheets of paper: addresses, phone numbers, a description of David Weir's car. "Some of his expenses have been paid by the same company that handles Ironwood's expeditions."

"How would you know that?"

"Ironwood surprised us in India, then Peru. We didn't want it to happen again, so Emil's been monitoring the expedition company, keeping track whenever it charters planes and boats, hires divers, pilots, what have you, for Ironwood. That's how we learned about the South Pacific expedition. And why Florian caught up with them in days, not months."

Su-Lin tapped the photo. "But this man, he's not expedition material. He's never been out of the United States. Never published in any journals.

Yet his expenses are being covered by the same company. If he has any connection to Ironwood's temple expeditions, we want to know."

Jess studied the photograph of the young man, caught again by the odd cast to his eyes. "He works in genetics?"

"That's the work of the lab he's in. He's a technician. Low level."

"Archaeology and genetics. Is there a chance Ironwood recovered remains from any of the temples?"

Su-Lin shook her head. "There was no indication of that in India or Peru, and the Polynesian site was underwater for a few thousand years at least. No bodies would survive that."

Jess scanned the printed sheets. Whoever he was, David Weir didn't seem to have done much of anything.

"Su-Lin, anyone can check this man out. I'd rather go to the South Pacific, see the temple for myself."

"You will. Just not yet. We're putting together a full expedition to the atoll, with armed security."

Jess started to protest further, but Su-Lin held up her hand. "Think about what happened, Jessica. Florian's death at a temple site could have several explanations, including involvement by Ironwood, but the attack on *you* . . . You must see the implications that concern us."

Implications? It took a moment for the realization to strike Jess.

"I was next in line."

"Exactly. Everyone in the Family knows there are twelve defenders and each one has two or three potential successors."

"Everyone in the Family . . ." Jess felt suddenly cold.

"No one outside the Family even knows that there *are* defenders, let alone who's next in line."

"Unless someone from inside the Family . . ." Jess felt her throat tighten. "What do we do?"

"Keep that suspicion to ourselves and move as quickly as we can to stay ahead of whoever it might be. Emil's in charge of the internal search, and no one can know the details." Su-Lin stood. "I'll make arrangements for your travel."

Jess nodded, all protest gone now, understanding what her cousin had left unsaid.

Someone in the Family was a traitor.

TWELVE

Late-night planes from Atlantic City International droned overhead, their lights flashing through breaks in heavy clouds the same color as the night sky. Their engines sounded distant, their power swallowed by thunder that still rolled up from the south. In the industrial park far below, the only thing moving or making a sound was a lone cable television installer, and he was completely out of place.

The only buildings within sight were mostly derelict or run-down: a printing plant, a few low-rise brick office buildings with heavy wire mesh over cracked glass panels on their doors and ground-floor windows, and an old, U-shaped warehouse converted into storage rental units. It was just past eleven on a Saturday night, and every window on the poorly lit and rain-wet street was dark—no telltale blue glow of a working television anywhere.

Still, there was a cable television van across the street from the court-yard parking lot of the converted factory. A sign on the back asked HOW'S MY DRIVING? Through small windows hidden in the dark areas of the van's colorful images of happy customers, a full suite of optical, infrared, and acoustical sensors scanned the warren of rental units across the street.

The van was the installer's destination. He reached the back of the vehicle and knocked twice, directing his gaze at the hidden port where the camera was positioned.

Then the rear latch clicked, and he yanked open the door and stepped up and into his office. The surveillance specialist gave him the bad news at once.

"They're talking about E.T. again."

Jack Lyle sighed as he settled into the swivel chair bolted to the floor of the van's back compartment. When he had started this case, it was challenging but straightforward: A copy of one of the country's most vital defense databases had been stolen, and the prime suspect was Holden Ironwood. All Lyle and his team of investigators had to do was prove who was responsible and stop him from selling it to America's enemies. Surveilling a petty criminal like David Weir to use him as an informant against a major criminal and potential traitor like Ironwood was a tried-and-true investigative technique. A methodical exploitation of such an asset should have resulted in an open-and-shut case.

Except for the damned aliens.

Lyle worked for the Air Force Office of Special Investigations' Region 7 detachment—the only detachment that didn't cover a specific geographical territory. Instead, Region 7 ran operations around the globe, and Lyle's cases routinely brought him into contact with the extreme cutting edge of the country's most advanced—and most secret—defense-related technologies. Ironwood's reputation as a notorious UFO fanatic was well known, and Lyle had initially discounted it for good reason.

In countless interviews, he'd heard top scientists and engineers lament the fact there were no crashed saucers in hidden hangars, no antigravity machines to reverse engineer, and no other miraculous outer space technology that would make their jobs easier. So, if the people at the apex of America's most advanced military R&D didn't know about alien spacecraft, then those spacecraft did not exist. More to the point, if flying saucers did exist, it was dead certain the civilians in the government would be incapable of keeping that information secret for more than, oh, about ten seconds, let alone since 1947.

Therefore, as far as Lyle was concerned, Ironwood's eccentric beliefs had no bearing on the air force case against him.

Until Weir and his nonhuman DNA came along.

No one in the AFOSI, including Lyle, knew what the hell *that* was about.

Colonel Kowinski had reported the genome on Weir's computer was some up-to-now unknown combination of readily identifiable human DNA and not-so-identifiable nonhuman DNA. "Anomalous" was what the colonel called it, which to Lyle meant she didn't have the personal expertise or resources to identify its origin.

Naturally, Kowinski had pressed him to grant her lab staff the necessary clearance to study the mysterious genome, but he'd refused. The fewer people who were part of this investigation, the less likely Ironwood would learn about it.

Kowinski had next made the case for him to bring in specialists of his own who already had top clearance. She went so far as to suggest this could be something of profound international and scientific value. She said the army would appreciate the air force's interest and enthusiasm. Like that would ever happen.

Lyle had refused again.

He had a higher-priority goal: protecting America.

That meant Holden Ironwood was first up, and all else was second—a decision that would make what was threatening to be a complex situation simple.

Or so he kept telling himself.

"How long this time?" Lyle asked.

Del Chang looked properly apologetic as he glanced away from his bank of surveillance equipment. The young man had lost his left leg in Iraq, and though the army no longer wanted him, he still skinned his scalp like a boot-camp recruit. The net result was Chang looked even younger than he was. That made him a perfect fit with the rest of the team. Everyone was young but Lyle.

Chang checked a notation he'd made in his duty log—a securely bound book with lined and numbered pages. "Ironwood called subject on subject's mobile at 21:57 hours, sir. They've been talking for—"

"An hour and six minutes," Lyle said. *Let's see the kids do that without a calculator.*

"Right," Chang confirmed. At least he didn't sound surprised.

Lyle looked to a monitor screen. He massaged his stiff knee, another unwelcome reminder of his own veteran status. Rain was not his friend these days.

The monitor filled with a blurred and shimmering infrared image of David Weir in his "lab"—one of the smallest rental spaces in the converted warehouse across the street. According to the floor plan Roz Marano had obtained from city files, Weir's unit came in at 102 square meters, about the floor space of a compact two-bedroom house, and apparently just big enough to house the equipment he needed to hunt Ironwood's Martians.

In the past fourteen days since his resignation from the Armed Forces DNA Identification Lab, David Weir had received deliveries here of approximately $130,000 worth of computer and lab equipment, all paid for by a subsidiary of Ironwood Medical Imaging Systems.

Over that same period, Lyle and his technicians had painstakingly tracked every phone call, text message, and e-mail Weir had sent and received. So far, annoyingly, everything matched the deal Weir and Ironwood had agreed to in the D.C. hotel: The kid was to search for so-called nonhuman DNA sequences in the genetic records of millions of individuals. That meeting and that first conversation, and all subsequent conversations, had been equally bizarre. Wall-to-wall aliens. Hidden outposts. Government conspiracies.

Lyle was convinced it had to be a smoke screen for something more down-to-earth: Ironwood's real agenda. The billionaire had to be using Weir as the equivalent of the magician's assistant, whose purpose was to distract the audience. Either way, whether the kid's involvement was intentional, or he was an unwitting pawn, he was an accomplice—and accomplices could be turned.

"Put them on speaker," Lyle said. He needed to concentrate on something other than these tight and uncomfortable confines. The air in the van was hot and dry from all the electronics, and there was no room to stretch out his complaining knee.

Chang flicked a switch, and Weir's annoyed voice came through the grille above his panel. Simultaneously, a small screen began displaying a rapidly moving green trace, visually mapping two voices as they were recorded.

Lyle settled back.

Ironwood's smoke screen couldn't last forever. Eventually, someone would make a mistake.

Someone always did.

THIRTEEN

"Because evolution proceeds by *chance*," David insisted. "That's why." Before Ironwood could interrupt him again, he held his phone close and continued in one breath. "So it *is* impossible that the *billions*—no, make that *trillions*—of *chance* occurrences that led to the evolution of humans on Earth happened in *exactly* the same way on *another* planet."

David inhaled deeply and sat back in the rickety office chair he'd drawn up to his makeshift desk. The walls of his new lab were soot-stained red brick with heavy wooden beams. The not-so-clean floor was splotched and cracked slab concrete. The hanging light fixtures on the twelve-foot ceilings were antique fluorescents, buzzing and flickering, washing everything below in sickly green.

He was a half hour and a world away from Ironwood's luxury casino resort in Atlantic City: close enough to be convenient, far enough away not to cost real money. *Bargains for billionaires,* David thought. Being cheap was either how Ironwood got rich or how he stayed that way.

"Two things wrong with that argument, Dave."

"Only two?" David tried to hide his frustration. Ironwood's incessant calls were making it hard to work at all. Still, he'd kept his word and paid for the equipment David had requested.

"First up, you're assuming that biology itself is blind. But you have to admit it's equally possible that it follows rules like every other science—universal rules. I mean, stars form wherever enough hydrogen clumps together, right? And that's no matter where or when. Why is that? Because those are the rules for how hydrogen behaves. So why can't that be true about life? What if the rules of biology make it so only RNA and DNA can carry genetic information?"

David winced and held the small phone away from his ear. Ironwood's voice blared from the speaker.

"What if only carbon-based life can get smart?"

David knew this conversation wouldn't end until Ironwood ended it. "So what's the second thing wrong with my argument?"

"Well, it just could be that Earth's some kind of alien farm, and we're the cattle."

David was glad he wasn't having this conversation by video, so Ironwood couldn't see him roll his eyes. "We've been seeded here, you mean."

"*Seeded. Engineered. Hell, we could be a galactic art project for all I know. But the fact remains: If aliens created life on this planet, it stands to reason they used their own biology to do it. Which means,*" Ironwood triumphantly concluded, "*their DNA can interact with ours.*"

David wanted to pound his phone on the worktable. Instead, unable to let the argument go, he made a counterargument. "The only thing wrong with that hypothesis is that there's absolutely no proof of it."

"*You mean, there didn't used to be proof—until you found it.*"

David's jaw clenched. "I have to get to work."

"*'Course you do. Got to know where they landed, and when.*"

"There's going to be another explanation."

"*Good man—spoken like a scientist. Doubt everything till you get the data that prove the hypothesis.*"

David mouthed a silent scream. "*If* the data exist."

"*They exist, all right. Just ask the government.*" Ironwood barreled on. "*Work hard, Dave. You've got my money. I want your results.*"

Then, mercifully—dead air.

David snapped his phone shut. What was it with people who didn't know the difference between facts and supposition? And what was it with his own inability to simply walk away from an unproductive argument?

His father had been easygoing, as much as David could remember. His mother, definitely so. Wherever his streak of stubbornness had come from, like his genetic peculiarities, it didn't seem to be from his parents. Overall, they had simply been accepting of life. When his father had died in the car crash at age thirty-two, David remembered his mother's grief was short-lived. *We go on,* she said. Nine years later, at the age of fourteen, David had recalled those words as he stared at his thirty-six-year-old mother in her open casket, taken in turn by cancer.

We go on. In his case, into foster care, finding freedom only when he went to college, a year ahead of his peers. Early on, he'd realized that everything died. It was the way of things. His mother had been right. *We go on.* He had.

Until eight months ago, when he'd discovered that his death was no longer an abstract future decades away.

Since then he'd experienced anger and frustration, especially when, late at night, he lay alone with his thoughts, imagining each breath, each heartbeat, was marking a countdown to the end of everything if he couldn't solve his problem. No fear, though. He couldn't remember ever feeling that. Just urgency and impatience.

His nightly phone call over, David rolled his chair across the concrete floor to another makeshift table. This one held fifteen unopened boxes of various reagent kits for use with the genetic analysis system still boxed up beneath the table. The DNA sequencer and its dedicated computer controller—about the size of a medium office photocopying machine—was for processing the DNA samples he'd told Ironwood he'd start to collect for him.

Now that he was able to work full-time, not in stolen evenings at the army lab, and now that he had the funds to buy openly from all genetic databases available, David anticipated the more rapid discovery of more clusters. To Ironwood, that meant more outposts. To David, it meant more chances to find others like him, and, most importantly, who among them had beat the odds—of all the cases he'd uncovered, none had yet. So finding more clusters meant more chances to find and turn off the genetic trigger that could kill him before he reached the beginning of the lethal interval, twenty-six years, six months.

Less than three months left.

Reason enough to get back to work now, resume his own investigation into his own genetic code.

To that end, he'd set up his own mini supercomputer. Already, the dedicated computing power of the three networked Apple Pro towers exceeded what he'd been able to access using his own account in the armed forces lab. The new screens, too, were larger and brighter and easier on the eyes than his old ones. He'd confirmed that on a few twenty-four-hour marathons. Everything else about his new lab, though, was decidedly low-tech.

His five worktables were nothing more than sheets of plywood on raw wood sawhorses. On the table with the screens, keyboards, and various drives, a gray and black rat's nest of wires and cables cascaded over the back and down to his computers and their battery backup. In another corner, deep in shadows, were four other tables laden with unopened boxes of lab supplies, junk food, and several cases of Red Bull. The cot and a sleeping bag were for the rare nights when the Red Bull stopped working.

He'd definitely reached that point now but doubted he'd be sleeping anytime soon. Ironwood's late-night phone calls and sheer obstinacy were partly responsible for his insomnia. More to blame was the new genome display on the large computer monitor on his makeshift desk—his complete genetic pattern this time, not just that of his mitochondria.

The genome on his screen told the story: The reality of his mtDNA results could not be denied. Fully 8 percent of his own DNA was nonhuman.

As he paged through graph after graph of his genome, David chewed at his lip, thoughtful. At the army lab, when he'd discovered that the peculiarities of his genetic structure were shared by a handful of other people, those individuals had had no other obvious relationship with him or with each other. The only exception to that lack of connection had been a few whose families clustered together geographically.

Those clusters had convinced David that the death sentence coded in his genes was a rare, recessive trait that his mother and father had carried, but on only one chromosome each. Both characteristics combined explained why his parents had lived past twenty-seven, and why the trait had persisted in the human population for so long without being identified as a medical threat.

It had been some of his searches online for more information about those regions that had drawn Merrit's and then Ironwood's interest to him. When they'd offered to buy his data, he'd scrubbed the army files and sold the first three data clusters. By that time, he'd already realized he'd either make a discovery worth something even to the army—it wasn't every day someone found nonhuman DNA in humans—or, with luck, he'd be dead before anyone could prosecute him. In any case, without the money, he'd be unable to do anything in time to save himself.

While Ironwood wanted to believe the origins of those three clusters with nonhuman DNA were alien, to David it was a given they were not. So far, however, he'd been unable to come up with a plausible, testable, alternate hypothesis.

So he'd decided to look next not just in the genetic profiles of other people but in those of other species, because Nature hoarded good ideas: If a particular sequence of amino acids accomplished something well in one life form, then the chances were strong the sequence would be conserved and passed on to other generations and, eventually, to other species.

Just this morning, he'd set his computers to comparing his own genes with those in twenty-eight other species. Following established protocols, he'd included seventeen specific mammals, plus a platypus, reptiles, amphibians, birds, and fish. He wouldn't know if he had a negative result until after his computers compared all the sequences, and that could easily take three days. A positive result, though, was a different matter. That could occur at any time, even with the first comparison.

David stifled a yawn and stretched. Time to call it a night. He instructed his computer to text his phone whenever, and if ever, it found a positive match.

He locked the metal exterior door and separate iron grate of his lab, then stepped out into the cloyingly humid August air. The evening's earlier rain had brought no relief, and it felt like more was on the way.

His black Jeep was one of three vehicles in the small parking lot edged on three sides by the converted warehouse. Another was a vintage Toyota truck that hadn't budged since he'd moved in. The battered pickup looked to be dark green under its thick coat of grime and dust. Two cinder blocks propped up the chassis where a rear tire was missing. The third vehicle, an old maroon Ford Crown Victoria, had initially captured his attention because it was the same model he'd seen Army CID agents drive on their visits to the lab. There was no apparent schedule to its presence here; sometimes it was parked in space number 27, and sometimes not. Reassuringly, though, he'd never noticed it anywhere else he drove in the area. Not at the local fast-food outlets, nor at the nearby Holiday Inn where Ironwood had parked him at a discount corporate rate until his few possessions from Maryland could be shifted to a local apartment.

David headed for his Jeep, pleased to hear only distant planes from the airport about a mile away, and the closer, faint electrical buzz of the lot's single light pole—a light pole that only held a light. Unlike the lab in Maryland, there were no surveillance cameras here.

He flicked the Jeep's windshield wipers on once to clear the last of the evening's rain, then drove out of the lot and onto the street, pausing briefly to check both ways. There was no traffic this time of night, only a cable van parked across the street. David made a mental bet it'd be on blocks when he returned tomorrow. This wasn't a district for leaving vehicles unattended.

He turned left, heading for the 24/7 McDonald's nearest his lodging. A shake and two Big Macs sounded about right—that stupefying combination should stun him into dreamless sleep. It was not as if he had to worry about what cholesterol would do to him at fifty.

He switched on his radio and kept pressing SEARCH until a talk radio station came on. He really didn't care what they were arguing about—any conversation was a better background noise than music, especially when he was working out problems. Someday he'd remember to get the kit that would let him plug his iPod into the Jeep's radio. Then he could play his collection of environmental sounds: recordings of the background noise of actual places, buildings, outdoor settings. He enjoyed visualizing the layout of the place where each recording had been made. He'd always been able to "read" the echoes and reverberations. The exercise was calming.

For now, though, he settled for talk radio, and he drove on while simultaneously following the political discussion on the air, trying to remember where he'd seen an Apple Store in Atlantic City for the iPod kit, and mulling over genes.

What he didn't do was realize that tonight, like every night for the past three weeks, he was still under surveillance.

This time, not just by the air force.

FOURTEEN

The screen in the cable van tracked David Weir's real-time position via a GPS beacon. Roz Marano had planted it.

"He's not going back to the hotel," Chang said.

"McDonald's," Lyle suggested. "There's one on Rupert." Weir ate like a horse.

Chang nodded and entered the departure in his log.

On another monitor, Lyle caught the flare of headlights in the converted warehouse's parking lot. Too much of a coincidence for his liking. "The Crown Vic's starting up. Run the tape back."

Chang brought up a different video display of the car now approaching the exit to the lot. Then, as that camera's image continued live on the first screen, he made time run backward on the second.

Lyle watched both screens until the Crown Victoria was out of range of the van's cameras, heading in the same direction as Weir's Jeep. On the playback screen, the Jeep backed into the lot, its headlights switched off, and Weir walked backward to his lab, unlocked the grate and door, then stepped back inside.

Now nothing moved in the parking lot.

Chang accelerated the reverse. After an hour of surveillance footage had sped by in two minutes, the conclusion was obvious.

"Sir, the driver was already in the Crown Victoria. I should have swept the lot with infrared."

Lyle was already speed-dialing Roz.

"Hey, boss."

"Road trip."

"Roger that."

Lyle's right knee clicked audibly when he stood. "You're here till the shift change. Keep the doors locked."

Chang patted the sidearm resting beside his log book. "Good to go, sir."

"Let's hope not." Lyle opened the back door and stepped into the night with relief. As hot as it was, it was cooler than in the van. A large jet roared by overhead, on an approach vector, landing lights captured in cones of glowing mist. Automatically, Lyle ID'd the twin-engined plane as an Airbus 319. He was good with planes.

Lyle donned his installer's ball cap before looking across the street to the warehouse lot. There were still lights on in unit 5. That one was leased by the owner of the Crown Victoria—Vince Gilden, who ran a used book-store in Mays Landing and had rented this unit two weeks ago, apparently to house extra stock. As a matter of course, Lyle had had a full profile run on Gilden, but the man checked out. Lyle made a note to revisit that.

Under a minute later, a black Intrepid turned the corner, stopped by the van, and Lyle got into the passenger side. Roz was at the wheel. She had a big grin for him.

"We going to follow him?"

Lyle tapped the nonstandard navigation screen in the center of the dash. The moving dot on the web of streets was Weir. A smaller, inset map showed the Intrepid's current position.

"No, we're going to follow whoever else is following him."

Roz was intrigued. "That's different. Has he got another agency tailing him?" Like every other member of his team, she liked to be in the middle of action, the wilder the better.

"Doubtful. I think it's the book dealer. Gilden." Lyle fastened his seat belt and rocked back as Roz took off.

"A civilian following our guy? Something's up."

"Unfortunately."

Lyle touched his own sidearm in his shoulder holster for reassurance. It had been years since he had used it anywhere but on the qualifying range—but that, like all things so far in this case, could change.

Waiting at a red light with no other cars on the road, David was tempted to call the radio station he was listening to and start a debate about what should be done about nonhumans walking among us. Just to see how quickly they'd hang up on him.

The light turned green. By habit, he checked the road left and right. Up ahead. Behind—

In his rearview mirror, he saw a car at the side of the road, maybe two hundred feet back, with its parking lights on. He'd just driven past that spot, and no car had been there.

He started forward.

In his rearview mirror, he saw the other car edge onto the road, its headlights still off.

For a few moments, David lost sight of the other vehicle as the road ahead curved. When it straightened, the car was there again, hanging back. Headlights now on.

He was being followed.

Either he was in the wrong place at the wrong time and he was a random target, or he was in the right place at the right time for someone interested just in him.

That decision tree was simple. Nothing he could do about army investigators. Even if he managed to elude them tonight, they'd be back. Casual crime? That was different. He had options.

David changed his choice of destination. This early in the morning, McDonald's wouldn't have enough people to deter a mugging or carjacking. He flicked on his blinker. He'd take the Atlantic City Expressway back to the Holiday Inn and drive right into the well-lit lobby drop-off. Goodbye mugger.

He made the next turn. The expressway overpass was clearly visible in the distance, its entrance and exit lanes picked out in lights.

He rechecked his mirror.

The car was still behind him.

A flash of lightning, then window-rattling thunder.

Up ahead slow-flashing orange lights smeared into halos on the windshield of the Jeep, and David pumped the brakes. The lights flanked signs warning that the expressway's entrance ramps were closed. Other signs pointed to the next closest entrance. *Great.* Another five miles on deserted surface roads.

He drove on past the blocked ramps, under the overpass.

Then the Jeep died. Engine, headlights, windshield wipers, radio. All out. David coasted to the shoulder. The Jeep came to a full stop.

A strobe of lightning, another roll of thunder. He looked in the rearview mirror. Saw no other car. Had the same thing happened to it?

David put on the emergency brake, pressed the hazard light button. Nothing. He took a small penlight from the glove compartment and switched it on. At least that worked.

He got out, grateful for the overpass above him sheltering him from the rain. On the off chance a battery cable had come loose, or something equally repairable, he pulled the hood up, confident he knew this engine well—4 liter, 6 cylinder, 12 valve, 190 horsepower. He could usually diagnose almost any trouble with it just from the way it sounded. Working on his Jeep was the closest thing he had to a hobby—doing something mechanical never failed to clear his mind.

Penlight in mouth, David peered into the engine compartment. The battery cables were still in place. He tugged each one to be certain they were tight. Then stopped. A small twist of red and black wire was where it didn't belong, running beside the bundled wires coming up from the alternator.

David took the penlight from his mouth and aimed it at the wires. Three possibilities instantly came to mind: tracking beacon, bomb, or remote kill-switch.

A new sound bounced off the concrete pilings of the underpass. The echo of a car approaching.

David straightened up, recognizing the configuration of the headlights and the parking lights. The other car.

It slowed, then pulled up behind his Jeep, motor idling.

David stayed where he was, penlight shining onto the battery cables. He had a flash where he visualized his situation in the same way he did arrangements of genes and chromosomes—as if looking down from above. Saw his Jeep. The other car. Himself beside the Jeep. The door of the other car opening—

"Having trouble?"

The driver stood behind his open door, a silhouette in the glare of headlights. The voice was familiar.

"I think the rain shorted out something," David said.

He heard the echo of another car. Coming from the opposite direction, driving slowly.

"Need a lift to a gas station?"

The driver was walking toward him. David recognized his face, didn't know his name.

"I'm Vince Gilden, by the way. You're David, right? We're neighbors. Back at the warehouse. I just moved into a unit at the back. We've said hello."

"The guy with all the books."

The driver smiled. "That's me."

David nodded, pulse steady but hammering in his ears. He'd only said hello in passing. He'd never said his name.

The second car was drawing nearer.

"Let me try one thing first," David said. He pocketed his penlight, throwing the Jeep's engine compartment into shadow. "Could you brace this?"

"Sure." Gilden put his hand on the Jeep's hood, at the same time darting a glance back at the car that was almost up to them. "Like this?"

"Perfect. Now here, hold this for me."

Gilden held out his hand, and David shoved the positive battery cable into it.

There was a sudden strangled cry, and sparks crackled from Gilden's hands as his body completed the circuit through the Jeep's metal frame and he flew back into the roadway.

By then, David was already halfway up the steep concrete embankment leading from the road to the overpass. The surface of the concrete was untouched by the evening's rain, and his Nikes gave him sufficient traction. He slammed to a stop behind a four-foot-wide piling, slowed his breathing, listening.

Heard two car doors open.

The second car. Samaritans? Or Gilden's "friends"?

He got his answer when an unfamiliar voice called out, "David Weir! We only want to talk!"

David stayed where he was. Whoever they were, they'd disabled his car. They could have talked to him at the warehouse.

Then voices, too faint to catch the words. The sound of a car trunk opening, closing.

"Weir!"

A powerful flashlight beam slashed over the concrete. David instinctively shrank back, but in the deep shadows of the piling, he was already shielded from the light.

"Come down," a different voice shouted, "or we come up after you!"

So there were three of them. No, two, David corrected himself. It was doubtful Gilden would be moving anytime soon.

"Last chance, Weir!"

David hesitated. The CID would never snatch him on a roadway in the middle of the night. Copying restricted personnel data from the lab's computers wouldn't warrant that kind of tactic. This had to be a case of mistaken identity. These people had him confused with someone else.

David began to dial 911. This was something the police could clear up.

A shotgun blast hit the overpass ten feet to his left, spraying him with stinging debris and dust.

For an instant, David thought he'd been shot. Then a series of images flooded his brain. Vivid snapshots. In one he was frozen in place behind the concrete piling, phone in one hand. In the next he was leaping from behind the piling. Racing up the embankment on the perfect angle. Tucking, rolling, dropping down to safety farther beneath the overpass.

Another shotgun blast.

Car tires squealing, voices shouting.

David rolled off the concrete, scanning the slippery grass slope leading up to the expressway.

He heard the rush of traffic overhead, wet tires on the asphalt. The rain intensifying. Lightning flashing.

He ran along the shoulder of the highway, waving for someone, anyone, to stop and help him.

Three cars roared past, splashing through pools of water, the spray soaking him.

A fourth car slid to a stop just past him and honked its horn. Its roof sported a lighted sign of smiling showgirls. A casino ad.

David ran to the cab, pulled the back door open, and jumped in, twisting around to squint through the fogged rear window at a rain-blurred stream of cars. No other car had pulled off behind them.

"Closest police station!" he yelled through the Plexiglas security screen. "Go!" Then he was thrown back as the cab accelerated so quickly it fishtailed and the side door slammed shut beside him.

He felt exhilarated. He was going to be okay. He'd never responded so quickly in his life. Then again, he'd never been shot at before.

That's when he finally saw the front-seat passenger. Half turned around, feeding a flexible tube through the payment slot in the security screen.

The tube was hissing.

FIFTEEN

"That's long enough," Lyle said. Weir's beacon hadn't changed position for two minutes—longer than any red light or traffic slowdown this time of night.

Roz slammed the black Intrepid into gear and pulled back onto the road. The car's rain-slicked tires spun for a moment, then gripped pavement, and they were off, flying through a red light—no other traffic on the road. Amber warning lights flashed ahead. "Ramp's closed," she said. "He might've been heading to the expressway after all."

The beacon had changed direction a few miles back. It was no longer tracing Weir's customary route to the closest McDonald's. Now it had stopped. Either the kid had noticed they were shadowing him or he was meeting someone. Lyle liked neither scenario. "I'm thinking he caught a ride."

"No way."

Lyle lamented the loss of conversational skill among his younger colleagues. *But, when in Rome . . .* "Yes, way," he said. "Gilden didn't know about our surveillance. If he wants to harm the kid, he could have done that at the warehouse. He's picked him up."

"What for?"

"To take him someplace, Roz."

They were heading into the curve of road protected by the expressway overpass. "Should be just ahead on the right."

A car loomed toward them. Too fast for the road conditions. Low and black. High beams flicked on, distorted in the rain.

"License!" Lyle barked.

Roz squinted ahead as the car rushed forward. "Lima Echo Delta—damn! Missed the numbers." She repeated the letters, added, "New Jersey plates. Black Bentley Continental. Sweet."

Lyle saw the Jeep. "Pull over."

Roz slipped in behind Weir's car. Lyle opened his door and stepped out, gun drawn. On the other side, Roz followed his lead.

The air was damp, cooling, but couldn't hide the scent of gunsmoke.

Lyle edged forward. He saw Roz sniff the air. She dropped one hand from her gun to pull a flashlight from her jacket, held it up like a dagger, shone it into the Jeep.

"Clear inside."

Lyle saw her crouch down. The flashlight beam shot out past the Jeep's tires.

"Clear underneath."

There was no sign of violence on the vehicle. No bullet hits. No damage from being forced off the road. No details for constructing a scenario of what happened here, harmless or not.

Lyle heard the snap of silicone gloves. A moment later Roz opened the driver's door. "Keys are in the ignition."

Lyle had a hunch. "Start the engine."

Nothing. Evidently, someone had installed a kill-switch in Weir's car so it would stop in a convenient place. "Kid's been kidnapped."

"Yeah?"

"Kill-switch. Gunfire." Lyle aimed his flashlight into the Jeep's back compartment. "There's his bag, too."

Roz reached in and retrieved Weir's backpack and unzipped it on the driver's seat. She drew out his black iPod, tangled in its earbuds.

That last piece of evidence convinced her. "Okay. So when you're right, you're right." The suspect had never gone anywhere without the device. That's why Roz had installed the beacon in it. "So who did it?"

"Vince Gilden. Aided and abetted by whoever was in the black Bentley. There can't be a lot of cars costing close to two hundred grand in New Jersey, so I don't think we'll have trouble finding a match with partial plates."

"I can find one for you now," Roz said. "Ironwood. He can buy Bentleys like peanuts."

Lyle wasn't convinced. "Ironwood talks to the kid five times a day. There's no sign of any trouble between them. Why grab him?"

"Maybe because you were right all along. All this talk about space guys *is* a smoke screen for something else they're doing. To talk about *that*, they have to do it in person."

"Easier ways to arrange a meet," Lyle said. "No. Someone else came after Weir."

"He's a lab geek. Who else would want him?"

"That depends on who the kid really is." Lyle's own search of Weir's cubicle in Maryland had revealed nothing significant about who he was and what he was up to. Only that one old photograph taken on an unremarkable family vacation—which meant it was definitely important, just undecipherable for now.

Something was going on with David Weir. The data he'd shown Colonel Kowinski was beyond her ability to identify. A batty billionaire had him holed up working some kind of mystery project. Then some new unknown had apparently kidnapped him.

Lyle's focus was still Holden Ironwood.

But the kid was getting interesting.

I'm in a spaceship?

David had just awakened in a roomy supportive chair that cradled him like those in a first-class aircraft cabin. He'd traveled that way once, on an unexpected upgrade. The rest of his surroundings fit the same comparison. Expensive. Curved wall panels, about three feet wide, each with a recessed pale oval that could be a window but was opaque for now. Subtly arched ceiling with overhead, indirect lighting concealed in a long center panel that ran the length of the cabin.

His nostrils flared, catching a lightly sour electric scent.

Now that *was* the smell of "aircraft cabin." He closed his eyes, heard muffled fans move the air. An electric hum—a generator—but there was no sense of movement, no sound of engines. He was still on solid ground.

He sat up abruptly, temples pounding, as he recalled another scent. Gas.

He remembered now. The Jeep cutting out. The book dealer—Gilden. Shotgun blasts. Running, escaping, all without thought. Then the cab. And the passenger. And the—

He shifted. Felt something hard beneath him. A seat belt lock. He half rose to look behind him. More chairs—but not arranged in aisles. More like conversational groupings. *A living room. In a plane?* Just past them a quilted leather wall, and in its center a closed door. He saw a number pad beside it. Security. There'd be an entrance code.

David turned around. Fifteen feet forward was a matching wall and door. Whatever craft he was in, it was huge. *A 747? Double-decker Airbus?*

A sudden shiver shook him. His T-shirt and jeans were rain-soaked. He couldn't have been unconscious long. Or been driven very far. Atlantic City Airport. It was the only place he knew nearby that could handle a plane this big.

Then he saw his phone on another seat a few feet away.

He stood up slowly, seeking any sign of a camera or a peephole, but saw none. Could someone have been clever enough to kidnap him with such elaborate logistics, yet be careless enough to leave his phone in plain view?

And did he care?

Decision made, he acted quickly. Launched himself at the other seat, scooped up his phone—it was on! Strong signal!

He punched in 911, tapped DIAL. The screen changed.

The call was going through.

He placed the phone against his ear. Heard—

Nothing.

The door in the wall behind him slid open.

"Put it back on the seat. Go back to where you were."

David turned to see a long-haired man in a black Windbreaker, hand on the open door frame. His full beard was the same color as his hair: rust brown streaked with gray. The man was no taller than he was, but his shoulders were much wider.

He reached into his Windbreaker, his intention obvious.

David dropped his phone, sat down.

He heard the door behind him close. Looked back. The man was gone.

Then the door in front of him swept open, and a woman entered. Young, in jeans and a light green shirt. Pale skin. Long red hair tied back. Her hands were bandaged—and in one of them, she held a small pistol, aimed at him.

SIXTEEN

As she studied David Weir, Jess reviewed Emil Greco's lessons on interrogation.

The sooner she could successfully complete this assignment for the Family,
the sooner she could take action of her own. Maybe even finish what Florian
had been trying to do: recover the lost Secret of the First Gods. She couldn't
wait to talk to Willem and find out what he knew, but she couldn't do any
of that, until she'd finished running errands for Su-Lin.

"Who are you people? Why am I here?" David Weir sounded more
irritated than afraid.

Jess took a seat a safe six feet away, resting her arm on the squared, upholstered arm so her P-3AT remained aimed in his direction. The pistol
was a small gun, barely ten ounces with a full load of six cartridges, but it
fired .380 hollow points, which gave it considerable stopping power for its
size. Dom LaSalle, the Family security chief for this trip, had insisted she
carry it.

Dom had also made her promise that if Weir did try anything, she'd
have him on the floor and bleeding to death before he took two steps.
Hollow points broke apart inside a body without passing through it, so she
didn't have to worry about piercing the fuselage of the MacCleirigh Foundation 787.

She began the script Emil had laid out for her. "Why'd you try to call
911?"

"Uh . . . so the police could come and get me out of this?" Weir looked
astonished by her question.

"I don't believe you," she said.

"Why not?"

"I don't believe you'd want to get the police involved in this."

"What is 'this'?"

"You tell me."

"You've got me mixed up with someone else."

"Is your name David Weir?"

"Yeah, but obviously *not* the David Weir you're looking for."

"David Michael Weir. Born Los Angeles. Parents deceased. No siblings. Social Security number nine one four—"

Weir cut her off before she could finish. "Okay, okay. So I'm that David Weir. So what? Why am I here?"

"I want to know what you're doing for Ironwood."

"Why?" She saw a flicker in his eyes.

"You work in genetics. What are you doing for him?"

"Will you let me go if I tell you?"

"I'll do worse if you don't." Jess worked the slide on her pistol for added intimidation. It had the proper effect.

"I'm giving him geographic genetic clusters for—"

"Explain."

"Uh . . . genetic clusters . . . they're a group of individuals who share certain genetic characteristics, who all trace their lineage back to . . . other individuals who lived in and around a particular region."

"Is that how you helped him locate the Azángaro temple site?"

"I don't know what Azángaro means or anything about temple sites. And I'll say it again. What does any of this have to do with me?"

"Azángaro's a province."

"Where?"

"Peru." She caught the flash of recognition in his eyes.

"In the Andes?" He stared at her. "One of the genetic groupings I isolated was centered there. Is that one of your temple sites?"

"Did you give Ironwood any other 'clusters' . . . for any other locations?"

"Two others. A cluster centered in French Polynesia and—"

"A place called Havi Atoll?"

"Maybe. I don't know where that is."

Jess's grip tightened on the pistol. *Florian.* Without this man's assistance, her aunt might still be alive. "It's part of French Polynesia. A volcanic atoll."

"How big is its population?"

"It doesn't have one. Just rocks."

"Sorry. I . . . the cluster groupings, they're only good for determining a general region. There's no way I could zero in on a specific island."

"What's the third one?"

"The last one I gave him was for India."

"What region?"

"It's on the Pakistan border . . . uh, Ganganagar. I believe that's a district of India."

"I know what it is." If this man was telling the truth—that his data could only point the way to a general region—then it was Ironwood who was processing those data to find the specific locations. Not Weir.

"Do you know what he's looking for?"

Weir hesitated. "Not really."

"Not really," Jess repeated. "That means you have some idea."

Weir frowned. "It's stupid."

"Not if telling me keeps you alive."

"Okay . . . okay, here it is . . . He's trying to find evidence that . . . that thousands of years ago . . . maybe tens of thousands . . . humans interbred with aliens."

"Aliens?" Jess had heard that Ironwood believed extraterrestrial visitations had happened in the past, but the idea of interbreeding was new.

"You asked and I'm telling you. Like a *Chariots of the Gods* sort of thing. You know, advanced beings from another planet came here and helped us build the pyramids."

A small vibration against Jess's leg interrupted. She shifted in the seat and pulled out Weir's phone. Dom had switched off the jammer that had prevented Weir's earlier call, and now Weir was receiving one. She read the caller ID.

"Who's MCP?" she asked. "Ironwood?"

"No. It's . . . Master Control Program." Weir shrugged. "A lame joke. It's my computer. At my lab."

Jess waited for a fuller explanation.

"It's running a long program. It can't have finished this fast, so it's probably letting me know it's had a positive match."

"Is your computer how you find the geographic clusters?"

"Yeah. It's comparing billions of amino-acid sequences. Sort of thing couldn't be done even five years ago. Not without a supercomputer."

Jess held up the phone. "Does this mean you've found another one?"

"Nope. I'm probably another few weeks away from doing that. If there is another one to find."

"But you've found three so far."

"Yeah."

"There're nine more." Jess no longer felt unsure about what to do with Weir. She flipped open a hidden cover on the arm of her seat, revealing a series of buttons. She pressed the one that summoned Dom LaSalle.

"How do you know?"

Jess didn't answer him. The interrogation was over. She'd made her decision, one she wasn't authorized to make. She stood and slipped her gun back into the holster in the small of her back. She wasn't doing this Emil's way anymore. Or Su-Lin's.

She was a defender. She'd do it her way.

SEVENTEEN

In all of New Jersey, there were only eighteen Bentleys of the model Roz Marano had glimpsed in the rain, and only one with the letters LED on its license plate.

"Owner is Mordecai Diego Rodrigues." Roz read from the screen on her laptop behind the wheel of the Intrepid. They were still parked under the overpass. Wishing he had coffee, Lyle sat beside her, watching the state police crime scene investigators load Weir's Jeep onto a flatbed trailer.

"Age sixty-two," Roz read out. "Occupation listed as consultant."

"To kidnappers?" Lyle asked. "Nice work if you can get it."

Roz frowned at him, tapped her keyboard. "Investment consultant. That's interesting . . ."

"Not these days."

"The kind of consulting he does. Art, rare books, antiques."

"Possible connection to Gilden?"

"Yeah, that's it. We're dealing with a gang of rogue book dealers."

"Address, Roz?"

More tapping. "He's in Mays Landing. Just outside Atlantic City." She gave him a hopeful look. "We could be knocking on the guy's door in half an hour. Find out where he was tonight."

It had been almost ninety minutes since Weir had disappeared. BOLOs—be-on-the-lookout alerts—were in effect for the black Bentley and Vince Gilden's maroon Crown Victoria, but both vehicles seemed to have vanished with the kidnap victim. Given those circumstances, Lyle doubted Mr. Rodrigues would be at home.

"Have the locals stake out his house."

"You don't want to talk to him?"

"The cars that were involved in this disappeared too quickly. They've got to be someplace close."

"Why don't we take it straight to Ironwood? He's at his casino. We could go shake him up."

Lyle understood the satisfaction that would come from such a move, but it wasn't feasible. "Ironwood's many companies give him more than three hundred domestic locations where he could be hiding the stolen database. Until we find out where it is, we're not knocking on any doors."

At least in that regard, Ironwood's theft of computer data from the air force was more of an old-fashioned crime than one of the cyber persuasion. Computer files with the plans for a new jet engine or directed-energy weapon could be e-mailed anywhere in a matter of minutes, if not seconds. Once stolen, they were impossible to retrieve.

The SARGE database, though, was literally massive. The computer terminology for its size—850 terabytes—held no particular meaning for Lyle. Its physical specifications did: Original or copy, with off-the-shelf commercial components it would take a fourteen-foot truck to move the storage units that could hold that much digital information, along with the necessary cables, power supplies, shelves, and cooling system. In fact, the database was so valuable, whoever stole it would make more duplicates. So they were talking several trucks.

Region 7 had tasked a team of specialists to monitor all the computer communications in Ironwood's corporate empire for any sign that the air force database, or selected parts of it, were being transferred to potential buyers. Lyle's goal was to find the actual, real-world location where all the truckloads of physical equipment were being maintained. "Shaking up" the prime suspect wasn't the best way to go about accomplishing that mission, no matter how much fun his junior agent thought that might be.

"We should go back to the kid's private lab," he said. "See if he left anything that points to a meeting tonight, or where he was planning to go."

Roz closed her laptop, disappointed. "Weir never leaves anything."

"Always a first time."

Lyle's phone buzzed. He read the ID, answered. "Yeah, Del?"

"He's back."

Lyle connected the dots. "Weir's at his lab?"

"Yes, sir. And he's not alone."

⸻

Jess was used to remote jungle huts, desert tents, and corroding ruins, so the half-finished state of David Weir's workroom didn't concern her. But the smell did. Acrid. Something like fermenting vinegar.

"There's the computer system I put together." Weir pointed under a plywood-and-sawhorse table at three silver-gray boxes with Apple logos on their sides. They seemed to be in a bed of tangled cables. "Not as fast as a purpose-built sequencer, but good enough for what I need it to do."

Jess took one of the metal chairs and positioned it to face the table with the computer screens as Dom circled the room, checking its high windows, being certain the front and back exits were securely locked.

She turned her attention to Weir. He was studying a screen with bands of color. Ever since she'd told him she knew there were nine more clusters to find, there'd been no more need to threaten him with a gun or confinement. He'd brought her and Dom here without protest. She still hadn't decided if she'd send him back to Zurich for further questioning by the Family, and she wouldn't make that decision until she had learned more about his work for Ironwood. Fortunately, Dom hadn't yet realized she was acting on her own.

"So why'd your computer call you?"

"Well, it appears I share a gene sequence with a pig. Hold on." He leaned down and typed on a keyboard. The screen changed. "Has to do with hemoglobin. No surprise. The program was supposed to filter out gene matches that are already known."

Jess didn't care about any of that. "Show me how you find geographic clusters."

Weir seemed hesitant. "It might not be that simple. What do you know about genetics? The human genome?"

"Assume 'nothing.'"

"Okay. So . . . human beings have forty-six chromosomes. That's twenty-three pairs, in the nucleus of all of our cells. Well, almost all of our cells. Then there's mitochondria that—you really need to hear all this?"

Jess nodded. "I do."

Weir pulled up a folding chair and sat down next to his computer table. "Okay, well, all chromosomes, human and mitochondrial, are made of bundled DNA. That's deoxyribonucleic acid—amino acids, nucleotides. There're four different types: adenine, cytosine, guanine, and thymine." He paused, but Jess said nothing.

Weir moved on. "We call those four types A, C, G, and T. You can think of them as chemical letters. They can go together in different sequences, making different words, you might say, and according to the way they're put together, like computer programming code, they tell the cell how to build certain proteins.

"Anyway, human beings have about three point two billion of these nucleotides—letters—making up our genetic information. The complete set is called our genome. But it turns out only about one percent of those three point two billion letters make up our actual genes. We've got about thirty to forty thousand of them setting our hair color, eye color, how tall we can grow, almost all of our physical characteristics, maybe even a lot of our mental abilities, probably our behavioral tendencies as well . . . So . . . by looking for specific differences in a person's DNA, especially in the DNA contained in their mitochondria, which are—"

"You're right," Jess said. "Maybe I don't need to hear everything."

"Bottom line—specific DNA differences can tell us where that person's ancestors came from."

This was what she had come for.

"You can map that?"

"*I* can't, but there's a research program—the Genographic Project—that's doing the work. They've created a map, and a timetable. A well-established one—of mutations. They're called polymorphisms, and they're in the human genome. And we can find that timetable on the Y chromosome of men and in the mitochondrial DNA of men and women."

Weir sat back, the fingers of one hand pushing back an unruly strand of black hair. He suddenly looked deeply tired.

"Knowing when and in which geographical regions those mutations arose is how we can track three major migrations of humans out of Africa in the past hundred thousand years. And that tells us whose ancestors originally went north into Europe, and whose went east into Asia, and whose settled India, Australia, and whose crossed into North America, and like that . . . all with reasonably specific dates."

"Do any of these markers prove what you say Ironwood believes, that humans interbred with aliens?"

Weir's dark, unusual eyes considered her. "There's absolutely nothing in mainstream genetic research to support his beliefs. Best I can figure is he's reacting to information he's getting from some other sources. What he calls 'archaeological and cultural anomalies.' "

Jess could guess what those anomalies might be. The Family hadn't been able to completely cover up all the physical evidence of its existence and influence through history. Though no legitimate researcher had ever managed to find a pattern in the few clues that remained in the open.

Weir glanced back at his three computer screens, which flashed with rapidly changing bar charts. "Look, Ironwood's not completely off base. The program these machines are running—the one I got the call about—it's comparing genes within the human genome to genes in other animals. I mean, we do share genes with all sorts of other species, and that points to all life on the planet arising from a common ancestor. But there's no compelling evidence that at any time in the history of life on Earth an extraterrestrial source of DNA was inserted into the process. No matter how much Ironwood hopes it was."

"No compelling evidence," Jess said. "Which means there *is* some kind of evidence, even if it's not that convincing."

Weir turned suddenly and looked toward Dom, and Jess followed suit. Her bodyguard was holding a finger to his earpiece.

"The car?" she asked. They had driven here in an armored Suburban. Rather than sound an audible alert, the SUV's alarm, if triggered, signaled Dom's phone.

Dom nodded.

"Go," Jess said. The Suburban was a tempting vehicle in a deserted neighborhood.

Dom pulled his Glock automatic from his shoulder holster, pausing only for Jess to draw her own pistol to cover Weir while he was gone. Then he sprinted for the room's back door.

"Uh, there's an alarm on that door," Weir said. "If he opens it, it'll—"

Click. The metal door was open and Dom was through it. No alarm.

Jess turned back to Weir. "The evidence," she prompted him. "That's not too compelling."

Weir was staring at the back door, now swinging shut, as if trying to work out how Dom had bypassed the alarm.

"David." She said his name sharply, as if trying to get a child's attention.

He gave her an odd look. "What's your name?"

Caught off guard, she surprised herself by breaking another of Emil's interrogation rules. "Jess. Jess MacClary."

"Well, Jess, in my experience, if you sort through a large enough random selection of genetic profiles, there're always a few individuals with markers that don't match any known human genome."

"How few?"

"Maybe one in a hundred thousand. But the markers are extremely rare. The Genographic Project? It's got about four hundred thousand genetic profiles. That means, at best, there may be four people in that database with unidentified mutations. Anything that insignificant is usually dismissed as an error, assuming they're even looking for it."

"So how did *you* find out about them?" Following his reasoning, with the world's population closing in on seven billion, Jess calculated there'd be at least seventy thousand people alive right now with unidentifiable DNA.

"I used to work at the Armed Forces DNA Identification Lab—"

"In Maryland. I know."

"Then you also know I had access to a database almost eight times bigger than the Genographic Project's. When I was doing quality assurance there, I happened to turn up a profile with nonhuman genes. I thought it was an error. I ran a check, and I found another individual with the same markers, and then another . . . and that's it."

"How'd you end up here?"

"I dug into the literature to see if anyone else had come across what I did. I figured somebody must have, and I wanted to see what theories they might have developed to explain them. A lot of the research in this particular area is . . . let's say, on the fringe of science. Someone on one of the Web sites I was searching—I thought it was the people who ran the site—sent me e-mail, inviting me to meet—"

"Ironwood?"

"Not till later. I ended up selling some data to a guy called Merrit who worked for him."

"And that data was your geographic clusters. And he's hired you to find more for him."

"Yeah."

Jess knew she was lucky Dom had stepped out to check the SUV. Su-Lin's instructions, which her bodyguard knew as well as she did, had been unequivocal: If Ironwood's technician had any connection to Florian's death, she was to ship him to Zurich without delay—and David had that connection.

Even so, Jess wasn't ready to reveal that to Dom or anyone else just yet. Not if she had a chance to advance Family knowledge of Ironwood's ability to find their temples—Florian had died because of it. This technician might have important information, and Jess knew that once Emil had David Weir in Zurich, she'd never talk to him again.

She spoke rapidly, summarizing what he'd told her, to be sure. "You sold Merrit your data for three regions—India first, then Peru, and then the South Pacific." Data that Ironwood had used to find and loot three of the Family's sacred temple sites.

David shook his head. "Two," he said, "and not in that order. The first datasets he bought were for Peru and French Polynesia. For the last one—India—Merrit was still in the field, in the South Pacific. A different guy took me to Ironwood. That's when he hired me directly. After I gave him my files on India."

Jess stared at him, making a connection that he couldn't. David's third cluster had only confirmed what Ironwood had already found. It hadn't led him to it.

Three years ago, the Family's longtime rival for ancient treasures had uncovered a lost temple of the First Gods in the Ghaggar-Hakra dry river valley of India—something the Family had searched for, for generations, and had finally decided was the stuff of myth. The Family's investigation of Ironwood's success where they had failed led them to conclude he was simply lucky. There were hundreds of significant ruins in that region, most still unexplored, and one of his teams had just by chance been the first to excavate at that location. The MacCleirigh Foundation had promptly pressured the local government to exclude Ironwood's dig team from the site and give the Foundation sole access.

Now, in just the past four months, Ironwood had located two more temples. *After* he'd bought David's data.

"Your turn, Jess. Tell me what you know about 'the other nine.' "

Jess considered her next move—one she knew Su-Lin assuredly would not approve. But centuries of library scholarship had led the Family nowhere. And now it seemed there was a chance to change all that. She, like all children of the Family, had been told that one generation of them would be called to change the future. What if this was the beginning of that call?

What if the key to discovering the Family's lost purpose was to locate all twelve of the lost temples of the First Gods and reclaim their mysterious artifacts?

What if, with this outsider's help, the Family could find the nine remaining temples the *Traditions* described?

And what if one of those was the *first* temple—where the Promise was made? Surely the Family would forgive her what she was about to do. She turned to David, prepared to make her offer.

The first burst of machine-gun fire tore through the warehouse door.

EIGHTEEN

"Shots fired! Shots fired!"

Roz Marano pumped the brakes, and the Intrepid slid into the curb a long block from the converted warehouse.

Lyle pressed his earpiece tight. "Who's shooting?"

The deserted street, glistening with rain, betrayed no sign of any activity.

Del Chang was reporting from the cable van positioned opposite the warehouse. He'd been describing the black Suburban and the man and woman who'd accompanied Weir into his unit—apparently at gunpoint. Then a green shape had moved on the night-vision screen.

"Shooter's on the roof."

Lyle and Roz were both out of the Intrepid now, running toward the warehouse, SIGs drawn, fingers off the triggers. Lyle heard a distinctive popping sound and echoes from the empty street—a submachine gun.

"There's someone returning fire from the ground!"

Lyle hissed at Roz to stop advancing. The junior agent flattened against the wall of a darkened building beside him.

Now more automatic weapons fire. Roz looked at him, eyes bright, cheeks flushed. "Is this when we wait for backup?"

"Wish it was." Lyle's earpiece squealed as Chang gave more details.

"Three shooters now. Two on the roof. They're concentrating on Weir's unit."

"Where's the third?"

"On the ground. Came around from the back. I think there was another shooter on the roof, but the guy on the ground popped him."

Lyle couldn't figure it out. Someone had kidnapped the kid. Someone brought him back at gunpoint. Now someone was trying to kill him.

Roz summed it up with her usual eloquence. "What's up with this guy?"

Priority one was still to preserve Weir as an asset to use against Iron-wood. Lyle figured he'd work the rest out later. "Del—give us an approach. We're going to take out the shooters on the roof."

Gunfire came in near constant bursts now.

"You should be clear coming up the side. They're directly opposite Weir's, shooting across the parking—whoa!"

"Say again!"

"The guy on the ground picked off another roof shooter. Someone else is returning fire from the unit, too."

The gunfire stopped.

"Last shooter might be withdrawing. Can't spot him."

"Let's go," Lyle said. "Close to the wall."

He and Roz ran forward.

"There he is! Far end of the building—two now. Confirm two shooters still on the roof. Still . . . what's that?"

Lyle's bad knee raged with pain with every footfall on the pavement. He cupped his hand over his earpiece. "Say again? Del?"

"They've got something big up there." A fusillade of sharp gunfire sounded. *"Big exchange from roof to ground. Sir, I think they've got a shoulder-fired—"*

That's when Lyle heard a short whistle and saw the lightning-quick streak of light that stitched across the street.

The cable van exploded.

Machine-gun fire pierced the metal fire door of David's lab, and, as Jess hit the floor, David scrambled for his computers, grabbed the wireless keyboard from the plywood table, then ducked beneath it. Gunfire *might* cause his death. Losing his data would guarantee it.

Hunched over, working swiftly, he typed a sequence of commands to copy the results of his latest run to disk just as the lights in his unit flicked off. *Power failure?* He listened intently, then relaxed. The battery backup for his computers hadn't chirped. *No power failure. Good.* Jess must've turned off the overhead fixtures.

He stretched up to check one of his screens to be sure the commands were correct, then hit ENTER in the same instant the thud of a thunderous explosion outside coincided with a brilliant flash of red light through the high windows of his unit.

Jess was gone. The metal door gaped open.

Silence.

David leapt to his feet, ran for his equipment table. He quickly sorted through a pile of padded envelopes to find the ones with the genome data disks he'd ordered from the University of California, Santa Cruz.

More rapid-fire gunshots.

He dropped back to the floor as bullets ricocheted around him. Heard a can of Red Bull hiss as it was punctured, saw dark streams of spraying liquid.

Flat on his stomach, envelopes in each hand, he saw Jess again. Bent over, struggling through the open door, firing her gun one-handed into the parking lot, the other hand dragging Dom inside. She hadn't run off—she'd gone for her bodyguard.

A burst of machine-gun fire peppered the concrete floor beside her, and she let go of Dom and flattened against the wall beside the open door.

David shoved the envelopes in his waistband, started forward on his hands and knees.

For a heart-stopping moment Jess swung her gun around to aim at him, but he kept moving toward her. "I'll get him!" David reached out for Dom, pulled him in.

Jess spun around in the same instant. A small magazine dropped out of her pistol's grip, and she slapped another one in place.

She fired into the parking lot. Six times, David counted. Then she slammed back against the wall as another round of machine-gun fire poured through the door.

For just a moment, her eyes met his. A dozen questions whirled through David's mind, unvoiced. Who the hell was trying to kill Jess? Was there any way out of this? How much ammunition did she have left?

Her red hair in wild disarray, she again reloaded as he tried to see how badly her unconscious bodyguard was hurt. The lab was dark. No light for a visual check, so David used his fingers. He unzipped Dom's Windbreaker, ran a quick hand over the man's T-shirt, stopping when he encountered body armor. Checked both Dom's shoulders. The left was wet and sticky. Felt the weak, rhythmic gush of blood.

Beside him, Jess leaned out to shoot into the lot again. Steeling himself for the loud bang of her gun, David yanked off his own T-shirt, folding it to make a compress. First-aid courses had been mandatory at the army lab.

He pushed the wad of cloth hard against Dom's shoulder. Kept the pressure steady.

Heard a groan. Good sign.

Jess stopped firing.

"How bad?"

"Ask again in twenty minutes."

She took another quick look into the parking lot. No response. No gunfire. She resumed position, back against the wall, gun ready.

Then from a distance came the wail of sirens. David cocked his head to listen. Four police cars and an ambulance from the east. Two more police cars from the south.

Jess touched David's arm, looked down at Dom, spoke quickly, clearly. "His full name is Dominic LaSalle. He works for Cross Executive Protection Services out of Zurich. He's licensed to carry his weapons here. The Suburban is registered to Cross."

She was giving him a cover story for the police, but he'd already worked out one of his own. Not only would it be truthful, it would satisfy the cops *and* protect his arrangement with Ironwood.

"He's your friend," she continued. "You were showing him your new lab. Someone tried to break in. To steal your computers. Dom drove them off before they could."

"I won't lie to the police."

"Those clusters you found? You're looking for an explanation for them, aren't you? I know what it is."

David almost relaxed the pressure on Dom's shoulder. Almost.

"Who was here with you tonight?" she asked.

Approaching voices, shouting, noisy. The flicker of angry red reflected flames in warehouse windows beyond the unit's open front door.

"Who was here tonight?" Jess repeated.

David made the only decision he could.

"Dom LaSalle. My friend the bodyguard. Lucky coincidence."

Jess holstered her gun in the small of her back and pulled out his phone. "You help me. I help you." She laid it on the floor beside him, held his gaze. "Expect a call."

Then she darted out the back door and was gone.

HAVI ATOLL 7,418 YEARS B.C.E.

Half a world away from the outpost being built on the shore of Cornwall, what would one day be an atoll was still an island.

Mordcai, Apprentice Master of the Star Paths, was grateful for the choice his elders had made in selecting this outpost's site. Some outposts were in cold and rocky regions, far from the center of the world. Others were along inland riverbanks, and one, which he had visited himself, was set high in a range of mountains where the Navigators themselves had once traveled. This outpost, though, was in the midrange islands of the Ocean and endured no extremes of weather. Nor had its construction offered many difficulties, other than the transport of building materials from larger islands hundreds of stadii distant.

Fortunately, the ahkwila *who inhabited the local islands had welcomed the* khai *and become eager students of the knowledge.* Ahkwila *wayfinders were common now, and trade routes among all the islands and even the great lands were established and secure.*

Those routes were what Mordcai charted now, on the great world map in the Navigators' Hall of Nan Moar. Beneath the precisely aligned silver starstones on the room's domed ceiling, with brush and rule the apprentice master carefully plotted the paths between the local islands, and beyond them to the other outposts across the world. In time to come, even if everything the Navigators warned against was true, the outposts would remain. And, Mordcai thought with satisfaction, these routes that he now charted, combined with the starstones on the ceilings, and the gifts on the altar, would ensure that the knowledge would never be lost. Nor would the way home be forgotten, no matter how much the world might change.

On this midsummer morning, Mordcai knelt on the polished stone floor of the hall among his paints and brushes, spools of twine, and precisely shaped bars and rules of iron. Despite the heat of the day outside, the room was cool, insulated by the outpost's thick walls.

He used a slender stone rod to scratch notations on a slate made easy to grasp by its woven wicker frame. In the warm amber light of a sputtering mollusk-shell oil lamp, he consulted a star path as recorded by Navigators' glyphs pressed into a thin sheet of gold. Only then did he work the number markings on his slate to accurately convert the position of a star that could be seen in the hemispherical dome of the sky

JUDITH & GARFIELD REEVES-STEVENS

to the cylindrical projection of the wall map. It was a calculation he could do easily enough without making marks, but he had two young students with him today, and the notations were for their benefit, to demonstrate the knowledge.

Adma, a true khai *female, eight years old, softly chanted each step of the conversion as Mordcai scratched them onto the slate. Her head was shaved, following tradition, as was her mother's, though Adma's obsidian skin was not oiled. The fine white sand spun up by the winds on the island had led the young* khai *to abandon the practice. So, like many of the true children here, Adma was an unsettling blend of the old and the new.*

Adma's fellow student this day was Lisafina, an ahkwila *female of twelve years. Despite being* ahkwila, *the girl was fortunate. One day, with Mordcai's help, she would rise to become an adept wayfinder of the islands. Even now, she knew the night sky well enough for her years, and could name each local wayfinder star as it rose above the horizon, although the abstract notion of changing spheres to cylinders was something his lessons had been unable to instill in her.*

Mordcai wasn't troubled by that, though. It was a known fact that different people, khai *or* ahkwila, *had different talents. While Lisafina would be a wayfinder, Adma could very well become a master of the star paths. The world had need of both.*

His calculation complete, Mordcai rose from his kneeling position and crossed the floor to the far wall, to count off the hexagonal cells spanning the distance from the Nan Noa quarries to Nan Moar. As he did so, Lisafina held the oil lamp close as Adma used a bone awl to etch a knotpoint into the plaster of the wall, precisely where Mordcai indicated. This close to the cool plaster, its damp sour smell overwhelmed the almost sweet scent of the whale oil burning in the shell.

The knotpoint he marked set the position on the open sea, beyond sight of any land, for a wayfinder to change heading from one particular star to the next. The second star was made easily identifiable as it rose above a horizon board, provided that board was held away from the eyes the particular distance set by the red knot in its wayfinder cord.

To sail from the quarries to this outpost, a wayfinder required a single horizon board, three different cords with a series of precisely measured and colored knots, and knowledge of only eighteen stars. To sail between all the local islands, and to the nearest great land, required knowledge of fewer than two hundred stars.

But to know the star paths between all twelve outposts and home—that is, to be able to sail anywhere around the world in any season—required knowledge of more than twenty-four hundred stars, plus the signs of the sea, of the clouds, and of the winds. Those who held that knowledge were star path masters, a rank to which Mordcai had dedicated himself five years ago, and a rank he might achieve in another five years of study. He'd be twenty then, and would spend his final few years traveling the world, looking for changes in the star paths, so that others might learn after him.

Adma used bright red plaster to fill in the hole she had made in the wall map.

Then Mordcai used slender fishbone needles to position a length of fine twine along the properly calculated arc between the previous knotpoint and this new one, in order to guide the route-marking he would etch and color.

As he brought his flint scribing tool to the wall, the ground shook.

Lisafina gasped, and a ribbon of flame trailed from the open lamp she carried and now spilled.

Adma looked at her fellow student with disapproval. "It's just the Earth growing."

Mordcai smiled. "Not quite, little one. The Earth's size hasn't changed in all the years it's been measured."

"At the equinox!" Adma exclaimed.

Mordcai nodded. It was common practice at an equinox to measure the size of shadows cast by perpendicular rods set at different known distances from the world's central circle. At the same time, young students were often tasked to demonstrate simple geometry. By using the differences among those measurements, they were able to calculate the circumference of the world.

Adma was proud to recite her knowledge. "But the land changes!"

"The land changes," Mordcai agreed. "So do the seas."

"But slowly!"

"Usually." Mordcai noted Lisafina's skeptical expression and chose to elaborate on his qualification. "I've been on mountains far inland and high above any sea, where I've found shells and the skeletons of fish. Such a thing would only be possible if, in time past, the tops of those mountains were underwater. So parts of the Earth do grow, but not the Earth itself."

Lisafina flicked her eyes at him in disbelief. So Mordcai turned that disbelief into a lesson as well.

"You're right to doubt the word of any one person, Lisafina. But I'm not the only one to have seen the shells and skeletons. And the more people who see something, the more times a thing is seen, then the more likely it is to be true."

The young girl remained resistant to the unfamiliar, a trait of the ahkwila, *Mordcai knew. "I haven't seen anything like that."*

"It's not possible for anyone to see everything." The apprentice master tapped the gold sheet, finely textured with the intricate glyphs of star paths. "That's why it's everyone's duty to record what's seen, so it can be shared with others and added to. That's how we learn."

The ground shook again.

Lisafina's doubt changed to worry. "We should go outside."

Adma objected. "We haven't finished marking the path."

"We can finish it later!"

Mordcai shook his head. Adma was right. Once begun, a task had to be finished. However, before he could devise a lesson about duty to impart this concept to Lisafina, he heard running footsteps in the corridor leading to the hall.

It was Qiamaro, a young ahkwila *apprentice to the builders, his face glistening with sweat from working outdoors, breathless from running and from fear. "The wall has fallen! Master Balihann . . ."*

He could say no more. He didn't have to.

In the central courtyard, the sudden movement of the ground had brought down an unfinished wall and its scaffolding. Dust still hung in the air.

It was true that Architect Master Balihann was dead. Mordecai could see a well-muscled leg and arm emerging from the tangle of wooden scaffolding that surrounded a fallen stone block, as a nest surrounds an egg. Thick blood pooled around what was visible of the body. As a group of khai *watched, a group of* ahkwila *builders worked frantically to position a makeshift lever to move the stone block.*

Adma, at Mordcai's side, was fascinated, and as her teacher, Mordcai made use of that.

"See the wound on the body's leg?" Mordcai pointed to where a splinter of stark white bone had punched out through the outer thigh. It seemed his good friend had been standing upright and died instantly when the block had crushed him, driving straight down onto his head.

"Where the bone is?" Adma asked.

"Correct. What does the nature of the blood there tell us?"

Adma stared at the wound and the bone and the blood, her young face contorted in concentration.

Mordcai gave her a hint. "Is the wound still bleeding?"

"No . . ." Then she had it. "That means the heart's stopped!"

"So . . . ?"

"So he's dead, and there's no hurry to remove the stone!"

"Very good."

Adma smiled up at Mordcai; then both looked over to the scene of the accident as they heard Lisafina wail.

The workers were removing two other bodies from the rubble, both ahkwila.

"I think that one was her father," Adma said.

"It was."

"Should we finish the map?"

"We should," Mordcai agreed, but he stopped Adma from going to get Lisafina. "She won't be finishing it with us. Not today."

Adma looked at him in puzzlement.

"It's not their way," Mordcai said.

That night, Mordcai and the other khai *disposed of Balihann's remains by fire, to prevent the spread of disease. Afterward, since the necessary business of elevating an apprentice to replace the master architect could not be finalized until the rubble of the fallen wall had been cleared, Mordcai went to the workers' camp near the beach. The public health traditions the* ahkwila *followed were, as always, a mystery.*

By firelight, the elder women of the workers' camp wept and sang as they cleansed the dead men. Mordcai saw younger women preparing long strips of cloth with which to wrap the bodies—cloth they wouldn't use for clothing but would waste on the dressing of a valueless corpse. At the same time, the men of the camp struck rhythmic, ritual poses around a large bonfire. Bellowing loudly, they were drinking large quantities of a liquid made from the root of the sava plant—not fermented, but potent all the same. Mordcai knew this behavior would last three days. There was no chance of the rubble being cleared until then.

Young Qiamaro had joined the men around the fire, but when he saw Mordcai, he left the others. A few moments later he offered Mordcai one of two half-coconut-shells filled with the sava drink. The apprentice master accepted it politely. He had seen how the drink was prepared—by groups of ahkwila *males chewing the roots, then spitting them into a communal bowl. He had no intention of consuming the resulting liquid unless it had been boiled to eliminate particles of disease. It had not. Boiling apparently also eliminated the drink's potency.*

"It's good you came," Qiamaro said in the true language. He spoke as if his lips were numb, and laughed lightly when he failed to make the proper click. "I have something to ask you."

"Of course."

"I would like a set of wayfinder's tools." Qiamaro swayed on his feet, obviously relaxed, though his eyes remained sharp and clear in the firelight. "A horizon board . . . a set of knotted ropes . . ."

"You want to change your apprenticeship?" It was likely Qiamaro was too old to ever study long enough to be a star path master. Still, becoming a pilot or a local wayfinder was a possibility for him.

The young ahkwila *surprised him.*

"Not for me. For Natano."

"Lisafina's father. One of the dead."

Qiamaro nodded and took a gulp from his coconut shell.

"Why?"

"To guide him."

"The dead man."

Another nod. "In the next life."

Mordcai moved to correct the youth. "That's not a known fact."

The youth rolled his head from side to side, as if his muscles had lost the necessary tension to hold his head erect. "Not for your kind, maybe. But for us, no doubt."

Mordcai regarded Qiamaro, curious. "Can you prove it?"

"*Can you?*"

"*I don't have to.*"

Qiamaro swayed, almost toppled, caught his balance just in time. "*You're going to be surprised, then.*"

Mordcai waited for enlightenment.

"*When you die, and you find yourself with the gods.*" Qiamaro laughed, spilled some of his drink, very cautiously balanced the shell again, and drank from it.

Mordcai reached out and put a hand on his shoulder to steady him. "*There are no gods, Qiamaro. At least, none that have made themselves known in a consistent manner.*"

The youth shook his head vigorously in denial and almost immediately looked as if he regretted the action. "*Look around you, Master! Where did all this come from—the sea, the land*"—he held up his shell—"*the sava! If not from the gods?*"

"*I don't know,*" Mordcai said simply.

"*Don't you want to know?*"

"*Wanting to know a fact is not an excuse to make one up.*"

Qiamaro shrugged, uncomprehending. "*Can I have the wayfinder's tools?*"

"*For Natano, the dead man.*"

Qiamaro nodded.

"*All right. I'll find a set,*" Mordcai said.

The young ahkwila *smiled his thanks, then half stumbled against the much taller apprentice master. "Now when you die, Master, Natano will be there with his tools to help guide you to the gods, too.*"

Mordcai sighed. *How could the* ahkwila *see the same world the* khai *saw, yet still not understand it?*

He tried once again to make the youth see reason.

"*Qiamaro, listen: Each time you drink the sava, it has this effect on you. Each time your fellow workers drink it, the same thing. That makes the effect of the sava a known fact. But your gods . . . beings that see us but we can't see them . . . beings that we go to when we die . . . Do you not see that being dead means to never exchange information with anyone ever again, that—to our knowledge—what happens after death can then never be known?*"

Qiamaro only stared at him as if his words held no meaning and never would.

Mordcai threw up his hands in frustration. "*There's no reason to accept that gods exist until you can prove they exist. I ask you again, Qiamaro. Can you do that?*"

Then the ground moved again. And again. And the first blast of incandescent lava shot up from the central peak of Nan Moar, sending red light flashing across the island and up against the sudden black cloud of scalding gas and smoke.

Mordcai and Qiamaro, khai *and* ahkwila *both, stared up at the tower of flame and destruction.*

"*I don't have to,*" Qiamaro said, then drained his shell.

Mordcai looked at the shell in his own hand and let it fall, concerned that he'd left the map unfinished. Just as he was wondering if he could make it back to the hall in time, the concussion of the volcanic eruption struck him.

Nan Moar was the first outpost to fall.

NINETEEN

"You sure you want to do this?" Roz asked.

Lyle stood before the one-way observation glass. On the other side, David Weir waited. He had been kidnapped, returned, then recovered in the middle of a firefight between two as yet unknown groups of trained and well-armed operators. Yet he didn't appear troubled by any of it.

"He hasn't moved, Roz. It's been an hour, and he hasn't moved."

Up until last night, Lyle knew he'd been running a straightforward espionage case: A vital defense database had been compromised, and Holden Ironwood was prime suspect. The case had three distinct operational phases of investigation. First, determine if Ironwood *was* guilty of stealing the SARGE database. If yes, then locate the storage site of the stolen data. Finally, recover the data and arrest Ironwood before he could sell it. The end.

Then David Weir had become involved.

Now a member of Lyle's team was dead and a Stinger missile had been fired on an American street.

"Is he asleep?"

"Eyes are open," Lyle said. "He blinks. He scratched his ear a couple of times."

"Then he *has* moved."

"The point is, he hasn't been screaming to see a lawyer. That's not normal."

Roz tapped his arm with the file he'd asked her to bring. She'd put the other item he'd requested in a small cardboard box on the table beside him. "That's what it says in here."

Lyle took the manila folder and flipped through its meager contents. A life reduced to a trail of paperwork. College transcripts. Bank records. Credit reports. Driver's license. Tax forms.

"He's *not* normal." Roz reached over and pulled a stapled two-page form from the back of the file. "Look at this." She handed him an Army CID security report. "When he joined the army lab, he needed to be cleared by Homeland."

The cover sheet was stamped DENIED. Lyle quickly scanned both pages, then shrugged. "I don't see anything to disqualify him from a basic clearance."

"Exactly. I called the investigating agent. He said there was nothing to investigate. No family to interview. No close friends. They couldn't gather enough information to make a judgment."

"Any chance Weir's in the witness relocation program?"

"Checked that, too. No record. And the photos we have from his driver's license since age sixteen? Same guy, same name, just getting older."

Lyle picked up the cardboard box, just in case his strategy worked, then started for the door to the hallway.

"Boss?" Lyle knew what his young assistant was going to say, just by the tone of her voice. She was worried he'd make it personal. "Del was my friend, too."

"Duly noted."

"Then go get 'im."

"I intend to."

Everything had changed, and David Weir knew why.

After months of false starts and dead ends, he finally had a promising lead to saving his life. Thanks to Jess MacClary.

His inner clock and stomach told him it was about 8:00 A.M. He couldn't remember when or even what he'd eaten last, but food would have to wait its turn. All he cared about now was getting out of here and waiting for Jess's promised call. The local police were just a momentary problem. After all, technically, he'd done nothing wrong. Last night or this morning. What he'd do about Ironwood, he'd think about later. Jess had been explicit: He could only work for her.

A faint rasp announced the unlocking of a doorknob mechanism. Besides the irritating hiss of air vents high above in stained acoustic tile, it was the first new sound in more than an hour.

A moment later the door banged open, as if the person in the doorway had meant to startle him. If so, it didn't work.

David recognized the man who entered, from last night at the warehouse. The local cops had deferred to him, even though he'd not been in uniform. No jacket. Blue short-sleeve shirt. Dark blue pants like those of a repairman. His white-streaked dark hair had looked flat, as if he'd been wearing some kind of cap.

He'd changed since then. Dark suit, white shirt, gray tie, boring.

The man closed the door and took a chair across from him. He put a cardboard box on the floor and a manila file folder on the table. David could read his own name on the tab.

"You want to call a lawyer?"

"Do I need one?"

"I don't know. Do you?"

"I'm a witness to the shooting. I wasn't armed."

"Oh, right, the shooting. At the warehouse where we found a body on the roof. And a federal agent killed by a Stinger missile attack."

That last statement did startle David. He'd been handcuffed and put in the back of a patrol car for questioning while one of the uniforms took over with Dominic LaSalle. Half an hour later, he'd been uncuffed and was on his way to police headquarters in Atlantic City. No one had said anything about a dead federal agent or a Stinger missile.

"Am I a suspect?"

"Oh, yes."

"But I wasn't the one doing the shooting."

"Who says that's why you're here?"

Okay . . . David thought quickly. Army CID? From the moment he'd downloaded his first files from the DNA lab, he'd known they could apprehend him, even planned that when and if the moment arrived, he'd confess to everything, share the discoveries he'd made, and hope for the best—but that had been before Jess.

"Nothing to say?"

"I don't know who you are."

"Jack Lyle." The man reached inside his jacket for a black leather badge case and flipped it open to show his ID. "Did Ironwood brief you on how to behave when you got picked up? Or maybe his lawyers did?"

Air force? David watched uncomprehending as the agent returned the badge case to his inner pocket.

"Not that it matters," Lyle continued, "but not only do we have proof that you've stolen government property, we know you've sold it. And the person you've sold it to . . . we can make a good case that he's reselling it to foreign buyers. Ever hear of the Economic Espionage Act?"

David hadn't.

Lyle drew the folder closer to himself, then leaned back in his chair as if settling in for a long discussion. "Why'd you abandon your Jeep last night?"

No matter who or what had pulled him in, David saw no harm in telling the truth, where he could.

"The engine died."

"There was a kill-switch in it. A radio-controlled one."

"I bought the car used. Must have been the previous owner's."

"Who was shooting at you?"

"People who wanted my computers."

"Not at the warehouse. Before that. Under the overpass."

That told David he'd been followed—by the air force. *Why?* "News to me."

The agent tapped the folder again. "What about Vince Gilden?"

"The bookstore guy? He rents a place at the same warehouse I do."

"You see him last night?"

"I saw his car. In the parking lot."

"How about Mordecai Diego Rodrigues?"

The name was unknown to David. "Never heard of him."

"Why didn't you call for a tow truck? When your car died."

"I don't have Triple A. Can't afford a tow truck."

"How'd you leave the overpass?"

David studied the air force agent, wary. If the man had followed him, he'd know how he'd left the overpass.

"I caught a cab. On the overpass."

"Where's the receipt?"

David shrugged. "Didn't ask for one."

"Where'd you go?"

"To meet Dom at the airport."

"Then what?"

"I wanted to show him my lab."

"Who was the girl?"

"Didn't catch her name. Ask Dom, she came with him."

"He's claiming amnesia from the trauma of being shot. Says he remembers nothing about last night. Doesn't even remember you. So how long have you known him?"

David gambled that Jack Lyle had no way to contradict him—for now. "A long time. Friend of the family sort of thing."

"What's your explanation for last night?"

"Burglars after my lab stuff, and Dom surprised them in the act."

The agent's finger flicked his file. "Was it worth it?" he asked. "Thirty thousand dollars—for the rest of your life?"

David answered truthfully. "Yes."

"Why?"

"You wouldn't understand."

"You're right. I don't. When you're convicted under the Economic

Espionage Act—and you will be—you're facing fifteen years' imprisonment. Per count. That's forty-five years, minimum. No parole."

David stayed calm. "They were *personnel* files, Agent Lyle. Not even complete ones. Colonel Kowinski can verify that I stripped the personally identifiable parts out. I only extracted geographical data from the sections about next of kin, family history."

Lyle picked up the manila folder, as if preparing to go. "I don't care if you lie to yourself, kid. I do care if you lie to me. You *stole* from the government while working for the government—a position of trust that you betrayed for money. You betrayed your country. That's what a judge is going to care about. Same goes for me."

David thought fast and hard. Long before he'd ever be tried, he'd die in custody if he couldn't find a way to make this man release him.

Then it struck him: If Ironwood was suspected of selling his data to a foreign buyer, then Lyle had probably been listening in to all of Ironwood's interminable calls to him. That meant he already knew what Ironwood was up to, so . . .

David had just been handed the advantage he needed. The air force needed something from him, even if Lyle couldn't or wouldn't say what that was. *What does matter is that he'll have to trade my freedom for it.*

"What do I have to do to walk out of here?" David said.

"I thought you'd never ask." The agent picked up the cardboard box, put it on the table, then took from it a gleaming silver object the size of a paperback. It was the kind of hard drive that could be plugged into almost any computer to provide extra data storage.

He slid the drive across the table. "Use this to find out where and how your data's being processed."

David couldn't believe his luck. Both he and the air force wanted the same thing.

TWENTY

In the light of the half moon, Merrit studied the two men with him on the beach. He'd probably have to kill one of them at the end of this conversation. He'd prefer killing both.

It was coming on midnight, and from more than a mile away blazed a kaleidoscope of light from Atlantic City's boardwalk casinos. The night was cool after a hot and humid September day. Merrit's black cotton trousers and shirt snapped against him in the breeze.

"C'mon, Merrit, we didn't know she was under surveillance." The speaker's name was Griffith, and he was angry. Probably because he correctly suspected he wouldn't be paid the outstanding half of his fee. "I mean, how could we?"

"By following her." Merrit left the word "idiot" unsaid but implied. "Establish her routine. ID her bodyguards."

"She only took one from the airport. Some guy named LaSalle."

"If you knew that, you should've known about the other people keeping her under surveillance."

"I know about them now, okay? I can still get to her."

Merrit doubted that. As long as Jessica MacClary remained on her family's private jet behind the layers of security at the airport, she was untouchable.

Amateurs, Merrit thought. He couldn't see any point in continuing this discussion.

The second man chimed in. "Listen, Nate—you know what my old man would say. You gotta let him try."

Nathaniel Merrit didn't like being called Nate, any more than he liked Holden Ironwood Jr. Still, Ironwood's brat had given him the distraction he needed.

"Yeah, man, gimme a chance to earn out," Griffith whined.

Merrit glanced up and down the beach to be certain their privacy would be undisturbed, that there were no unwanted watchers on the distant piers. "Okay, here's the deal I'm willing to make." He dropped his KA-BAR down his sleeve and into his palm as he saw his target relax.

"Pay attention," he said.

Reflexively, Griffith and J.R. both eased closer.

Merrit locked eyes with the man he was going to kill and brought his knife up in a single sweeping motion to puncture the chest below the sternum and drive into the heart.

Except the target caught his hand first.

"No!" Griffith cried.

A challenge. Merrit's sudden smile reflected his approval. A fair fight was preferable to a simple execution. He'd still win anyway.

Locked like lovers, he and Griffith pushed against each other, muscles rigid, straining, trembling with the effort, the blade easing toward one chest, then the other.

Close up, Merrit saw glistening sweat in every pore of Griffith's face. Saw crazed determination in the man's wide-open eyes. Smelled his sour breath—mints over something with garlic. His last meal.

The contest lasted twenty seconds. Griffith's pupils widened an instant before his grip on Merrit weakened, knowing his fate.

Merrit's knife turned, pressed in, and this time it met no resistance, only yielding flesh.

Griffith's hot, foul breath escaped him in a whisper. His pupils expanded into darkness, became black holes.

Merrit released him, and the body fell.

"You didn't have to do that," J.R. said—but Merrit heard excitement in his voice. Inappropriate emotion. Death was just the stopping of a process. A regular occurrence. Inevitable. Sometimes profitable.

"Yes," Merrit said. "I did."

"Yeah? What if the surveillance wasn't for her?" J.R. stared down at the dead man's wide-open eyes, at the bloodstain slowly growing across his Caesar's T-shirt, glistening in the half moonlight.

Merrit rechecked the beach, the piers. No movement. "Who else?"

"Maybe the guy."

Merrit pulled his own shirt away from his chest, inspected it for blood spatter, saw nothing. He'd still burn it, though. All his clothes. He had seen those *CSI* shows. "The guy?" He pulled his knife from Griffith's chest and wiped the blade on the dead man's shirt. He'd destroy the weapon, too.

"You know. The lab geek from the army."

Merrit stopped his cleanup. "Weir? He was *there* with *her?*"

J.R. looked at him as if he had missed the first half of a conversation. "That's what I said: She was at his lab when Griffith took his shot."

"What the hell was she doing with Weir?"

"How should I know?"

"You didn't think it was important to find out?"

"C'mon, I didn't even know it was his lab until I got copies of the police reports." A truculent J.R. pointed at Griffith's body. "He didn't either. So you *didn't* have to kill him."

Merrit, against all the grounding principles that directed and controlled his life, grabbed J.R. by the shirt. Ironwood's whelp was thick with muscles but had no idea how to use them.

"You decided on your own to take out a *MacClary?* What do you think your old man would say about that?" He shoved Ironwood's son away in disgust. J.R stumbled and fell onto the cold sand by the corpse.

"Well, you started it," J.R. said, like a kid on the playground. "You killed her aunt. You know what those people are like. Everything's 'family' to them. Sooner or later, she'd have come after us if we didn't get her first."

"Those 'people' are my concern, not yours."

"Okay, okay." J.R. sullenly shook sand from his shoes before awkwardly getting back to his feet. "So I messed up. But you're supposed to keep me out of trouble. What would the old man have to say to you?" At his mention of his father, loafers in hand, J.R. looked down the beach, toward the casinos. The Encounters resort stood out with its otherworldly green floodlights.

Ironwood senior was still in residence this week. So something was going on, Merrit knew, but his speculation went that far, and no more. If Ironwood thought he had a need to know, he'd be told.

"I want copies of all the police reports," Merrit said. There was no sense in creating an enemy here. Once Sr. was gone, Jr. would have a few billion dollars to burn. That could buy a lot of revenge before he squandered it.

"Why?"

Merrit pictured himself snapping J.R.'s neck. It wouldn't take three seconds. "I want to find out about the surveillance. Who they were watching. Who they were."

J.R. shoved bare feet back into his loafers. "Well, *I* can tell you *that*. It's in the reports. Air Force Office of Special Investigations."

Merrit was surprised. "Air force? Not Army CID?"

"Yeah, but you have to leave them out of it. I shouldn't have even mentioned them. It's sort of a secret between me and the old man."

"Too late. What's the rest of it?"

J.R. shrugged. "He took something from the air force. It's how we've been finding the outposts. But don't worry, Weir doesn't know, so he couldn't tell them anything."

J.R. only had part of it right.

There was just one way to be sure David Weir couldn't tell anyone anything—and Merrit planned to see to it at once.

TWENTY-ONE

Jess let the words of the memorial service drift over her, unheard. She found her comfort in their familial setting, not their content.

The contemporary Episcopal Church of the United States was just another veil that offered sanctuary to the Family. The Line MacClary had come to the American colonies as public followers of the Church of England. After the American Revolution, the MacClarys had joined in the common mood of the new country and supported the formation of an independent church whose bishops would no longer need to swear allegiance to the British king. In the Americas, as in Europe and Asia, the changing fashions of the pageant of history were little more than camouflage for those who lived to serve the First Gods.

Thus, in Boston's Cathedral Church of St. Paul, Jess readily found her true beliefs reflected in everything around her. Like the ancient Shrine of Turus, this public place of worship showed private evidence of the Family, to those who knew.

Built in 1819, almost a century before it became Boston's Episcopal cathedral, the Church of St. Paul owed its existence to, among other notables, Paul Revere, Nathan Hale, and John Hancock. The building committee for the church structure itself had included William Appleton and Daniel Webster. Though none of the five was a defender, each had been among the 144 of the day who knew the truth of the Family. As a result, St. Paul's looked like no other Christian church of its time.

Instead of the Gothic architecture popular in the America of that era, the Cathedral Church of St. Paul was a distinguished example of what came to be called Greek Revival. Its graceful exterior of limestone blocks and sandstone columns mirrored the classic lines of Greek temples supported, in turn, by Ionic pillars.

Even more intriguing, the church's Greek Revival style matched that of the secular government structures of the nation's capital, where the Family also worked behind the scenes. In Washington, D.C., the Family's goal was not to gather or influence political control but to help create a strong national banking system to protect their assets. It took three attempts, and almost a century, but the U.S. Federal Reserve's twelve regional banks eventually secured the ancient MacCleirighs' future in the New World.

The interior of St. Paul's, despite more than two centuries of repair and renovations, bore even clearer signs of the Family's influence. The altar of the old church was built in the style of a Chamber of Heaven, complete with its hemispherical ceiling. More telling, above the altar hung a dramatic cross lacking the traditional proportions of a crucifix in which the upright stand was longer than its crosspiece. Instead, each arm of St. Paul's cross was the same length, as in the Family's bladed cross. Only the position of the circle on the cross had changed. In the cathedral's cross, the ancient symbol of the Family now encircled the intersection of the cross's arms. Yet, when seen in the proper light, when the cross's wedge-shaped arms cast shadows, that circle divided into twelve segments, not four. The Twelve Restored.

So when Jess gazed upon the cross of St. Paul's, she saw the symbol of her faith, and today she drew the strength she needed from it.

Publicly, Florian MacClary had been reported dead of a heart attack in French Polynesia. The medical records provided by her personal physician in Boston established she'd been undergoing treatment for angina and had been urged to have bypass surgery. A second physician, in Papeete, Tahiti, had forwarded the paperwork from the autopsy, officially confirming the cause of death was what her own doctor had feared. In accordance with her wishes, Jess's aunt had been cremated, and her ashes scattered in the great southern ocean.

All of it was a lie arranged to suit the purposes of Family business by the MacCleirigh cousins who were everywhere, working for smooth passage of the Family's assets between the generations.

In truth, Florian had been lost at sea, without witness. Today's supposed affirmation of her religious beliefs as a member and supporter of St. Paul's had no connection to reality. Only the tears shed for her were real.

As Florian's adopted heir, Jess accepted that she was the focus of the afternoon's events. She'd dressed in a simple black linen sheath and tied her bright hair with a black silk ribbon. She displayed her silver Tuareg cross openly, as did almost a third of those in the cathedral who sat apart from other, less intimate friends of the deceased. Each of those pendant crosses differed slightly, no two exactly alike.

The remembrances, hymns, and silent prayers finally ended, and Jess rose and walked down the long aisle to stand beside the open doors that led outside. Taking a place to the right of her in the reception line was the Reverend Noreen Enright, who had baptized her in this cathedral, and who had returned from retirement to conduct Florian's memorial service. The elderly reverend seemed troubled by Jess's pendant. Not because the cross that hung from it wasn't traditional—tradition was not often an issue with the Episcopal Church—but because of the deferential way Jess was treated by the others who wore crosses similar to hers.

Yet the reverend asked no questions. Not even as those others, one after the other, took Jess's left hand, dipped their heads, even bent a knee as if in service to her. The MacClarys were longtime benefactors of the cathedral, and odd behavior, when combined with wealth and generosity, could be explained as charming eccentricity.

When the last of the mourners disappeared through the doors, into the late-afternoon September sunshine that still bathed the verdant Boston Common opposite St. Paul's, Jess turned to Reverend Enright to ask permission to stay a few minutes longer. The reverend made no objection, offering only to sit and join her in prayer. Jess declined politely, and the cleric touched her shoulder in sympathy, then left.

Jess was alone.

She returned to the altar. To the right was an oversized color photograph of her aunt. Smiling, vibrant.

She slipped into a pew on that side, next to an arching spray of silver-green eucalyptus bound with fragrant thyme and garlanded with acorns—ancient symbols of protection, of the restful sleep earned through courage, and of immortality. Eleven identical sprays adorned the ends of other pews. Twelve remembrances from twelve defenders.

None but Jess had come to say farewell in person, though, for just as no defender could marry another, ensuring the Lines remained distinct, no defender could attend another's funeral rites. Another way of ensuring safety from one's enemies.

Jess bent her head as if in prayer and gave her heart over to her grief for the woman who had become her second mother, who had given her so much, and yet hidden so much more.

Yet, even now, her training kept her alert. She heard careful footsteps approaching, and they were not the light steps of Reverend Enright. Instinctively, she brought both hands to her cross.

"Jessie . . . *het is I.*"

The soft words spoken in Dutch shocked Jess with joy. She turned. "Willem?"

Incredibly, he was there. Willem, Line Tasman. Defender of Macao. Florian's partner, her lover, her one true love. By all the traditions of the Family, he was not allowed to be here—but here he was.

The black skin of Willem's shaved scalp shone in the warm light of the darkened church as he held out his arms to her, his embrace tightening with her first words. "I can't believe she's gone."

Then Jess leaned back, looked up, eyes questioning. Like her, Willem wore mourning black. His suit trim, his shirt collarless. Beneath his jacket, though, she'd felt a gun.

"You're taking me back to Zurich, aren't you?"

"Why would I do that?"

"Su-Lin sent you."

He held a finger to his lips, conspiratorially. "Ssssh, the others think I'm still in Iceland, on the Snæfellsjökull dig."

"Then why are you here?"

Willem looked up at the altar, to the image of Florian. The photo had been taken on a sailboat in spring. The sea was brilliant blue behind her. Sunlit strands of her short, windblown hair created a halo. Her unguarded face was radiant.

Jess understood. This was something else she was learning for herself: Sometimes, even defenders broke the rules. Just as she had with David Weir.

"Now why would Su-Lin send me to take you back to Zurich?"

"My first assignment as defender. And I botched it."

"Oh, well. Off to the Shop with you for a few years of academic exile." Willem squeezed her hand, released it. "Tell me about this 'botched' assignment."

"His name is David. David Weir."

"And he is . . . ?"

"The researcher? For Holden Ironwood? Su-Lin wants to know if he had anything to do with what happened to Florian. Willem, she told me all of you knew about this."

The Defender of Macao's broad forehead creased in surprise. "Not me." He steered Jess back to the pew and took a seat beside her. "From the beginning."

Jess shared with Willem everything she knew. How Ironwood's technician had come to the Family's attention during Emil's surveillance of the billionaire's charter operations. How Su-Lin had ordered her to bring him to Zurich if she found any connection to what had happened in the South Pacific.

Then she told him how Dom had arranged David's capture, what she'd learned from questioning him, and what she'd discovered in his research lab.

Willem's astonishment, and his elation, were the equal of her own.

"He can *locate* the lost temples?"

"Not exactly," Jess clarified. "What David does is find a general area to search. Then Ironwood takes his information and somehow pinpoints an exact location. That's why I didn't want him to go to Zurich. I have a way to have David work for us instead of Ironwood."

"Money?"

Jess shook her head. "He's a scientist. You know the type. When I told him that his genetic clusters led Ironwood to three temples, but that there were nine more out there to find—that's when I got to him. I think he'll do anything to find out how *I* know that."

She put a hand on Willem's arm. "Don't you see, Willem? The First Gods brought one of our twelve lines to each temple site—so his analysis must have picked up a unique MacCleirigh gene. I think David's found long-lost cousins of ours. Five, six, maybe even more times removed. Because when a MacCleirigh line left a temple site, some of their offspring must have stayed behind. That means their genetic legacy is still there *today*."

"It *sounds* reasonable . . ."

"But?"

Willem put a large hand over hers. "What I'm about to say isn't blasphemy. You have to believe that. Hear me out."

"It's all right. I mean, about the Secret. I know it's been lost, but—"

He interrupted her. "This is something different. Something else that's missing. From the written *Traditions*."

Jess withdrew her hand. "What about them?"

"For a long time now, Florian and I have . . . had . . . been working on a different way to read some of the passages. When that second temple was discovered in Peru"—Willem paused, choosing his words with great care—"it was strong confirmation for what we were looking at."

When Jess said nothing, Willem forged on. "Some of us have come to believe that the First Gods walked among twelve *different* families."

Jess didn't understand.

"Jess, the twelve lines of the MacCleirighs today are *modern* branches that broke off from the *single* MacCleirigh line in the past fifteen hundred years. We don't know who the other eleven families were or what happened to them."

His words dropped into the well of silence in the empty church, and their ripples swept Jess into an unknown sea.

"You've seen the sun map in the Shrine?" he asked.

Jess nodded, mute with bewilderment.

"Then you also know the First Gods walked among us almost nine thousand years ago. That's a huge gap in our records—seventy-five hundred years. A lot could happen over that much time. A lot *did*. Eleven other original families were most likely lost along the way." He looked toward the photo of his lost love. "Or maybe they're still out there, still hiding like we are, following traditions of their own."

"But our *Traditions*—"

Willem's voice was solid with conviction. "*Nothing* I'm saying contradicts them at all. The First Gods did arise from us and walked among us. They scattered humanity on the Twelve Winds, built the Twelve Temples around the world, gave us their gifts, guided the birth of civilization.

"But of those twelve original families, only one remains, Jess. Ours. The MacCleirighs. Yet even the *Traditions* say we'll never know what actual names the First Gods gave us, because names themselves are transitory. We do know that MacCleirigh *is* one of the oldest names from our part of the world, so it's as good as any."

"Does anyone else know about this?"

"Of course. Florian and I, we told the others what we were thinking, the areas we were investigating. All Su-Lin requested was that we restrict knowledge of our speculation and our findings to the other defenders. Until we could be sure."

"I thought all defenders were equal."

"That's why the table's round."

"So how can Su-Lin tell you what to do?"

Willem seemed surprised by the question. "She's in charge of the money."

Jess was surprised in turn. It was something she'd never considered before. The MacCleirighs, at Florian's level—and, by extension, hers— were independent of any monetary system. Jess had always taken it for granted that she'd be provided with everything she needed: tuition, travel expenses, a limitless Foundation ATM card . . .

"It's a considerable undertaking to send fifteen archaeologists into India for six months," Willem said. "To mount an expedition such as that, even we have paperwork to fill out. And there's always more to do than the resources available."

"And Su-Lin decides how the resources are allocated?"

Willem shrugged. "Su-Lin. Andrew. One of the others. Control rotates among us all. If I weren't in the field so much, I'd even get a turn. Su-Lin's based in Zurich these days, so she's the final arbiter."

Something else Florian didn't tell me, Jess thought.

Willem put a hand on her shoulder. "Back to you and your 'assignment.' Do you see now why this researcher of yours might not be detecting

MacCleirigh descendants in India or Peru or Polynesia? Because, if Florian and I are correct, then the MacCleirighs are descendants of a single line associated with a single temple. Probably somewhere in Northern Europe."

"Then what *is* he detecting?"

"Without knowing more, I couldn't guess."

"There's another possibility, you know. You could be wrong."

Willem grinned. "Now you sound like Florian." His grin faded. "So what've you decided to do? With this David Weir."

"I'm not sure yet. I guess I need to get a new chief of security first."

"What's wrong with LaSalle?"

Jess stared at him, startled. "Willem, they tried to kill me again last night. Dom was shot . . . wounded . . ."

"Who tried to kill you?"

"Ironwood's people. At least that's what Su-Lin thinks."

"You used the word 'again.'"

"The first time was in the Barrens. The Canadian Territories. I was at a pipeline site. You haven't heard any of this?"

Willem's face was tight as he made her go through all the details. By the time she'd finished recounting the attack on the warehouse lab, his incredulity had been replaced by open anger.

"You have only four bodyguards around this church," he said. "They didn't even see me."

"They probably recognized you. I'm fine."

"No, you're not. You should have a full detail outside. Three armored vehicles. It's outrageous Su-Lin allowed this." A strange look crossed Willem's face. "You did tell her of this new attack?"

"Of course. Dom's in the hospital. I told her everything. Except about David. I told her my first talk with him was inconclusive but that I'd be following up."

Willem's face clouded with concern.

"What's wrong now?" Jess asked.

"It makes sense that I didn't hear anything about last night. They could be trying to get word to me in Iceland. But for no one to have told me about what happened in Canada—Jessie, that's almost a month ago. Any time there's an attempt on a defender's life, we *all* have to know. For our own safety."

"But . . . Su-Lin knew. I had helicopters following me in Zurich. Decoys."

Willem shook his head. "That's standard for any of us there. Something's wrong." His eyes flicked to the side, caught by some movement at the back of the church.

Reverend Enright was waving a hand at them, walking toward them. "Mr. Tasman?"

Willem got to his feet. "Whatever you find out from this David Weir, tell me first. Not Su-Lin."

"Willem, what's going on? What's wrong?"

"We're all supposed to know *everything*. The Twelve Restored. No secrets." His eyes locked on hers. "Su-Lin's holding something back."

Any solace that St. Paul's had offered Jess evaporated.

"Don't trust her," Willem said.

TWENTY-TWO

"What happened?"

Such a simple question. Such a complicated set of answers, none of them good.

Su-Lin Rodrigues, Defender of São Paulo, considered the image on the small video conference screen on her desk. The huge window behind the Defender of New York was flooded with daylight. Andrew McCleary's forty-fifth-floor view of Manhattan would be impressive today. Here in Zurich, her office had no windows. Only carbon-fiber-augmented, blast-proof walls. Individual defenders on their own, as Andrew was in New York, were well guarded, so elaborate security measures weren't often needed. The MacCleirigh Foundation building, however, made a tempting target for the Family's enemies.

"You said our associate in the Ironwood organization wouldn't fail a second time."

For that, at least, there was a straightforward explanation.

"He didn't. He subcontracted the assignment."

"We should have handled this ourselves."

Su-Lin preferred to have Andrew's cooperation but, if necessary, she was prepared to act on her own. Even in the best of times the Family was a fragile construct. If a schism among the twelve defenders were even suspected, it was all but certain the Family would splinter into opposing factions. That, inevitably, would lead to the revelation of its existence and the collapse of the Foundation.

"There's no need to panic, Andrew. You and I eliminated Florian without direct involvement, and—"

He interrupted. *"But we needed to be rid of them both! Jessica is just as dangerous to us as Florian ever was. You know what will happen if more temples are found."*

He was right. For generations the MacCleirigh Foundation had thrived because its members supported it with devout zeal and no thought of personal reward. The Foundation's steadily accumulating wealth and influence were simply regarded as secular by-products of the Family's holy mission, set by the First Gods themselves: to defend the First Gods' Secret until their return.

For generations that status quo existed undisturbed, and the flock in turn became gullible and easily led because, in truth, the Twelve Restored were no longer defending some mythical Secret. They were defending the Foundation's assets. Then the first temple had been found, and what once had been myth became reality. Many within the Family now believed the discovery heralded the imminent return of the First Gods and the completion of the Family's mission.

To Su-Lin and her closest ally, Andrew, it heralded the potential end of the Foundation itself and, more importantly, control of the MacCleirigh billions.

"No more temples *will* be found, Andrew. At least, none that'll last long enough for the Family to examine."

"What about Havi Atoll?"

"The demolition team is on-site. It'll be dealt with by the end of the week."

"And if Ironwood finds another?"

"Then our associate will inform us, and we'll take care of that one, as well." Su-Lin was losing patience. With the current state of the world economy, managing the Foundation's holdings deserved her ongoing attention more than Andrew did. Four displays beside the video conference screen streamed disappointing data from New York, the NASDAQ, Toronto, and the Bolsa de Valores de São Paulo. It was another bad day. She was needed elsewhere.

"Focus on the positive aspect of this, Andrew. As long as we destroy the temples whenever and wherever they're found, the Foundation remains safe."

"Only if no one else finds out what we've done."

"How could they?"

"A third attempt on Jessica can't help but raise suspicion."

"There's always confinement."

"That's no longer an option."

Su-Lin's voice sharpened. "Is there something you haven't told me?"

"Willem's in Boston. He was at the memorial. He spoke with Jessica."

"Why didn't your people stop him?"

"They never saw him. My source was the memorial officiant. She called the firm to inquire about Florian's regular donations—if they'd be continuing."

Su-Lin shut off her financial displays. As a team, Willem and Florian had represented a real and present danger to the Foundation's security.

Given Florian's penchant for fieldwork in remote and often dangerous areas, she'd been the less troublesome of the two to eliminate. Her death while on expedition had raised no questions. Her rebellious successor should just as easily have been terminated during a violent protest against a Canadian pipeline, with her death a regrettable coincidence. Instead, with Jessica still alive and Willem now in contact with her, it was as if nothing had changed: The Foundation was still in peril.

"We have to assume they told each other everything."

"About his and Florian's theories, the attempts on her life, yes, of course. But as yet they have no reason to suspect our involvement."

"Unless we do something foolish and confine Jessica to the Shop."

"I agree. Willem would ask too many questions."

"No more half measures, then."

"No more subcontracting."

"I'll send someone I can trust. To bring her back to Zurich."

"How does that help?"

"Her plane won't make it."

"Expensive, but . . . for the best. And Willem?"

"Use your firm's people to find him. No Family involvement."

"And once they've found him?"

"We have to know if he's talked to anyone else. Especially Emil or Victoria. They'd be vulnerable to his theories."

"Knowing Willem, finding that out could be a lengthy affair."

"For the sake of the Family, cousin, we don't have a choice."

"For the sake of the Family . . . What about Ironwood?"

"Not our concern."

"Even if he keeps finding temples?"

Su-Lin switched on the financial displays. This crisis, like others she'd dealt with before, now had its solution.

"That's over, Andrew. Our associate tells me that however Ironwood managed to make those discoveries, he won't be making any more."

TWENTY-THREE

Armed with a 9 mm Glock and a new matte-black, KA-BAR Becker knife, Merrit exited the elevator, prepared to kill.

He felt no more personal responsibility for what was going to happen than would the bullet he'd fire from his gun. Viewed rationally, the target had caused his own death, a marked man the instant he stole from the military and could link Ironwood to his actions.

Merrit nodded to the security guard in the private elevator alcove and continued on his way. He had full access throughout the resort, even here. Most of the fortieth floor in the South Tower of Ironwood's casino was reserved for whales—those gamblers who could be counted on to regularly lose millions, no matter how troubled the economy. There were twenty-two private suites on this level, each at least eighteen hundred square feet, some larger, with Jacuzzis and lap pools, screening rooms and fireplaces, gourmet kitchens and mirrored ceilings: as many pleasures and distractions as required to keep the whales from migrating along the boardwalk to the Taj Mahal or Caesars.

It had only taken a few words to Ironwood about the attack on the warehouse lab—Merrit had been careful to call it an attempted robbery—and the target and his computers were promptly shifted to a safer location, within Encounters.

Merrit straightened his sports coat and his shoulder holster, then pressed the call button on the suite's door-entry panel.

A moment longer than he liked, the door swung open.

"Merrit." David Weir's surprise was an unspoken question.

Merrit pushed past him, into the marble-tiled hallway, through to the great room. "Get packed."

"What's up?"

Weir closed the door and followed him into the high-ceilinged room. Here, black club chairs on thick white shag carpeting were angled toward a black-and-white-veined marble fireplace and a wall of windows that showcased the Atlantic. This time of night, though, even the ocean views were black. There was little to see but the navigation lights of passing ships and watercraft.

Merrit walked to the windows, found their controls, and started the heavy blackout curtains along their track. At the same time, he scanned the room to confirm they were alone. The usual inhabitants of rooms like this were seldom on their own. Weir, it seemed, did not need company.

"What's going on?" Weir asked.

"You're getting an apartment in the Marina."

"Thanks, but no thanks." Weir gestured to the dining alcove. The large glass-topped table in the mirrored room was covered with new, high-end computer equipment. "This is all the room I need. No commute, and I get room service."

"Not anymore. The suite's too expensive." It was the perfect explanation for anyone who knew Ironwood. "Get your jacket."

"Right now?"

"Right now."

Weir didn't look happy, but his shrug conveyed acceptance. "Okay, but I have to make a stop first." He hit a few keys on his computer, then picked up something rectangular encased in shiny silver. A computer hard drive. "I found another cluster for him."

Merrit held out his hand. "I'll deliver it."

"It'll just take a minute." Weir checked his watch. "He's on some conference call to Hong Kong right now, and as soon as he's done, he wants to see me."

Merrit adapted smoothly. "I'll go with you."

"Suit yourself." Weir stopped at the hall closet and pulled out a jacket.

Merrit held the suite's door open. "Don't mention the Marina. He's liable to change his mind and send you back to the sticks to save himself a few bucks."

"Don't I know it."

Merrit closed the door behind him, his plan unchanged. Weir would still be dead by midnight.

* * *

"England?"

"Southwest tip," David said. "About a thousand square kilometers."

"Cornwall!" Ironwood beamed. If this fourth cluster proved out like the last three, he'd have the new outpost's location within a mile—without using any of his expensive toys.

He paused as a new thought struck him, held up Dave's shiny hard drive, its glossy metal case reflecting the Roswell Suite's warm desert colors. A comfortable thirty-five hundred square feet, the penthouse was decked out in full Santa Fe style, complete with a two-hundred-strong cactus garden and a series of original Georgia O'Keeffes on faux adobe walls.

"I seem to remember you saying you'd need a month or more to come up with this."

"The new database from Santa Cruz. It's perfect for my kind of research—smaller, presorted. Saved me time."

"Okay, then . . . You boys want a drink?"

"Sure," David said.

Merrit shook his head a touch too emphatically.

Ironwood looked from one to the other and back again. "In the kitchen, Merrit. Diet cola. Lots of ice. Thanks so much."

Merrit disappeared down a long hallway bordered on either side by tall ficus trees in terra-cotta pots.

"How's he treating you?" Ironwood asked.

"Fine." David's answer came a touch too quickly.

"Un-huh." It was time to have a talk with his security chief. David Weir was a valuable resource, to be handled with care. "Well, don't forget you work for me, not him. I don't want him interfering."

Ironwood picked up the phone and speed-dialed his son, who answered after one too many rings. A cacophony of sounds assaulted him. The gaming floor.

"Get up here." He disconnected without waiting for J.R.'s reply.

Merrit was back from the kitchen, carrying two tall green glass tumblers, filled to the brim with cola and clinking ice.

Ironwood took his and tapped it against David's. "To truth."

David tapped back. "And justice and the American way."

Ironwood heard the cynicism in the young tech's voice. "Still not buying it, are you?"

"About aliens? No."

"Got a better theory yet?'

"Yeah. The nonhuman polymorphisms are SINEs."

Ironwood grinned appreciatively and glanced at his security chief. "This boy just goes down fighting, doesn't he?" Drink in hand, he ambled back to the huge, overstuffed couch and its mounds of canvas pillows worked in traditional Navajo designs. He swept the newspapers to the side and settled back.

David took one of two matching chairs. Merrit stayed on his feet. "Someplace else you have to be?" Ironwood asked.

"No, sir."

"Then take a load off." Ironwood raised his glass as Merrit reluctantly sat down on the second chair. "So, SINEs . . ."

"Short interspersed elements. Retroposons."

"Which tells me exactly nothing."

"A type of noncoding DNA."

Ironwood had no time for jargon, technical or otherwise, but he wanted to be sure he missed nothing of importance. "Meaning a little bit of DNA that doesn't actually do anything."

"Not as far as we know," David admitted. "But the interesting thing—depending on whose study you look at, of course—is that it accounts for anywhere between ninety-five to ninety-eight percent of human DNA. About fifty percent of that, in turn, is just endless repetitions of small sequences."

Ironwood took a sip of cola before answering. "I know all about junk DNA, Dave. It's one of the best indications that something other than evolution's been tinkering with human genes."

He took a moment to enjoy his young researcher's instantly wary look. "In fact, I've been told that for every *other* animal species on the planet, junk DNA shows up in regularly spaced safety zones or some such . . . you know, separating the active genes from each other."

Ironwood used his free hand to indicate a series of building blocks. "Here's an active gene, then bang—bang—bang—fifty thousand repetitions of pure junk and then—bang! Another active gene. Then another fifty thousand repetitions, and so on and so forth. Correct me if I'm wrong here, but I believe that *uniform* distribution is what you academic types call *statistically* smooth.

"But now, if we're talking *human* DNA? There's *nothing* uniform about that. A bunch of 'active' genes strung all together, then a few hundred thousand repetitions, then another 'active' gene, then maybe only two thousand repeats. Whatever. It's all a big mess. Completely random. Like someone got in there and moved things around willy-nilly. Like we were designed by committee, as the old joke goes."

Predictably, David did not agree with him. "All of nature's random. Evolution is fueled by random events."

"I know the standard screed, son. And I quote: 'When a random mutation confers an advantage, that particular animal has more offspring, so the mutation expands through a population generation after generation.' What you're forgetting is that it's only a mutation's *first* appearance that's random. As soon as it appears, and it's *useful,* then random *stops.*" Ironwood snapped his fingers for effect. He glanced again at Merrit, but the security chief was checking something on his phone, his attention elsewhere. "Seems to me, Dave, you're deliberately missing the whole point of what I'm saying: Natural evolution created a regular pattern in every animal's genome—*except* for ours."

David took the bait. He was already shaking his head. "Look, what *you're* forgetting is that we're a pretty recent species. As far as anyone knows, modern humans have only been around about two hundred, two hundred fifty thousand years on the outside. Most geneticists would say that's probably not long enough for a clear pattern to even show up in our genome."

"You're missing a key point, son. I'm not talking humans. I'm talking hominins. All the species and variations that led to *Homo sapiens*. Going back two million years to *Homo habilis*. Heck, even further back, like about fifty million years ago, when our branch of mammals essentially *stopped* adding more of that noncoding junk DNA. But the rats? *They're* still adding it. And what I want to know is: Why's our DNA and our genetic development so much different from every other natural species on this planet? Answer me that, if you can."

He lifted his glass in a mock salute, then coughed as David surprised him.

"I don't have a problem with aliens visiting Earth. I'm just saying there's no evidence yet that convinces me it's already happened. But if you ever do get that kind of proof, it's not going to be astonishing.

"I bet the universe *is* filled with life. I think intelligence and tool using confer an advantage, so somewhere, yeah, there probably are other intelligent beings. And if they don't blow themselves up, then traveling from one star to another is an engineering problem. In two or three hundred more years, maybe even a lot less, we'll most likely know how to build machines that can operate for centuries in interstellar space and think for themselves. We'll probably be able to freeze humans solid for centuries, too, so some of us can make the trip."

The small gray handset on the table chirped. Ironwood squinted at its display. J.R. was in the hall. About time.

David wasn't finished with him, though.

"However, if you think aliens came here *fifty* million years ago and engineered the DNA of some primate knowing . . . *knowing* . . . that they were setting into motion a chain of events that would end up with modern humans—you're not talking about aliens, or science. You're into the supernatural. Divine intervention."

Ironwood waved a hand at David—they'd pick this up again, soon—and tapped an entry code into the handset. The odor of stale smoke and alcohol entered with his son.

He held out David's hard drive to J.R. "Deliver this."

J.R. took it from him. "This his?" He cocked his head in David's direction.

"It's mine," Ironwood said.

"Right. I'll take it down."

"You do that."

As if he thought the meeting had ended with J.R.'s departure, Merrit was on his feet before the door had closed.

David stayed seated. "You know, maybe if you tell me how you're processing my data, I can give it to you a different way. A better way."

Ironwood heaved himself to his feet. He needed to get down to the Red Room, tell Keisha he knew where to start her search for outpost number four. "I got that covered, Dave—but thanks."

David stood up, too, carefully placing his half-full glass of cola on the table. "Have to admit I'm curious, though. I mean, you and I are using the same data, but I'm only finding areas. You're finding outposts."

"Not your concern, son. Just stick to what you're doing."

David finally took the hint. "No problem. Forget I even asked. Stand by for cluster five."

Now Ironwood was curious. It had always been "if" and "maybe" before with his young researcher. "I thought these clusters were hard to find. What's changed?"

"Well, one cluster could have been a statistical fluke. Two, same thing. Now that we're up to four, I'm guessing there's a pattern."

As they walked together to the foyer and the suite's private elevator, Ironwood felt the glow of satisfaction. "Well, now, if there's a pattern, Dave—and I guarantee you'll find there is—there's only one reason for it. Aliens."

David held up his hand as if signaling a stop, then split his fingers between ring and middle. "Then all I can say is, Live long and prosper."

Ironwood chuckled, then put out a hand to restrain Merrit before he could leave. "You'll stay and we'll talk."

Merrit's eyes were locked on the young researcher.

"You two have plans?" Ironwood asked.

"No," Merrit answered.

"Good. Dave, don't go back to work just yet. Relax. Go see the show downstairs. Call Ellie and she'll get you a ticket. Got a suit with you?"

"No, sir."

"Go down to Berlatti's. Tell Tony I said to fix you up."

Ironwood watched the elevator doors close on David before he turned to Merrit.

"Anything I should know about you and Dave?"

"I had to finesse the robbery at his off-site lab, but I kept the company in the clear."

"It *was* just a robbery, right?"

Merrit answered without hesitation. "No question. The police reports I saw, they seem to think it's a gang that specializes in high-end lab equipment. Steal it here, resell in Europe. No interest in computers."

There was something Merrit wasn't telling him, Ironwood was certain, but experience had taught him that, if pressed, the security chief would just give his standard reply: The less his employer knew about certain events that might edge the law, the better. Plausible deniability by any other name.

Ironwood headed back to the sofa. "Here, I want to show you something."

He rifled through the newspapers scattered around the sofa and found Sunday's *Boston Globe*. It was already folded open to the obituaries. He tapped one entry.

"You know anything about this?"

Merrit dutifully scanned the obituary indicated.

Ironwood had already read it several times. Florian MacClary. Philanthropist. Adventurer. Noted archaeologist. Coronary in Tahiti. The small photo the paper ran was from twenty years ago. She'd been a knockout.

"She was on your tail, wasn't she?"

Merrit shook his head. "I knew their foundation was down there. I didn't know she was with them." He handed the paper back.

Ironwood wasn't through with him. "You see the date she died? They were only a few *days* behind you, at most. Took them a year to figure out where we found the outpost in India and get the government to turn it over to their dig team. Nearly two months before they got up to the one in the Andes. But this time, the MacCleirighs almost got to this one before you did. How's that possible?"

Merrit studied him as if coming to some decision. "I didn't want to tell you until I was sure. I believe they have someone on the inside."

"You saying one of *our* people has sold out to *them*?"

A slight smile twisted Merrit's face.

"Not one of ours. Yours. David Weir."

TWENTY-FOUR

David wanted to run but couldn't yet, and walking slowly, the South Tower corridor seemed endless. As soon as the door to his high-roller suite closed behind him and he was out of range of cameras, he raced to the cabinet in the dining alcove where he'd set up a transmitter—just another odd electronic component among many, nothing anyone would notice.

Two days after meeting Agent Lyle, he'd installed on his computer a tracking program, originally designed to monitor warehouse inventory. Just before leaving the suite with Merrit, he'd switched on the program's transmitter. Since then, it had sent out a query radio signal every five seconds, each query answered in turn by a self-powered RFID, a radio-frequency-identification tag. Half the size of a credit card, the tag was hidden inside the hard drive he'd delivered to Ironwood, and Ironwood had passed on to J.R. The same hard drive given him by Jack Lyle.

The air force already knew Ironwood was buying geographical data from David, to find his outposts, and now they wanted to know where the data were being processed. That's what the tagged hard drive was supposed to tell them.

It was all that Lyle had said, but it was enough. As soon as he'd been set up in Ironwood's resort hotel, David had taken apart the air force hard drive without breaking the tamper seal he knew would be there.

Examining the RFID tag inside the drive had been easier—it was an off-the-shelf model modified with a longer-lasting battery. That accounted for its relatively large size. Standard RFID tags, like the ones hidden in casino high-denomination chips, were considerably smaller. Some were barely visible to the human eye. That size of tag, however, was only possible if batteries and transmitters weren't required—in effect, reducing the tags to little more than passive reflectors of whatever radio frequencies were beamed at them.

Fortunately, the outsized air force model in Jack Lyle's hard drive was active—capable of transmitting a signal under its own power—and that made it modifiable. Now it was transmitting on frequencies different from the ones the air force would be monitoring, presumably from a vehicle they'd parked near Ironwood's casino.

Despite altering the air force's tag, David had complied with what Agent Lyle wanted and had delivered the tagged hard drive into Ironwood's hands. Not doing so would mean the government would bring charges of economic espionage against him. What he *didn't* intend to do was share what he learned immediately. Not till he discovered what Ironwood learned from his fourth data cluster, because *that* was what Jess MacClary wanted to know. In exchange, she'd promised to tell him how *she* knew there were twelve clusters—and that information might save his life.

Ironwood, Lyle, Jess, and me, David thought. All interested in the same thing: something buried in his data. But only he knew the first nonhuman DNA sequences he'd discovered were his own. That meant that until he knew who he was, or what he was, and how to escape the death sentence encoded in his genes, all three of his employers were going to have to wait.

In the dining alcove of his high-roller suite, David sat hunched forward over his computer, fingers flying across the keyboard to bring up the RFID tracking log on the monitor. The twelve queries and responses each minute for the past hour were recorded in columns of numbers. Though he could have mapped the tag's position visually, he'd decided not to have anything on-screen that anyone else might recognize. Besides, from Encounters tourist casino maps and the emergency-exit plans posted on every floor of the North and South hotel towers, he'd already built up a mental picture of the complete resort.

Guided by the coordinate numbers of each query and response, David began placing corresponding dots on his mind's-eye layout, tracing J.R's route after exiting the Roswell Suite, descending in the private elevator to the casino's main floor, across the gaming area and . . . where?

He visualized the casino's marketplace—a long sweeping thoroughfare, like that in an indoor shopping mall, where the lucky few regularly surrendered casino winnings for overpriced luxury goods. J.R. had walked partway along that sweep, taken a turn, headed in a straight line, and then—

For just over a minute, the signals didn't change location.

Waiting for another elevator?

Then two more signals—the beginning of another straight-line movement.

The signals cut out.

The conclusion was obvious.

J.R. was in a shielded area, screened to prevent the detection of electromagnetic radiation from whatever was inside. It was a standard security measure for sensitive computer installations, which meant—

Success. The air force's tagged hard drive had done exactly what Agent Lyle had wanted it to do: It was in Ironwood's secret data-processing center, where Ironwood was somehow extracting specific locations from the general regions David's genetic clusters indicated.

He visualized again the resort's layout, J.R.'s path, and—

He pushed back from the computer. He'd seen exactly where to go next.

The casino's test facility. What the staff called the Red Room.

Merrit was annoyed but not surprised to see Ironwood's son already in Encounter's surveillance center. When it came to security issues involving Ironwood's personal projects, only he and J.R. were cleared to handle them.

Dominating the room was a state-of-the-art video-switching console where five operators busily monitored a bank of twenty surveillance screens. Presented on those screens was a constantly changing montage of views from the hundreds of cameras that watched the casino's lobbies, corridors, and gaming activities. The position of most cameras directed at the public areas was fixed, but in the gaming areas, false ceilings hid a network of "eye-in-the-sky" cameras, any of which could be moved to cover any table, any slot machine, anytime.

Merrit pulled J.R. aside, out of earshot of the operators, to deliver the story he'd worked up when he'd returned to Weir's high-roller suite and found him gone.

"Your father wants us to watch Weir. If he tries to leave the hotel, we bring him back. If he makes a phone call, we listen in. If he passes anything to anyone, we go get it. He left his suite about eight minutes ago. We're here because we lost him on the main floor and we're waiting for the system to pick him up again."

J.R. shrugged. "Okay by me."

Merrit returned to the video console. As a standard procedure, the surveillance center automatically scanned every camera's signal using Viisage facial-recognition software. The goal was to identify known casino cheats and VIPs, as well as to keep a record of returning customers. Now, on Merrit's order, the Viisage operators bypassed the automatic-scan function and directed the software to look only at video from the main floor— every frame.

Five minutes earlier, the system had tracked Weir from his suite to the gaming floor, then lost him as he entered the crowded retail area.

Five minutes more and J.R. became restless with the lack of progress. "He's probably quit the building already."

Accepting the idea, not its author, Merrit instructed the operators to pull video of the past ten minutes for all casino entrances—even those backstage away from publicly accessible areas—starting with the main entrance lobby, where taxis and limousines queued and hotel guests arrived.

The Viisage software obediently began locking onto every face that appeared, overlaying each with lines and dots to isolate distinct features, matching each resulting mathematical profile with that derived from the photos of Weir taken for his resort keycard.

No match.

Still, Merrit was patient. No one could beat casino odds forever. Not even David Weir.

TWENTY-FIVE

Today the Red Room leader's T-shirt read, WHAT PART OF $\Delta x \Delta p \geq \frac{1}{2}h$ DON'T YOU UNDERSTAND? Ironwood didn't understand any of it, but appreciated the humor of its message even more as a result.

As Keisha Harrill typed in the location he'd given her, Ironwood watched letters begin appearing in the search window on the Red Room's nine-foot screen. Not that any other members of her team were paying close attention. Frank, the flannel-shirted mathematician, was arranging M&M's in patterns on the lunch table. Two of the other six technicians stared into workstation screens dense with indecipherable symbols, while the other four were deep into some computer game involving armored soldiers blasting away at unarmored aliens.

"That it?" Keisha asked, finishing. "Tintagel?"

"Ground zero," Ironwood confirmed.

"Okay," Keisha said, "the new cluster's probable range covers more than a thousand square miles. Any particular reason we start at this specific spot?"

"Historic resonance. It's the birthplace of King Arthur. So the legends say." He added the last sentence so she wouldn't have to.

Keisha smiled. "Bringing up the satellite."

On the main screen, a section of the Cornish coast materialized. From a virtual altitude of about a mile, the aerial image looked to Ironwood like a jigsaw puzzle piece with two small promontories separated by a gouged-out shoreline.

"Rough and rocky, boss. Any specific place we should begin?"

"The castle ruins."

"And they are where, exactly?"

"Eastern edge of the westernmost peninsula, smack-dab where it joins the shore."

"Smack-dab it is." Keisha manipulated her remote control.

The aerial image expanded, centering on the area Ironwood had just described, and he found himself looking at blocky white patches—stone walls, their outline defined by shadows against a rectangular base, also white, that stood out against dry brown ground. The stored satellite image was softened by its extreme magnification, as if the viewpoint were from only a few hundred feet above target.

Keisha shot him a questioning glance. "Compared to some of the other sites we've checked, that doesn't look old enough."

"It's not. The earl of Cornwall built it in 1233. But don't forget what they all did back then. One big dog after another, marking each other's territory."

"There's something underneath?"

"Veritable layer cake of goodies. Seems the earl knew all about the legends of Arthur having come from there, so he had his castle built in an old-fashioned style, even for then. Before that, it was a Celtic fortress or maybe a monastery . . . something with religious significance. Before that, it was Roman."

Keisha had already created a crosshairs overlay on the castle ruins and was expanding the image again when she stopped. "We talking about searching in the same time frame as the other sites? Nine thousand years, more or less?"

"I would think so. Why?"

"Sea level was a lot lower."

Ironwood knew that. "End of the last ice age."

"Remember Polynesia? That atoll was underwater."

"Because of a volcanic eruption."

"Well, that probably contributed to the change in elevation, but nine thousand years ago, sea level was maybe sixty, seventy feet lower than it is today."

"You think we should start this search underwater?"

Keisha turned back to the screen and tapped the remote against her open hand. "Thinking about the one in India . . . the pathways leading up to it . . . the way it was positioned to look over the river that used to be there . . . If we're talking about the same philosophy of building, and we're thinking there's an outpost in this area, I wouldn't look for it *under* the castle."

"Where, then?"

Ironwood watched the large screen as she used the remote again and the aerial image shrank, then shifted until the crosshairs fell over a striking rectangular gouge in the coastline, almost exactly between the two peninsulas.

"Take a look at the color of the water."

Ironwood saw what she meant. In the span between the promontories, a distance of about a mile, the sea was a pale milky blue. Just off the tips of both, it changed almost instantly to the dark green cast of deep ocean.

"You think the outpost's somewhere between the two promontories?"

"That's where I would've built docks and warehouses," Keisha said. "But . . . if I was going to build an outpost like the one in India, *this* is where I'd carve in the paths leading from the docks to the site."

The crosshairs shifted again, moved over the rectangular gouge.

Ironwood stared at the small smudge that was the ruins of the castle, built over the ruins of the fortress where King Arthur might have been born. It would be so satisfying to find an alien outpost under those ruins— but there was a reason he paid Keisha as much as he did.

"You know what you're doing. You make the call."

Keisha waved the remote through the air, and a circle appeared on the display, with the odd gouge dead center.

"Okay, ladies," she called out to the others, who, with the exception of Frank, were now watching the big screen. "Start your engines. We're doing a targeted outpost search. Those cliffs. One hundred meters back from the edges, starting inland, radiating out. Let's build the grid. Frankie— you, too."

At the lunch table, Frank scooped up his M&M's, stuffed some into a shirt pocket, and the rest into his mouth before shuffling over to his own station.

"Gonna stick around, boss?" Keisha asked.

Ironwood was tempted. "How long to search the cliffs?"

Keisha hit some keys, watched some numbers change at the bottom of the screen. "They're about ninety feet above current sea level, so if we start there . . . say ten search grids? Nineteen with overlaps. Half-meter slices moving up. Two minutes a grid . . ." She did the math. "If there's nothing there, we'll know in about twenty hours."

"And if there's something?"

"Hey, if it's in the *first* grid, we'll know in two minutes."

"Give me a call. I'm just upstairs."

Keisha held up the remote. "At least get the party started."

Ironwood smiled and took the control.

"The big blue button at the top," Keisha said. She turned to her team. "Switching to SARGE."

Ironwood pressed the button, and all the colors on the display changed to the arbitrary false shades that made it easier to distinguish different materials.

"Aaannd . . . they're off!" Keisha said, as the screen began flickering with the rapid appearance and disappearance of the wireframe diagram of an outpost.

Ironwood handed back the remote and left them to their fun.

Fifteen feet above them, David Weir remained, uninvited, and saw everything as it happened.

━━ ━━━━ ━━

Merrit's eyes stayed on the casino's security screens as his hands moved over the security console's switches, sliders, and keyboard to follow the advance and retreat of video frames illustrating David Weir's journey through the retail arcade more than an hour ago.

Seeing Weir go into a souvenir store, he called up surveillance footage from inside it, then watched as Weir purchased a sweatshirt and two baseball caps, received a large shopping bag, and then stuffed his knapsack and jacket into it.

Merrit went back to the arcade camera records. This time he followed Weir in the midst of shopping tourists as he moved through the mall, his face blocked by a ball cap. For every store window Weir stopped to check out, Merrit zoomed in to examine the items on display, but found no pattern other than crude misdirection. Whatever Weir was up to, the kid knew he would be tracked, and had done all he could to delay his inevitable detection.

Finally, Weir reached the end of the arcade and slipped into a men's room. There was no coverage inside. Was he switching to a new disguise?

After fast-forwarding five minutes, it became obvious Weir wasn't coming out.

"What's he doing in there?" J.R. said.

Merrit suddenly had it. "Stay here. Keep watching that door." Weir was no longer in the men's room because there was another way out—a locked door marked MAINTENANCE, which led to the hotel's service corridors, below and above its public areas.

"Where're you going?"

Merrit was already on his way out. He didn't know how Weir had figured it out, but he did know where he was going.

The last place on Earth he'd ever see.

━━ ━━━━ ━━

The dimensions of Heaven matched those of the room beneath it.

The difference, David noted, was that up here, the only solid floor space was the metal-railed balcony ringing the outer walls and linking to an open network of crisscrossing metal catwalks. Below the balcony and catwalks, a grid of thick wires was suspended above undulating, clear plastic panels, whose undersides formed the ceiling of the room below. The grid of wires supported sixteen cameras, each pointing straight down at the plastic panels.

Though clear from above, the plastic panels were mirrored when viewed from below so the network of overhead cameras would not be detected as their focus shifted from table to table, dealer to dealer, player to player— their God's-eye view searching for any sign of cheating. In casino lore, that was why a room like this was "Heaven."

This particular Heaven had been easy to enter. From the maintenance area of the men's room, David had taken a backstage staircase to the hidden level set between the casino's main floor and the first convention floor. From there, a second set of blank-walled corridors had led him here. Protected only by a card reader, the door had snicked open the moment he'd held his reprogrammed keycard to it.

He edged farther along the balcony to reach the control station for the centralized surveillance system: a four-monitor console with rocker switches, a dial for cameras, and a single joystick. No indicator lights, though. The cameras trained on the room below were not switched on.

David ran a finger over the controls. One rocker switch was labeled TEST. *Perfect.* A manual option. He switched it on.

Then he turned a camera dial to select a camera. Number 14. Using the joystick, and watching on one of the console's four monitors, he moved it until—

He saw the air force hard drive on one of the computer workstations in the room below.

Then he saw Ironwood and a woman with beaded dreadlocks tracking flickering images on a wall-sized computer screen. Satellite imagery of a coastal area. Unfamiliar to him.

Without audio, David could only observe, not listen, as the huge display abruptly changed color, then changed again.

A moment later, Ironwood left, but David stayed, watching what he knew had to be a search program flashing into action, comparing the imagery on-screen to a three-dimensional shape unknown to him.

The speed with which the algorithm worked was stunning. The image changed every two minutes, presumably the amount of time it took the algorithm to finish with one search grid and move on to the next.

Using the joystick, David moved camera 14 to focus on each of the room's other workstations, and discovered that their smaller screens—each with its own intent attendant—held portions of what was on the larger screen.

Minutes stretched to an hour, and he took the opportunity to further study details of the Red Room. A thick bundle of cabling ran from the workstations to what seemed to be a retrofitted internal wall that sectioned off half of the available floor space. Whatever was behind that wall was beyond the reach of any camera.

Two hours into the search, David was back on camera 14 and saw signs that, of the eight technicians in the room below, seven were packing up their cases, getting ready to leave. One man, in torn jeans and a plaid shirt, continued working.

Half an hour later, the last man was still there, slouched now in a chair at a conference table, one knee bouncing up and down, endlessly arranging M&M's, green only, in complex fractal patterns.

David directed camera 7 to observe the lace of candy grow, so he was watching as, moments later, the man jerked back in his chair, sending M&M's skittering across the table to the floor. At the same time, through the ceiling, David caught a faint electronic beep.

David dialed up camera 14 and angled the joystick to get an oblique, downward view of the quicksilver, flashing 3-D wireframe model now fixed in one position on the large screen, slowly blinking on and off.

The man below agitatedly dug through all his pockets, stopping only when he discovered his phone in his flannel shirt. He punched in a number, and waited . . . waited.

David knew what was wrong. The phone wouldn't work inside a room that blocked electromagnetic transmissions.

It took another few seconds before the man apparently recalled the same and bolted for the room's one exit, presumably to make his call outside.

Whatever the algorithm had been set to find, it had found.

David saw his chance and took it.

TWENTY-SIX

The instant the door below closed, David had his knapsack on and was sprinting onto one of the metal catwalks, where he reached down and lifted up a ceiling panel. Easing over the railing, he lowered himself until he was hanging through the opening.

Six feet below his sneakers was the candy-littered table.

David dropped, rolled to one side as he landed, and fell off the table edge, colliding with three wheeled office chairs before he struck the floor, unhurt. At once, he scrambled to his feet and ran to the workstation connected to the air force hard drive.

The big screen was still awash in information.

Centered against a background of random color splotches, the wireframe pattern continued blinking on and off in one place. A strip of coded numbers ran along the screen's bottom edge. David didn't recognize the program, which meant he had no time to explore how to save a file.

He did, however, recognize elements of the screen's layout, enough to recognize the local network operating system. He hit the CTRL + ALT + PRINT-SCREEN keys.

A window promptly opened on the workstation display, asking him where he wished to send the print request. He was offered a choice of several printers, plus five auxiliary drives where the image file could be saved for later printing.

David selected Jack Lyle's drive, and a smaller window popped up showing the progress of the write request. It was startling how slow that progress was: three minutes to write the data on the big screen to his drive. The nine-foot display wasn't simply showing an image file. It apparently contained a massive amount of other data.

He tapped his fingers against the side of the workstation, considering his next move. This combination of software and hardware had found its target within a few hours. Even if he erased the results, they'd be easily reacquired. He'd need to do something more to be sure Jess MacClary had information that Ironwood didn't—and couldn't—get.

He decided to erase the search database itself. He overrode the sysop function, typed in his command, hit ENTER.

It was simpler than he'd hoped. No security measures had been considered necessary and none had been taken to protect the isolated workstations, likely because they had no physical connection to any other computer network, or to the Internet, and were contained in a room impervious to radio transmissions.

On-screen a progress window opened: The system would need four hours to erase the entire database.

David knew it was unlikely the process would be allowed to continue to completion, but even an hour would help. Until they restored their database, Ironwood's team wouldn't be able to reproduce their results.

He left the big screen and ran back to Jack Lyle's hard drive, checked its progress. Thirty seconds left.

Then he heard the thud of footsteps, and a door slammed open.

In Heaven.

Merrit stood in the open doorway to the security facility above the Red Room. He moved his gun in a two-handed sweep from left to right, scanning for movement as his eyes adjusted to the unnatural underlighting. There was no one in the observation room.

Then he saw the camera console. It was powered up. Images on all four screens.

He stepped onto the metal balcony and looked down at the Red Room for the first time, seeing only a bank of gaming consoles, computer stations, and equipment. No personnel. No Weir.

The next thing that registered was the missing ceiling panel.

Weir *had* been here—and because the only way out was past three former marines with shoot-to-kill orders, he was still there.

Merrit ran onto the catwalk and dropped over its railing through the missing panel to the table. He was on his feet in a heartbeat, gun in hand.

The catwalk above clanked.

"You're not supposed to be in there!" J.R. called down. Then a pained grunt announced his clumsy drop beside Merrit.

"Weir's trapped in here!" Merrit swept the room with his weapon, seeking anything large enough to hide a man.

The room was clear.

Merrit pointed to the cylindrical door. "Where does that go?"

"The computer room. Even I can't go in there."

Merrit was already spinning the revolving door to open it. He entered the cylinder, rotating it until—

It was like stepping into a meat locker. In the dim light, he could see his breath. He could also see, in the enclosure's center, eight metal shelving units, five feet high, eight feet long. Each was stacked with what looked to be stereo components or DVD players, all identical—black fronts dotted with a constellation of small blinking lights. The components were on brackets that kept them a few inches from each other, top and bottom, side to side. Each shelving unit was back to back with another, with hundreds of multicolored ribbon cables woven in between.

Gun held ready, Merrit explored the stacks, alert for anything that would betray a fugitive. He stopped by the wall closest to the crowded shelves. A large ducting tube hung from the ceiling, directly over a stack of wooden crates. The tube, obviously arranged to blast cold air straight down onto the shelves, had once been joined to the wall and a large air-conditioning outlet. Now it dangled free.

Merrit moved on. No matter how haphazard an installation this room was, it was still in a casino, where the interiors of large air ducts were always subdivided into smaller ones so that no one could crawl through them.

But he found no other potential hiding place for Weir.

The cylinder door rotated again, and J.R. poked his head through. "The old man's going to go apeshit if he finds out you were in here."

Merrit knew he wasn't wrong about this. Weir had been in the upper level, and he couldn't have eluded the guards outside the only exit. He *had* to have come in here.

"There's got to be another way out."

"Like that?" J.R. pointed to the dangling wall duct.

Merrit shook his head at J.R.'s ignorance of his own family's business. "Standard casino building rule. It's subdivided."

"Wanna bet? That one got added for all this computer junk. Subdividing, that costs money, right?"

Merrit swore. Ironwood's damned cost cutting. He grabbed one of the crates and stacked it on another under the air-conditioning outlet. "Where does the duct come out?"

"The roof, probably. Above the convention floor between the towers."

"Get up there. Take guards with you. But if you hear gunshots from the duct, tell them to back off, understand?"

As soon as he was alone, Merrit pulled himself onto the top crate, then leapt up to catch the edge of the outlet. He scaled the wall and pushed deep into the ductwork.

Weir would never reach the roof alive.

Still in the chilled computer room, David was in the floor-level inlet of the retrofitted air-return duct, his fingers numb from holding closed the vent screen.

When Merrit entered, he'd just squeezed in. There'd been no time to refasten the screen that concealed him. If Ironwood's security chief had bothered to bend down and peer in, even without a flashlight he'd have seen his prey, and that would've been the end.

Literally. David had seen the gun.

Ironwood's assurance that Merrit was not to interfere with him was no help now. Merrit had gone rogue, and there was no time to wonder why. He'd reach the roof in minutes, and then he'd come back here.

David carefully latched the vent screen before turning around and crawling deeper into the ductwork. A few feet along, he stopped and, with eyes closed, listened intently. He placed the sounds of the casino, one by one, on the mental map he'd formed of the whole resort, with his own position a dot in a three-dimensional wireframe.

Finally he heard noises that could guide him out: the far-off but unmistakable rumble of a truck backing up, the whine of its gears, the beep of its reverse alarm. If he followed that sound profile . . .

Five minutes later, David fell out of the retrofitted duct and into the steaming-hot blanket of moisture-heavy air that enveloped a casino loading dock. In the impersonal cacophony of trucks and carts, his arrival passed unnoticed, and, pulling a cap out of his knapsack, he joined a few off-duty employees exiting and walked out with them.

But when he reached the parking lot, he ran.

TWENTY-SEVEN

Less than sixty seconds after Weir left the casino, Jack Lyle took a call from an agent in one of three surveillance vans on the outskirts of Encounters: Weir was running.

For now, Lyle ordered pursuit only, no interference. While he'd been questioning Weir in Atlantic City police headquarters, a team of AFOSI technicians had installed a new SIM card in Weir's phone. It could still make and receive calls as before, but now its GPS function could not be switched off. For added backup, the team had also replaced the tracking devices in Weir's iPod and digital recorder.

As long as those three units were operational, and the target himself was under visual observation, Lyle was willing to cut him some slack. The kid could be late for a movie, out on some errand. There was still nothing to track in the Ironwood investigation—the RFID tag in the hard drive hadn't been switched on yet.

Thirty minutes later, Lyle's willingness to give Weir the benefit of the doubt evaporated when a second report said the target was now in a cab on the Atlantic City Expressway, heading for the airport.

By the time Roz swung the black Intrepid into the driveway of his Best Western, Lyle's team had pulled the passenger lists for all flight departures in the next few hours. Weir's name wasn't on them. By the time Roz had Lyle halfway to the airport, the team had the reason for omission.

The target was on his way back to the city at the wheel of a metallic gold Cadillac DTS, rented at the airport.

Lyle checked the Intrepid's navigation screen as it tracked the progress of the Cadillac. He had a few new questions. Why go out to the airport to rent a car when the casino could provide one? More to the point, who was paying for it? There'd been no activity on any of Weir's credit cards for weeks.

The Cadillac made an unexpected turn. Well before reaching the city, the car exited the expressway onto the Garden State Parkway. Weir was going out of state.

"Do we think he's an errand boy?" Roz asked. She began changing lanes to take the same off-ramp Weir had. The New Jersey daytime sky had been almost gray with the haze of heat, but now it was turning indigo as sunset neared, bringing a welcome drop in temperature. Traffic was light, and Roz was able to hang back a safe distance.

"Delivering his next batch of data to the SARGE database? Too easy."

"It sort of makes sense."

"Except he didn't switch on the hard-drive tag."

"Maybe he did and it's broken," Roz said. "Or maybe he agreed to anything you said to get the hell out of Dodge."

"I did scare him pretty good."

"Maybe someone scared him better."

*   *   *

"How on earth did this happen?"

Ironwood's voice was tight with indignation.

An error message flashed on every screen in the Red Room, including the big one.

"This room was off-limits to everyone!" The big man stabbed his finger at the open panel in the ceiling. "How is *that* not part of this room?!"

Merrit remained calm. "I had no say in the security arrangements."

"Then who—?" Ironwood's gaze settled on his son. As if restraining himself with difficulty, he turned away to a woman at the closest workstation. She was bent over her keyboard, typing rapidly.

"Keisha . . . how bad?"

The woman leaned back in her chair, hands behind her head. "The program he set up? It erased and overwrote three percent of the database before I could stop it. I figure we lost about six million square miles."

"We still have Cornwall?"

Keisha shook her head. Her beaded dreadlocks swayed. "All of England's only about fifty thousand square miles. We lost that in the first few minutes."

"Frank. You saw the screen, right? Before everything got erased?"

"Un-huh."

"The search was positive?"

"Un-huh."

"So the program found what it was looking for in Cornwall?"

The woman prompted him. "In the first dataset, Frankie."

"Un-huh," Frank said. "It found it and stopped."

Merrit saw her smile of relief as she turned to Ironwood. "The good news is we know it's there. Since it was in the first search grid, we also know where it is to within a mile."

Ironwood didn't look or sound reassured to Merrit. "This isn't some barren stretch of desert or hidden valley. Those castle ruins are a tourist attraction. I can't send in a full-scale dig team."

The woman turned back to her screen, typing while talking. "We know the search started at sea level. That means the outpost ruins aren't more than ninety feet deep. You could send in a couple of geologists to take some echo readings. Map the stratigraphy. I can even do a rough estimate of where the search ended based on when Frank called to report it." She shot a glance over her shoulder at Ironwood. "Give me an hour. I'll narrow the location to a thousand feet or so."

Ironwood looked happier. "Okay . . . okay . . . that sounds doable." He nodded as he worked something out. "I own an oil company over there. Royal Sovereign. I'll get them to send some geologists."

Ironwood turned to Merrit. "I'm going to need a team in Cornwall by next week, and then—" He broke off. "Keisha, how long to restore the full database from the backup?"

"If you'd let us connect over a network, I could do it in less than a day."

Ironwood frowned. "No transmissions. The government can't find it if we keep it off anything they can intercept."

"Okay. How about I make a list of the subsets that were erased. You can give that to whoever it is that knows where the backup is. They can load those subsets onto spare components and bring them back here to swap for the blank ones."

"How long would they take to do that?"

The woman paused, considering. "For copying the subsets and swapping out the components? No more than a day. Add to that whatever time you need for transportation."

"Say two days."

"Then we'll be back in business in three."

Ironwood turned to Merrit again. "It's not as bad as I thought. We should be okay."

"What do we do about Weir?"

"He'll be back. He still needs my money."

"Don't be so sure. Remember what I told you—there's a good chance the MacCleirighs got to him."

"You have any proof of that yet?"

"I'm working on it," Merrit lied, "but, to be safe, I think it's a good bet that whatever data he gave you, he'll give it to them."

"So? Won't do their Foundation a spit's worth of good. We're talking a thousand square miles of England. How're they going to search that? It'd take them years."

"Maybe not." All eyes turned to Keisha. "That hard drive's gone. The one J.R. brought down. It was plugged into my workstation."

"What kind of damage we looking at here?" Ironwood asked.

"Enough," she said. "He could've done a screen capture and copied the final search coordinates to that drive."

Merrit ran with the gift she'd given him. "He can sell that to the Mac-Cleirighs."

Ironwood's face flushed red. "They'll get to the outpost before we do! They don't care about history. The way they steal and hide and lie . . ." He shook his head in disgust. "They're part of the conspiracy to withhold the truth. Probably in bed with the government.

"Merrit, you get yourself to Cornwall ASAP. I want you to follow whoever those people send in, let them lead you to the outpost, and then you do whatever it takes to keep them out until we have everything we need from it. Understood?"

Whatever it takes.

Merrit finally had the orders he'd been waiting for.

TWENTY-EIGHT

David had been driving for five hours, hadn't slept for almost twenty-four. He felt rumpled, sticky, and ravenous. Even so, as instructed, he had reached Faneuil Hall in Boston at 10:00 A.M.

A week ago, mixed in with his other equipment deliveries arriving at the casino, he'd received a prepaid phone he hadn't ordered. He'd called the number on a note included with the phone, and Jess MacClary had answered. She told him to call again the moment he isolated the fourth cluster, and she'd tell him how to get the information to her. She wanted her specialists to start working with it the same time as Ironwood.

David had called her yesterday, only minutes before Merrit's surprise visit to the high-roller suite. She'd told him where to pick up a rental car and where to meet with her. They hadn't spoken since, so Jess didn't know what he was bringing her: not a general region, but the precise location of another temple.

He'd more than delivered on his promise to her. Now it was her turn.

He pulled the Caddy into the lot close by the hall, grabbed his knapsack, and got out. The morning air was surprisingly crisp after the heat of Atlantic City. The sky here was brilliant blue. He saw the first tinge of gold and red in the leaves of the city trees that edged the parking lot.

Why she'd told him to meet her here, he didn't know. Faneuil Hall, which she'd pronounced to sound like Daniel with an *F*, was a weathered redbrick building. Four stories tall, with rows of arched and multipaned windows, the structure was crowned by a white wooden bell tower. It was also, oddly, faced with redbrick versions of Greek pillars.

Now that he was here, the request that he go to the building's east side made more sense, because that side faced a market area, its walkways already crowded with shoppers. It was busy and therefore safe.

Hands in his pockets, knapsack over his shoulder, David walked along a pedestrian-only street toward the hall, past vendors' carts cluttered with impulse items for tourists, from leather cell phone cases and healing crystals to small framed photographs of local attractions.

The rising and falling murmur of carefree voices was a welcome distraction after the monotonous soundscape of the long drive from Atlantic City. Until a gun pressed into his ribs and a calm voice said, "You run, you die."

▬▬ ▬▬▬▬ ▬▬

Another name for Faneuil Hall was the Cradle of Liberty. The original structure on its site had been built in 1742. Samuel Adams and other firebrands of the era had given speeches here, urging the American colonies to declare their independence. None of which had anything to do with the MacCleirighs.

The original hall burned down in 1761 and was rebuilt in 1762. Fourteen years later, in 1776, the American colonies succeeded in winning their independence. Yet, it wasn't until 1806, when it was clear the winner of that war would survive and a new current of history could be charted, that the MacCleirighs put their stamp upon Faneuil Hall through the efforts of Charles Bulfinch, Line McRory.

Bulfinch was not a defender, but one of the 144 possessing knowledge of the twelve lines of descent. He was also one of the first native-born citizens of the new country to become a professional architect. Echoing the deep MacCleirigh history that only he and a handful of others in the Family knew, he'd added to his 1806 redesign and reconstruction of the hall a decorative redbrick façade suggestive of Greek pillars—Doric on the first and second floors, Ionic on the third.

Eight years later, the Family's invisible hand moved from Boston to the heart of the new country as Bulfinch was appointed Architect of the Capitol by President James Monroe and placed in charge of rebuilding the structures burned by British forces. Benefiting from a Family education, Bulfinch helped usher in the Federal style of architecture, inspired by the Greek Revival movement that found expression in the signature, temple-like designs of the capital's government buildings, as well as in Boston's Cathedral Church of St. Paul.

Jess had chosen Faneuil Hall not because it was a monument to commerce but because she knew it well. The east façade's main entrance with its impressive three-story, domed ceiling and encircling balustrade for shoppers was too open for her assignation, but in the building's opposite end was a large auditorium, complete with a white-column-flanked raised stage. Behind that stage was a small anteroom, out of the way and seldom used when there was nothing scheduled for the stage. Perfect for a private meeting.

The narrow anteroom was windowed on one side with a single row of vintage, bubbled panes that looked out onto Quincy Market. Beneath the windows was a row of straight-backed chairs. Dusty white file boxes, sealed with tape, were stacked against one wall. Beside them, an empty wheeled coat rack listed. Overall, the space had the feel of an unused store-room, not much of anything.

David arrived in the strong grip of Jess's new bodyguard, Nils Behren, a hulking figure with long blond hair who towered over him. Nils also carried something silver, the size and shape of a small book.

"David," Jess said. "I—"

Nils waved the metal case, interrupting. "We might have to move locations. His phone was rigged to transmit its location, and he had two transponders in his bag. One in a music player, another in an audio recorder."

"Did you know about this?" Jess asked David.

David shook his head. Strands of black hair fell across his face. His eyes were deeply shadowed as if he hadn't slept. Despite the cool fall air, he wore only a thin black T-shirt and jeans.

Jess looked to Nils. "Where're the transponders now?"

"Simon's taken them on the subway. He's wearing Weir's jacket and cap."

She had another question for David. "Is Ironwood tracking you?"

"Maybe, but it could also be the air force . . . the Office of Special Investigations. Espionage cases."

Jess didn't understand, but didn't let it show. Not with Nils as a witness.

"Let him go, Nils." She gestured for David to take one of the chairs. She sat close to him and had Nils move across the room for privacy.

She lowered her voice. "You'd better tell me everything."

David did. Leaving her with even more questions.

"That's how Ironwood's finding the temples? He's using something he took from the air force to analyze your genetic data?"

"From what I saw, I think he's tying into air force spy satellites. However he's doing it, it requires a huge computer installation. The air force agent—"

"Jack Lyle?"

"Yeah. Lyle. He wants Ironwood more than he wants me. That's why he tagged the hard drive—the one your guy took from me. Lyle wanted to see where Ironwood took it, but I changed the tag's operating frequency so I could track it and the air force couldn't."

"Where did Ironwood take it?"

"A secure room in his casino."

"And the air force still doesn't know?"

"They will."

"When?"

"When I tell them."

"Why would you do that?"

David hesitated, as if he had been about to say one thing and decided on another. "So I won't get locked up for fifty years."

"You can't," she said. He didn't, couldn't, know the stakes.

Something flickered in his dark eyes, but David's next words made Jess forget all else. "Look, that hard drive your guy's holding? It's got an image file on it. It's from my latest cluster—it shows the location of another site. Another of your temples."

A fourth one! I have to tell Willem . . . Jess struggled to conceal her elation.

"This time, *you* can get there first," David said. "Before I left, I started an erase program in Ironwood's system—he can't rerun his search for a couple of days at least. So if you just tell me how you know there're twelve clusters out there, we're done. And I can go see Agent Lyle."

Jess shook her head at his naïveté. "How do you know Lyle won't raid Ironwood's casino, confiscate the computer, and find out what he was using it for? That would mean the air force would find out about our temples."

"Why would that matter? You think the government is interested in—" David stopped. "Does this have anything to do with aliens?"

"That's Ironwood's fairy tale. Not ours."

"Ours? Who are you working for?"

Jess was skirting the very limits of what was permissible to share with outsiders. Nils was here to protect her, but he was also here for the Family.

"I'm . . . part of a nonprofit group doing scholarly research. Ironwood's been looting important sites we believe should be preserved. If the air force goes public . . ."

"What's the harm in that?"

"Considerable."

"From archaeological ruins? How important are they?"

"If you want to know why I believe there're twelve genetic clusters"—there, she'd successfully distracted him—"then you can't tell the air force about Ironwood's computer system."

"Then they'll lock me up and . . ." David hesitated, looked at Nils, who stared back at him. "Great incentive."

Jess took another risk. "Maybe there's another way. What if I can make it so the air force still gets Ironwood but drops its charges against you?"

"I'm listening."

177

"If we can't clear you, we could set you up in almost any research position you're qualified to hold. In any country you like. Under your own
name, or a new one, if it comes to that."

"Who did you say you were working for?"

"My research group?" Jess asked innocently. "We don't exactly have
a—"

"No. I mean, which country?"

"No country. We're a . . . family business."

"Family. This interest you have in the geographic clusters I've been
finding . . . any specific connections between those temples and your
'family'?"

Instinctively, Jess looked to Nils, far enough away that he couldn't hear
this forbidden conversation. She turned back to David. "Yes, we believe
so."

"Tell me about the number twelve."

Jess's phone vibrated. She read the display and walked away from David, careful to keep her back to both him and Nils.

"Willem, where are you?"

"The temple at Havi Atoll is gone."

Jess had never heard Willem sound afraid before. "Gone? How?"

"Demolition charges."

"Ironwood?" Jess felt the rush of a terrible, overwhelming anger.

*"No. The team . . . I don't know how it's come to this—they were sent by Su-
Lin and Andrew."*

Jess's voice rose in shock. "What?"

"They don't want anyone to find the temples. Not even us."

She didn't want to believe it. Couldn't believe it. "But why—"

*"They . . . know I'm . . . in the country, Jessie . . . they . . . they know . . .
we spoke . . ."*

Jess's fingers tightened on her phone. His words were coming now in
ragged gasps. He was running.

"End the call." It was Nils.

Jess turned to face him and a Glock, a stubby silencer attached to its
barrel.

"End the call."

"Willem, I—" Jess heard a sharp noise, a groan, then silence. She looked
at her phone's display: CALL FAILED.

She was truly on her own now. She addressed Nils with her full authority. "I am Defender of the Line MacClary. Put down your weapon."

"I have orders to take you back to Zurich." Nils raised his Glock to
sight between her eyes. "Preferably alive. Defender."

"If you don't put the gun down now, they'll come in shooting," David said.

Jess's bodyguard didn't change his stance. "Who?"

"The air force. There's another transponder in my sneaker. It's been transmitting audio."

Nils swung his gun around to aim at David. He snapped his fingers. "Give me the shoe."

"Sure thing." David pulled off his shoe and tossed it.

And in the same instant Nils reached out to catch it—

—Jess's knife found his neck. Nils roared as he spun, gun firing with a silenced puff and the sound of breaking glass. Shards exploded from a shattered window.

Jess was already on the ground and rolling. Safe from his second shot as well.

Nils swatted at his neck, his fingers seeking the silver blade she'd thrown. She'd missed the carotid artery, but blood spurted from a gaping gash. His head twitched to one side, as if she'd compromised deep tendons.

He yanked the knife out with a triumphant cry, only to be struck a moment later by David smashing into him.

Both men fell to the wooden floorboards. Nils struggled to train his gun on David.

Then Jess's boot struck Nils's temple with all the force and precision Emil had taught, and the result was instantaneous.

The Glock flew from Nils's hand as his arms flung wildly outward and his head lolled back and hit the floor. His neck tightened grotesquely, bending toward its uninjured side. A pool of blood spread beneath his cheek as froth escaped his mouth. He coughed. Gurgled. Tongue protruding. Then he fell silent, stilled.

Jess picked up her knife from beside the body, used Nils's Windbreaker to wipe it clean, and slipped it back within her Tuareg cross.

"Was that the truth?" she asked quietly as she retrieved the Glock. "About your sneaker?"

David had retrieved his sneaker and the hard drive. Still breathing heavily, he stood over Nils. "No. Just wanted to make him put down the gun." His gaze shifted to her cross. "Defender of the Line MacClary?"

"According to the rules my family plays by, because you heard that, I should kill you, too."

She didn't bother adding that she hadn't meant to kill her bodyguard. Or that everything she believed, everyone she'd trusted, all of it was threatened somehow because of him.

Not even Willem could help her now. *What were Su-Lin and Andrew doing? What if Florian* . . . Jess stood, transfixed, as terrible thoughts of lies and betrayal swept her mind.

"You still want to find those temples?" David held out the drive to her. His voice was steady, unafraid.

Jess took a deep breath, committing to the mission of her life. For Florian and Willem. For the Family.

"We have to go," she said.

"Where?"

Jess held up the hard drive. "Let's find out."

TWENTY-NINE

Jack Lyle, impatient, pretended to study a rack of hand-tooled leather belts. His real focus was the main entrance to Quincy Market's Faneuil Hall. He'd stationed four uniformed Boston police officers at the other entrances. Plainclothes detectives were on their way, but until they arrived he couldn't take the search for Weir inside.

Then his phone buzzed in his jacket pocket, and even those plans changed.

"You ready for this?" Roz asked. She was on the street behind the hall with two more police officers and the man who'd mistakenly believed that wearing Weir's jacket and cap, and carrying his knapsack, would be enough to throw the AFOSI off track.

After parking on Congress Street, on the far side of the hall, Lyle and Roz had followed Weir and witnessed the clothing transfer taking place, just before a second man with long blond hair pushed Weir into the hall, apparently at gunpoint.

"Make it fast," Lyle said.

"The locals ran the decoy's ID. His name's Simon Moretti."

"And?"

"Cross Executive Protection Services, Zurich."

Lyle saw the connection at once. "Same as Weir's 'friend' at the warehouse."

"Bingo."

"Is he talking?"

"Only to say he's not doing anything illegal. Wants us to arrest him or let him go."

"Is he armed?"

"Glock. Extra clips. Licensed. The knife's questionable."

"Cell phone?"

"Yes, but we can't touch it unless we arrest him. And can I say again I don't know anyone except you who doesn't carry a phone twenty-four seven?"

"The knapsack had the iPod and recorder, right?"

"That's affirm."

"Then charge him with illegal possession of government property and

181

interfering in a federal investigation. Then do that thing you do to his phone."

"Hack it?"

"That's it."

"Something else not so good to report . . ."

"Don't make me beg."

"We found the hard-drive cable in the knapsack. Moretti's not talking, but I'm thinking Blondie lifted the hard drive first."

"Can you turn on the RFID tag?"

"I just tried. Either it's not within a mile of here, or our boy-genius changed its operating frequencies."

"Wasn't it supposed to send an alarm if Weir tampered with it?"

"I'm guessing he's better than we thought."

"Well, change the frequencies back."

"Easier to try to find the new ones he switched to. You think Weir could be Ironwood's middleman for selling SARGE?"

"Why use the hard drive we gave him?"

"Overconfidence—maybe he thought we wouldn't notice?"

"Or he's gone into business for himself."

"Time to bring Weir in?"

"When the detectives get here," Lyle said. Using the kid as a way into Ironwood's organization had been a promising option, but it hadn't worked. They'd need a new strategy for taking down the billionaire.

"They're pulling up now."

"Good. Put me through to whoever's in charge and—" Lyle broke off. He'd just heard a sound, two sounds: breaking glass and a ricochet. No gunshot. Except . . .

Knots of startled shoppers were pointing to the north side of Faneuil Hall. To what, specifically, Lyle couldn't see—but a uniformed cop could. He was heading in that direction, fast.

"Roz, cover the doors now! Shots fired!"

Lyle broke into an awkward loping run. His right knee felt unreliable.

Then two figures burst out of the hall. A slim red-haired woman in a tan jacket, and—

Lyle hobbled forward, knee forgotten, shouting, "David Weir!"

The two figures increased their speed, pushing past innocent civilians.

Lyle swore, reached into his jacket for his ID, took his eyes off the fugitives for an instant to find another cop. When he looked up, the two fugitives had stopped. They faced him from across the street.

The red-haired woman had a gun. Weir was beside her.

"Get down! Get down!" she shouted.

Lyle raised his hands in the air and limped forward slowly. There was no way she and Weir could get away.

"Put your weapon down!" he shouted back. "You're sur—"

She fired!

Lyle tensed, furious with himself for misjudging the situation so badly. *But . . .*

Three more rounds.

She missed? Lyle thought. Then he realized he heard screaming, whirled around to see—

Shoppers scattering from a body. A gun fallen from an outstretched hand. Lyle registered the black Windbreaker and in that moment realized he'd not been her target. She'd tried to protect him, not shoot him.

Lyle lowered his hands and saw a second gunman strong-arming an elderly shopper, using her as a shield as he fired back at the red-haired woman.

The screams diminished into whimpers and frightened cries. Most of the onlookers had fled or were lying on the concrete, heads down, terrified. Uniformed police were running into the square, guns drawn.

"Release the hostage! Drop the weapon!"

Three cops circled the shooter with the human shield. The gunman hesitated as if calculating the odds, dropped his Glock, pushed his shocked captive away. Three seconds later, he was tackled.

Two more cops zeroed in on Lyle. "Not me!" he protested, flashing his badge. "Her!" He turned to point, but the woman and Weir were gone.

Then Roz sprinted into the square, gun drawn. Lyle waved her toward a long market building past some trees. "That way! That way!"

He put on a burst of speed to catch her, every second step a shock of pain.

"Who's the redhead?" Roz panted.

"Weir's going to tell us," Lyle promised and meant it.

Side by side they rushed into South Market Hall.

* * *

Halfway through the five-hundred-foot-long South Hall, Jess swerved down another aisle of market stalls, and David matched her move for move, the hard drive welded to his hand.

Over the thrum of huge industrial-sized fans that echoed off the low wooden ceilings, he'd heard an offsetting lag in the pursuing footsteps. Jack Lyle. The AFOSI agent had favored one leg when he'd entered the interrogation room in Atlantic City. He wasn't alone. There was a second pattern—lighter, female.

"This way!" Jess veered toward a side exit, and David followed.

They exited the building onto a narrow street, one-way toward the harbor. No sign of pursuit outside. No police cars. But—

"Sirens." David judged the shrill, undulating waves from the northwest. "Four police cars . . . five . . ."

Jess swiftly assessed the area. She pointed to the two tall buildings across the street. Between them, a dark opening, no wider than an alley. "Over there."

She darted across the road, David at her side, both narrowly missing the moving cars. More sirens. More police. "Three more . . . from the south. One ambulance from the north."

"How do you know that?" Jess led them into safe cover between the buildings. "Tell the difference, I mean. Let alone count them?"

David wasn't sure himself; it was just something he'd always been able to do. "They're using different systems. It sounds like the cops have Federal Signal PA300s. The ambulance's got a SignalMaster pattern from a Smart Siren 2000. I can count them from the phase offsets . . . in the echoes."

Jessica gave him a puzzled look for just a moment; then they were out in the bright sunshine again, on another, busier street, one-way in the opposite direction.

David looked up, alert for cameras.

They were on every corner.

He gestured to them. "That's how they'll track us now."

"Let them." Jess glanced to her left, then zigzagged through four lanes of clogged traffic, clearly trusting that he'd follow her. He did.

The hard reflective surfaces of the soaring modern towers caused David to lose precise count of the converging sirens. Still, he estimated they had under a minute before at least one vehicle would sight them.

Just past an office tower up ahead, he glimpsed another redbrick building patterned with multipaned, white-framed windows like Faneuil Hall. It was a smaller structure, but to his untrained eye it seemed roughly the same vintage. The street in front of it was wide, with a ring of old cobblestones set into a redbrick concourse.

The wail of sirens came from every direction now, and David had to concentrate even harder to sift relevant data out of the noise that enveloped them.

Jess was almost five feet ahead of him, running.

"Where're we going?" David called out to her.

"Subway!" She waved past the old redbrick building to an MTBA subway entrance. STATE STATION, the sign read.

"No, Jess! Too many cameras!" But she was already on the sidewalk, steps from the subway entrance.

A siren punched through the din, and David turned to see a police car, rooftop lights flashing, squeal to a stop on the one-way street behind them. A sedan and two SUVs prevented it from turning onto the street he and Jess were crossing now.

An amplified voice—from a 100-watt PA300 siren with a noise-canceling microphone—blared over the whooping wail. *"Clear the lane! Clear the lane!"*

A black Suburban with tinted windows screeched to a stop directly across the street from them, riding halfway up the sidewalk. Two tall men jumped out. Dark jackets. Muscled. Elite bodyguards. Like Nils.

"David!" Jess tugged on his arm. "Move!"

A wash of sounds from enameled tiles, cinder-block walls, and exposed metal structural supports assailed David as he and Jess thundered down shallow steps to the subway concourse. The last three stairs they jumped, sprinting for the ticket booths and turnstiles.

"Orange Line." Jess raced to her left. David kept pace with her.

She slowed for a few steps as she reached inside her jacket and pulled out a plastic card. "That one!"

David ran where she pointed, to a tall turnstile of interlocking metal bars—impossible to jump, no room for even a child to squeeze through. Jess slid her card through a reader. Something clicked.

"Go!" she cried, and David pushed the bars forward and the turnstile moved like a revolving door, delivering him to the other side.

A moment later, she joined him from a second turnstile. "Southbound," she commanded.

They ran again to another set of stairs heading down. David looked back in time to see one of the black-clad men stopped by the turnstiles, digging through his pockets.

Another level down, the walls were smudged and cracked. David smelled wheel grease and ozone. The distant rumble of an approaching train danced off unforgiving surfaces, smooth tile and rough concrete all combined.

For just a moment on the platform, they stopped to catch their breath. Here the concrete pillars were painted glossy orange. The safety zone at the platform's edge was yellow, chipped and streaked with dirt. The only light came from rows of old fluorescent tubes that buzzed. A breeze was building from the tunnel.

A distinctive bass note grew stronger in the distance. David automatically recognized it. A Hawker Siddeley engine, electric. Less than a minute away

"Let's go," Jess said.

"Where?" By now, the two bodyguards would have bought their tickets. They'd arrive about the same time as the train.

"The tunnels."

"They'll know exactly where we've gone." David pointed out three cameras. One at each end of the platform, another above the entrance corridor

"You have a better idea?"

David suddenly saw himself from above, on the platform. The sound of the train rushing from the tunnel made ripples over the scene. They interfered with other emanations from the cameras. Like watching a secret passage open in a solid wall, he saw the three dead spots where the emanations didn't reach. Where the cameras couldn't see.

One was down the platform to the left of the third last pillar.

"Yeah, I do." He grabbed her hand and pulled her past the handful of people on the platform, to the third orange pillar. Jess looked startled but didn't resist.

He stopped on one precise spot, positioning her shoulder to shoulder with him.

"Cameras can't see us here."

"They'll know which train we're in."

"We won't be in one."

The first car of the subway appeared at the end of the platform. The car's upper half was white; its lower, orange. The station banner above the motorman's windshield spelled out its destination: OAK GROVE.

"We're going in the tunnels?" Jess looked confused.

"Nope."

The train huffed to a stop; the second to last car was right before them.

The doors puffed open. Two riders exited. None entered. The car was empty.

"David?" Jessica whispered.

David suddenly turned to her and cupped his hands. "Up on top!"

Once again he was relieved she didn't hesitate, no matter how bewildered. She put both hands on his shoulders, her foot in his hands, then leapt up as he gave her the needed extra momentum.

She rolled onto the car's roof, braced her feet against the concrete overhang that divided the lower ceiling of the platform from the much higher one in the tunnel, and kicked off, pushing herself farther up along the roof's curve.

A warning chime sounded, cautioning riders that the train doors would be closing in five seconds.

Then came the sound of running boots in the entrance corridor. The bodyguards.

The doors were sliding shut as David tossed the hard drive to Jess. Then he jumped as high as he could, hands up to—

Jess grabbed at one of his hands as his other found the edge of the car's narrow rain gutter. Just enough to give him leverage. David's sneakers squeaked against the glass window as he swung halfway up, one foot catching the curve of the roof. Then the train lurched into motion, quickly gaining speed, and with a pull from Jess, he heaved himself onto the rooftop.

Immediately, he flattened down, as Jess already had beside him. The concrete tunnel ceiling supports whistled past, inches overhead.

David risked turning his head to see a narrow strip of the platform shoot by.

On it two black-clad figures looked left and right at the passing train, but neither one looked up. Then they were lost from sight as the train car plunged into a dark void lessened only by light streaming from its windows over blackened walls.

David was immersed in the rhythmic clack of wheels against steel, the electric whine of the engine, the complex interplay of all the sounds echoing in the closed space as the train rushed on.

A patch of daylight flashed over them, and just as quickly disappeared. But not before David caught a strobelike image of a wall-mounted metal stairway, and an overhead grate, twenty, thirty feet above the track. If there were more of those staircases, and he and Jess could lift the grate . . .

Jess's hand reached out to his as she spoke up over the rumble of the train and the tunnel. "We make a good team."

David agreed, but for a reason she was the first to hear. "Those genetic clusters, the ones linked to your temples. The same markers are in me, Jess. I think we're family."

THIRTY

Merrit was in the South Tower high-roller suite that was still set up with Weir's computers. Gratifyingly, his prey had conveniently provided the means by which he could be located and eliminated without subterfuge.

It was obvious that Ironwood's researcher had been in the observation area above the Red Room. It was equally obvious what he'd been doing there. One of the overhead cameras was still trained on the nine-foot computer screen.

Weir might have erased the results of Ironwood's search, including the parts of the database allowing it to be repeated, but the overhead camera had recorded what had been found.

Half of what Frank Beyoun mumbled as he worked to re-create what the overhead camera saw, Merrit didn't understand. The image the camera had recorded was what the mathematician called "keystoned," and apparently he needed a special program to correct that. He also needed another program to improve the focus. Even then, when it did, the image revealed a string of numbers at the bottom of the screen so blurred that Merrit couldn't read them.

Helpful as always, Frank explained that since he knew that the string of numbers consisted of one group of eight numerals and one group of seven numerals, and he also knew the first four numerals in the first group and the first three numerals in the second, he could teach the program how to resolve the other numerals. Or something like that.

It took two precious hours, but Merrit's new best friend finally delivered. Frank wrote the numbers down for him: the longitude and latitude of Ironwood's fourth outpost, to a precision of ten feet. It was the site where the MacCleirigh Foundation and Weir would be going as quickly as they could.

So would Merrit.

First, though, he'd have to thank Frank. Personally.

Agent Roz Marano had worked a miracle. Again.

"He must've had a really huge image file on the hard drive." She pointed to the computer Weir had used in the quick print shop located less than a mile from Harvard University.

Ten hours ago, she and Lyle had given up the foot chase from Faneuil Hall—just in time, as far as Lyle's ruined knee was concerned—when the police radioed they had the fugitives on camera. They weren't kidding. In Boston, those cameras included the police's own network, as well as the even more extensive system installed and run by Homeland Security to protect the city's unique historical landmarks.

Nine hours ago, Lyle had used Roz's laptop to review the recordings of the chase. Street cameras showed Weir and the red-haired woman fleeing into a subway station. A few seconds later, the MTBA concourse cameras had picked up the pair as they'd passed through the turnstiles. The woman had used a fare card bought the previous day with cash in a store without surveillance cameras. Impossible to trace.

More transit cameras tracked the two to the southbound Orange Line platform. As a train had arrived, they'd run in full view toward the end of the platform, only to duck behind a pillar. Coincidentally—though Lyle was not at all convinced that it was a coincidence—that particular pillar was one of three small areas on the platform that the cameras couldn't cover. It was from that spot that they'd simply vanished.

That had left the RFID tag as the last hope. Weir had still been carrying the tagged hard drive when he'd run into the subway station.

From the kit of equipment that filled half the trunk of their AFOSI unmarked car in a custom Kevlar-lined bin, Roz had retrieved radio-tracking gear that let her listen for the RFID's signals.

She picked up nothing.

That was when she'd started transmitting a coded pulse that would, she claimed, reset any changes Weir might have programmed into the tag.

Four hours later, two Boston police surveillance vans, one FBI van, two Homeland Security command post vehicles, and four air force staff cars had cruised through Boston and the surrounding regions following a precise grid pattern, using equipment similar to Roz's, transmitting the same reset-and-respond pulse.

His own effort to assist them had been to ask Andrews Air Force Base to launch an uncrewed Global Hawk drone. They'd done so only after his request had ascended the chain of command to the Pentagon and the Air Force Chief of Staff. Even so, a mere nine hours after Weir and the woman disappeared, the Global Hawk began transmitting Roz's reset-and-respond pulse over the Greater Boston area, and the sensitive antennas of the drone's EADS electronic intelligence system began listening for the tag's reply.

Within forty minutes, the tag was detected, stationary. The location was the print shop where he and Roz were now.

Two police cars had been there within eight minutes, but they were twenty minutes too late. By then the tag was no longer responding. A print-shop clerk confirmed that two people answering the descriptions of the fugitives had been there and paid with cash for half an hour of computer time and for a poster-sized print from the shop's largest printer. The small shop didn't have security cameras in the parking lots front or back. There was no way to tell what Weir and the woman were using for transportation.

When the police called to report, Roz instructed them to keep every-one away from the computer Weir had used. She and Lyle arrived forty minutes later.

The computer was now protected by a web of yellow police tape on a small gray desk that reminded Lyle of a library carrel.

"He needed this computer," Roz reasoned, "because he had to convert the file into something he could print out. Which he did."

"Any idea what he printed?"

Roz typed on the computer's keyboard, then frowned as she read the text that appeared on the screen. "Whatever it was, he wanted to keep it to himself. He overwrote all his work files a bunch of times. There's nothing to recover."

Lyle was about to move on but saw Roz hesitate. Very encouraging. She typed again. Grinned. "He sanitized the computer, but not the printer."

"So we can get a copy?"

"Maybe not the whole file, but depending on how big the buffer is, at least a third of it. Maybe two-thirds." Roz did something, and the screen changed to show yellow text against a black background. "Give me five minutes and we can print out whatever data are left in the spool file."

Five minutes later, Lyle stood by a large machine through which a sheet of heavy paper moved like a cloth through an ancient wringer washer. Lyle didn't mention the similarity to Roz. He wasn't about to sound even older than he was.

The image forming on the paper was like a wildly colored piece of abstract art, random except for a string of numbers that ran along one side, and a few strange collections of letters that appeared here and there.

"Any idea what that is?"

"False color of something," Roz said, "but it's definitely some kind of map."

Lyle was a big fan of maps. They showed locations. Locations meant destinations. Journeys to destinations could be tracked.

The page finally rolled out from the printer—two-thirds complete. In the middle of a field of splotchy, garish colors was a three-dimensional line drawing of a building of some kind.

Roz handed it to him for a closer look with a reminder that Ironwood was always talking to Weir about using his data to find alien outposts. "Maybe that outline is what they look like."

Lyle frowned. "That would mean all those lunatic conversations were legitimate."

"Truth and fiction, huh?" Roz took the awkwardly sized sheet back. "I'd say this is a shoreline. Somewhere. What do you bet Geospatial can figure out exactly where it is?"

"Just don't tell them about the aliens."

Roz smiled. "What makes you think they don't already know?"

Late that night, the scholars stood in silence as Stoneworker Apprentice Atlan counted aloud in the center of the observatory ring. Other than the young female's strong voice, the only sound was the rippling of the dark cloth that wrapped the encircling sun stones, covering all the sighting gaps but one. For the accuracy of this test, the night breeze must not be allowed to deflect the weighted cord Atlan swung as a pendulum, her arm braced on a small wooden frame.

"Three hundred sixty . . ." Atlan neared the critical stage of her count. "Three hundred sixty-one . . ."

Her instructor, Stone Master Nazri, stood several steps behind his student, monitoring her count of each full swing of the pendulum she held, following her sight line to see what she saw. The elderly scholar, frail and, at twenty-five years, stooped with age, wore a white cloak so the other scholars could see him despite the darkness of the new moon. All the torches and lamps had been extinguished to allow the apprentice's eyes to remain sensitive for her task.

Nazri raised his hand so the other scholars would know: The next few counts would be close.

"Three hundred sixty-two . . ." There was no hesitation in Atlan's voice, no indication that, in only moments, she might achieve the reward of four years of study, or be forced to wait another year for her advancement. "Three hundred sixty three . . . three hundred sixty-four . . ."

Nazri raised both hands as if to frame his student.

"Three hundred sixty-five . . . three hundred sixty-six and gone!"

At the same instant, Nazri swept both hands down, indicating that the timing star had indeed moved behind the right-hand wooden post and disappeared at the moment his apprentice's pendulum completed its 366th full swing.

Now it was only a matter of handiwork for Atlan to complete this final test.

As if this were simply an ordinary day and another lesson, the young apprentice, almost twelve, walked with measured pace to a cutting table, the leather soles of her woven footwear crunching against the dry ground of the viewing yard. Two younger apprentices were there with oil lamps, which they quickly lit with fire moss kept smoldering in metal cages. Other apprentices went purposefully from torch stand to torch stand, bringing light to the circular yard.

Ten days earlier, Atlan had constructed her sight line and timing gap. With little more than fine rope, sharpened wooden stakes, and some marking tools, she had drawn an arc of a great circle in the finely packed soil of the yard. The length of rope she had used to draw the arc was the radius of the circle. When she then pulled that rope taut between two points on the arc, the section of the arc created in that fashion equaled one-sixth of a full circle—exactly 61 of the 366 degrees by which the star path masters measured the great circle of the sky. One degree for each sunrise in a year.

With other lengths of rope and wooden stakes, she had used basic geometry to further divide a portion of that arc into its individual degrees, resulting in two sighting posts exactly one degree apart.

It was a known fact that a pendulum of a given length always completed its swings at a constant rate. So the challenge Atlan faced was to precisely measure a length of fine cord that would make a pendulum that completed 366 full swings in the time it took a star to move between the sighting posts—one 366th part of a day. In time to come, that span would be measured as three minutes, fifty-six seconds.

For her final test, one that would elevate her from apprentice to master, Atlan had been allowed ten nights to refine the length of the cord. Then, this night, she demonstrated to her master and the scholars of the observatory the preciseness of her craft.

Atlan pulled her cord straight atop the cutting table, using sharpened iron awls to mark the length of it on a polished rod of fire-hardened wood. Then, with a serrated, carved bone saw, she cut the rod to the exact length of the pendulum cord.

She presented the rod to Nazri, and the wizened scholar took it to a round stone altar. On the stone, an iron rod rested in a shallow trough that precisely fit it. An apprentice builder carefully removed the iron rod, then used a whisk of feathers to be sure the trough was free of dust and debris.

Oil lamps glowed and sputtered at the edges of the altar stone as the other scholars gathered around it.

Nazri gently lowered the wooden rod into the trough.

It fit exactly.

Atlan had demonstrated that she could travel anywhere in the world and with a few simple tools create a precise unit of measure that would allow her to construct observatories and libraries and outposts, according to common plans and known facts.

The other scholars, having seen the result, went back to their studies.

Nazri gave his student the highest praise possible. "Well done."

She bowed her head, apprenticeship at an end. "Master."

He gestured with a trembling hand to have her look up at him. "No. We're the same now, Stone Master."

Atlan drew in a breath at hearing that title. She knew what was to come, but had no idea what it might mean.

The next morning, Atlan met with Nazri and three other stone masters outside the observatory's central chamber, set apart from the other low stone buildings of the scholars' community. The plaster walls of the structure glittered in the brilliant summer sun—tiny flecks of mica mixed with the yellow pigment produced a sparkling point of light, not for decoration, but for distant ships approaching during daylight. The wind was heavy with the promise of rain later in the day. At this hour, though, the sky was a brilliant blue, the clouds small and distant and pure white.

Atlan, now wearing the cloth trousers, cloth shirt, and stiff leather protective apron of a stone master, breathed in that morning air as if noticing it for the first time. The day felt new to her. Her life was about to begin again. On that hilltop of baked white soil and rock, looking out over the interior ocean that one day would be called the Mediterranean, she believed she could see the curve of the world, believed she could feel the world spinning in its endless dance among the other bodies of the sky, as timeless and predictable as the swinging of a pendulum and the known facts of geometry.

Her studies had made her part of the pattern of all that was known, and all that was still to know. There could be no greater fulfillment.

"Are you ready?" Nazri asked her.

She clicked her answer.

"Then the doors are yours to open. Paid in blood."

Atlan was puzzled by her former master's words. Knowledge sometimes demanded a heavy price. Bridge ships could disappear forever on voyages of discovery. Inland expeditions set out, never to return. But to wayfinders and star path masters on solid land, where was the danger?

The other masters stepped aside in silence. Atlan approached the doors of the central chamber, placed her hands under the wooden crosspiece that kept them secure, lifted it—and cried out in surprise and pain.

Blood pulsed from a lattice of shallow cuts on her palms and fingers.

She looked to Nazri, but he had no sympathy.

"You said you were ready."

Atlan had come too far to give up now, or question those who had taught her, and anger was not in the nature of the khai. *She turned back to the crosspiece and found there was nowhere she could place her hands to avoid the thin blades lining its underside.* The price of knowledge, *she thought. So Atlan lifted the crosspiece, knowing that because of the pain, she would remember this day forever. And perhaps that was the reason for it.*

The doors gave way.

▆▆▆▆ ▆▆▆▆▆▆ ▆▆▆▆

There was a stone meeting table in the center of the torchlit chamber. The domed ceiling held the familiar constellations of the White Island. The encircling wall held a map of the world, clearly marked with trade and transportation routes, though

195

some were different from the ones she knew. Still, Atlan had been in enough similar chambers to wonder why this one was open to star path masters only.

As Nazri bound her wounds with strips of white linen, the other masters placed a wayfinder's case on the meeting table. The curved wooden chest was larger than any Atlan had seen before, and the silver panels inset into it were somehow different. The star patterns she saw on one specific panel made no sense at all.

"What kind of case is that?" she asked.

Nazri finished tying the linen around her bloodied hands. "An old one."

The masters worked the strips of wood that locked the case, sliding one after another in the proper sequence to release its lid.

Without ceremony, they swung open the hinged top of the case. Inside, Atlan was intrigued to see, there were no standard wayfinder's tools. No lenses, no cords, no horizon boards. Instead, there was a large roll of vellum.

The masters placed the roll of supple leather on the table and removed the case. "Unroll it," Nazri said.

With hands made clumsy by her bandages, Atlan untied the cord that kept the vellum bound. She smoothed it on the table, seeing many other dark dried streaks of what she presumed was blood from other new masters who had also fallen victim to the bladed crosspiece.

On the vellum was a map, faint in the torchlight. From the texture of its markings, Atlan saw it was a rubbing. The thin hide had been placed over a relief map, then shaded with charcoal.

"It's an island," she said. In her mind, she rotated the outline of it, trying to match it with other islands whose outlines she knew. Something about it was familiar but, as with the altered details on the world map that surrounded her, Atlan couldn't quite place the differences.

The other masters stood silent, watching, expressionless.

"Look closer," Nazri said.

Atlan lifted a corner of the parchment to improve the lighting on it. On one part of the island, she saw the faintest outline of a familiar cross—the mark of the Navigators. She felt a thrill of recognition.

"This is a rubbing from the Great Hall."

"Look closer."

Atlan was no longer aware of the throbbing pain in her hands. She had never been to the White Island, never seen the Hall of the Navigators itself nor the treasure that filled it. From her lessons, though, she knew each part of it in her heart, each map and chart and table memorized exactly. As the image of the Hall's great map rose in her memory, she realized what was different about the surrounding wall map in this chamber. It wasn't that the trade routes on it were unfamiliar—the outlines of the land were subtly changed.

With that realization, like lightning caught by a scholar's spool of copper, Atlan suddenly recognized the outline on the vellum.

Her breath caught.

"You see it?" Nazri asked.

"It's a map of Har Madhyh. This island."

"But?" Nazri prompted.

"Har Madhyh is two islands— and this map shows it as one."

This island on which the observatory had been built, which one day would be called Malta, had a sister island to the northwest, separated by a narrow strait less than a single stadon across—a quick boat ride or a short swim.

Yet this map, judging from its relief shading, showed the two islands joined as one, with a valley where the strait ran today.

As smoothly as the interwoven strips of wood had moved to unlock the unusual wayfinder's case, Atlan pictured the known facts falling into position.

"This is how the Navigators saw Har Madhyh."

"It is," Nazri agreed.

"But it is not as Har Madhyh is today."

"It is not."

Atlan had been trained in logic and deduction. The end result was obvious.

She looked at her fellow masters in the torchlit chamber. They were no longer expressionless. They were grim.

Atlan said the only thing that could be said. "We must do what the Navigators did before us."

"Even if we do, the White Island won't survive what's to come," Nazri said. "Neither will our outposts. We'll perish as they did."

Atlan didn't share her fellow masters' pessimism. She looked around the chamber with its wealth of information. But not enough information. "As individuals, yes. That's a known fact. But as a people, perhaps not."

Nazri and the other masters regarded their newest colleague with interest as she ran her bandaged hand across the smooth stone surface of the meeting table.

"We need to leave more than maps," she said. "I have an idea."

THIRTY-ONE

Andrew McCleary found the whole affair distasteful, especially since it should never have been allowed to begin in the first place.

The interrogator waved something near Willem Tasman's face, and the man twitched back into consciousness. The only reason he hadn't fallen from his chair was that he was tied to it.

The Defender of Macao was being questioned in an old residential building in Queens. Not Andrew's favorite place in the city, but safely removed from the offices of McCleary Adams & Intrator LLP. The sound-proofing built into the deceptively plain and artistically aged walls also added a measure of protection. This room, and others like it, had been useful over the years, whenever the needs of the Family had required certain actions to be taken that were best kept hidden. A sliding panel in the next room led to a corridor that ran to an underground parking area—perfect for discreet removals.

"You can make this stop anytime," Andrew reminded him.

His captive said nothing.

The interrogator, a bland-looking man in his fifties, but one of Cross's best, looked to Andrew for further guidance. The session had lasted more than an hour, which explained why the subject kept passing out.

Andrew decided to try another approach. He waved the interrogator aside and stood before Willem's wooden chair beneath the room's single harsh light.

"If you tell me what I need to know, I'll make sure Jessica is safe. There's nothing I can do for you, but I can protect her."

Finally Willem spoke. Only a single word, but it was the first he'd said since he arrived from Boston and the hood was taken from his head.

"Why . . ."

"You know the answer. For the Family. Everything I do is for the Family."

Andrew's phone vibrated silently in his jacket pocket. He told the interrogator not to resume until he returned, then went into the next room.

"Any progress?" Su-Lin asked.

"None whatsoever. What about you?"

"She's gone to ground, and it's obvious Florian taught her all her tricks."

Andrew knew exactly what that meant. Defenders were supposed to be completely supported by the Foundation. They had no need for private wealth because anything they could ever want would be provided without cost or question. It was a perfect way for whoever held the purse strings to keep control. Which is why, from time to time, more willful defenders, like Florian or Willem, would work outside the system and amass their own resources, beyond Family oversight.

Florian had been particularly adept at diverting Foundation funds to her own use, and had actually reached the point where she had been able to personally underwrite her own expeditions. Now, it seemed, Jessica was following in her aunt's footsteps.

"Any ideas where she's gone?"

"There's no electronic record of her leaving America, so she's using false passports."

"Are you certain she's left?"

"Cross found her and David Weir on security tapes from Terminal 7 at JFK airport. They're going through them all to see which flight they took—Canada, Japan, Spain, Australia, Britain . . . a great many places they could end up, and Cross can't cover them all in the time we have."

"If she's with Weir, we know where she's hoping to end up."

"A new temple."

"Exactly. But we can't allow that to happen. We'd lose everything we've—"

"Just a minute . . ."

Andrew looked at his phone in disbelief. Su-Lin had put him on hold. What could be more important than saving the Foundation?

His annoyance vanished when she returned to the call with good news. *"We have them. They flew British Airways to Heathrow. Cross is checking the passenger lists against passports. We'll have the names they're traveling under within the hour. Then we'll be able to do a full survey of hotels and car rental companies."*

"What if England isn't their final destination?"

"Then we'll keep tracking them. In the meantime, we're sending a demolition team from Zurich to London. If she's found a temple on British soil, by tomorrow morning we'll only be a few hours behind them."

"Then do we need to continue this unpleasantness with our friend from Macao?"

There was a long silence. She was either weighing all the variables or checking the markets.

"We shouldn't risk having him disappear so close to Florian's death. When he dies, it will have to be seen as an accident, and we'll need the body."

"It might take him a few weeks to heal, so he's recognizable."

"A few weeks should be fine."

Su-Lin's decisiveness made Andrew feel better than he had for ages. Willem and Jessica might not agree, but their sacrifice would be for the greater good. For the Family.

"Perhaps we could arrange to have Willem and Jessica perish in the same accident."

"She's too dangerous," Su-Lin said. "I don't want her alive for a few more weeks. I want her dead tomorrow."

THIRTY-TWO

"How does this work?"

Tucked into the high wingback chair in David's room, Jess looked and sounded jet-lagged. She'd wrapped herself in a gray flannel bathrobe and slipped her bare feet under her.

It was midnight, local time. David was still in the same jeans and navy pullover he'd been in for hours. He snapped on the pair of thin silicone gloves that had come with the testing kit.

Three days ago, they'd been running for their lives beneath the streets of Boston. Now they were settled in a fussy Victorian bed-and-breakfast in the north of Cornwall, under new names. The Canadian passport that carried David's photograph identified him as Mark Alexander Askwith.

Three phone calls were all it had taken for Jess to arrange their flight and journey. In addition to what seemed to be unlimited funds, she had access to resources that effectively trumped government regulations. David hadn't asked for details.

He tore the seal on a slender foil pack and withdrew a small scraper.

"I'm going to collect some skin cells from the inside of your cheek—with this."

The scraper resembled a cocktail swizzle stick—a long white plastic rod with a flattened end that had a few scallops in it, like a worn-down comb.

"I'll put your sample in the vial with the preservative, and then we send it to your friends at Cambridge for comparison with mine."

When David had explained the test he'd like to do to confirm that he and Jess were distantly related, she'd asked him which English university could run it. He'd said Cambridge, and she'd made another phone call. The sample-collection kit had been waiting for them at the Goring Hotel in London the night they arrived. It seemed her family had been long-term benefactors of the University of Cambridge. Since it was founded. In 1209 C.E.

"I'm asking them to look specifically at the hAR regions on chromosome 20."

"Because that's where you found your anomalies."

"The most significant ones, yes." David made sure the small vial of preservative was ready. It was a bullet-sized container of translucent plastic, the tip sharply tapered. "The four clusters I've found so far aren't exactly like each other—there are markers unique to each of them—but all four share the same haplotype around the hAR region."

"Haplotype?"

He knelt down before her. "Open," he said. Jess opened her mouth, and he lightly began scraping the inside of her cheek. "Have you heard of the Human Genome Project?"

Jess nodded, the small movement awkward in the circumstances.

David removed the scraper, examined it. At its flattened tip was a small buildup of white mush. "It was the first attempt to list the genetic structure of every human chromosome—some three billion base pairs. Took thirteen years and three billion dollars, and that was just for one person's genetic code." He broke the end off the scraper, dropped it into the plastic vial, capped the vial, and shook it.

Then he opened the packet holding a second sterile scraper. "Some parts of chromosomes are so difficult to take apart that, realistically, we know maybe ninety-two percent of the human genome's DNA sequence in detail. Open." He scraped at the inside of her other cheek. "This is for the backup, in case anything goes wrong with the first. Anyway, the point is, given the cost and the difficulty and the time required, most researchers have to work with big chunks of DNA from specific sites on specific chromosomes. Done."

David snapped the end of the second scraper, placed it in the second vial, and capped it.

"Does that work as well?" Jess swung her legs down from the chair, stood up, and stretched.

"Yeah, it does. Because genes tend to get passed from one generation to the next in big chunks called haplotypes."

David peeled off his gloves, then began attaching ID stickers to the vials containing Jess's samples.

"It's the same technique researchers use to figure out when humans migrated out of Africa tens of thousands of years ago. Haplotypes tell them the routes the different groups of people took as they spread out over the rest of the world."

"I remember you told me that. Three major ones, right?" Jess said.

David nodded. "It's likely there were lots of migrations, but not all of them were successful. For example, we know there were modern humans living in Israel somewhere between ninety and a hundred and twenty thousand years ago, but around the ninety-thousand-year mark, humans outside of Africa disappear from the fossil record. So none of the genetic lines from those first migrations survived. That means"—he dropped her vials into the slot of the collection box next to the two vials that held his samples—"everyone alive today can be traced back—genetically at least—to one of those three major migrations out of Africa, starting about sixty-five thousand years ago."

David placed the consent forms he and Jess had signed earlier into the sample box, then sealed it. The signatures matched the false names on their new passports.

"So what about your clusters of nonhuman markers?" Jess asked him. "Which route did those people take?"

David took a moment to answer. The small room's overwhelming fragrance of lavender potpourri was almost suffocating. "Well, that's the strange thing. The genetic anomalies I've found . . . they're not unique to any of the migrations. They show up in populations everywhere."

"If everyone has them, how can they be anomalous?"

"Because everyone doesn't have them." Jess still didn't know the death sentence those markers bestowed on him and a few unlucky others, maybe even her. From her mentions of other members of her extended family, David knew that many of them lived a normal span of years. However, for now there was no way to know if that was because they had a variant of his genes that overcame early death, or because they had nothing genetically in common with him.

Until the tests were run and David knew one way or another if he did have a connection to the MacCleirighs, he saw no point in revealing his secret to Jess. At first, that decision had been to protect his privacy. Now, he realized, it was because he didn't want to cause her worry.

He sat down on the edge of the room's white iron-framed bed. He chose his words carefully to tell her just enough and not too much.

"It's as if nine to ten thousand years ago or so—when humans had spread out across the world—somehow a new set of identical haplotypes just appeared. All at the same time and in at least four different populations."

"Your four clusters," Jess said. Her green eyes were bright, clear. Interested in what he had to tell her.

"Exactly. So here's the problem. Someone might be able to make the case for some kind of trade or connection between the South Pacific and Peru back then, but there's no way to connect the people in those two sites—at that time—to the clusters in India or in Cornwall."

"Except my way."

"The First Gods?" David shook his head. "What I should have said is there's no way to *scientifically* connect the sites. *Stories* just can't do that."

Jess looked chagrined. "Stories. David, do you know you could be the first person in years . . . maybe centuries . . . maybe *ever,* to know about the First Gods outside of the Family? I can't believe I even told you."

David found himself wishing he could tell his own story to her. Instead, he tapped the small box beside him. "Might not be a big deal that you did. If the DNA test shows we've got the same anomalies, then you and I are cousins."

He couldn't read the strange expression that flashed across her face. It was as if he'd said something with special significance to her.

"But you don't believe," she said.

"In God, or First Gods? No, I don't—can't. There's no evidence. At least, none that's testable, scientific."

"Like Ironwood's aliens." Jess's eyes met his, unflinching. "I'd get into so much trouble saying this to my teachers, but . . . what if they're the same?"

"Your gods were aliens?"

"No. No." Jess waved a dismissive hand at him. "The other way around. The *Traditions* clearly say that the First Gods rose from the people. They didn't come to us from the sky or from anywhere else."

"The *Traditions.* Your bible." David felt he had no footing here. Religious beliefs were a matter of faith, and faith didn't lend itself to rational debate.

"There's nothing supernatural in the *Traditions.* That's one of the ways we know it's the truth."

"How can the idea of gods not be considered supernatural?"

"Because of where the First Gods came from."

It was obvious to David that Jess's next words were a straight quote from her *Traditions.*

" 'For forty generations man hid in darkness like the beasts, and knew not fire nor grain nor the markings of the heavens and the measure of the sun and moon and stars. Then, in the fortieth and first generation, the people of darkness captured fire, and did sow grain, and by the measure of the sun and moon and stars, did reap it. And these things and others they took to their children and to their parents so they would not fear the darkness, nor hunger, nor would they fear the confusion of days.'

"How much clearer could it be?" she asked. "It doesn't say, 'The people from the sky.' 'The people with green antennas.' It says, 'People of darkness.' The same people mentioned in the verse preceding." She tapped a finger to her chest. "Us. Humans. People of darkness living in caves and grubbing for our food until—until the First Gods rose from us and gave us the tools of civilization so we could rise from that darkness and become gods ourselves. At their side.

"You want to know why our scripture isn't some collection of fairy tales like any other religious text you'd care to name? Because it reveals *truth* that's supported by reason, not unthinking faith."

However unfounded her beliefs, David accepted they were sincerely held, like Ironwood's. "Well, it's different, at least," he said.

For the first time, David realized he was enjoying the company of someone else as much as his own. He searched for a way to prolong this strange conversation, fearing if he didn't, Jess would return to her room and their day together would be at an end.

"Tell me more," he said.

And she did.

In modern times, the scriptures of the Family were called *Les Traditions de la Famille,* after the classic French translation by René Quinton, guardian of his line at the turn of the last century, and a shining example for children of all twelve lines as to what they should aspire to be. Quinton, a renowned scientist and physician who had saved tens of thousands of lives with his discoveries, had based his translation on earlier works in Latin, Hebrew, and ancient Greek that dated back to between two and three thousand years ago. With multiple copies having been passed down through generations of MacCleirighs, the scriptures were complete, and, even having been copied by hand and translated so many times, there were few discrepancies among the different versions.

The oldest form of the Family scriptures, though, was in cuneiform, dating back to almost five thousand years. One hundred and seventy-eight clay tablets—approximately one-third of the complete work—survived and were now preserved in the repository maintained by the Claridge line in Australia.

On those tablets, fired by scribes who had traced their lineage back to the time of the First Gods, and from whom Jess's own lineage could be traced forward, the world and the universe were described in terms that contradicted millennia of common wisdom and superstition, yet were confirmed in modern times.

In the scriptures of the Family, the Earth was said to have been formed by forces unknown and was older than any person could comprehend. It was also described as a sphere, and it moved around the Sun as the Moon moved in turn around the Earth.

There were no demons or angels or wars in heaven in *Les Traditions.* Not even a god at the beginning. Not until the First Gods arose from humans, just as life was said to have arisen from the land and sea—not through the intent of some supernatural mind, but because it was the nature of things.

These scriptures, with statements most other religions would find blasphemous, were the reason why the MacCleirighs had remained hidden, their faith disguised throughout recorded history.

Over the centuries, as the scattered lines of the Family perfected their strategy of hiding in plain sight, the scholars among them began to assemble the evidence that the truths in their scriptures—so at odds with what other religions maintained—actually did reflect the natural world.

MacCleirigh money and influence prodded the Enlightenment into being, gave birth to rationalism and an explosion of science. One after another, the truths of the Family scriptures were revealed to be *actual* truths, measurable by the tools of science.

Yet, as Jess told David, her teachers emphasized that there were no statements in the scriptures reflecting knowledge that early humans couldn't have had. There was no mention of atomic theory. No discussion of medical concepts beyond those that wise observers at the time might note; hygiene was critical to maintaining health, the scriptures said, but they made no references to why that might be so, not a word about bacteria.

Les Traditions de la Famille, then, were exactly what they themselves said they were—the writings of humans who had been present at the birth of the First Gods, and who had been charged by those gods to be their representatives on this world, defending their secrets until their gifts could be shared by all people, everywhere.

People. Not aliens.

So the *Traditions* said.

"How's all that stayed secret?"

Jess shrugged. "By not talking about it. Like I'm doing now."

"For seven thousand years?" David struggled unsuccessfully to soften his skepticism. "That's something like three hundred generations." The numbers arranged themselves in his mind. "One hundred and forty-four people in each generation means forty-three thousand individuals who knew all this, and not one of them ever tried to betray the Family, or was estranged, or got drunk in a bar and spilled their guts?"

"Not completely."

David took her smile to mean he hadn't insulted her.

"Of course," Jess admitted, "some of the stories from the *Traditions,* and from the Family's other writings, *have* leaked out for all sorts of reasons—that's human nature. You can find them in other cultures, other legends.

Even other religions. Where they came from, though, that's not open knowledge.

"The Family's done studies of generational secrets, particularly of the dynamics of keeping them successfully. Three conditions have proved particularly important." She ticked them off on her fingers: "One: stability over time. The Family's certainly had that. Two: strong selection criteria for choosing who to tell the secret to. Very few. You being an exception. Three: nonconfrontational posture. We've never tried to impose our beliefs on anyone, so we have nothing to prove. People tend to ignore us because we're not a threat, and that leads back to our stability."

The lamplight illuminated half her hair. *Like half a halo,* David thought. *An angel's halo.*

"Next question." Jess's half-grin told him he'd been caught staring.

"Okay. What's the Family actually been doing all these years? And why?"

Jess's hands went to the silver cross she wore, the gesture seeming more reflexive than intentional. "The First Gods rose from humans, which means the seeds of godhood are in each of us. They gave humans the gift of civilization, so that we could be freed from fear and labor, and become wise. When we are wise enough, in time we will become gods ourselves at their side."

To David, Jess's words seemed less an answer to his question than a ritualized response derived from unquestioned repetition: childhood training. "You say, 'in time.' How much time? Do the *Traditions* say how long this is going to take?"

Jess shook her head, and a few strands of her long red hair floated free, gleaming in the light. David had to blink to keep his concentration. "All we know is that everything will change when the First Gods return to us."

"They left?"

She kept her hands on her cross, but David saw her fingers tense. "Nine thousand years ago. Ever since then, each one of us who reads the *Traditions* has been faced with what we call the Mystery of the Promise. We know what the Promise is—the *Traditions* make that clear. The First Gods *will* return to us, and that's when their Promise that all of us, all of humanity, will become gods at their side will be fulfilled. So the Family protects the knowledge they gave us, and adds to it, preparing for that day. We just don't know when."

The way she spoke said more to David than her words. It was as if she needed to convince herself, not him. As if something else about this ancient mystery were bothering her. Something she wasn't sharing with him.

"Why did the First Gods leave?" he asked.

"We don't know."

"Any idea where they went?"

"The White Island."

"The White Island." He studied Jess. "You don't know where that is, either."

The way she turned the cross in her hands told him he was right. "There's a new theory—new questions—every generation. Does the word 'white' refer to a color? Is it an industry? A practical facility for making linen shrouds thousands of years ago? Or was it a place of purity? A physical location like Mount Ararat? An actual island? Atlantis? Malta? A place of ice and snow like Greenland or Antarctica? Or, in the end, just a philosophical state of mind?"

"What do you think?" David asked.

"If we knew why the First Gods left us, maybe we could figure out where they went." She seemed about to speak, changed her mind, stood up. "I need to sleep."

David stood, too, still reluctant to say good night. "Big day tomorrow." He glanced at the heavy curtains covering the window, as if he could see through them, through the night, to Tintagel Castle, less than five miles distant.

He walked to the door with her. She hesitated in the open doorway. "When we get those results back, you'd better be one of my cousins. Otherwise, after everything I've told you . . ." She didn't finish the sentence.

"Don't worry," David said. "Tomorrow, we'll find a new temple. That's my promise."

So quickly that David knew there was no thought behind her action, Jess lifted the thin silver chain with its silver cross from around her neck and placed it around his.

"I give you the Twelve Winds of the world," she said, the rhythm of recitation in her voice again, "because no one knows where one will die."

Then, cheeks blazing like her hair, she turned away, and was gone without another word.

That night, David lay back in bed with her cross in his hand, thinking of the Twelve Winds and where they might take him in his own quest.

Like Jess, he didn't know where he might die, either.

He only knew when.

Sleep did not come easily.

THIRTY-THREE

As far as the public and press knew, the FBI's 6:00 A.M. raid on the En-counters casino and resort was part of Holden Ironwood's ongoing legal battles with the Treasury. Special Agent Jack Lyle, Agent Roz Marano, and eleven other specialists from the Air Force Office of Special Investigations—all wearing blue FBI Windbreakers and photo IDs—went unmentioned in the press briefing.

It took less than an hour to locate the isolated computer installation that Lyle had gambled was hidden in the casino. There, with the exception of the mysteriously missing billionaire himself, Jack Lyle found everything he wanted—but nothing he could use.

In the walled-off, climate-controlled portion of the Red Room, Captain Trevor Kingsburgh, a computer specialist on loan from U.S. Space Command, wearing civilian clothes and an FBI jacket, delivered the bad news.

He showed Lyle and Roz one of the data-storage units he'd removed from the block of eight metal shelving racks in the center of the chilly room. "The good news," the captain said, "is that the installation has eight hundred and fifty one-point-five-terabyte hot-swap drives like this one. If it's set up with a standard configuration, that works out to about five hundred and seventy drives to hold the entire SARGE database, two hundred to manipulate it, cache, and cross-sort searches, and eighty or so units as redundant spares."

Lyle let those figures slip past him, focused on something more important. "Yet you don't seem happy."

"Every drive I've examined has been wiped clean. So there's unlikely to be evidence that SARGE was ever used here."

Roz jumped in before he could. "No way you can erase eight hundred and fifty terabytes in an hour."

"Not through software," Kingsburgh agreed, "but look over here." He carried the drive to a small worktable. "Recognize those?"

Roz picked up something that to Lyle looked like a large handheld hair dryer completely sealed in red plastic—no air vents. There were five others like it on the table, each with a long electrical cord and standard plug. "It's an old bulk eraser. Generates a powerful magnetic field. It's designed to erase videotapes by the box load."

Roz wasn't happy, either. She turned back to Kingsburgh. "Are you going to be able to reconstruct anything that was on them?"

"We'll check them all, sector by sector, but . . . hold those erasers within a foot of the drives for a few seconds . . . that's all it takes."

"I didn't see any bulk erasers in the other room," Roz said. Her eyes narrowed. She was getting an idea. Lyle began to hope. "So I'd bet the techs didn't get a chance to use them on their workstations."

The junior agent headed purposefully through the cylindrical door to the other side of the Red Room. Lyle and Kingsburgh followed.

There was an AFOSI technician or an air force specialist at each of the eight workstations at the back of the room. At the conference table, two of Ironwood's programmers waited, hands bound by plastic restraints.

One was Keisha Harrill, a young woman about Roz's age, with dreadlocks, jeans, and a T-shirt showing a large green dinosaur above the words NEVER FORGET. Lyle didn't get it, but Roz thought it was funny. Naturally.

The other prisoner was Joost Chatto, a tall, awkward man who had his head down, intent on studying something fascinating on the floor, or maybe it was the knife-sharp crease ironed into his jeans.

Both Harrill and Chatto had been in the Red Room when the AFOSI technicians had entered. Both had thus far refused to answer any questions. That generally meant they knew something. Their turn would come.

Lyle waited, patient, as his junior agent zeroed in on one of the AFOSI technicians at a workstation. After a quick conversation, the two consulted the technician's thick red binder with SECRET emblazoned on its cover; then Roz stood behind the tech as he typed. Both looked pleased by the text that appeared on the screen, and Roz came back to tell Lyle why.

"Slam-dunk. We found a subdirectory on the local hard drive that lists files in the SARGE format. That should be enough to establish that the workstation had access to the SARGE database."

Captain Kingsburgh still wasn't happy.

"Might not be that simple," he said. "Like I said, two reasons for concern—the fact that all the drives have been wiped, and the fact that this installation isn't big enough for what it needs to do."

"Why not?" Lyle asked.

"That partial printout you turned in, of the unknown coastline. Its level of resolution is at least six times greater than anything SARGE can produce. Plus, it's showing a structure at something like ninety meters underground. At best, SARGE can only go two to three meters below the surface—and that's with favorable soil and moisture conditions, not the kind of rocks we've got in that image."

Lyle saw no reason to admit defeat. "So what else do we need to find?"

Kingsburgh looked over to the retrofitted wall that cut the room in half. "For a global database with that level of detail . . . we need to find at least another thirty-five hundred drives to go with the eight hundred and fifty in there. All networked together." The captain shifted the unit he carried to his other arm. "If I were you, I'd start looking for a few more heavily air-conditioned rooms."

"We won't find them," Roz said to Lyle.

"Because?"

"Because there's no outside network here. These workstations connect to each other and to the drives in the air-conditioned room, and that's it. There's not even an ordinary phone line leading out of this place, so there's no way they can access any other database or network."

"Then we've got a problem," Kingsburgh said. "However that printout was generated, it had to come from something more than just the SARGE database. Because they're processing a lot more information than what they could've stored here."

Roz looked around, searching for inspiration, Lyle knew. "Then how about this? Somehow Ironwood's managed to get access to a second database, similar to SARGE, but . . . better."

Kingsburgh glanced around to see if anyone was within earshot. No one was, but stepped closer anyway and dropped his voice. "The EMPIRE satellite constellation that produced SARGE, the synthetic-aperture radar technology the satellites use . . . we're the only country with that capability."

"Then another possibility," Lyle said. "If we can keep EMPIRE a secret from other countries, could other countries be keeping their version of the same technology secret from us?"

Kingsburgh made quick work of that idea. "Why would Ironwood steal the SARGE database to sell to another country if the other country already had a better version?"

"Unless . . ." Roz said slowly.

"Don't stop there," Lyle prompted her.

"What if Ironwood's not interested in *selling* SARGE? What if he's the end user?"

Lyle was impressed. Something new he himself hadn't considered. "So . . . he obtained a copy of SARGE for himself . . . and also bought or stole a similar database from China or Russia—"

"Or Switzerland," Roz said.

The captain from U.S. Space Command looked confused. "Switzerland? They don't have spy satellites."

Roz looked at Lyle, silently asking permission.

He nodded. "Go ahead."

"When our inside man, Weir, disappeared," Roz began, "he was being shot at by operators working for a private security firm based out of Zurich. Cross Executive Protection. Then, two weeks ago, we picked up another guy who worked for Cross, who'd been in another gunfight that Weir also was involved in."

"Except," Lyle added, "two weeks ago, the Cross operator was apparently trying to protect Weir. The day Weir disappeared, the Cross operators were trying to stop him."

The captain thought that over, then stated the obvious. "Weir made a deal with Cross and then reneged."

"He made a deal with someone," Lyle agreed. "Your line of work, ever hear of the MacCleirigh Foundation?"

Kingsburgh hadn't.

"Neither had we. Turns out, that's the entity that owns Cross, and it's the company's only client."

"Private army?" Kingsburgh asked.

"Close enough."

"What kind of foundation is it?"

"Scholarly research and such. Funds archaeological digs, university grants, museums . . . everything seems aboveboard."

"Seems?"

Lyle shrugged. "They have that private army. Or, at least, a private security force. And that force has some kind of connection to Weir."

"If you were running Weir as a way to get into Ironwood's organization, maybe Cross or their employees were doing the same. Weir's the pawn caught in the middle."

"If so," Lyle said, "here's the big question. Is the MacCleirigh Foundation trying to get to Ironwood to buy the SARGE database from him, or are they the ones who sold it to him in the first place?"

"You think a scholarly foundation is involved in international espionage?"

"There're so many left turns in this case, I don't know what to think. The Foundation's worth billions, tens of billions, so maybe that's how they make their money: buying and selling state secrets."

"Worth looking at," Kingsburgh suggested.

"We will." Lyle waited to see if the captain would say more, but he didn't. Time to move on. If Kingsburgh didn't have any secret store of classified knowledge to share . . .

The captain got the hint. "I'll check the rest of the drives. See if they missed erasing one." He headed for the cylindrical door to the sealed half of the room.

Roz gave Lyle a stern look.

"What now?" he asked.

"Some reason you didn't mention the elephant in the room?"

"Yes. I'd like to keep my reputation as a rational investigator."

"They're Ironwood's aliens, not yours. This is about what he believes, not you."

"It's a cover story, Roz. You know—Tony Soprano says he's going to pick up the cannolis, and he really means the illegal goods, to throw off the Feds."

"So what's Ironwood talking about with Weir if he's not talking about real aliens? Russians? Chinese? The Swiss?"

"You're not telling me *you* think aliens are real."

"What *I* think doesn't matter. What does matter is that Ironwood believes. Don't we have to start looking at this case from his perspective?"

"Fair enough," Lyle said. "So what do you think that is?"

"I think Ironwood *is* the end user of the database." Roz's eyes were bright as she made the most of her chance to persuade him to her way of thinking. "Think about it: He's obsessed with finding his alien outposts. He thinks they're thousands of years old—that's archaeological. The SARGE database, able to look underground, that's got to be a valuable archaeological tool, wouldn't you say? The MacCleirigh Foundation, they fund archaeological expeditions. So SARGE is valuable to Ironwood *and* the foundation—no enemy state need apply.

"What it comes down to is that maybe this isn't an espionage case. Maybe this is just some modern-day Indiana Jones and SARGE is this year's Holy Grail."

It was a good argument, but it wasn't on point.

"Whatever perspective you want to choose," Lyle cautioned, "the database is stolen government property, and each moment it's in the possession of someone other than the United States government, we're at risk."

"No argument."

"You could have fooled me."

"So . . . what do we do now?"

Lyle knew he had several options: He could attempt to interrogate the programmers at the table, but, since they'd already asked for their lawyer—

tellingly, the same one—there was obviously some kind of plan in place and none of them would be talking soon. He could wait to find out what Captain Kingsburgh might discover, provided Ironwood's people hadn't managed to erase every hard drive, but odds were they had. He could search Ironwood's other facilities—but, if there were other large computing installations in one or more of them, it was also a good bet they were already being disassembled.

"Only one thing we can do."

Roz gave him a sly smile, as if she knew what was coming.

"We need more information," Lyle said. "Geospatial has to identify the shoreline in that printout."

"And then . . . road trip?"

"Road trip."

THIRTY-FOUR

"I wonder what it was like." Jess spoke quietly, as if in church.

David stood beside her on the bluff overlooking the Atlantic Ocean. Fog and mist filled the morning air. A hundred feet down, they could just make out slow waves gently frothing against the dark stones of the rocky beach. Beyond that, only haze. Even the cries of seabirds were indistinct.

"When do you think it was built?" David asked.

First thing this morning, he and Jess had copied the coordinates from the printout they'd made in Boston to a topographical map. According to that, and their handheld GPS unit, they were standing over what Ironwood hoped would be an alien outpost and what Jess believed would be a Family temple. Whatever it actually was, the site, carved out of the shale of Cornwall, lay some ninety feet below them.

"Nine thousand years ago."

"Sea level would have been lower," David said. "Sixty feet, at least."

Jess flashed him a smile, as if he'd said something that amused her.

"What I meant was, how many people lived here? Were there ships? Piers? Festivals? Shops? What did it smell like? Did they have kilns for pottery? Ovens for bread? What was their world like?" Jess paused, as if overwhelmed by possibilities.

David offered his own approach to the unknown, distant past. "Well, their technology would be different, but the people would be just like us. Same emotions. Wants. Needs. Human nature doesn't change."

"The First Gods were different."

David let it go. He, Jess, and Ironwood were in the same boat. All seeking proof. All running out of time to find it.

"There!" Jess held her binoculars to her eyes, lenses pointed down to a bluff wall across a two-hundred-yard inlet.

They'd been walking along the pathways and cliff edges for over an hour, waiting for the fog to burn off. The ruins of Tintagel Castle proper, maintained as a tourist site, were a mile to the southwest of the temple's location, but here and there among the bluffs, clearly visible, were the remnants of stone walls and eroded steps. None was old enough to date back to the time of the temple, but David could see the effect they had on Jess. The Cornish site was more than a church to her. It was the Holy Land itself.

"David—there's a discontinuity in the strata! Twenty feet up, just to the left of the whitish splotch."

David aimed his binoculars at the cliff and saw the streak of white. "Above the three boulders?"

"That's it! You can see the slate and siltstone layers are interrupted by a conglomerate inclusion."

"The jumble of stones?"

"It's artificial."

David saw nothing but natural rock. He lowered the binoculars. "How can you tell?"

"Trust me, I'm a geologist."

"Seriously, Jess. How can you look at something that thousands of others have seen and tell it's artificial, when they haven't?"

"Because I can see igneous inclusions all through the local strata. Around here, the locals call those 'greenstone' or 'blue elvan.' So common no one notices them. That discontinuity down there? For the most part, it's no different from a thousand others along this part of the coast."

"For the most part?"

"Igneous rocks form from magma, so an igneous inclusion in Cornwall shale tends to be solid."

"So?"

"Look closely at that inclusion down there. It's not solid. It's a conglomerate—a mixture."

David lifted the binoculars again as Jess's voice directed him. "A long time ago, somebody could have filled a tunnel or cave with rubble or mine tailings or leftover quarry material. Over time, something cemented that filler, most likely minerals deposited by groundwater seepage. End result? It looks solid. For the most part. See it now?"

"Sort of." He returned the glasses to her. "Sealing something off? You're sure of that?"

"If I wasn't looking for it, I'd probably miss it," Jess admitted. "But remember, we've got this." She held up the topo map, folded to show the outline of the temple she had sketched on it. "See how it lines up?"

She turned the map so it became oriented to the view they faced. David nodded. "There's a tunnel there."

Jess's voice betrayed excitement rising. "Half of it's gone by now, collapsed with the shale as the bluff erodes. But five meters farther in, it should open into this main structure."

David preferred practicality to dreams. "Any idea how we get through five meters of 'conglomerate' without jack hammers and dynamite?"

"We don't have to." She gave him an odd look and tapped her finger along the edge of the sketch. "Look closer."

David looked across the inlet, made the connection.

"There's a cave."

By sunset, the sky was clear, an unbroken sweep of deepest blue, shading to black with a thin band of fiery red sketching the far horizon. The waves were little more than a slow pulse, no splashing. The scent of the Atlantic faint. Sea and land birds silent.

The only sound that David registered was the sharp click and clatter of stones struck by their sturdy workboots as he and Jess lugged their packs along the shoreline base of the bluff, having timed their approach to attract the least notice.

The grounds of Tintagel Castle closed at sunset, so there were few cars parked there, and no one else on the unlit scenic pathways to notice two figures in dark coveralls on the rocks below. There was just enough light left to reach what they'd seen that morning, without having to use their flashlights. The cave opening in the bluff was five feet above the high-tide line.

They dumped their gear on the stony ground. Two large backpacks with metal frames, and a smaller canvas bag.

David leaned against the near-vertical slope and made a stirrup with his hands to boost Jess up. As soon as she gained the opening, he tossed the packs and bag to her. A moment later, he scrambled up to join her.

The opening was six feet across and four feet high. Room enough to crouch, not stand.

In the falling light, they checked for watchers. Detected none.

Then they turned from the opening, pulled their flashlights from the packs, and switched them on. Guided by bright beams, they stayed low and moved deeper into darkness, their packs and the bag left behind for now.

They weren't the first explorers of the stone-strewn cave. David noted the empty Guinness beer cans, fast-food wrappers, broken glass, and other signs of assignations.

Twenty feet in, the cave suddenly expanded, and he and Jess both straightened up with relief. The rocky ceiling was at least a foot above their heads.

David took a deep breath, inhaling moist air, its sea scent concentrated. Jess consulted her electronic compass. The GPS unit didn't work here—no access to the positioning satellites.

"Are we close?"

"We are." Jess shone her flashlight ahead and up to the left. The circle of light it cast rippled over the rough walls to the ceiling. There was a dark shadowed band there, a gap.

She went to it, reaching up with a small knife to chip away at loose stones.

David heard a change in the sound of the knife's impacts just as she whispered, "There . . ."

His flashlight beam joined hers.

Jess rapped her knife point against a different type of stone. It was smooth, finished with a sharp edge.

"It's carved," she whispered.

David understood. "I'll get the packs," he said.

The work was tedious but not difficult; the shale loose and easily moved. After two hours of scrabbling and scraping, they had cleared enough away for Jess to worm her way through the opening between the cave and the tunnel.

David heard her muffled report. "It's clear." He pushed their packs through, then followed.

They rested for a few minutes, sitting on the floor. It was damp and cold.

David snapped two lightsticks, shook them to activate the chemicals inside, then threw them along the tunnel, one near, one far.

The near one revealed in pale green light a bowed wall near collapse, its carved stones bulging out, apparently held in place by thick deposits of some sort of mineral buildup that resembled thick ropes of melted wax. Similar accumulations threaded down the opposite wall of the narrow tunnel and from the ceiling.

It was evidence of Jess's earlier explanation. Millennia of groundwater seepage leaving its mark.

The far lightstick had landed beyond a mound of rubble from a section of wall and ceiling that *had* collapsed. Here, the passageway, though constricted, had just enough room for them to squeeze through.

In the reflected white light from his flashlight and the green glow from the lightstick, Jess's face was smudged by dirt and sweat, and her tightly braided hair was covered in stone chips and dust. But her eyes were bright, alive.

"We've never beaten Ironwood to a temple before," she said.

David selected a rugged Olympus digital camera, one of six that Jess had bought so they wouldn't have to fumble with swapping memory cards or downloading on-site. "We should start documenting this," he said. He shot the length of the corridor, the ceiling above, the relatively undamaged wall to one side, a detail of the stone blocks making up the uneven floor. By the time the first series was complete, both he and Jess were momentarily blinded by the multiple flashes. They waited another minute for their vision to recover, then continued.

Fifty feet farther and they found a branching.

David held the compass to align with the map as Jess focused her flashlight on the temple sketch. Vapor from their exhalations swirled through the beam of light. The still air was colder now, dense with moisture. Though clearly audible, all sound within the contained world of wet stones and rough textures had strikingly diminished echoes. Under other circumstances, David knew he'd have recorded this unique ambience to add to his collection. But that was then, not now.

"We're after this." Jess touched the image of a circular structure in the temple sketch. "Should be that way." She shone her flashlight along the left branch of the corridor. "A hundred feet or so."

The beam revealed a massive pile of debris. Closer than a hundred feet.

Jess activated another lightstick and dropped it on the floor.

They approached the rock pile.

Once again, David hoisted Jess up, and, flashlight in hand, she called back to him that the way was clear.

The first thing that struck him was that this time, sound echoed. The second—no sign of water damage on the other side. Not to the floor or walls or ceiling. David asked Jess if she could explain the change.

After easing once more into her backpack, she directed the beam of her flashlight to the ceiling. "Could be the strata above this part. If it's igneous, then it's impervious to groundwater compared to shale. Any water trickling down from the surface would hit it, then seep across it. It'd be moving toward the cliffs and the other damaged parts, leaving this section relatively dry."

She shone her flashlight along the floor and, without further word, moved ahead, quickening her pace.

David took a moment to sling his own backpack over one shoulder, grabbed the small canvas bag with the cameras, and hurried after her.

He caught up, about eighty feet along the way, where she'd halted, staring at the wall on their right.

David saw planked doors of old gray wood, warped and twisted, bound with rusted metal—and, directly opposite the doors, a second passage-way, a ninety-degree T-intersection.

"David, look. They're untouched . . . someone . . . someone closed these nine thousand years ago and . . ."

Jess's hand moved forward, then stopped as David reached out to re-strain her. "Better take some pictures first." The doors would never sur-vive being opened, and none of their tools and equipment could preserve something so old and fragile.

He pulled out the camera and quickly took another series, then cracked and shook a new lightstick and dropped it to the side. "Up to you now," he said.

Jess took a deep breath, then pushed gently on the left-hand door.

In near-silent slow motion, the soft rotted wood crumbled to the floor, the corroded metal beyond support.

Jess bit her lip but shone her flashlight ahead. Gasped. "It's there . . ."

She stepped through.

They were standing in a room that Jess had already described to him. David's flashlight beam now doubled hers, illuminating the circular space, which was perhaps twenty-five feet across. At its center was the table—a disk of stone eight feet wide on a central stone support just over three feet high. Carved lines divided the tabletop into twelve equal wedges, and in each wedge was a different indentation. All were empty.

Jess brushed the dust from one hollowed-out space, touching its angu-lar shape, two branching lines. "We're too late. Again." She couldn't hide her disappointment.

David played his flashlight over the encircling wall and saw something unexpected. "You didn't tell me about this."

Jess looked up. "A map . . ."

"Of what?" The image at first glance didn't make sense to David.

"The world!" Jess's voice rose in wonder. "See?" She directed her flashlight at one spot on the wall. "There's Africa, but it's upside down. Putting north at the top of a map is just a convention, and whoever drew this chose the other way."

Together, they turned slowly in a circle. As their twinned flashlight beams swept over the entire wall, the map was revealed in colors seemingly as bright as the day they'd been painted into the plaster. Brown and green for land, blue for water, with smooth arcs of black and red lines crossing oceans.

"A map of the world? From nine thousand years ago?" David swung his flashlight's beam around to what was clearly the Mediterranean, but a

Mediterranean in which Sicily was a continuation of the Italian boot, instead of a separate island. Other parts of the continental outlines seemed equally crude and imperfectly detailed, though if the map were in fact that old, he couldn't fault its lack of precision.

"It has to be," Jess said. "There . . . what's that?" The beam of her flashlight moved in, wavered, and David saw Western Europe, and its extension—England, still attached. And on the southwesternmost tip of that extension—

"Cornwall," David said. Then he saw something more. A mark on their approximate location. Two intersecting blades topped by a circle. Like the cross that Jess had given him. She saw it, too.

"Our sign, David . . . This *was* built by our—"

David grabbed for her flashlight, switched it off along with his.

Footsteps.

THIRTY-FIVE

Merrit shone his flashlight and aimed his gun along the damp and dis-integrating passageway as J.R. trudged up behind him. "I need to see it," Merrit said, suppressing his irritation. He'd underestimated the enemy in the South Pacific, not anticipating the MacCleirighs would pay his divers to betray him. Ironwood's son wasn't a competent associate, but at least he couldn't be bribed.

J.R. swore, voice shaking with cold, as he pulled the sheet of paper from his Windbreaker.

Frank Beyoun had produced the printout before Merrit had perma-nently relieved him of the inconvenience of being arrested with the rest of the Red Room team. It showed the outline of one of Ironwood's alien outposts over a close-up of the ground surface high above them now.

Merrit studied the map to confirm his plan. The dead-end passageway from the opening in the bluffs was the only easily accessible point of entry for the entire outpost complex. Weir and the MacClary girl weren't armed, and there was nowhere they could hide. Their glowing lightsticks also marked their trail.

Merrit turned off his flashlight. This would be over very soon.

Then it wouldn't matter how much noise J.R. made.

Lit only by the green chemical radiance of the lightstick in the passage-way, David held up his hand to signal silence, listening.

"Two people," he whispered. "First passage. Before the branch."

"The lightsticks lead right to us," Jess whispered back.

"Any idea who it is?"

"Ironwood? Who else would have a map of this place?"

David knew. He spoke softly, urgently. "Merrit's here to kill us."

Jess immediately unzipped the top of her coveralls and reached inside for a small pistol.

David was startled. "How'd you get that?" They'd carried nothing but a few quickly purchased clothes and toilet articles on their flight to En-gland. There was no possible way that gun would have escaped detection.

Jess didn't answer. She was already edging toward the open doorway. David stayed with her.

The sound of rocks scattering created an instant mental image for him of Merrit and his accomplice pushing through the large debris pile. They'd be here in a minute. David glanced behind him. The details of the wall map were being swallowed as the lightstick faded, sapped of its strength by the cold floor. "Jess," he said as quietly as he could, "is there another way out of this chamber?"

She shook her head.

More stones fell. Running footsteps now. Past the rocks. No flashlights. Guided by the dying lightsticks. David had a sudden thought. "We could blind them."

"For a second, maybe."

"Enough to run down one of the other two corridors?"

"*If* there're no other obstructions—they both go two hundred feet straight before they hit another branch. No cover."

"You could shoot first."

Jess nodded, and David realized she'd already planned to do that.

A foot scraped loudly; someone cursed. Loudly.

David knew the voice. "J.R.—Ironwood's son," he breathed.

"How close?"

He cocked his head, intent. "Twenty feet."

"Ready at ten," Jess whispered back. "Hold the flashlight as far to the side as you can."

David held up the flashlight and silently began the count. *Nineteen, eighteen, seventeen . . .*

Merrit stopped, his free hand raised to make J.R. hold position. He took a moment to attain situational awareness. He smiled as he saw the green lightstick lying on the floor. Ironwood's treasure room would be ahead and to the right, and the tunnel—duplicating the one he'd swum through in the Pacific—would be on the left, directly opposite the entrance to that room.

He guessed—no, he *knew*—that his quarry was already in the chamber, and it would be wise to assume they'd heard him approaching. Or, to be more realistic, that they'd heard J.R.

Not that that would change anything. Weir was a civilian, and thus unskilled. The MacClary girl, though, had turned out to be more of a problem than expected. She'd survived J.R.'s ill-considered grab in Canada and fought back well in Weir's lab.

Merrit considered the situation from her perspective. She had the same map he did, so she'd know there was no escape route. *When we get close enough, she'll leap out and start shooting,* he decided. Maybe, for the advantage of a second or two, she'd try to blind him with a flashlight as well.

Covering his left eye with the palm of his hand, Merrit told J.R. to do the same but not to move until ordered. Then he put his back against the wall and slowly and silently began to advance again, his Glock 9 mm leading the way.

Sun Tzu, a thousand years earlier, had summed it up best: In a situation such as this, with no possible escape, an adversary could only fight to the death.

Merrit asked for nothing more.

Ten . . .

David held his breath to improve his hearing. *No footsteps.* Either Merrit had stopped at about fifteen feet, or he was moving forward with exceptional care.

He lightly touched Jess's arm, pointed to his ear, shook his head. She'd have to risk making the first move. They couldn't wait for Merrit and J.R. to suddenly appear in the doorway.

Jess held up her left hand, two fingers and a thumb.

David nodded, understanding. *A silent count of three.*

She folded in her thumb first, then a finger.

He tensed to lunge.

The first explosion struck the corridor.

The force of the blast blew Merrit and J.R. backward.

Merrit hit the stone floor hard, any sound of the impact lost in the deafening thunderclap that reverberated around and through him.

His first thought was that the girl had gone insane. That she was destroying her temple so Ironwood couldn't claim it.

His second thought was for his gun. The Glock was no longer in his hand.

In the dark and dust-filled chamber, David and Jess scrambled to their feet. David held his hands to cup his ears, still ringing from the explosion. Jess held her hands over her mouth, trying to stifle coughs.

They swayed on their feet as another explosion shook the ancient chamber. Something metallic dropped to the floor from high overhead and, unseen in the darkness, clattered like a spinning coin.

"This is deliberate." Jess's voice was tight with fear. Not for her life, David knew, but for the loss of this place, this echo of her family. *My family, too?* "But who? It can't be Merrit. Ironwood wants this place as much as we do."

"Who else knows about the temples?"

The thunder of a third explosion assailed them, its impact different from the other two. This time, not all its energy was channeled through the corridors. David began to build a sound image. Someone was blasting in, forcing a different opening.

Jess was horror-struck. "Take pictures, David! Fast as you can. We have to make a record!" Jess rushed back to the door, gun held ready.

David sprang into action. The first three sites had all been looted, without artifacts and ornamentation. But in this one, the ornamentation, the world map, was pristine. If the chamber didn't survive tonight's attack, then at least the information in it would.

He found their packs and pulled out a fresh camera. Standing with his back against the stone table, he began taking photos swiftly, moving the camera to the right a few degrees after every flash. He went all the way around the room, capturing the map.

"Ceiling!" Jess said.

David looked up, snapped a flash, then checked the image on the camera's display.

The chamber's roof was hemispherical, like a planetarium dome, but studded with metallic disks, silver. They'd flared in the lens flash.

He grabbed a second camera, chose a setting to reduce the flare, completed a full sweep of the ceiling.

Now for close-ups of the map. David picked up a third camera, realized he'd need more light. He held a lightstick up. "Jess . . . I have to see the map."

"Do it!"

He cracked the lightstick, shook it. Looked for Cornwall. Found it.

He snapped a close-up of the bladed-cross mark, the sign that showed where to find . . .

He paused, stood back, then moved the lightstick across the mural on the wall. *There.* Another bladed cross on an island in the Mediterranean. *And there.* In sub-Saharan Africa.

The thud of boots. Shouting. *German?* "Jess—"

She twisted around, gun in hand, her silhouette wreathed in green-glowing dust motes. "Did you get it?"

"Yes!" David stuffed all the cameras he'd used into his coverall pockets, discarding the canvas bag and backpack, leaving nothing that would identify them. Protein bars, water bottles, digging tools, batteries, a first aid kit . . . everything was expendable except for the memory cards in the cameras.

"Did you get it *all*?"

"Yes! Jess, we have to go." *They were almost here. Couldn't she hear them? At least eight* . . . David shook his head. His ears still thrummed with the white-noise rush of the explosions. There could be more than eight . . .

A glint of something metallic on the floor caught his eye. It was the source of the coinlike sound he'd heard when the second explosion shook the walls. One of the ceiling disks had dislodged. He picked it up, then ran to Jess, still by the doorway. He heard the nearby sound of whispers, the rustling of heavy fabric, the click of metal . . .

This time she heard them, too. "The lightstick!"

David berated himself for not thinking of it first, sprinted back for it, and shoved it inside his coveralls, restoring protective darkness.

The other lightstick they'd left outside had been shifted by the explosion, but it still glowed and lit the entrance to the intersecting passageway.

"This is where they'll come first," Jess said, her lips by his ear. "We have to find someplace else to hide." She pointed to the other passage.

Neither he nor Jess had checked it. No way to know if it was blocked or clear.

"On three?"

David nodded.

Gunfire.

⸻

Merrit and J.R. were crouched in darkness, even the outlines of their bodies hidden by the rock pile behind them, beyond the reach of the glow from the lightstick at the entrance of the treasure room.

"We gotta get outta here!" J.R. started to get up, but Merrit grabbed his shoulder, forced him back down. Merrit knew exactly what was happening; he just didn't know who was behind it. Whoever had blasted their way in here wasn't interested in preserving anything or anyone. It was doubtful they'd leave witnesses.

He threw a lightstick over the mound of debris he and J.R. had just scaled, and its light winked out on the other side, safely out of sight. The water-damaged passageway beyond led back to the small opening in the bluff. That would be his escape route. By using explosives to blast through from the other side, the intruders had revealed they didn't know about the shoreline cave.

"First we get Weir. Then we go."

"What about the girl?"

"She can't deliver your father to the Feds."

"My father's safe?!"

It was true. Ironwood's escape, long planned and often rehearsed, had gone off like clockwork. The moment Merrit's inside source from the Atlantic City police alerted him to the staging of an interdepartmental task force at police headquarters preparing a raid on Encounters, Merrit had roused Ironwood and the helicopter pilot kept on standby to ferry VIPs and whales between the casino and local airports.

Twenty minutes later—more than an hour before the raid began— Ironwood was on his way to Philadelphia International on the resort's Sikorsky. By the time Encounters was surrounded, Ironwood was airborne in a private 777. As much as his employer hated flying, it was preferable to prison, and the jet had the range to take him beyond reach of the U.S. government.

All of these precautionary moves were simply a holding action— denying the government the advantage of surprise. Ironwood could only stay away from the day-to-day operations of his business empire for so long. Nor would Ironwood's empire remain an empire for long if the government announced the billionaire had been charged with theft of classified military computer assets.

Merrit felt vindicated. He'd predicted that Weir would be turned by the air force investigators, and that's precisely what had happened.

But Ironwood's son was thinking of himself as usual. "So if my father's safe . . ."

"Only for a few days," Merrit cautioned. "Maybe less if the Feds go public. But when I get rid of Weir, that threat's over."

"We have to kill the girl, too."

"Why?"

"She knows too much."

"About what?" Merrit asked. Then he heard running up ahead, commands shouted in what sounded to be German.

"Who the hell is that?" J.R. said.

Merrit was already on his feet, rushing forward. "Stay here!" He sensed movement far along the corridor straight ahead and, more from instinct than rational thought, fired three times into the darkness, then dove to the ground fast and hard as an answering volley of automatic fire sprayed overhead, sparking and ricocheting off the walls.

The instant the volley ended, Merrit darted forward again, firing as he rolled to the side, just avoiding a burst that stitched across the floor where he'd been moments before.

He was past the dimming lightstick now, the entrance to the treasure room on his right. The opening on his left was closer.

Merrit fired twice more, then threw himself into the intersecting corridor as more bullets whined past him. He positioned himself with his back to the far wall and assessed his situation. To his right was the passageway that duplicated the one he'd swum through in the South Pacific. To his left, across the width of the passageway he'd just escaped, was the entrance to the treasure chamber. At his back were the shooters. Somewhere in the direction he faced was J.R.—presuming he'd survived the gunfire.

Merrit dropped the magazine from his Glock but caught it to avoid making noise. He quietly slipped another into place. His eyes were becoming accustomed to the almost complete absence of light. The faintest of pale green rays still shone from the almost exhausted lightstick that lay a few feet back in the direction from which he'd come.

A harsh voice called out, echoing against the stones. "Throw out your weapon and you won't come to harm!"

Merrit risked a glance into the intersection, keeping alert for sounds of movement.

In that glance he saw, in the doorway leading to the treasure room, two silhouettes in the watery green light.

Weir and the MacClary girl.

David yanked Jess back from the entrance. "It's Merrit!"

"Throw out your weapon!" the harsh voice in the corridor called again.

The unknown gunmen were edging forward, along the wall that led to the half-open doorway to the chamber.

"Did he see us?" Jess whispered.

"Couldn't miss us."

"But the others, they don't know we're here."

"Maybe. Can't be sure."

"So we stay quiet, hope Merrit draws their attention, and—"

Sudden scuffling, a round of automatic gunfire, a dark shape hurtling toward them.

Now they weren't the only ones inside the chamber.

Merrit rolled back to his knees and held his Glock on his hostages.

"Put your guns on the floor—very slowly—then slide them away."

"If we had them, you'd be dead." That was MacClary. Weir didn't speak.

Merrit wondered if J.R.'s silence down the passageway meant he'd caught a bullet. Could be good news all around.

He got up, gun held steady. "Okay," he said. "New orders. You're going to charge across that passage when I say. I'll cover you."

"I can't outrun a bullet."

"Theirs or mine. Your choice."

Merrit allowed himself a smile. His plan could work. Since the gunmen didn't know about the entrance to the cave, they couldn't know these two were in here. They'd be expecting J.R. or him. So when Weir stepped into the corridor . . . Merrit smiled again. The other shooters would do his work for him, and when they came in to check the body, that's when he'd have them.

"Get ready to run." Merrit stepped back so he could see directly out the doorway. Weir was standing, his back to the wall. The girl was still hunched over on the floor beside him.

Merrit saw movement, shifted his gaze. The girl had reached up to hold Weir's hand.

"Now!"

Weir turned his head suddenly and ducked down to cover Jessica Mac-Clary with his body. In the seconds it took Merrit to wonder why, the grenade landed in the corridor outside the entrance and—

Seconds after he heard the rustle of the thrown grenade, the thunderclap of its explosion deadened David's hearing to a high-pitched whine. Simultaneously, he saw Merrit thrown back as if a wave of light had crashed over him.

Merrit hit the stone table, and his limp body sprawled across it, unmoving.

The sudden wall of heat was startling, sucking the air from David's lungs. He could feel Jess clawing at his chest to pull out the lightstick he had hidden in his coveralls.

She scrabbled to her feet and held the lightstick up, lips moving. David couldn't hear a word. Only the whine.

Jess pointed to the entranceway. Carved stone blocks. Loose shale.

It was collapsing.

David reached for her hand, and together they ran through the doorway. No flash of gunshots met them.

Left or right? Or straight ahead?

David squinted down the corridor to the right. Thick billows of dust were lit by wild flashlight beams that swung back and forth like swords of light through a waterfall of falling rock. Whoever was responsible for the explosions, they'd blasted through from the other side, not come in from the shore. There was no escape in that direction, and the T-intersection ahead was a complete unknown.

The only path remaining was the way they'd come.

He and Jess ran to the left, stopping only when they saw a body, face-down, before the pile of rocky debris. David started to reach for the body, to turn it over. A flash of light. Another. Something sparking.

Jess's hand was on his shoulder. He saw her lips move, read her urgent words. *They're shooting! Run!*

Leaving the body unexamined, they scrambled up and over the debris pile, falling down the other side. They stumbled down the damp, chill passageway until—

The slightest perceptible sounds began to penetrate the still-persistent whine in David's ears. A far-off rumble. Creaking stones. The whisper of an ocean breeze. They'd reached the tunnel to the inlet cave.

Jess first, then David, dove headfirst through the slick, wet opening, leading down to where they could run again. Where the rocky ceiling became too low, they crawled forward on their hands and knees.

The air quickened, fresh, alive, from the sea outside. David saw pale moonlight shine through the narrow opening just ahead.

He felt a warning hand on his shoulder and turned to see Jess hold a finger to her lips as she pushed the lightstick back into the pocket of his overalls. Next, still on her stomach, she eased past him, until she was just inside the opening, looking out.

A moment later, she relaxed and waved him forward.

It was safe.

Dropping five feet to the broken shale below, they landed on the shore beneath the bluff.

Jess grabbed David. *The cameras?* she mouthed. *Do you have them?*

David patted his pockets. *Yes,* he nodded.

They ran again.

THIRTY-SIX

It was raining. The rocks underfoot were soaked and slippery. And though local time was three thirty-five in the afternoon, Jack Lyle was still on Eastern Daylight Time and starting to think of dinner and bed. He hadn't slept on the red-eye from Kennedy to Heathrow, but the journey had brought him to the coastline on the printout identified by the National Geospatial-Intelligence Agency. Cornwall.

"Any of this making sense?" Roz asked.

She held a large black umbrella for both of them. They each wore a bright yellow rain jacket with a checkerboard band of reflective tape, courtesy of the Devon-Cornwall Constabulary. The umbrella kept the rain off, but the wild waves crashing not twenty feet away created mist and spray that went everywhere.

The local police were inured to these conditions—the rain hadn't slowed them. They'd done an exemplary job of securing the site of . . . whatever this had been.

Fifty feet along the stony shoreline, at the base of a near-vertical cliff, yawned the jagged edges of a huge hole created by explosives. It had been cordoned off by traffic-control barricades and yellow tape, as had a second explosive opening in the cliff wall, higher up and another twenty feet farther away. Police and a hired civilian crew were now moving in and out of both openings, digging through the rubble to get some idea of what had happened here and why. They'd already brought out a number of carved stone blocks, and the police had called in local historians, still in transit.

"You tell me," Lyle said. "It's definitely not a secret military installation."

"Still, someone used military assets to find the underground structure inside that cliff," Roz said.

"Someone?" Lyle mopped beaded moisture from his face. "How about David Weir and the woman he's with? Or Ironwood's outfit?"

"But they all wanted to find whatever's in there. Real bad. So why would they try to blow it up?"

"Doesn't look like they *tried*, Roz. Looks like they blew it up real good."

"Which could mean there's a third party involved."

"I really wish you hadn't said that."

"Because that's what you're thinking, too, right?"

"Right."

Roz sniffed, then wiped her own face free from spray. "Which could confirm Ironwood stole the SARGE database for his own use—"

"As you so helpfully suggested."

"—and not to sell it to our nation's enemies, of which there are so many."

"Just because he has his own use for it doesn't mean he doesn't plan to sell it. And remember, he's altered it some way, to add more detail. Could be Ironwood's so keen to find his . . ." Lyle couldn't bring himself to say it.

Roz could. "Alien bases?"

"Yeah, those. Could be he's made a deal with the devil. Or *a* devil, at least."

"So what about party number three? Someone's blowing up those bases. Who might that be?"

Lyle tried to focus his thoughts as pragmatically as possible. "In the real world, which would be the one I inhabit, it could be whoever it is who wants the database for themselves, and wants to hide the fact that SARGE can be used to find underground complexes." He looked at his partner, knew what was coming. "And in your world?"

"Simple. Someone already knows what the alien bases are and doesn't want Ironwood to find them."

Lyle was too tired and too cold to play the game anymore. "Do you honestly believe that's what's in there?" He looked down the rocky shore to the first explosive opening. Most of the police were gathered there now. Two were on radios. Something had caught their attention. "Something built by aliens?"

"Honestly?" Roz asked.

"Preferably."

"If the aliens are smart enough to get from wherever they live to where we live . . . and they really don't want us to know they were here . . . then they're smart enough to do a better job at hiding their bases. I don't have any idea what's in there, or who built it, but it's homegrown."

Lyle studied her closely "So that's not an alien base."

She shook her head. Drops of water fell enchantingly from her soaked hair.

"Yet you still believe in aliens."

Roz smiled.

Lyle sighed. He felt his phone vibrate, fumbled with the police rain-coat, pulled out the buzzing device in time, answered.

"Agent Lyle, it's Colonel Kowinski."

"Yes, Colonel?" Lyle made a point of leaning close to Roz so she could hear the conversation. Roz rolled her eyes, hit a button.

Kowinski's voice was now on speakerphone. Who knew?

". . . the nonhuman DNA," Kowinski said, then paused as if expecting a response.

"Say again, Colonel. You broke up."

"I said, my team has been able to identify the source of the nonhuman DNA in the files that David Weir stole."

"Okay, I got that. Neanderthal?"

"Not even close. The source is David Weir. He was sequencing his own DNA."

"Colonel, are you telling me . . ." Lyle hesitated, searching for the appropriate words.

Roz had no such trouble. "Colonel Kowinski, Agent Marano here. Are you saying David Weir isn't human?"

The colonel's reply was characteristically brusque and noncommittal. *"I'm staying out of any interpretation of these results. All I'll go on the record with is to say that Weir's genetic structure contains sequences that are not typically found in the human genetic code."*

Lyle waved Roz off, found his voice. "And off the record, Colonel? Can you give us anything more to go on?"

"Off the record . . ." There was a long pause, enough to make Lyle check the phone's display to be sure it was still connected. *"Off the record, he doesn't have a human genetic structure—and he's not the only one."*

Lyle put it together as quickly as that. "The other files he was selling, they're for people with the same sort of . . . wonky DNA?"

"He found thirty—out of three million."

This time, Roz held up a hand to seek permission to speak next. Lyle nodded.

"Colonel, Marano here again. Is there any way to figure out where the anomalous DNA came from? Can you be sure it's not just some kind of random mutation?"

"Let me be clear about this, Agent Marano, any mutation that shows up in thirty different families from four different locations isn't random. I don't know where it came from. And, second, unless someone *can give me clearance to bring in some outside specialists, I can't even go looking."*

"I understand," Lyle said. "Let me get back to you, Colonel. And thank you."

"I'll be here." The call clicked off.

Lyle didn't want to consider the implications of what the colonel had found, but he knew he had to. As crazy as it was, could there be any connection at all in this case to extraterrestrials?

Roz apparently guessed what he was wrestling with. "Y'know, *we* don't have to have an opinion about aliens for this investigation. All we need to know is what Ironwood's opinion is, and that's pretty well established."

She was right, and Lyle felt embarrassed to admit it. He hadn't been tasked to solve a bigger mystery here. His job was to find the SARGE database, keep it from falling into enemy hands, and arrest the people responsible for its theft. After that, Roz and Kowinski could play *X-Files* to their hearts' content. For himself, he planned to go fishing.

He made his decision. "Trail's gone cold here. We catch the next flight back home and focus on the interrogation of Ironwood's computer team."

"Works for me," Roz said.

Lyle handed her his phone. "Make the arrangements."

Before Roz could place the call, two paramedics hurried past them, boots crunching on the rocks. They were carrying a folded stretcher toward a knot of workers and police by the cliff opening.

"Someone hurt?" Lyle asked.

"Someone in the rubble," one called out as they rushed by.

Lyle and Roz exchanged a glance and fell quickly in behind them. Roz struggled to close the big black umbrella, failed, tossed it aside.

They arrived on the scene just as a dirt-covered body was carefully lowered down the cliff face to the waiting police and paramedics.

The body twitched, alive.

Lyle pushed through the police beside the stretcher and flashed his badge. "You know him?" an officer asked.

Even through the dirt and blood, Lyle did. "Don't book that flight," he told Roz. "We're staying."

On the stretcher before him was an asset better than David Weir. Someone even closer to Ironwood and his illegal activities.

His son.

THIRTY-SEVEN

"What now?" Jess asked as she moved her chair closer to David's. Twenty-four hours ago, she and this man had been in yet another race for their lives, this time along the rocky shore of Cornwall, and she still couldn't say she knew anything about him. Nor why, the night before that, it had seemed so natural to share her secrets with him and give him her cross. The only explanation had to be that he *was* Family.

The computer screen in front of David was three feet across, its colors intense. The small workroom was quiet, the air-conditioning cool. The absence of windows added to the almost cocoonlike environment. The room was designed for optimal concentration on the work at hand: usually geological mapping, but now archaeological reconstruction.

"All the photos are loaded in from the memory cards," David said. "We'll sort through them, pick the best ones, then have the software stitch them together to make a seamless image."

He began typing on the computer's elaborate keyboard, and the screen displayed a rich green backdrop on which the corporate logo of Haldron Oil appeared to float. Haldron was one of dozens of energy conglomerates that based their headquarters in Aberdeen, and unquestioned access to their facilities had been easy to arrange. Not because of the Family's influence, but because of Jess's own. She'd been on assignment for Haldron in the Barrens.

On her rushed flight to Zurich, just one month ago, she'd dictated her report on the nature and origin of the buried bodies found by the company's Arctic pipeline crew. Charlie Ujarak's wishes notwithstanding, the early North Americans who'd lived in that long-vanished village were not related to the contemporary Inuit population of the region.

That report had saved Haldron Oil both time and money, on the order of months and millions. It also hadn't hurt that Haldron's project manager, Lionel Kurtz, had formally credited Jess with saving his life. She didn't care about being thanked. She was just relieved he hadn't died because of her.

"Here goes," David said. "Tell me when to stop."

Jess moved closer to the screen. The images they were about to see, no one had seen for thousands of years. There could be nothing more important for her. For the Family.

David tapped through three overexposed photos until he came to the first image of the wall map. The hair on the back of Jess's neck bristled. It was an exquisite piece of artwork, the colors pure and the execution polished. There was nothing primitive about it.

"Those lines crossing the oceans," David said as they worked, "they could be shipping routes."

Jess had been thinking the same thing.

"So, my question is, is this a map made by a culture that managed to chart the entire globe about nine thousand years before Europeans did, and history somehow forgot about it?"

"My family didn't forget," Jess said.

"No, really, Jess. To map the entire world by ship, that's the work of generations. Hundreds of voyages, at least. Maybe thousands if you think of all the ways ships can be lost at sea." He lifted an eyebrow. "I know your *Traditions* say the First Gods were advanced, but this advanced?"

"The *Traditions* tell us the First Gods scattered us to the Twelve Winds. They don't say how. But it makes sense if we went by sailing ships—they're wind-powered."

"And then what? All your ships sank?"

"All our ships . . . left."

"To the White Island." David studied the image on the screen. "Do you think that's on this map?"

Jess found she couldn't answer, but that was exactly what she hoped. Of the eight temples remaining to be located, there was still a chance to find a table that held all twelve lost artifacts. Before Su-Lin and Andrew could destroy them.

David tried another way to break her silence. "I admit I don't know a lot about history."

"But?"

"Some people think we were preceded by an earlier, more advanced civilization, that it was wiped out by a global catastrophe, and that became the source of our legends of a universal flood. What if that's what happened to your family's First Gods?"

"You're talking about the Sea Kings," Jess said. Every member of the Family was aware of history's fringe theories describing a fantastical advanced society in the dim past, if only because some of those theories owed their origins to certain misremembered stories of the Family itself. "Sometimes they're called Atlanteans."

"As in the Lost Continent?"

"Exactly. But you can file those stories with Ironwood's aliens. There's no solid geological record of a global catastrophe in historical times. Not even in the Family's records."

"What about all those mammoths flash-frozen in Siberia?"

"Urban myth," Jess said. "Lots of mammoth carcasses in Siberia, but—without exception—there's significant decay. All that's left is bone and tusks, hide and hair. There's never been a perfectly preserved find. That young mammoth they dug up on television a few years back? It froze before rotting because predators had torn it open and eaten its internal organs. Wasn't much more than a shell."

"Then how about a huge meteor or comet impact?"

"Again, lots of those in historical times, but most impacts cause localized effects, not global."

"You said 'most.' So some aren't?"

This was her territory of expertise. "There's a good case for a series of significant impacts eight to ten thousand years ago. Some of them might be connected—parts of the same body, a shattered comet or meteor, striking different locations at almost the same time. Others . . . well, their timings are too far apart to be anything other than individual events.

"But there is one well-documented impact that took place about twelve thousand nine hundred years ago. Something big detonated over the Great Lakes region of North America. Some say it coincides with what's called the Younger Dryas—an anomalous cooling period that lasted over a thousand years in the northern hemisphere. Sort of a localized version of nuclear winter. There's evidence to suggest that particular climate change was responsible for disrupting the continent's Clovis culture."

She stopped to explain. "They're the first people to establish themselves in historically significant numbers in North America."

David was still with her. "But it took a thousand years?"

Jess nodded. "The cooling lasted that long. Clovis culture probably collapsed over a generation or two."

"So not an instant catastrophe?"

"Well, there's suggestive evidence of huge fires in regions that were close to the projected impact point. But overall? No, not instant, at least, not in the way other impacts affected other people."

"So, if there was no global disaster to wipe out the First Gods, what do you think happened to them?"

"They didn't vanish without warning. The *Traditions* say that they *told* us they were leaving. To go to the White Island. And they promised to come back. They just didn't say when."

"Or why."

Jess hesitated. David couldn't know he'd just touched on the real mystery of the Family. One that had cost Florian her life—and threatened his, and hers. "Or why," she agreed.

Thankfully, David's attention was back on the image of the ancient map. "What we do know is that they marked the location of the Cornwall temple on this. And I saw the same cross on an island in the Mediterranean, in Africa, India . . . I know there were others, but I didn't see everything I shot. Who knows what else they marked?"

"Only one way to find out," Jess said.

David pressed the key to start the program.

In less than a minute, the Haldron mainframe quilted together sixty-seven separate images. The completed picture—an extraordinary world view—filled the screen side to side.

The first thing David did was click on the command that rotated the image, so that north would be at the top.

"Where do we start?"

Jess took a deep breath, excited, apprehensive. "Cornwall."

David expanded that section of the map, and they began. In less than twenty minutes the two of them completed the work of lifetimes. Twelve temples around the world.

"Anything else?" David asked.

In addition to the four already known, the digitally preserved map showed the same bladed cross marking a location on Malta, two in Africa, and one each in Tibet, Indonesia, the American Southwest, the tip of South America, and the maritime region of Canada. Red lines drew connections to all of the temple locations accessible by sea. Black lines marked overland routes and linked ports, none of which were temples. The map showed more than forty separate locations on those routes.

However, beyond the twelve temples marked with the bladed cross, there was no thirteenth site that suggested the location of White Island.

"Jess, what language were the *Traditions* written in? Originally, I mean."

"The earliest one we know of is in cuneiform, like I said. Before that, we're not sure. But, whatever written language it was that the First Gods gave us, it's most likely the source of all the other written languages that appeared around the world, all at the same time. Same thing for agriculture. The fertile triangle in the Middle East, rice cultivation in China . . . agriculture began around the world, all at the same time. Standing stone observatories. All of those things are their gifts to us."

"Right." David drummed his fingers beside the keyboard. "What I was wondering was, is there any chance 'White Island' could be a mis-translation, or have other meanings?"

"It's not quite that simple." A strange thought struck Jess. This was like a children's lesson, one she had had to learn herself. Because the term it-self didn't come just from the *Traditions*. David had asked her earlier how her Family had managed to keep all their secrets, and the truth was, they hadn't.

"In some ways, if you think about it, my Family's really not so different. Lots of cultures tell the story of how they were given gifts by mysterious visitors. The Aztec legends say that strangers came from a place called Aztlan. That's been translated as 'White Island.' The dwelling place of Hindu yogis with supreme knowledge was called Shveta-Dvipa. That also means 'White Island.' And the Tibetans—they believe a 'White Island' will be the only part of the world to escape disaster because it's the eternal land. So it's not just us."

David wheeled around to stare at her, as if she'd just said something striking. "But land's not eternal, is it?"

"Sorry?"

"You know what's wrong with this map?"

"It's not precise?" Jess could see that. How could it be, given the age of it and the conditions under which the First Gods had charted the world? Of course it couldn't match modern cartographic techniques.

"Maybe the differences aren't a matter of precision." His face alight with some idea, David turned back to the map on the screen, touching it as he spoke. "England joined to Europe. Sicily joined to Italy." He glanced back at her. "At Cornwall, the sea level nine thousand years ago would've been at least sixty feet lower. So how low would it have to be for the world to look like this map?"

Jess thought back to her most basic introductory courses in geology. "Well, England and the continent were definitely joined by a land bridge. Another twenty to twenty-five feet down would be enough to expose it—but that would've been another thousand years or so even earlier than that map. Sicily and Italy, I'm not sure. Whenever they were last joined, it could be a function of sea level, or of earthquakes, or some combination of both."

"So we've got a map that's obviously important. It shows the location of the temples, but not the White Island. And it seems to be based on charts that were prepared at least a thousand years prior to it being painted on that wall."

Jess couldn't tell what he was driving at, if he was driving at anything. "That's *if* our assumptions of dating are correct. Maybe the temples were built nine thousand *eight* hundred years ago. Then there's not as much difference between the time the charts were drawn up and the map was painted."

"Still, there'd be a difference, Jess, and if they were making charts over, let's say a few centuries, then the mapmakers would have to have been aware of a pretty significant rise in sea level over that time."

Jess still didn't get it. "Okay . . ."

"So the land isn't eternal. *This* map's going to go out of date."

"This map? There's another?" Jess looked at the screen again, wondering what she had missed. "Is it painted over something? Like a palimpsest?"

David grinned, almost as if he were teasing her again. "Not over something. *Under* it." He reached into his pocket, but before he had brought out what he was searching for, Jess had it.

"The dome," she said. "The disks on the ceiling are a star map." The name had been there all along. "*That's* why it's called the Chamber of Heaven!"

David held out the metal ceiling disk he'd retrieved from the chamber floor. It had eight tacklike points on one side, presumably to hold it in place in the plaster. On the other side, it was simply a highly polished disk of some silvery metal that remarkably hadn't tarnished.

"To make a map of the world as good as this, your ancestors would have to know navigation, which means they'd have to be good astronomers."

"The sun map," Jess said. Her thoughts tumbled over one another. "Carved on the meteorite. They *knew* the planets orbit the sun. They *knew* Jupiter had moons, that Saturn had a ring."

David nodded. "To see the moons and the ring, they had to have telescopes at least the equal of Galileo's. They also had some pretty good math to work out the orbits."

He laid the disk on the desktop beside the keyboard, used a trackball to move the map to one side, and started typing.

"Let's put together the photos of the ceiling map."

David's next words made Jess forget their need to outrun the ruthless killers who were after them.

"You know, if we can figure out a date for when that map was made . . . when we see the pattern of the ceiling stars, we should be able to figure out where you'd have to be to see them."

"A location," Jess said. Then David said what she was thinking.

"Maybe *the* location. White Island."

THIRTY-EIGHT

"What's the plan?" Roz asked. "Good Cop, Bad Cop? Or Bad Cop, Worse Cop?"

"Not necessary. I think this one's going to be easy." Lyle peered through the glass partition into the infirmary of the Lakenheath RAF Base, home of the U.S. Air Force 48th Fighter Wing. On the only occupied bed inside, Holden Ironwood Jr. was patched up and on a morphine drip.

"Famous last words."

"Watch and learn, Roz. And don't let any medical staff through that door once I'm in there."

"Yes, sir. No matter how loud Junior screams."

Lyle didn't comment. He slowly and silently turned the doorknob, waited a moment, then jerked the door open noisily.

On the bed, the patient's eyes fluttered open, but since he could only turn his head slowly, exactly how much of his delayed reaction was due to drugs, and how much to injury, Lyle didn't know. Nor did he particularly care.

He held his ID up, though he doubted the groggy man could read anything on it. Again, not important.

"Jack Lyle, Air Force Office of Special Investigations. We're going to talk before you're processed."

The man on the bed licked his dry lips, running his tongue along the edge of the stained dressing that covered his face from his cheek to his mouth. According to the medical reports, Ironwood's son had been shot twice—a graze to the shoulder and a more serious hit through his left calf. He'd also suffered multiple scrapes and superficial puncture wounds along the right side of his body. The injuries were consistent with being trapped in the partial collapse of the tunnel the rescue workers had found him in. Plus, his left arm was broken in three places, and his left shoulder dislocated. The face scrape was an added insult.

"Wh—at?" Holden Jr., a.k.a. J.R., spoke slowly, but, according to the monitor beside his bed, his heart rate had definitely speeded up.

"Processed," Lyle repeated. "I'm turning you over to the MPs this afternoon for transport to Leavenworth."

J.R. was becoming more awake with each passing moment. "Leavenworth?"

"Military prison."

"I'm under arrest?"

"No. You're a captive." Lyle always enjoyed this part.

J.R. struggled to sit up, failed, his panic growing. "Wait, wait, wait . . . start over."

Lyle identified himself again, then said, "You are an enemy of the United States who has been captured and who will be—"

"No! Stop it!"

Lyle waited.

"I'm not an enemy. I'm a U.S. citizen."

"Who's involved in a conspiracy to steal vital defense-related assets and sell them to foreign powers. You got caught. You'll be spending the rest of your life in Leavenworth."

J.R. let his head slump back on his antiseptically white pillow and stared at the ceiling. "I want a lawyer."

"Civilians get to talk to lawyers. Military captives get to talk to me."

J.R. glared at Lyle. Lyle didn't look away. "Something to say?"

"I wanna talk to my father."

"I can arrange that. All you have to do is tell me where he is."

J.R. blinked, finally awake enough to realize the game he was actually in.

"That's right. He got away," Lyle continued. "The big fish. But, as consolation, we have you. Pulled out of a hole in the ground in England. A country, by the way, that has no record of you having entered it. Impressive, but also confirmation that you have sophisticated partners. In the conspiracy."

"There's no conspiracy. My old man—" J.R. caught himself.

"Your old man what?"

J.R. closed his eyes. No doubt, Lyle imagined, visions of life in maximum security danced in his morphine-addled mind.

"What do I have to do?"

"Answer some questions."

"Like what?"

"Where Holden Sr. is. Where the database is. How he got it. Who he's selling it to. What—"

"He's not selling it to anyone!"

"What's he doing with it, then?"

"Looking for . . . for that underground pile of crap you pulled me out of. Ruins, you know? He's found a couple of those old places. All over the world."

Score one for Roz, Lyle thought. "Who's helping him do that?"

J.R.'s face twisted. He winced at the pain the movement caused him. "Nathaniel Merrit. He's the bastard who left me down there. He does all my old man's dirty work." He looked Lyle in the eye. "There's your killer. It's not me."

Lyle concealed surprise, changed tactics. He'd been expecting J.R. to name China or Russia or some other unfriendly country as the entity helping Ironwood exploit the SARGE database. Not an individual.

"Who'd he kill?"

"I tell you what I know, I don't go to Leavenworth?"

"You cooperate, I cooperate. Remember what I said: You're not the big fish." Lyle left the rest of the deal unspoken. It was still too early to expect Junior to give up Senior. He'd have to be eased into it. "Now, this man Merrit. Who is he? What's his connection to your father? And who'd he kill?"

J.R.'s mouth twisted into an unpleasant grin; then he groaned as his cracked lip split.

But he told Lyle *everything*.

"Yes, I know, I know, it's a real mess," Ironwood said to his wife of thirty years. "Never really thought it would get this far. Bet you never did, either." He paused, pensive. "What was that you'd always say? 'Holdie, the trouble with you is that when you want something, you want it all. Never did learn to settle. Or share.'"

Ironwood sighed and scratched his head through the straw hat he wore. The Vanuatu sun was strong this afternoon, and the sweat rolled down his scalp and face in a never-ending trickle. Still, it'd been almost three years since he'd last talked to Nan. He could take the heat a bit longer.

"Never did," he told her. "Never did at all."

Bracing one hand on the white marble gravestone, he awkwardly knelt to adjust the bouquet of flowers he'd brought. Birds-of-paradise. Her favorite. Just as this island paradise had been. "Let me get that," he said. He brushed aside a few yellow leaves that had fallen from other bouquets, the ones he had delivered every day. "Have to talk to Etienne about that. Got to have you looking neat. Know how much you . . . Aw, Nan. Miss you, Little Girl. Miss you something terrible."

He put both hands on the gravestone incised to Nancy Lou Ironwood, beloved wife and mother, and rested his head against his arms. "But I had this all worked out from the beginning, and we'll get by," he whispered to her. "We always do. You and me."

He heard footsteps in the gravel and looked over his shoulder.

Crazy Mike was standing twenty feet back along the white gravel path that wound through the low shrubs and fluttering palm trees of the cemetery. Crazy Mike was native to the island. He ran the main house here and drove the Rolls as needed.

The young man scuffed his sneakers in the gravel again, not wanting to interrupt, but he held out a phone.

Ironwood gave a grunt and pushed himself to his feet, brushed the white stones and dust from the knees of his khakis, and straightened his hat. "What've you got there, son?" He started back down the path to his driver.

"Phone call, Mr. Woody. For you."

Ironwood hesitated. There were maybe ten people in his head office who knew how to get in touch with him, but they used the encrypted satellite phone back in his house on the harbor. He had no idea who among them would know that Crazy Mike was his driver, let alone know his driver's mobile number.

"Who?"

Crazy Mike shrugged, shoulder bones jutting sharply through his blue-and-white-flowered shirt.

Ironwood took the phone. "Who the hell is this?"

"Holden Ironwood?"

"I asked first."

"That you did. Jack Lyle. Air Force Office of Special Investigations."

Ironwood waved his driver away and began to walk along the path. "You're a resourceful man, Mr. Lyle. Is it 'Mister'? You got a rank?"

"Agent Lyle will do."

"'Course it will."

"And I'm not that resourceful. I got this number from your son."

Ironwood felt an icy band around his chest. "Did you now."

"I need you to come home, Mr. Ironwood."

"Is that a threat?"

"Up to you. Technically, you're untouchable. But you know that. No extradition agreement between the U.S. and Vanuatu. Not even formal diplomatic ties. And I understand Ironwood Industries has made some significant investments in schools and infrastructure down there, so I'm guessing the local government wouldn't be in too much of a hurry to change the status quo."

Ironwood wasn't about to be taken in by Lyle's easygoing manner. Sharks swam in those waters. He used the same technique himself.

"If you say so, Agent Lyle."

"That's technically, of course. Operationally, well, you know the United States government isn't in the habit of letting its enemies walk around free in any country.

So one way or another, you will be coming home. It's just that if you fly back in your own plane, it'll be a more pleasant experience than returning in a cargo jet. Bound and gagged."

"I'm not sure I understand, sir. What's this talk about me being an enemy?"

"Let's not play games. You know what you stole. Your son's told us everything. Even told us where to find Frank Beyoun's body."

Ironwood came to a sudden stop on the gravel path, as startled as if he'd been slapped. "Frank? What happened to Frank?"

"No games. Your son's already talking. We show photos of what's left of Beyoun to the rest of your 'Red Team,' you can count on them wanting to start talking, too."

Ironwood stared at the horizon, at the soft white clouds above the blue Pacific. Didn't see any of it. "What happened to Frank?"

"Your man murdered him, Mr. Ironwood."

"My man?"

"Nathaniel Merrit. Head of your security. Former marine. Though I doubt they'd want to claim him as their own. We have him down for at least two other murders as well. All on your orders."

Ironwood erupted, shocked to his core. "That is a lie!"

"Not according to your son."

Ironwood took off his hat and wiped his brow. This was wrong. Horribly, impossibly wrong. "Listen to me, and listen good, Agent Lyle. I never gave Nathaniel Merrit or anyone else such 'orders.'"

"Then come back and we can straighten it all out."

Ironwood looked around the cemetery. Couldn't see a bench, didn't want to sit on a gravestone, but he couldn't stand.

He saw a twisted root stump and dropped down on it to catch his breath, his legs spread wide in front of him, hand on knee to brace himself.

It had been such a simple undertaking. Dave's genetic clusters, the SARGE database, underground maps leading to alien outposts. Evidence of visitation . . . it all would finally turn the world on its head with the truth. How had something so straightforward, so *necessary,* led to murder?

"Mr. Ironwood?"

"I'm here."

"Will you come home, sir?"

Ironwood looked back to Nan's gravestone. There was space in the plot beside her. Eventually, he'd be there beside her. Not just yet.

"Agent Lyle, we're going to sort this out."

"I agree. Best place to do that is back here."

"All right. But first you've got to do something for me."

Far too quickly, far too smoothly, Lyle answered, *"I'm listening."*

Ironwood shook his head. The poor SOB. Expecting him to strike a deal. More like a bargain, and one he planned to cram in the agent's craw. "I'm going to presume you found a copy of your database in my casino."

Lyle said nothing.

"I'm going to further presume you've seen one of the products of that database. A printout, let's say, of a site in Cornwall, England. Is that right?" Ironwood took a deep breath, prepared if need be to wait for kingdom come, because the first person to break silence would be the one with the most to lose.

Finally, *"That's correct."*

Ironwood released his breath. He was still in business. "Good man. Then, if you haven't already done so, Agent Lyle, I suggest you have an expert examine that printout. To figure out how much information is in it. And then tell you how the heck all that information got squeezed out of your precious SARGE. You following me?"

"Don't make such a big thing out of it, Mr. Ironwood. We know you accessed another database."

Gotcha, Ironwood said silently. He closed his eyes to savor the moment. "No, Agent Lyle, I did not. You tell your expert all that information came out of *your* database, and your database alone. If he can't tell you how I did it, I can. And that answer fits on one computer disk. You tell him that, and then you call me back and *I'll* tell *you* what kind of a deal I'll cut for you to get that disk."

"You don't want to play it this way."

"You set the rules, son, so don't throw a tantrum just 'cause you lost a round. By the way, in case you want to go changing those rules or something foolish like that, so far I've had no intention of turning SARGE over to someone who doesn't share my love for my country. But I promise you, any of your friends come parachuting out of the sky to throw me into a Globemaster or what have you, then SARGE and my disk are going to end up exactly where you don't want 'em to end up. You got that?"

"I gave you a chance to do the right thing."

"Now I'm giving you the same opportunity. When you get your head straight, you call back. Have a nice day."

Ironwood snapped the phone shut. He had to make this right. If he didn't, how could he ever face Nan again?

THIRTY-NINE

"At least the Cornish temple was destroyed."

"That is the least of it, Andrew," the Defender of São Paolo hissed into her microphone. "They're *both* still alive!"

The silence that followed was oddly flattened by the noise suppression built into the headphones she wore, essential for helicopter flight. In theory, the elegant cabin of the Foundation's Dauphin Eurocopter was quiet enough for passengers to carry on an unassisted conversation. Nevertheless, when the aircraft transported the Family's defenders, for privacy and security the pilots and passengers wore communications headsets.

"Cross found them once," Andrew finally said. *"So they will be found again."*

Su-Lin didn't think that was likely. Jessica was too much like her aunt Florian. She'd be aware what the Cross attack in the temple meant: that all her efforts to cover her tracks had failed. That the Family had been literally minutes behind her.

"Jessica will not repeat anything she's done since we lost her in Boston. She won't use public airports. Who knows how many passports she has, but she won't use any of them more than once. She's going to be impossible to follow now."

Su-Lin looked out the large passenger window at the lights of the city. Different parts of Zurich glowed different colors, reflecting the era of the various lighting systems clustered below. Rich orange in the oldest sections. Actinic blue along the modern thoroughfares. Sickly yellow where newer lights strove for anemic efficiency. It was a jigsaw pattern of time, and Su-Lin thought it fitting that she was above it all, just as her ancestors had remained behind the scenes of the city, from its beginning.

It was intolerable that she even faced the prospect of losing her position, and her power, all because of other people's mistakes.

"Perhaps we don't have to follow her."

Su-Lin had no idea what he meant. "Give up, you mean?"

"Not at all. Consider her position."

"Andrew, if she has even a tenth of Florian's wealth, she has all the options money can buy."

"*No, she doesn't. Think, Su-Lin. She's not doing this on her own. She needed David Weir to find the temples, and David Weir—*"

Su-Lin broke in. She understood. "He needed Ironwood."

She could almost hear Andrew's self-satisfied smile. "*And, as our associate told us, that particular source of aid is at an end.*"

It only took a moment, then Su-Lin relaxed. "She's going to the Shop." It was the only place Jessica could go now to continue her search for the Family's past.

"*That's where I'd send the next team from Cross.*"

However, there was a potential problem in taking such drastic action in the Family's most secure archive: its Australian director, Victoria, Line Claridge. The Defender of Canberra had proven herself independent enough that her loyalty could not be assumed.

"We'll have to be careful. Victoria was Florian's friend."

"*She knows what's best for the Family.*"

"I'll speak with her," Su-Lin decided. "Sound her out, find out if she's heard from Jessica. But, Andrew, it might not be wise, or even possible, to count on Victoria's assistance."

"*We do have other friends in the Shop, don't we?*"

Andrew was right. Regardless of Victoria's help or hindrance, there were those on her staff who could always be counted on to do the right thing.

High above Zurich, Su-Lin placed the first call to Australia.

FORTY

It was David who caught the first clue: Orion was upside down.

Between them, he and Jess could only name four constellations: the Big and Little Dippers, Taurus the Bull, and Orion the Hunter. The last was reproduced by seven silver disks on the domed ceiling of the chamber, but David noticed something different about the arrangement of the four outlying stars. Seen from the northern hemisphere, Orion was most often in the southern sky, and the stars that were farthest apart were to the left. On the dome of the Cornish temple's inner chamber, that pattern was reversed.

At Jess's request, Haldron Oil's director of exploration sent over Burt McGilford, a soil engineer in the Aberdeen office, whose hobby was astronomy. The moment he saw the star map, he pronounced it a chart of the southern sky. Then, in a dense Scottish brogue, he pointed out several other constellations that neither David nor Jess had heard of, including the Telescope, the Microscope, and the Air Pump.

The most significant, though the smallest, was Crux, the Southern Cross.

In the northern hemisphere, McGilford explained, observers had Polaris, the Pole Star, to indicate the north celestial pole. In the southern hemisphere, there was no star in a similar position, so observers had always relied on the Southern Cross, tracing its long arm southward for four and a half lengths to find the other celestial pole.

David and Jess were familiar with the use of stars for navigation, and their question for McGilford was: How could they calculate the specific place on the planet where the specific stars on this map could be seen in this specific configuration?

"You can't." The Cornish chamber's star map, which matched far southern skies as seen from South America or Africa or Australia, could only be used to calculate latitude—the measure of how far a point was above or below the equator. Latitude, McGilford emphasized, was relatively simple to ascertain. Longitude—how far east or west a point was from an arbitrary starting position—was not. Precise navigation, he explained, required calculating both latitude *and* longitude.

That led the engineer into a treatise about how, in modern times, the arbitrary starting position—0°—dividing the Earth into western and eastern hemispheres had become the line of longitude that runs through Greenwich, England. To be able to calculate how far east or west a point might be from the Greenwich Meridian, two separate pieces of information were required: the positions of particular stars above the horizon, and the time those positions were observed. Precise timekeeping was so necessary for the art of navigation, the oceangoing powers of the seventeenth century—France, Spain, and England—offered prizes amounting to millions of today's dollars for anyone who could devise a way to accurately determine longitude at sea. The first reliable method had been a new type of clock, invented in the late 1700s by a Yorkshire carpenter, that kept accurate time even on a moving ship.

"People sailed around the world before the 1700s," David said. "How did they make maps without knowing longitude?"

"There're plenty of other methods that were in use, y'see." The amateur astronomer smoothed his mustache, enjoying this unusual call on his expertise. "The trick was to have an almanac of celestial occurrences, such as when a particular star or planet would be moving behind the Moon, or the arrangement of Jupiter's four major moons, or—"

Jess interrupted. "Sorry, but what about Jupiter's moons?"

"Well, their orbits are as predictable as any other, and the fact that there're four of them has them behaving like the hands of a clock—different arrangements of them occur only at specific times. That means, if you're having an almanac showing the arrangement of the Jovian moons at midnight in London, when someone in Australia is seeing that exact arrangement, they'll know what time it is in London, and then they can work out what time it is for them where they are, and that's how they'll calculate their longitude. Easy enough to do on land, but a sight more difficult on the heaving deck of a ship at sea."

"Possible, though?" Jess asked.

"Aye. All you're needing is a telescope that'll let you resolve the moons. In fact, it was Galileo who first saw those moons, and who first came up with the idea of using them like a giant clock in the sky."

Jess's face lit up, and David knew they had another clue.

"The sun map!" Jess said as soon as she and David were alone again. "It's the time stamp that says when the stars in the chamber were observed. That's how we know."

The inscribed meteorite was the only artifact ever recovered from a Chamber of Heaven. Of the three sun maps known to be in existence, one was in the MacCleirigh Foundation in Zurich, far below their corporate tower in the Shrine of Turus. The other two, retrieved from the temples in Peru and the South Pacific, were in Ironwood's possession.

In her last communication before her murder, Florian had confirmed that the diagram on the Polynesian meteorite was identical to the one on the sun map in the Family's Zurich shrine.

Jess's eyes flashed with her excitement. "If each Chamber of Heaven is like every other one in layout and in size, then the world maps are probably the same. Same for the arrangement of stars on their ceiling domes. Identical. Since the stars can tell us the latitude they were observed from, and the sun map can give us the longitude, all we have to do is put them together and—"

"We've got the exact point on the globe from which they were observed."

"The one point that's not marked on the map," Jess agreed.

"The White Island." David looked thoughtful.

"You're not convinced. Why?"

"Everything you've told me about the First Gods says they were teachers. They gave people gifts of knowledge."

"Including astronomy." Jess quoted again from the *Traditions*. "'The measure of the sun and moon and stars . . . so they would not fear the confusion of days.'"

"And they created that world map, which we're assuming shows the location of all their temples, and the routes between them."

"Right . . ."

"So why hide the White Island?"

"Because, if that's what the missing location *is,* it's not hidden at all. The answer's in the Chambers, and the First Gods left us everything we need to find it."

"Except, if the sun map's the key, we don't have one. Your family does, and so does Ironwood."

Jess had the perfect answer to that problem. "We only need the information on it—and I know where to find that."

"Stochastic resonance," Captain Kingsburgh said.

Jack Lyle folded his hands on the tabletop before him and looked across the room at the four fifty-inch video screens. One displayed the life-sized image of the U.S. Space Command computer specialist seated at a matching table in Colorado Springs. The other screens showed two uniformed air force image analysts to either side of him. The paneled wall behind Kingsburgh and his associates was identical to the one behind Lyle and Roz

Marano. The illusion cast by the two videoconferencing studios that this meeting was taking place in one location, not two, almost five thousand miles apart, was nearly perfect. Though Lyle would've been just as happy with a phone call.

"Enlighten me, Captain," Lyle said.

"It's counterintuitive, but simply put, it's a method by which an overlay of noise or static—that is, random information—is applied to an existing signal, making the detection of subthreshold information—the parts of a signal that are technically just below the limit of what we should be able to detect—much easier to, um . . . detect."

"Easier," Lyle repeated. "Now you're speaking my language. How much easier?"

Kingsburgh rocked his hand back and forth. "In signal analysis, we gain four to five times the sensitivity, more or less."

"And you think this is what Ironwood has done to increase the amount of information he's been able to extract from the SARGE database."

The captain's chin jutted out. Lyle read that as a defensive gesture. "It's an approach, Agent Lyle. The only plausible one we can think of. But if Ironwood's being truthful, he's managed to retrieve considerably more information than should be possible, even with this technique. I mean, the ground-penetrating, synthetic-aperture radar used by the EMPIRE satellites—that system can't possibly penetrate as deeply as the Cornwall printout indicates. Not even under optimal conditions.

"Our guess is there's some kind of radiation scattering going on and he's managed to develop an algorithm to isolate that from the main signal. How's that even possible? We don't know. But if he *is* being truthful . . ." The captain's next statement clearly was as painful to utter as it was for Lyle to hear. "It's probably the most important advance in geospatial intelligence since satellites. With this technique, the world becomes transparent. There is literally no place left for our enemies to hide, short of digging a mile-deep hole."

"So this is something that we need?"

"It's a game changer. Whoever controls that algorithm wins."

That was enough for Lyle. "Thank you for your input, Captain, and thank you to your staff."

Kingsburgh nodded; then he and his analysts left their studio.

Lyle sat for a moment, contemplating the image of the empty room thousands of miles away.

"We're going to have to make a deal with Ironwood, aren't we?" Roz asked.

"Let's not go there yet."

"We have other options?"

"One in particular."

David's body told him it was midnight, but the sun blazed overhead, and local time was early afternoon. He felt raw, his hearing still affected by the explosions in the Cornish temple. Jess seemed more collected. She'd slept soundly on the flight from India and showed no sign of time-zone confusion.

Four hours after their impromptu astronomy lesson, David and Jess were on a Bombardier Global Express XRS leased to Haldron Oil. Twenty-five hours later, with a single refueling stop in Bombay, they'd changed planes in Sydney, New South Wales. Four hours more and they were in Australia's Northern Territory.

Twice they'd been processed by immigration officials, and both times Jess had produced new passports with new names. American for India, Canadian for Australia.

"How about I drive?" Jess already had her hand on the right-side door of a dusty white Toyota Land Cruiser in the Thrifty Car Rental parking stall.

David shrugged, not inclined to argue. He opened the Cruiser's left-side door and climbed into the passenger seat. Its leather covering stuck unpleasantly to the back of his already sweat-soaked shirt. The cabin itself was uncomfortably hot, even with the vehicle parked beneath an awning.

A Haldron employee had met them in the Sydney airport with a packet of outback gear and clothing. They'd changed on the plane north. Now they were in khaki shorts and short-sleeved shirts, long white socks and leather boots, and wide-brimmed hats. David held his hat on his lap. He'd wear it later.

"You're sure about this?"

Jess turned the key in the ignition. The diesel engine started rough, evened out.

"They've tried to kill you twice now," he added. "So knocking on their door might not be the best idea."

Jess adjusted the air vents to direct the air-conditioning at her face. The outside temperature was over 100°F. The southern hemisphere was moving toward summer.

"Su-Lin didn't tell Willem about the people who came after me in Canada," she said. "So whatever she's doing, whatever she's hiding, she believes not all the other defenders will agree. Willem was my aunt's . . . great love."

"I thought defenders weren't supposed to get involved."

"They're not supposed to turn on each other, either. Victoria Claridge was a good friend of Florian's. If Su-Lin didn't share news about me with Willem, my guess is she hasn't told Victoria."

"What if you're wrong?"

"Then this is where I'd end up anyway. Locked up in the Shop in the middle of nowhere. I'd rather think about what'll happen if I'm right."

"So would I," David said. His future was now tied to hers. Without access to her family's records, he had no chance to improve the genetic odds of his survival. Or even find out if survival was possible.

They drove from the lot to the entrance to Roger Vale Road, following it to the two-lane highway that led to Alice Springs, the small town located in what was almost the exact geographical center of Australia. Before they reached the Alice, Jess took a sharp turn onto another two-lane road that passed for an outback highway and started driving east.

"How far?" David asked.

"Fifty klicks."

The landscape was startlingly orange-red, flat and dusty, broken by stark and endless hills to the north. But for the sparse olive-green and dun-colored desert plants and grasses here and there, it might as well have been Mars. "You weren't kidding about the middle of nowhere."

"That's the whole point," Jess said. "In the event of nuclear Armageddon, the Family's collection would survive. Of course, ten years after we moved everything out here, the CIA built a satellite ground station ten miles to the west of town, and the whole area became a target."

"You didn't move again?"

"Apparently we're far enough underground. It's an old mine that we took over, then excavated even more. Very impressive."

"How big?"

"I don't really know. I've been there four times, and it seems to go on forever. I'm told it houses close to a hundred and sixty million individual artifacts." She glanced away from the monotony of the road for a moment. "That's more than the Smithsonian—*all* the Smithsonians."

"You're just . . . saving stuff?"

"We study it. Preserve it." She sounded defensive. "It's what the First Gods asked us to do."

"But they gave away knowledge, and you're hiding it."

"That's unfair, and you know it."

The Cruiser rocked as Jess swerved to avoid a snake sunning itself on the open road. "How many times was the Library at Alexandria looted by invading forces? How many Mayan codices were burned by the Spanish? Books and artwork burned by Nazis? The Taliban shelling the Afghani

Buddhas? The Qin Dynasty of China didn't just burn books, they buried scholars alive. Who can even comprehend the loss in human knowledge, human arts, human experience, that's been brought about by centuries—by millennia—of religious and political extremism and intolerance?

"That's why we keep our beliefs to ourselves. Why we adopt the religion and the culture of whatever time and place we're in. So we *don't* stand out, *don't* attract attention. So we can *protect* human knowledge from human ignorance, and hatred, and fear."

"Until the First Gods come back." David closed his eyes against the glare. He had heard this before.

"Until then."

David's eyes opened. Jess's hands were tight on the wheel, her knuckles white. Her attention fixed on the unchanging road and landscape.

He'd just heard something that he *hadn't* heard from Jess before.

Doubt.

FORTY-ONE

Ironwood was on a small dock in Port Vila harbor, buying fish for dinner. It was another of the many reasons he enjoyed the island nation he'd adopted. In addition to its no-extradition-to-America rule, haggling over prices was frowned upon, and it was considered rude to tip. Apparently, at some point in its past, some wise politician had also decided income taxes were rude as well, because Vanuatu didn't have that annoying custom, either.

He paid the fair price for a fine barramundi and had the fish wrapped in brown paper for his driver to carry in the string bag already swelling with glossy purple eggplant, bright yellow grapefruit, and ripe brown pawpaw. Farther down the weathered dock was a stand that could be counted on to have the largest prawns. He moved on through the crowd of local shoppers and Australian tourists to make his next purchase.

But Crazy Mike stopped him, phone in hand.

Ironwood checked the time. It had taken Agent Jack Lyle almost two days to analyze the Cornwall printout and get back to him. A bit faster than he'd anticipated. No matter; the outcome would be the same.

He took the phone and selected a section of the dock between two vendors' stalls where he could lean against the rough wood safety rail and have a private and profitable conversation.

"So what did your experts tell you?" Ironwood kept his tone amiable, a man in control.

"Tell me about what?" The voice on the other end of the call was unexpected but familiar.

"Merrit?"

"Sorry to call you this way, but the satphone could be—"

Ironwood lowered his voice with effort. "Where are you?"

"Probably better you don't know. The Cornwall thing, it didn't go the way we hoped."

"Go on."

"The MacCleirighs got there first. Makes no sense, but they demolished it."

Ironwood felt the phone tremble in his fist. How far was his security chief going to take this fabrication? "Where's my son?"

He heard Merrit exhale—this from a man who never broke a sweat.

"There's no good way to tell you this. He got caught in the explosions, the cave-in. I tried to pull him out, but . . . he didn't make it."

Ironwood had to concentrate on every word he spoke, to keep rage from consuming him. "Then why's J.R. in the custody of the air force? Telling them things even I don't know?"

Merrit hesitated. *"I saw the tunnel roof fall in on him . . ."*

"What'd you do to Frank Beyoun?"

"The programmer? Nothing. Haven't seen him since—"

"Frank is dead, Merrit. My son says you killed him."

"I didn't. Why would I?"

"That last day, when Dave gave me that hard drive, there was something going on between you two. Did he take off because of you?"

"Your handpicked genius stole from you and hooked up with your enemies, and you're blaming me because he ran?"

"Florian MacClary. She died in Tahiti. Now I'm wondering if you killed her, too. I have always considered this . . . 'difference of opinion' between me and that misguided foundation to be a gentleman's disagreement. But if my boy's right, you've turned it into some kind of war."

"He's lying. That's all I can say."

Ironwood had a flash picture of his son lying wounded in a hospital, ready to bring down everything his father had worked to build, the legacy of truth he wanted to leave to the world. *Because I saw only what I wanted to . . . heard only what I wanted to . . . ignored the evidence . . .*

He wrenched his thoughts away from what he couldn't change.

"Then prove it. Explain it all away, to me, in person."

"Why? So you can trade me to the air force for your son?"

"The air force isn't interested in you. Now answer: Will you come here and defend your good name?"

"What do you think?"

"I'll take that as a no." Ironwood disconnected.

He also took it as a declaration of war from a murderer.

His quest for the truth had just become a quest for survival.

"Doesn't look like much," David said.

"That's the point," Jess answered.

Thirty miles from the town of Alice Springs, with no other sign of human habitation in sight, she slowly drove the now-filthy Land Cruiser along the winding red-dirt road, through a wide-open gate in a sagging chain-link fence that offered little more than a suggestion of security.

In the distance, past a weathered tin guard shack, was the beginning slope of a massive sandstone outcropping. Just past the shack was a sun-bleached and wind-scoured sign. It was a directory of storage and file-management companies, listing loading docks each could be accessed through. A wooden barricade arm beside the guard shack was down, ostensibly preventing entry to the continuation of the road beyond, though a car could easily drive around it.

Jess stopped the big SUV in front of the barricade.

"What now?"

"Won't be long."

Less than a minute later, a crunch of dirt, and another vehicle approached from off road. A Land Rover Defender. The much-dented and dust-filmed white vehicle had extra fuel cans strapped to its roof rack. It looked antique, but even through closed windows, David heard its engine. It was new and powerful.

The driver got out, no sense of urgency about him. He wore knee-length tan shorts, a sweat-stained olive drab shirt with epaulets, thick boots, and what David decided was an Australian version of a cowboy hat. A second man stayed in the vehicle.

Jess lowered her window as the man approached and rested her hand on the open sill. The position looked awkward to David, and he noticed the tips of her thumb and index finger touched.

"G'day," the driver said. "Looking for something?"

"I'm on a long journey."

"Which direction?"

"West to east."

The man's attitude seemed to change. He scratched lightly at his throat with two fingers, then bent down to look past Jess at David. "Can you vouch for him?" the man asked.

"No," Jess said.

"Fair enough. I'll let herself know you're on the way."

"Thank you."

"No worries." The man walked back to his vehicle, swung in, and used a radio mike.

"Was all that some sort of code?" David asked.

"Some of it."

"So why couldn't you vouch for me?"

"It's a different meaning. He wanted to know if you were Family. I said you weren't, so he had to be careful of what he said."

"What if I am part of the Family?"

"Then I'll teach you the codes myself."

The barricade arm swung up, and Jess drove on. Ahead, beside an industrial-sized propane storage tank, David glimpsed for the first time the opening in the sandstone cliff, wide enough and tall enough for three double-decker buses to drive in, side by side. It dwarfed the Toyota as they drove through.

The volume inside could easily accommodate a doubles tennis court. Three other white Land Rovers were parked along one red-hued wall whose grooves and lines suggested it had been carved from solid rock.

Jess switched on the Cruiser's headlights, and, at the back of the artificial cave, David counted three loading docks with standard garage-type doors.

Halfway to the docks, she parked beside the wall and told David to leave the luggage and come with her.

The sign on the metal personnel door between two of the loading dock doors said hours were by appointment only.

Jess stood before it, waiting.

David looked up to the vast raw-rock ceiling and saw security cameras looking down.

The metal door opened.

The woman before them was young, with a slight build. A soft black cloud of hair framed a caramel complexion and clear sherry-brown eyes. Despite the pervasive red-desert dust, her shirt and jeans were immaculate.

"Bakana," Jess said.

"Defender." The young woman half knelt, took Jess's left hand, and kissed it. She glanced at David. "He's not on the journey?"

"He will be. I want Victoria to meet him."

Bakana stood, and David saw the appraising look she gave him. Not so friendly.

She led them into a hall, which ended in the distance with a closed door. Lit by overhead fluorescents, a series of innocuous and simply framed prints of local landscapes graced both rock walls.

Halfway down the hall, Bakana ushered them into a lounge area on the right. They were to wait while she made the arrangements. There were drinks in the cooler. She shut the door behind her.

David studied a remarkably ugly chair covered in what appeared to be orange burlap. "Anything I should know?"

Jess rummaged through the cooler and pulled out two water bottles. "You're my fiancé." She held one up questioningly.

David nodded. "Okay . . ."

She tossed him a bottle, then opened one for herself. "It's the only way to get you in here. Simpler than the truth."

David twisted off the bottle's cap and took a long swig. He knew he'd become too comfortable with lies, but as death drew near, things he used to worry about no longer concerned him.

The rest of the lounge furniture was as ugly as the chair, and at least thirty years old. A ring-stained wooden coffee table was piled with well-thumbed magazines. They ranged from *Modern Documents Management* to the requisite copies of *National Geographic* from decades past. "It's not what I pictured."

"They get government inspectors from time to time. Drivers for the trucks that bring in supplies. This is what they expect here."

"What are you expecting?"

Jess didn't answer. She drained the last of her water and dropped the empty bottle in a recycling bin.

David sensed more than doubt in Jess now. Fear.

Nathaniel Merrit sat calmly in the chair by the window of his hotel room near Heathrow.

On the desk beside him were the supplies from the clinic—the ones they'd given him, and the ones he'd stolen.

Right now, his attention was on the bottle of co-dydramol tablets. He was waiting to see if he needed more. Pain, the warrior's mantra went, was weakness leaving the body. But his back had been badly wrenched when he'd slammed into the stone table in the treasure chamber. The flesh over his rib cage on the right side had been slashed by the shooter he had had to kill to escape the collapse. And his ankle . . . he'd sprained that making a simple four-foot jump from one of the openings blown out of the side of the cliff.

It had not been his night.

The only thing that had made the fiasco in Cornwall even remotely acceptable was that he'd caught sight of J.R.'s body in the passageway, by the rock pile, just instants before the ceiling collapsed.

By then, he'd already suited up in the black Nomex jacket and helmet of the first shooter who'd entered the treasure room searching for survivors. Merrit had strangled the man so quickly he'd had no time to shout a warning. He'd dropped the other two shooters on the way out. Dressed as one of their partners, he'd made use of his advantage and opened fire first.

Now, though, with J.R. alive and squealing to the air force, his escape from Cornwall was no longer step one in cleaning the mess Ironwood's brat had left him.

His arrangement with Ironwood was over, and that was a problem. His ex-employer had resources, and motive, to silence him. To survive, Merrit knew, would require even stronger resources.

Fortunately, he also knew where to find them.

FORTY-TWO

Jess followed Bakana through a cluttered warren of low-walled cubicles.

The administrative facility at the end of the hall was more window dressing. Once every year, for the benefit of occupational health and safety officers and business-license issuers, MacCleirigh Foundation researchers came up from the underground caverns of the Shop to play the parts of office workers. For now, though, the cubicles were silent and empty. Every desk and chair was draped in heavy sheets of plastic, the red dust everywhere.

Bakana carefully pulled the cover from one of the filing cabinets against the back wall. She drew out the middle drawer, and Jess placed her hand inside, palm down, fingers splayed to fit within a set of plastic pegs. A flash of white light. A soft chime. Then a panel in the wall beside the cabinet smoothly moved aside.

Bakana went through first.

The open staircase spiraled downward to another, larger room, equivalent in size to the cave where Jess had parked the Cruiser. At the room's far end gleamed the huge steel disk of a fifty-ton blast door. It was open to reveal a circular passageway as wide as a two-lane road.

Once through, it was a short walk to a bank of elevators that descended five levels deeper underground. Jess knew that if she had misjudged the extent of Su-Lin's power over other defenders, it was possible she'd already been declared an enemy of the Family. If anything was going to happen to her, it would be now.

The elevator door whisked open. Cool air washed in. Jess braced for attack.

It didn't come.

"Such news!" Victoria, Line Claridge, Defender of Canberra, swept Jess into a quick embrace. Her turquoise eyes were as startling as ever in her deep-tanned face. Her white-blond hair was straight and chin length.

Jess relaxed momentarily. Su-Lin hadn't sent out an alarm. Her cover story about David and marriage, concocted quickly on the plane, only had to hold until they got the sun map images.

"My office?" Victoria suggested. "So you can tell me all about him."

"Lots to tell," Jess said.

Victoria winked. "Time for true confessions."

Victoria's office was like the workplace of any other academic who had too many projects and too little time. Journals and papers and open books feathered with sticky notes covered both desks, each shelf, and every piece of furniture.

The Defender of Canberra transferred one of those piles from the edge of a dark green leather sofa to the top of another pile already on the floor. Jess settled in as instructed while Victoria took her own chair, checked her laptop, then folded it closed. She stripped off her Velcro-fastened sandals and, with a sigh, lifted her calloused feet up on the only clear corner of her desk.

"Jessie, Su-Lin's worried about you."

Su-Lin . . . not David or my marriage. Jess returned to full alert. "When did you talk to her?"

"A few days ago. She said you went missing in Boston after Florian's memorial, after saying something about going to the Pacific temple site. Before it's been secured."

There was a chance, Jess realized, that Victoria knew exactly what she was doing. There was also a chance that Victoria was merely Su-Lin's unwitting ally, being used to find out if the new defender might implicate others in her rebellion against the Family.

There was one way to find out. Strike first.

"The Polynesian temple's been destroyed," Jess said.

"What?" Victoria swung her legs down. "How?"

"Underwater demolition."

There was a knock on the door. Bakana was there. She held a tray with a covered china teapot, cups, and a plate of Tim Tams. She looked apologetic, apparently aware she had interrupted something.

Victoria asked her to put the tray down on a relatively stable pile of books, then leave. Bakana closed the door without being asked.

"Was it Ironwood?"

"No," Jess said. "Su-Lin." Victoria's strong-featured face betrayed only bewilderment. That, paired with her convincing shock about the temple's destruction, gave Jess new hope.

"Why ever would Su-Lin destroy something so valuable? And if she did, how would you know?"

Jess took a deep breath, hoping she wasn't making a mistake. "Willem told me. Just before he disappeared."

"But Willem's in Iceland."

"He came to Boston for Florian's memorial."

Victoria started to say that was against all the rules, then reconsidered. "They were very fond of each other."

"And Su-Lin didn't tell him gunmen tried to kill me in Canada, just before—"

"Gunmen?!"

"Then she didn't tell you, either."

"When did this happen?"

"Three days after Florian was murdered."

"Jessie, dear, you'd better tell me everything."

David woke with a start. He'd nodded off in the ugly orange chair waiting for Jess to return, or for someone else to come for him.

She'd said it'd be impossible for him to see the real underground facility here, but as soon as she'd spent a few minutes speaking with her host, he'd be allowed to enter the first level, where the main living quarters were housed. He could rest there while she used a computer terminal to call up photos of the sun map. She'd also said there would be several astronomers she could contact, funded by MacCleirigh Foundation grants, who'd be able to interpret the arrangement of planets in the meteorite's inscriptions. That they would know if a particular date could be inferred.

David checked his watch to see how long he'd slept. *An hour and a half?*

He stood up, muscles sore and stiff after Cornwall and the forced inactivity of a day spent in planes. His stomach rumbled. He hadn't had a real meal for days, but the closest thing to food at hand was a can of Coke.

He went to the door, opened it, saw no one in the hall.

"Hello?"

No one answered.

David didn't know how this place ran, but something wasn't right. Not for a security-obsessed outfit like Jess's family.

Coke in hand, he started down the hall toward the closed door at its end. He was guessing that that was where Jess had gone with Bakana.

The door was unlocked when he tried it. He walked into what seemed to be a mothballed office. Everything was wrapped in plastic.

"Jess? Bakana? Hello?"

Silence.

David took another sip of Coke, considering his next move. Then he heard someone in the hall, moving fast. *Finally.*

He went back to the door, pulled it open.

The driver of the Land Rover was charging toward him. He had a gun.

David slammed the door shut—

But he'd swung the lightweight door so hard, it banged open again just as fast. The driver fired.

— —— —

Jess sat in anxious silence as Victoria stared up at one of the few paintings on her office walls, its ornate frame squeezed between the overstuffed bookcases. It was a portrait of Sir Francis Bacon, one of the 144 of his day. It was also a Family painting, and he held one hand in the gesture of the empty scroll. His other hand grasped his Tuareg cross. In the edging of the purple cloak that draped the famous scholar, the words SCIENTIA PO-TESTAS EST were worked in gold threads: *Knowledge is power.* The phrase was one of many from the *Traditions* that Sir Francis had revealed to the world, much to the chagrin of his cousins.

"Do you believe me?" Jess asked at last.

Victoria turned away from the portrait, and Jess saw new creases of concern on her cousin's sun-weathered face. "It's not that simple. You've given me no motive, or real evidence. Without that, how can I, or any of the rest of us, believe Su-Lin—and *Andrew*—want . . . and have *already* acted, to erase our heritage? There's no basis for removing them from the Twelve."

Jess blinked. "Is that possible? Can a defender be removed?"

"Supposedly, though I don't think it's ever happened. The most I'm aware of is that a few defenders have left active service and ended up in our libraries. 'Taking on lives of permanent scholarship,' I believe the Foundation calls it. But that's more like being in exile than being removed." Victoria frowned. "You see, that's the problem with what you've told me, Jessie. The Foundation's so big, our resources so formidable, any defender should be able to pursue any line of inquiry, without question. That's always prevented disputes among us."

"What about the allocation of those resources? Willem said there are never enough in a given year to do everything that everyone wants to do."

"That's true in any academic setting. But if one of our personal projects isn't approved one year, it's approved the next. We're all equal, dear. That's why the table's round."

"But . . ." Jess felt desperation rising, all thoughts of the need to acquire the sun map image sinking below a new threat. If she couldn't convince Victoria, there was every likelihood she'd corroborate Su-Lin's misgivings about the new defender's readiness—*and I'll end up in a "life of permanent scholarship."*

She spoke with urgency. "Victoria, listen, that's *not* how Su-Lin is behaving. She didn't tell you about the attack in Canada—and she was supposed to. Think about that, please. She told you she was worried about me, but she *didn't* tell you she'd already sent Cross personnel to bring me back to Zurich—at gunpoint. She's already destroyed one temple, and probably the one in Cornwall, too. Think of what else we'll lose if we don't stop her!"

"I have been listening, and, frankly, Jessie, you've just weakened your argument."

Jess stared at her cousin, uncomprehending.

"You made it clear that you and your David, and Ironwood and his people, were the *only* ones who could have known about the temple in Cornwall. That leaves only one reasonable assumption: Ironwood is responsible for its destruction. Which means, it's likely he's also responsible for what happened in Polynesia. And I wouldn't put too much on Willem, just now. He's been distraught since he lost Florian. Their 'association' with each other wasn't unknown to all of us."

For Jess, though, one action outweighed all others. "That doesn't change the fact that Su-Lin's withholding information."

"What would you have me do?'

"Exactly what *she's* doing. Don't tell her anything I've told you."

"About . . ."

"About anything, especially David."

"David." Victoria looked thoughtful. "When do you get the results of the genetic testing back?"

"Another two days for the preliminary results. Apparently, they'll be able to tell if we're related right away. It'll take a bit longer than that to work out the precise details."

"Well . . . at the very least, it would be fascinating if it turns out there's a genetic marker that identifies the Family. It'd certainly make sense. And it would make it easier for you to bring him into the 144."

Jess understood. Spouses of defenders automatically became part of the Family's inner circle, though sometimes the training period could last years.

"What about . . ." Victoria hesitated. "The White Island?"

"Not till we decode the star map."

"Then what?"

"Ideally?" Jess knew what she wanted to do but wasn't sure it was possible. "Ideally, I'd like to go to whatever location the star map points to and see what's there—and, somehow, get word to all the defenders, and all the 144 at the same time. If Su-Lin and Andrew are destroying temples, that would stop them."

"Because everyone will know."

Jess looked at the portrait of Bacon. "Knowledge will give us the power to preserve knowledge."

Victoria thought that over, and Jess held her breath when it seemed her cousin had made a decision.

Then the deafening scream of a siren made them both cup their ears.

"What is it?" Jess gasped.

Victoria raised her voice to be heard above the din. "The blast door! It's closing!"

━━ ━━━━ ━━━

David raised his hands in a reflexive yet futile attempt to block bullets, but the gun was a Taser, and it fired darts. They struck the can of Coke he held, sparked, and deflected from their target.

Reacting instantly, David slammed the door again in the same heartbeat the driver lunged forward, and the sound of its connection with his face was solid. The door slowly opened, and the man staggered forward, blood spurting from his nose and lips.

A month ago, David wouldn't have known what to do.

Now he did.

He swung, hard, and the man dropped to the floor.

David thought quickly. There had been two men in the Land Rover that had intercepted him and Jess. Driver *and* passenger.

He checked the hallway. Empty.

He bent down, patted the man's pockets, and found keys and a small plastic box with extra darts for the Taser gun. He used the man's belt to secure his hands. Then he locked the door to the hall. His eyes swept the cubicles, chairs, and saw—

Something that broke the pattern.

The back wall of filing cabinets, the one unit without a plastic shroud. Its middle drawer was open.

David ran to the unit, looked in the drawer. A biometric hand scanner—Jess and Bakana *had* come in here.

David dragged the unconscious man back to the cabinet, freed his hands, and placed one of them on the scanner.

A soft chime sounded, and a wall panel slid aside.

David retied his captive's hands, then stepped through the opening.

He was at the top of a staircase that wound down into a vast artificial cavern with a massive vault door at one end. The door was disklike, shining stainless steel, open to reveal a large tunnel.

The only other ways in or out of the cavern appeared to be three smaller, unprotected tunnels. David guessed those led to the loading-dock garage doors he'd seen when he and Jess drove in.

The conclusion was obvious: The Shop lay beyond the vault door.

He started down the stairs. A cry rang out behind him.

The second man. The Rover's passenger was in the opening to the staircase, shouting into a radio.

A siren soared into earsplitting life. On the floor below, spinning lights flashed into action, smearing wild reflections in the vault door's sheen.

The air shook as the deep rumble of powerful hydraulic pumps began.

The silver disk was closing.

FORTY-THREE

The blare of the siren drowned out Jess's shout of "Why?"

Victoria grabbed her laptop and rushed for the door. "We only shut it for drills and—"

She stopped dead. Bakana stood in the open doorway. "You need to stay in your office," she said.

Victoria tried to push past her assistant, but Bakana took her arm and firmly forced her back. "You need to stay here." The assistant glared at Jess. "You, too."

Victoria wrested her arm free, furious. "What is this about?"

Jess knew the answer. "Me."

Bakana closed the door behind her. From the hallway, Jess could hear running footsteps, the rise and fall of worried voices. The scholars working here would be hurrying to do exactly what her cousin had done: retrieve their computers and vital notes. Just in case.

"You have no right to detain either of us," Victoria said.

"I'm doing this for the Family."

Jess knew why this was happening. "No, you're not. Whatever Su-Lin's told you, it's not true."

"Why would she lie?" Bakana looked back and forth between her two captives. "She's a defender like the two of you. You both know things I don't. The 144 know things I don't. Keeping knowledge secure is how the Family survives. But now *you*"—she pointed at Jess—"you're threatening everything we are with your stories of a false temple! You're helping Ironwood!"

The siren stopped abruptly. The sudden silence was unnerving.

"The door's closed now. We're sealed in for at least a day." Victoria held her laptop to her chest. "I agree with you, Bakana. We do need to keep some knowledge hidden. That *is* how we survive. But, having been a defender for more than twenty years, I can tell you that not all of us at the table agree with one another. I'm going to call Su-Lin. I'm certain this can all be sorted out."

Bakana held her position blocking the door. "They want Jessica back in Zurich. Just to talk. That's why they don't have guns."

"Who doesn't have guns?"

"The people from Cross." Bakana stepped aside as the office door began to open. "They're here to take her back."

David rushed for the vault door as the sirens wailed and the immense steel disk ponderously shifted, gaining momentum. Without breaking pace, he glanced back.

The Rover's passenger was halfway down the spiral staircase. David recognized the blocky black weapon he carried. A Taser gun.

He raced on. Getting past the vault door was his only chance of escape, but the huge disk was already halfway through its arc—in ten seconds, it would be closed. Behind him he heard the clanging of the metal stairs end as his pursuer reached the ground.

Ahead of him, the opening to the tunnel narrowed, nearly covered by the immense steel disk. David twisted sideways, skidding into the five-foot depth of the locking frame, slipping through just as a crackling Taser dart sparked off the disk's outside edge and the towering cold bulk closed.

Safe.

The hydraulics growled to a stop, and the door's locking pegs sprang out to hold it fast.

The siren stopped.

David moved. Felt resistance. Something held him. He twisted, awkward.

His shirt. The tail of it caught in the door.

He yanked on the trapped fabric. No success. In frustration, he pulled his khaki shirt open, ripping buttons off, finally pulling free and turned to keep running, just as a third Cross bodyguard Tasered him.

Bakana backed away from Victoria's office door as the bodyguard pushed a figure in ahead of him.

David fell to his knees, and Jess rushed to kneel beside him.

Seconds later, she looked back at Victoria. "He's alive because they used darts this time. In Boston, their orders were to kill."

"Why the change?" Jess demanded. The Cross operative in olive drab outback gear didn't answer her. With the hypertrained resolve of each recruit in what was, to all intents, the Family's private army, he slipped a new cartridge into his Taser.

"Orders are to take you both to Zurich. Uninjured, if possible."

Jess saw Bakana's look of surprise at the threat of violence. Victoria continued to say nothing.

Jess touched David's smooth bare chest. Barbed electrodes were still hooked into his skin there. Blood oozed from the impact points.

He moaned, still not coherent. The disruptive effects of the high-voltage, low-current shock did take some time to wear off, but Jess thought it odd he showed no signs of recovery yet.

She turned back to Victoria. "In Boston, Su-Lin wanted David and me dead. Now she doesn't. That means she needs information from both of us. She wants us to tell her how to find the temples."

Jess ignored the astonished faces of the operative and Bakana. All that mattered was what Victoria would do.

The Defender of Canberra evidently made her decision. She spoke to the man with the Taser, her voice authoritative, commanding.

"You are in my domain. If you expect to leave with your prisoners, you'll do me the respect of telling *me* why you're taking them."

The operative hesitated, and Jess guessed that Su-Lin had ordered him not to reveal anything. Not even to the Shop's director.

She saw Bakana, conflicted, look from the bodyguard back to her superior. Aware that she was watching history.

Jess suddenly wondered if *this* was one of the stories she would tell the Family's children someday.

"You should speak to the Defender of São Paulo," the operative finally said.

"I intend to. But right now, I'm speaking to you."

David moaned again. The sound distracted the operative, and he reached down for the wires trailing from David's chest, to pull them free. "He should be fine now." But in one quick motion David ripped the darts from his chest himself and used them to slash at the operative. The man reeled back, startled, his face streaked with blood as he raised his Taser to fire again, and—

—fell back as David grabbed a heavy book from a shelf and slammed it against his head.

David scooped up the Taser and backed away, waving the weapon at Bakana as he ordered her to stay by the fallen man. Though David's hand was shaking and his face was ashen, blood still dripping from ragged chest wounds, it was obvious to Jess that he'd deliberately acted to persuade the operative, and her, that the Taser had debilitated him more than it had.

"Let's just find what we came for," he told Jess, "and get out of here."

Bakana found her voice. "You can't get out of here. No one can."

"I can wait for the door to open," David said. He looked at Victoria. "You are going to open it, right?"

Despite what she'd just witnessed, Victoria maintained an air of imperious calm. She pulled out a dusty black phone from under a stack of papers. "Jessie, I agree with you that something's not right, and that Su-Lin's somehow involved, but you still haven't convinced me she wants the temples destroyed. There's just no reason for it." She lifted the receiver, ready to place the call.

Before Jess could make one last attempt to convince Victoria to help her, David spoke.

"Sure there is," he said. "What about the Family secret?"

It was as if a sudden chill had frozen everyone in the office. Bakana and the operative turned to stare at him. Victoria stood with the handset of her phone halfway to her ear.

Jess knew what David was about to do: Defend *her*. She tried to warn him off. "David—"

But David was oblivious to the hurricane he was about to unleash.

"I couldn't even begin to guess what this facility cost," he said. "What it took to get a blast door into the center of Australia. How Jess can get fake passports, charter planes halfway around the world . . . It's like money doesn't exist for you people."

"Your point?" Victoria asked. She was looking straight at Jess, the unspoken question in her eyes. *How much have you told him?*

Too much, Jess knew. Then David made it worse. Much worse.

"The MacCleirigh Foundation, your 'Family,' exists to search for the temples. So tell me, what happens when they're found?"

"There's more to us than that." Victoria's voice was even, but Jess knew that outrage was beneath it.

"Not a lot," David said. "It's pretty much the fate of all institutions. They're formed to achieve a particular goal, but when they get big enough, rich enough, they put their first goal to the side and work only to ensure their own continued existence.

"The Family's no different," he continued. "Look what Jess had to go through to get you people to finally listen to her. If Su-Lin destroys the temples, then the Family's search will never end and the MacCleirigh Foundation goes on forever. End of story. But thanks to Jess, you've got something bigger to think about now. If you do find all your temples, including the White Island, and maybe even rediscover the big secret that you defenders lost—no matter what that secret is, no matter if it's still even meaningful after so many centuries have passed—the Foundation will have fulfilled its goal and it's all over. Right?"

Victoria replaced the handset. Jess didn't have to look at Bakana or the operative. She knew what she would see. Shock. And condemnation. David had just made it clear that the Family's newest defender had knowingly broken its most sacred vows.

Her cousin seemed to have aged in only moments. "Jessica . . . how could *you* betray us? Florian chose you herself."

Jess refused to capitulate. "David *is* one of us, so I told him everything."

"Even if he is," Victoria said with finality, "he's not a defender. Now he knows too much. Unfortunately, he's not the only one."

Her gaze swept the room, including Bakana and the operative.

"What you've done, Jessica . . . It's out of my hands. Our traditions give me no choice." Jess heard the finality in her cousin's words. "None of you can ever leave this place again."

FORTY-FOUR

"Are you ready?" General DiFranza asked.

Lyle sat at a console at the end of the central table in the Emergency Conference Room of the National Military Command Center. It had been three years since his last visit to the Pentagon, and that had been for an outdoor memorial service. He had never been at the heart of the nation's military command structure, and had never imagined being in a situation where three generals with eight stars among them would be looking to him to take action. The others in the room—Captain Trevor Kingsburgh and his two air force communications specialists, five analysts from the National Reconnaissance Office, two from the National Security Agency, and six other unsmiling civilians who pointedly had not been introduced to him—were icing on this particular cake.

The only good thing about what was about to happen was that Roz Marano wasn't present to say the wrong thing at the wrong time. Even if it turned out to be the right thing, as it often was, it would be to the wrong people. *Small mercies,* Lyle thought.

"Yes, sir," he said. He looked down again at the cheat sheet the Department of Justice had prepared for him.

"Bulldog?" DiFranza said. "How're your boys doing?"

Carter "Bulldog" Tyrell was the other three-star general in the room. He was checking the progress of an aircraft currently depicted as a blue triangle on one of the six large display screens on the double-story wall to Lyle's left.

The aircraft was an MC-130H Combat Talon II that had just completed its second inflight refueling over the Pacific. On board was a team of twelve Air Commandos from the 1st Special Operations Wing unit operating out of Nellis Air Force Base, Nevada. They were en route to their first staging point on their mission: Christchurch International Airport, New Zealand, the USAF's most southerly operational foreign airbase. It was just under two thousand miles from Vanuatu.

Bulldog covered the small mike on his headset and answered DiFranza's question. "ETA three hours. On-site eight hours after landing Christ-church."

DiFranza, Lyle, and almost everyone else in the room checked two of the other large screens on the left wall. One showed a crisp surveillance photo of Ironwood's sprawling home in Port Vila, Vanuatu. The other screen of interest was a world clock. In eleven hours, it would be 3:00 A.M. in that region of the Pacific, a definite advantage for the air commandos who'd be able to see in the dark with thermal imagers.

If Lyle's phone call didn't go well, then Holden Ironwood was going to have visitors on his island paradise.

"You're on, Jack." DiFranza gave Lyle a pat on the shoulder, then stepped away to let him work. Lyle nodded at the airman seated beside him. The airman pressed a single button on the console.

Lyle picked up the black receiver in front of him and heard the faint hollowness of a satellite connection, then the distinctive buzz of a Vanu-atan phone ringing. Only once.

"Ironwood." Lyle was surprised at Ironwood's harsh tone, as if he'd been expecting a call other than one that could guarantee his personal safety.

"Jack Lyle."

At that, Ironwood's usual bonhomie returned. *"What can I do for you, Agent Lyle?"*

"Well, sir, I've checked out the Cornwall printout as you suggested, and I'm ready to talk. But I'm going to need some additional assurances from you."

"You're ready to talk. I like that. How many people you got listening in on this call, son?"

Lyle didn't have to think about his answer. "Let me see. I'll count." Half the room looked surprised by that comment, but Lyle knew the only way he had a chance of gaining Ironwood's trust was to be completely honest. "Including me, there're twenty I can see. Couldn't tell you who else might be listening up the line."

Ironwood seemed pleased with his answer. *"And where are all you fine people calling from?"*

DiFranza shook his head at Lyle.

"Let's just call it a secure and undisclosed location. But you're impor-tant, Mr. Ironwood, and from the amount of brass in this room, it's safe to say you've got our attention."

"Then it's your move, son."

Lyle knew what the first step was but glanced down at his cheat sheet anyway. "First, we need to be certain your method for extracting infor-mation from the SARGE database is real."

Ironwood snorted. *"You already know that. That's why you've got twenty people in that room."*

"No, sir. We don't know it. And we can't take your word for it. Bottom line, we need a copy of your disk."

"Son, give me credit for having half a brain, will you? If I give you that disk before we come to a satisfactory understanding, you won't need me. We make our deal based on my guarantee that the technique on that disk—let's call it an algorithm so you know what you're bargaining for—works the way I say it does. Then, when all's said and done, if I've been playing you, you can lock me up in Area 51. You're already protected in this arrangement, so I'm not showing you squat. Move on."

DiFranza gestured for Lyle to do so.

"How many copies of the database did you make?"

"You got the one in my casino. I've got one other backup that's operational, in what you could also call a secure and undisclosed location. And then a second in the same facility that's just a stack of unconnected drives."

"We'll need proof of that," Lyle said. It was on his checklist, but he knew what Ironwood's response would be.

"I'll say it one more time: You're already protected. Anything I tell you that turns out not to be true, my deal's over. I know that. Why don't you?"

Lyle looked over all the other demands the DoJ had put down on the sheet, each one carefully prioritized and bulleted. He knew Ironwood wouldn't go for any of them. So why bother?

"Listen, Mr. Ironwood." Lyle held out the receiver, crumpled up the sheet of paper. "Hear that? That was the list of demands they gave me. They're done."

He heard Ironwood laugh.

"So now it's your turn. What do you need from us?"

Ironwood answered so quickly and concisely, Lyle realized the billionaire had his own list prepared.

"First, full immunity from any and all charges related to my 'acquisition' of the database for myself, my son, and everyone else who aided and abetted me, especially my fine programmers." Lyle looked up to see one of the civilians give him a nod—that demand had been expected and could be worked out.

"Second, immediate cessation of all probes and audits by Treasury, and a guarantee that no new probes or audits will be launched as retaliation." Another civilian waggled her hand back and forth—maybe something could be worked out.

"Third, and most important of all, immediate and complete disclosure by the White House of all documents and other evidence relating to the ongoing cover-up of the government's knowledge of UFOs and alien visitation."

Roz would have loved to hear that one. Lyle lifted an eyebrow at DiFranza, but the general was frowning, looking over at another civilian who shook his head once.

He was still trying to make sense of that exchange when DiFranza came closer to whisper, "Can't release what doesn't exist."

"Uh, that it?" Lyle asked Ironwood, thrown off his rhythm.

"I think that's enough for you fine folks. All I ever wanted was to get the truth out. Do that for me, and I'm a happy man."

"Well, all right, so here's the consensus." The next words were some of the hardest Lyle had ever had to say. "Full immunity we can talk about. Shouldn't be a problem." He had to pause then, to let the disgust he felt shake out and sink to the bottom of his gut. Then, "The Treasury thing looks to have some complications, but it seems something can be done."

"Let's get to full disclosure."

"Well, that's the thing. I'm told that the government can't release what doesn't exist."

"The hell it doesn't."

"I'm being honest with you here, Mr. Ironwood. I've dealt with enough bleeding-edge technology cases to have heard rumors of some great store of alien technology. And, guess what? I haven't. There are three Air Force generals in the room with me right now, all honorable men, and they have no knowledge of what you want, either."

"Agent Lyle, you haven't been listening to me. I didn't go to all the bother and expense of getting a copy of your database to sell military secrets to the Red Chinese. I did it to find buried evidence of alien visitation. Visitation that is still going on today, that the government knows about, and that the people of the world deserve to know about, too."

Lyle looked to DiFranza. DiFranza looked to the unsmiling civilian. The civilian shook his head once. DiFranza took the phone from Lyle.

"Mr. Ironwood, this is U.S. Air Force General Lou DiFranza."

Lyle couldn't hear Ironwood's reply, but the general looked surprised by it. Then very surprised. "He hung up." DiFranza passed the phone back to Lyle, spoke to his fellow general. "Bulldog, as of now, you are go on Operation Clawback."

Lyle pushed away from the table and stood up. True, he had failed to make a deal with Ironwood. It was also true, now, that no deal had to be made. The Air Commandos would have his target in custody within eleven hours. Back to the States within a day of that. Justice would be served after all.

Still . . .

He walked over to DiFranza. "General, if I'm out of line, I never asked this question. But when Ironwood wanted evidence of UFOs released, and that civilian—"

"Dr. Satomura. Psychiatrist," the general said promptly. "Works extensively with Special Operations Command on hostage situations, ransom demands, areas of that nature." He laughed, though Lyle thought laughter was a touch unfair.

"I see what you're getting at, and no, there are no UFOs. No alien UFOs, that is." The general leaned in conspiratorially close. "It's no secret we have a lot of, let's call them 'interesting' aircraft flying, but none of them are from Mars. Mak Satomura, he's been through negotiations like this before, and when the subject makes an impossible demand, like wanting the government to bring someone back from the dead, or trading something for the president, or evidence of UFOs, that's a sign that further negotiation is unlikely to produce a satisfactory outcome. So when Ironwood made that screwball demand, he was letting us know he never wanted to make a deal in the first place."

Lyle had no reason to doubt that the explanation of the exchange he'd witnessed between the general and the civilian was a good one. But Roz? She would have had a completely different interpretation of it.

"Ironwood, he actually believes in UFOs and aliens, you realize," Lyle said.

"Lots of people do, but they don't put the safety and security of the United States at risk to pursue their delusions. He's dangerous, Jack. You did an exemplary job proving he stole SARGE. You got his accomplices and his son in custody. And you tracked him down for us. That's outstanding work. Now we'll take it from here." DiFranza held out his hand, and Lyle knew a dismissal when he saw one.

He shook the general's hand. "Thank you, sir."

"We'll let you know how it plays out."

"I'd appreciate that."

Lyle left the Emergency Conference Room. A marine corporal escorted him to the Pentagon's Metro entrance and watched as he passed back through the security scanners.

Lyle walked to his car in the lot under the pedestrian bridges, trying to decide why he felt so troubled.

He *had* done his job. Ironwood would be apprehended.

For all the man's crazy talk, though, after speaking with him directly, Lyle's instincts were telling him the complete opposite: Ironwood wasn't crazy.

Lyle drove off, deciding to put some distance between himself and the

Pentagon listening posts that heard in real time every cellular phone call placed within a three-mile radius of the building.

He needed to talk to Roz.

He needed to ask her the question he couldn't ask anyone else.

What if Ironwood was right?

FORTY-FIVE

"Has it all been a lie?" Bakana asked. "The Secret's *lost?*" She looked pale, close to tears, stricken by the revelations that had been forced upon her.

Victoria was dismissive of her bewilderment. "You shouldn't have heard any of this, but you have. Su-Lin was right to act to confine them."

"Bakana, everything David said is true," Jess said.

"There's a way to settle this," David said to Victoria. He still held the Taser. "Get Jess and me a detailed image of the sun map. Have an astronomer derive a date from it. Match it to the star map from the Chamber of Heaven. Then let everyone in the Family know the location of the White Island."

"You can't know the two maps will give you that location."

"You can't know they won't. Unless you try." He aimed the Taser at her. "The laptop. Use it."

Victoria crossed her arms. Her refusal unequivocal.

"Consider this, then," David said. "The First Gods shared their knowledge and gave you a secret to defend. Whatever it was, your Family lost it. Jess is giving you a chance to get that back. But you won't even let us go looking for it. You'd throw away the Mystery of the Promise—just to preserve your own domain."

"Finished?" Victoria asked.

"That's up to you."

"Fine. Put the weapon down. My security people are outside that door by now."

"You never called them."

"The blast door's closed. It's an emergency, and I'm not out there. I don't have to call them."

"Jess, can you check?" David kept the Taser leveled on Victoria. The defender stayed where she was, unreadable.

"I'll have to open it," Jess said. There was no glass in the door, no way to see into the hallway outside.

"Go ahead."

She slowly turned the brass doorknob in the dark wooden door, opened it about an inch, and—

—the door flew open as a young man burst in, seizing her by the throat with one arm as he aimed a gun at David.

"Put it down, mate." His Australian accent was strong. He wasn't an operative from Cross in Zurich. He was one of the Shop's—and Victoria's— personal security guards. His weapon was unknown to David, but it was a firearm, not a Taser.

David made one last attempt to reach the scholar inside Victoria. "When did you become so afraid of the truth?"

"Put down the weapon," she said, "or I'll tell him to shoot you."

David looked at Jess, saw only despairing resignation in her eyes. So he took a step to put the Taser on the corner of Victoria's desk. The guard moved to retrieve it. In that split second of inattention, his gun moved off target as Bakana tripped him.

"Bakana! No!" Victoria cried.

David was already grabbing for the Taser as Jess leapt for the guard. The impact of her body threw him off balance. His gun swung up, fired blindly, and as he fell back, he struck his head on the sharp desk edge. His eyes lost focus, then closed as he slumped, unmoving.

As if in a trance, Bakana picked up the guard's gun.

Jess held out her hand.

Bakana gave it to her. "The promise *must* be kept," she said. Then she turned apologetically to Victoria and—her hand flew to cover her mouth.

The Defender of Canberra was in her chair, bloody hands pressed to her chest, staring at Jess with incredulity. "You've ruined us *all* . . . you've . . ."

Then she stopped as if seeing something at a great distance, and sighed her last breath. Her head fell forward.

Jess turned to David, stricken. "How did this—"

There was no time for regret, just action. "Bakana, how do we get out of here?" David asked.

Victoria's assistant gulped, struggled to speak. "The . . . the blast door's sealed. She was . . . she was right . . . it'll take a day—"

"No," David said. "There's got to be another way." He turned to Jess. "Talk to her."

Jess put out a hand to steady the unnerved assistant. "Bakana, your instincts were right. This is about more than just me. It's about all of us—the Family. I never wanted anyone to be hurt, but we have to learn the truth. It's important that we find a way out of here. Can you help us again? Please?"

Bakana shook her head, apprehensive. "I don't know. I don't know. Victoria . . ." She sobbed.

David tried again. "This is a bomb shelter. Something with such a prominent entrance has to have another hidden exit. In case the main way out's covered in rubble after an attack."

The Cross operative swayed as he got to his feet, bloodied and sore from his fight with David. "Can you really find the White Island?"

"If we get out of here, yes," David said.

The young man staggered to Victoria's desk, ignored the body in the chair, and opened the screen of the laptop.

"Find what you need in here, and I'll show you the way out."

Jess knew she *had* betrayed everything she'd worked for all her life, everyone she'd ever known.

Victoria had been right.

But so am I, she thought.

"Here're the photographs," Bakana said. Somehow she'd rallied, rationalized her participation in the events that had led to a defender's death. As a researcher in the Shop, she was an expert in using its cataloguing system and found the sun map files in less than a minute. She turned the laptop around. "Is this what you need?"

David and the Cross operative had carefully laid Victoria's body on the floor and covered it with a throw from the back of the leather couch. Then they had tied and gagged her security guard. Bakana had warned them there could be up to three others in the Shop, depending on whether or not they were inside when the blast door closed. So far, no one else had shown up at the office door.

"That's it." The image on the screen was a close-up of the diagram etched on the meteorite Jess had seen in the Shrine of Turus.

The photo's sharp side-lighting gave high relief to the details. The six planets were there, each at a different point along its circular orbit. One moon for Earth, four for Jupiter, and a ring for Saturn.

"Is that what you expected?" Jess asked David. His simple search to unlock his personal genetic heritage to save his life had been swept into her own quest for the survival of her family's whole existence. But she felt no guilt. Too much had happened. Her life and David's were somehow intertwined: Neither of them could solve their mystery without the other. And with hunters on their trail, from the Family and from Ironwood, there was no way back for either of them.

David frowned. "Not sure. The planets all orbit at different speeds, so how often do they take on this particular arrangement? Is this the whole diagram?"

Jess thought back to the artifact in Zurich. "This doesn't show the decorative bands."

"Do you have a photo of that?"

Bakana tapped a few keys, brought up another image. Now the diagram was smaller, but the entire cut face of the meteorite could be seen, including two engraved bands around the solar system. The outer band was a narrow ring of thin radial lines. The inner band, an apparently random pattern of dots.

"Those are the stars in the zodiac," David said. "Whoever made the map might have imagined different constellations, but the stars would be the same."

Jess confirmed it. "That's the consensus."

"Then I bet that's the key. An astronomer could tell us when this specific configuration took place. You know, Mars in Aquarius, Saturn in Gemini. All at the same time. That kind of thing."

"Bakana, is there an astronomer here we can talk to?" Jess asked.

"Tomasso. He'll be in the archives."

David looked at the bound and gagged security guard. "We'll have to leave him behind."

"I can lock the office." The Cross operative wiped dried blood from his face with his sleeve.

"What about the other security guards?"

"If you trust me enough to give me the gun, you can be my prisoners."

Without a moment's hesitation, Jess took the gun from David. She dropped the magazine from the grip, checked the chamber to be certain it was clear, then gave the gun to the operative.

"Now we trust you."

Jess, David, and Bakana kept their hands on their heads as they walked slowly through the long hallways of the Shop. The operative, whose name, he volunteered, was Niklas, walked behind, empty gun in hand, Victoria's laptop under his arm. The Taser hung from a clip on his belt, but the Taser's cartridge was in the pocket of Jess's khaki shorts.

Scholars who watched the four of them pass made no attempt to interfere or even question what was happening, even though all must have known how extraordinary it was to have the whole Shop in lockdown. Jess understood why they turned away: Not to know everything was normal in the Family, and so, for most, the habit of questioning had died.

That's what David was trying to tell me . . . and Victoria . . . that this is what we've become, she thought, as scholar after scholar stepped aside or averted his eyes, her eyes. *Unquestioning slaves to tradition, suppressing knowledge that doesn't fit. Is this how we lost the Secret?*

They made only one stop, when Niklas slipped into a storage room and brought out another olive drab shirt for David, to cover the evidence of his chest wounds.

Soon after, they reached the central core of the underground facility—a ninety-foot-wide, five-hundred-foot-deep shaft straddled by a Goliath crane, a device common to shipbuilding yards. In the fifties, the crane had lowered and raised the tunneling equipment and mine borers that carved out the archive level, and in the nineties, once again, for its expansion. The Shop's Goliath was operated only occasionally now, when oversized shipments arrived for safekeeping.

Personnel and smaller loads made use of two open wire-cage elevators in opposite corners of the shaft. The larger of the two cages accommodated loads up to a small car's mass; the smaller held ten people. Niklas and his apparent captives entered the smaller cage.

Slowly and noisily, the wire-cage elevator now descended past a seemingly endless string of low-power bulbs connecting the small square of light above to the small square of light below.

The cage clanked as it reached bottom, and its sliding metal door rattled as it opened to admit its passengers to the hard rock floor of the archive tunnel. Scored and grooved, the lines on the tunnel walls and ceiling ran parallel with the narrow pipes carrying wiring, and the large round ducts for ventilation.

Tomasso Moretti was in chamber 314. Short, round, mostly bald with a wispy fringe of faded brown hair that floated around his neck and grazed his shoulders, the Family astronomer was sitting at a computer workstation, staring at a complex graph that showed a thin red line flashing between different points on a grid.

To Jess, the juxtaposition of a state-of-the-art computer in an enormous rock cavern crammed with towering shelves filled with boxes, books, and antique scrolls was business as usual. But it wouldn't be to David. Jess wished she could hear his impressions, get his viewpoint again, the way she had in Cornwall. She wondered if they'd ever talk like that again. She hoped so.

The Shop astronomer was so engrossed in his work, he was startled when Jess touched his shoulder. Still, he was delighted to have visitors—he had so few. It was clear he hadn't noticed the blast-door siren, either, so they didn't have to tell him anything of what had happened.

Jess put their question to him.

Moretti cocked his head, intrigued and honored to assist a new defender. "It's not a very difficult problem to solve," he said. "The solar system's dynamic, always changing, and for any specific arrangement of planets to repeat *exactly* . . . Well, that's something that could happen only in something more than, oh, a trillion years."

He became more animated as the implications filled him. "Since the sun will die long before that—expanding to consume the inner planets in just a few billion years from now—*no* specific alignment of planets will ever repeat. Which means each moment of the planets' combined journeys is unique."

David voiced his lack of understanding. "I thought planetary alignments were more common. Every fifty years, or hundred and fifty years. Something like that."

Moretti welcomed the opportunity to enlighten him. "Ah, but the term 'alignment' is very loose. You see, astronomers are easy to please. We say the planets are aligned when they appear in the same small *section* of the sky. That's maybe within five to ten degrees of each other. Now, for some small groupings of planets, that does happen with greater frequency. But"—Moretti held up a stubby finger to emphasize his point—"*never* exactly the same. And mathematically, well, it's easy to see that any two planets might come within a *particular* alignment quite often. Any three planets, a bit less often. Any four, less often still. And," he concluded with pleasure, "with the addition of more planets to the equation, the odds of repetition quickly escalate to . . . well, to literally astronomical proportions."

Jess realized the lonely astronomer could keep them here for days as he discoursed about the stars. She exchanged a quick glance with Bakana and Niklas. Niklas tapped his watch, and she nodded. Someone was bound to discover Victoria's body soon, and her remaining security guards would hunt her killers.

"So," she said, "you *can* tell us the date the sun map shows, from the alignment of the planets?"

The astronomer shrugged, disappointed but not surprised to be cut short. "*Si, simplice.* Though, of course," he qualified, "depending on the accuracy of the depiction of the planets' position, it might not be possible to achieve a precise date. More of a range, I'd say."

"What magnitude?" David asked.

"Perhaps a month, plus or minus a few days."

Jess smiled. "Thank you, Tomasso. Anytime you're ready."

"*Prego.*" Moretti accessed a program that controlled a telescope in Hawaii funded by the MacCleirigh Foundation. It took him less than ten minutes to run the clock backward through the centuries until the positions of the five classical planets and Earth matched the alignment against the stars on the sun map.

"*Velò*," Moretti said and leaned back in his chair.

Jess read the date range on the computer screen.

August 10–25, 8254 B.C.E.

David handed the astronomer a flash drive no larger than half a stick of gum. "There's a star map on this. Can you tell us where an observer would have to be on that date, to see these stars?"

Moretti pushed out his bottom lip in contemplation. "I'll need to assume a time of day. Maybe local midnight, but . . . why not?" he said.

This time, it took almost twenty minutes, and the answer came out in a string of numbers: longitude and latitude.

64° 48m 34s S 60° 54m 49s W

"That's not right," Moretti said.

"Why not?" Jess asked.

The astronomer called up a new program that displayed the Earth as a globe. He copied the longitude and latitude into a search window, hit RETURN.

The globe rotated to center the coordinates; then the image zoomed.

"See?" he said. "It's too far south. It must be an error."

Bakana and Niklas were confused; not so Jess and David.

On-screen was a mass of land from which a narrow peninsula stretched northward into the Great Southern Sea.

The home of the First Gods. Her hope unspoken, Jess turned to David, and for the first time she saw the same emotion there.

"Antarctica," he said, "but that's impossible. People have never lived there. Couldn't live there."

Jess understood what only those brought up with the *Traditions* could know. "People of darkness, no. They couldn't. But the First Gods were more than that, David, this was their home. The White Island." Jess said the words with reverence as Moretti gaped at her.

In that shared moment of discovery, of hope for even greater enlightenment, the next words spoken were "Hands on your heads!"

FORTY-SIX

"How dare you!" Moretti stood to face two of Victoria's security force. Their guns were drawn. "Jessica MacClary is of the Twelve Restored, and I'm of the 144."

"The Defender of Canberra is dead," the taller guard said. "These people are responsible."

The astronomer stepped back, stunned. "Victoria . . ."

"I'm under orders from the Defender of São Paolo," the guard continued. "I'm to take MacClary and her accomplices to Zurich."

Unloaded gun in hand, Niklas moved between Jess and the two gunmen, turned so the Taser on his belt was out of their sight. The moment he did so, Jess began to unhook the weapon.

Whatever they were planning, David knew they needed more cover. He edged closer to Jess, ready to act when she needed him.

The taller guard addressed Niklas. "Victoria Claridge was shot. We need to inspect your gun."

Niklas held steady. "She was alive when I left her office with my prisoners. She sent me down here to get information from Dr. Moretti. This is a defender affair. Do not interfere."

"Give me your weapon," the guard repeated. He advanced toward Niklas.

The young operative suddenly began shouting, "You will not harm a defender! Put your weapons down now! Now! Now!"

Instinctively, the guards moved back as David heard the click of the Taser cartridge as it locked into place. He started forward. Jess could take out one guard with the Taser, but not two. Then David froze as he saw what she and Niklas were doing. The operative had held out his hand behind his back, and Jess had slapped into it the magazine she'd pocketed for his unloaded gun. Then, seamlessly, they'd shifted into a new position, shoulder to shoulder, each facing a guard. Niklas with the still-empty weapon. Jess with the reloaded Taser.

"Weapons down! Weapons down!" Niklas and Jess shouted at the same time.

"Whatever you're doing, stop!" the two guards commanded.

David knew the standoff could only last a moment more. Then he saw his chance. All attention was on the four with weapons. No one was looking at him.

He tensed to leap between the guards and Jess and Niklas. If a bullet found him, it wasn't as if it would cut his life short by much.

Moretti acted first. "Enough!" The astronomer brought his chubby fist down on a control at his workstation, and the chamber's overhead lights shut off.

In an instant, the guards were shapes backlit by the open doorway. A second more, and one guard fell with a Taser dart in his chest as David threw Bakana down and covered her with his body. The other guard fired once, blindly into the dark. By then, Niklas had slapped the magazine into his weapon.

Three quick gunshots and it was over. The sudden quiet broken only by the groaning of the Tasered guard. Huddled behind his workstation, Moretti reached up to his console, switched on the lights again. Immediately David looked for Jess. She was unhurt. So was Niklas. He got to his feet, helped Bakana to hers.

Leaning against his console for support, Moretti brushed back disheveled strands of hair, trying and failing to regain lost dignity. "The location is real?" he asked in a shaking voice. "The White Island is part of Antarctica?"

"I believe so," Jess said.

"Then the Mystery of the Promise . . . it's solved?"

Jess took his hand. "I promise on the First Gods, whatever I find there, I'll tell you. I'll tell everyone. Everything."

"Defender," Moretti whispered and kissed her hand. Then Bakana took Jess's other hand and knelt beside the astronomer.

David could understand why. There was no more doubt in Jess's tone, and he wished he could share that strength as well.

———

Half a mile beyond the central shaft, some twenty minutes after they'd fled Moretti's section of the cavern through a secondary exit known to Niklas, he directed them through an unsealed entrance and into another vast chamber. Moving quickly, he led them past a remarkable set of free-standing walls some forty feet high, built from precisely shaped stones with a pinkish cast.

"What are those?" David asked Jess.

"Walls from Petra. They're from the earliest city built in Jordan. Too much Family iconography in the decorations. So we brought them here."

Family iconography. The walls were banded by a frieze of charioteers in battle, which, though ancient looking, bore signs of recent reconstruction. One wall, in particular, drew David's attention. A large opening in it was edged with carved pillars wrapped in oak leaves. Sculpted above was a medallion inset with twelve wedges, each carved with a distinctive symbol. In the very center of the medallion was a carving of a cross similar to the one that Jess had given him.

A sudden thought caused him to pat the pockets of his khaki shorts. *Yes.* It was still there. He'd concealed Jess's cross for safety when they'd arrived here.

Niklas didn't even glance at the walls from Petra, halting only when he reached a tower of crates stacked on the floor between two impressive figures, six feet high, on wooden pallets. The sculptures were strongly reminiscent of the Egyptian Sphinx, except the faces were those of men, not lions.

David had heard Jess call this room from treasures chamber 248. How many other rooms and treasures were hidden down here? How many, if not all, of the world's—and Ironwood's—mysteries could they solve?

Niklas opened a metal door behind the crates, and Jess went through it first.

"Lights?" David heard her ask as he and Bakana joined her. They were at the base of a tunnel that slanted upward.

Niklas gestured to a rack just inside the doorway. It held a dozen emergency flashlights, hand-cranked, no batteries required. "Follow the slope uphill," he said. "It'll take half an hour to reach the outer door."

"Where do we come out?" David asked.

"Don't worry. There'll be transportation."

"Niklas, you're not coming?" Jess asked.

"I'll slow them down here."

Jess turned to Victoria's assistant. "Bakana?"

"I won't tell anyone what I know, Defender. Solve the Mystery. Tell us everything."

"No more secrets," Jess promised her. Her eyes met David's.

The tests, David thought suddenly. He still hadn't told Jess what his nonhuman markers might mean for both of them. *What if she's marked for early death?* He pushed down the disturbing possibility, seeking the comfort of logic as always. From the number of her older relatives just in the Shop, there could be variations that held hope for both of them.

"No more secrets," David lied.

A half hour later, they reached the end of the inclined tunnel, only to encounter a crude airlock of sorts. A series of three doors, all metal, two painted battleship gray, long ago put in place to keep out radioactive dust after a nuclear holocaust. With David's help, Jess took particular care to reseal each door properly with the handwheels like those on watertight doors onboard ships.

Next to the first door she took the time to raid racks of emergency supplies and, more importantly, pouches of sterilized water. There she also found Australian army rations, complete with tubes of Vegemite.

When they opened the third door, chilled desert air spilled over them. It was night, and above them stars dazzled, with the Milky Way a waterfall of light. When David told her he'd never seen a night sky like this one, she told him that she had, in the Barrens, though the northern sky held other stars and shimmering auroras.

The cool night air was welcome on Jess's legs as she tipped her head back, staring upward with him. Together they searched for and found the Southern Cross. The rest of the stars, most unique to the southern hemisphere, remained unknown to both of them. Even so, that didn't make them unfamiliar.

David gave voice to what she was thinking. "The same stars *they* saw."

Silently, she walked on with him, over a small rise, until they could see the transportation Niklas had promised. It was only a few hundred feet away in a small cleared section of ground that held a sun shelter with a corrugated metal roof. Beneath were a water tank, a chemical toilet, and two dust-covered Land Rovers, the same model as the one that had met them on arrival.

David's question was in his eyes. "Safety station," Jess said, "for the guards patrolling the area. Your car breaks down out here in the summer, you can die."

They made quick trips to the no-frills facilities, then inspected the two vehicles. The keys were on the floor mats by the drivers' seats.

After making sure that one of the Land Rovers started and was fully fueled, Jess threw the other set of keys into the scrub. The brief respite from the memory—and the horror—of Victoria's violent death was over. Niklas, Bakana, and Tomasso Moretti had freed them, but she and David were on their own now. There'd be no other Family help.

Jess climbed into the driver's seat unsure of the next step, and David took the navigator's seat beside her. There was a GPS unit on the dash, and at her suggestion he powered that up.

They were about two miles from the entrance to the Shop. There were no roads out here, but there was a trail of GPS waypoints marking the path back to Highway 87.

"Where they'll probably be waiting for us," David pointed out.

"Right. So . . . where do we go?" Jess held her breath, hoping David would somehow figure out what she could not. A way they could make good on her promise to Niklas and Bakana, and Moretti.

"Antarctica."

"How? Even I can't manage that on my own."

"So we'll get help."

"From whom?"

"Someone who wants to get there as much as we do."

The night was clear, but the wind was bitterly cold. Tel'Chon struggled to keep his furs pulled tight as he trudged through the snow to the common house.

It was late, and he knew the ahkwila *workers of Nikenk would be asleep, dreaming no doubt of another snowfall that would keep them indoors tomorrow. But* khai *shipwrights and tallymen would be working still, by the light of their whale oil lamps, tying knots in their colored threads to record the outpost's production. Those who didn't sleep could be dangerous because they reported directly back to the Fleet Masters in Carth. If they recognized his presence here, and knew the rumors of what he had done, what he carried, and of what he planned with his fellow scholars, it could be the end of everything.*

Solon opened the door when Tel'Chon knocked, hurried him in, then closed it again, unrolling insulating layers of fur over the door to seal it from the icy wind. The common room was warm, and Solon's head was uncovered, revealing her shaved scalp, lustrously oiled.

The others were waiting at the table by the fire. Six of them now, banded together in secrecy. Oil lamps cast flickering light upon their dark faces. The smoky aroma of the burning oil mixed with the rich cypress scent that rose from the rafters and walls and the table itself.

Nikenk had been established to log the cypress forests of this land that one day would be called Patagonia, and the White Island was dependent on its output, first for the shipyards, and more and more with each passing year for fuel.

"Do you have it?" Solon asked.

Tel'Chon reached within his furs for the leather sack he carried. From it, he took his precious, deadly burden.

It was wrapped in the purple cloth of a scholar, and he put it on the long wooden table for the others to open.

"There," he said. "Paid in blood."

He saw the expressions of his fellow conspirators then, as they realized the rumors were true.

Holch pulled away the cloth, and for a moment everyone in the room stared in wonder at the golden book from the Hall of the Navigators. Such a thing had never been seen before outside the walls of Carth.

Carefully, Holch turned the leaves of gold, reading the glyphs and calculations. "Does this prove it?" he asked.

Tel'Chon stood close to the fire, banishing the cold. Through the stone flue, he could hear the wind howl outside. No one remembered a winter as bad as this one. "The numbers are recorded there. Scores of lifetimes' worth. They're as we suspected. And feared."

Azotekay left the table, to add more logs on the fire in blooms of crackling sparks. Like the others, Tel'Chon could see, she was troubled by the paradox before them.

"If the numbers are recorded in the Navigators' own hand, why won't the scholars accept them? If a fact is known, why would anyone make an argument against it?"

Tel'Chon lived in Carth, and knew that the influences that the scholars faced there had nothing to do with their studies. "The change we see," he told the others, "is a known fact, but an expensive one." It was vital they understand that if the scholars of Carth were to accept their proposal, then the people there would be disadvantaged. Shipments of fuel and building materials from Nikenk would be reduced, and the collapse might come sooner than predicted.

Solon approached Tel'Chon as if seeking the fire's warmth herself. She wore leather trousers and a shirt, and a brightly colored woven vest, the type made by the ahkwila here. It seemed odd to see her in clothes not meant for a true person.

"Are you concerned that, if we go through with this, we might be responsible for causing the collapse of our own home?"

"The collapse will happen anyway." Tel'Chon pointed to the Navigators' book. "The sea rises, the land changes. Not in the lifetime of one khai, but the Navigators saw it in their time, just as we see it now. If we take this action, then at least when the collapse comes, not everything will be lost. If we do nothing, then it will be the end of everything that we are, and everything that we might become."

Coscol, the eldest among them, rapped the table. It was time to decide. "The plan before us is simple. We'll divert two shares of our logging operations to build additional bridge ships and use them to establish colonies away from the middle of the world. Change might come to one colony or another, but not to all."

Solon was unconvinced. "We can't hide that much production from the shipwrights. They'll demand to know where the extra ships have gone."

Tel'Chon had the answer. "I've just crossed the Storm Sea from Carth. Conditions are worse than I've ever seen. More ships lost in that passage than ever before. All we have to do is prepare manifests showing the ships have set out for home. Then, if they don't make it . . ."

"If they discover what we're doing, they'll kill us," Solon said.

Tel'Chon had already faced that possibility. "Our lives for our people? The equation seems balanced."

"What if it's not enough?" Solon asked. "What if the change does affect the

world, and the scholars continue to reduce the numbers of us allowed to enter the Hall of the Navigators?"

To Tel'Chon, the answer was simple. "Then there's no hope for anything, and it won't matter."

"Hope is not a quantity that can be measured," Solon said.

In the end, they voted to undertake the plan and build the ships to spread themselves and their knowledge around the world. That journey and that mission was something the Navigators, for all their recorded wisdom, had never undertaken, and they had paid the price.

For the seven who sat at the table in Nikenk, it was clear. What was the purpose of studying history, if not to learn from the mistakes of those who had gone before? And what was the purpose of history itself, if it was not remembered?

FORTY-SEVEN

"Knowing what we know about Ironwood," Roz said, "we could have saved a whole lot of trouble by looking here first."

"Agent Marano," Lyle told his partner, "I don't need to hear that now. Or ever."

He and his task force were in the parking lot of a self-storage lot in Roswell, New Mexico. Less than a mile down the road was the Roswell Industrial Air Center, used by American Airlines, the New Mexico National Guard, and various aircraft maintenance companies. Once upon a time, as Roz had put it, it was the Roswell Army Airfield, site of the infamous Roswell crashed flying saucer story of 1947.

"At least we know the guy has a sense of humor."

"Let's hope it's just that." Lyle saw her questioning look but didn't bother to explain.

He, Roz, Captain Kingsburgh, two NRO technicians, and three other agents from AFOSI, together with Keisha Harrill, Ironwood's lead programmer, had pulled up to the self-storage site in three unmarked white vans and a rented Chevy TrailBlazer. Harrill, who'd been arrested at Ironwood's casino, wore an orange jumpsuit, white sneakers, and handcuffs. Roz said the ensemble was actually fashionable, perp orange being the new black-and-white stripe.

One of the AFOSI agents fitted an ordinary plastic pail around the heavy padlock that sealed the rolling garage door of unit 27. A second agent, wearing thick, insulated gloves and a face shield, poured liquid nitrogen into the pail. Two minutes later, he removed the pail, and the first agent swung a sledgehammer at the frosted lock, shattering it like glass. Ironwood had warned them not to waste time trying to cut through the nanosteel alloy—it couldn't be done.

The third agent shoved the garage door open and went inside to turn on the overhead lights.

"Thar she blows," Roz said.

On metal racks, spread more widely than they had been arranged in

Ironwood's casino, were half the 850 1.5 terabyte hot-swap drives that contained the SARGE database.

Lyle entered the cool and harshly lit enclosure. Concrete-floored, it measured ten by thirty feet. As described, there was a hole cut conveniently through the drywall to unit 28. That was where the other half of the drives were kept, joined to the first half by a thick bundle of cables.

A small beeping sound began, and Lyle looked over to a metal folding table with four computer screens and keyboards. A light on a stack of incomprehensible equipment was flashing in counterpoint to the beeping.

"Tell me that's not a bomb," he said.

Kingsburgh peered at the light. "Temperature alarm. We should close the door to keep the air-conditioning in." He motioned to one of the NRO techs.

The door came down. The beeping stopped. "Is this what you anticipated?" Lyle asked.

Kingsburgh was already at one of the keyboards, scrolling through lines of text. "Seems so."

"Okay, then. I'm going to have to stand outside to make the call."

Kingsburgh held up his phone. "I'll be on this. Send in your better half."

Lyle didn't bother to ask who Kingsburgh meant by that. He tugged the garage door up, went back to the van he'd arrived in, and held out his hand. Roz gave him the satphone. He made the call.

"That you, Agent Lyle?"

"Yes, sir, it is."

"You find it okay?"

"Right where you said."

"Does Keisha say it's all copacetic?"

"I hope you don't mind we're having our own people check it out first."

"Just as long as you stick to the deal."

The deal, Lyle thought. He was still trying to comprehend the deal.

Twenty-four hours ago, two hours before the Air Commandos reached Vanuatu, Ironwood had called the Air Force Office of Special Investigations headquarters in Crystal City, Virginia, and asked to speak with Lyle. He was using his satphone, and AFOSI patched him through to Lyle at home within a minute.

Then Ironwood said he had another proposal to make, and Lyle said he was listening.

"Clemency as before. Treasury protection as before. And no UFO evidence demands."

At the time, Lyle sincerely felt disappointment. He liked picturing Ironwood's face as the Air Commandos burst into his home, bound, gagged, and cuffed him, and gave him a ride, military style, back to America. But the forces upstairs were willing to deal if it meant the billionaire revealed the location of the stolen database, so . . .

"I can make that work," Lyle said.

"I haven't finished, son. What I want is your guarantee, in writing, of the first two conditions, and one more."

"Go ahead." Lyle felt no pressure. He checked his watch. The Air Commandos were almost at Ironwood's front door.

"I'll tell you where I'm keeping SARGE, you take Keisha there, and you let her run one last search for me, just like that one in Cornwall. Shouldn't take more than a day, then you send me the results and you can pack it all up and ship it to wherever you want. We'll be done."

As Lyle considered that, General DiFranza's voice joined their conversation, momentarily surprising him, until he realized that, of course, some, if not all, of the twenty or so personnel who had been in the Pentagon for his first call to Ironwood would have been rounded up to listen in on this one.

"Mr. Ironwood, it's General DiFranza. Don't hang up."

"No such intention."

"If this search you're requesting has anything to do with any sensitive location that could harm the United States or its allies—"

"Put a sock in it, General. You think I'm an idiot? I hope you do end up thinking there's something sensitive about what this search turns up, because then you'll just be confirming what I've been saying all along. So either way I'm a happy man. Now is that a deal, or is that a deal?"

"One search," the general said.

"Here's my fax number. I want to see it all in writing."

By the time the Air Commandos were in position, the deal had been signed, and Ironwood had told them where to go.

When Kingsburgh confirmed the entire database was online and operational, Ironwood read out a set of coordinates. General DiFranza, monitoring this unorthodox procedure from the NMCC, had the coordinates checked and, in under a minute, gave authorization for Lyle to pass the numbers to Captain Kingsburgh of U.S. Space Command, and on to Ironwood's programmer in orange.

The numbers didn't appear to have any military significance. They designated a site on the Palmer Peninsula, Antarctica.

Lyle had taken the coordinates in, personally. Roz had accompanied him without asking, and he'd allowed her to. It would have been cruel to cut her out of the end of the case that had consumed them both.

Kingsburgh was under strict orders not to let Harrill have any direct access to the database, so Ironwood's lead programmer sat back from the metal table on a cheap rolling office chair and told the air force captain how to proceed.

First, he input the coordinates. Then, on the screen before him, an aerial photo appeared of . . . of white. That was all that Lyle could see. Next, Harrill told the captain to zoom in, and the white expanded to more white, and finally some random black shapes appeared. Black rocks partially covered by snow, Lyle decided.

"Toggle the false-color control, bottom left," Harrill said. Kingsburgh used the mouse, and the screen switched from white with black to white and a garish purple-blue. "Now switch to SARGE. Bottom right."

The white areas magically disappeared, replaced by a rainbow assortment of bright colors.

"Whoa," Roz said to Lyle. "What happened?"

"I believe we're looking through the snow to the actual terrain."

"Cool."

Then Harrill gave Kingsburgh a set of step-by-step instructions having to do with setting the initial depth and resolution of the slices they were going to examine.

At this point, Lyle stopped paying attention. He had had a long talk with Roz about the exchange he had seen between DiFranza and the civilian who had been identified as a psychiatrist. Roz accepted that the general's story might be true—that a criminal who asks for something impossible in a negotiation isn't really interested in closing the deal. However, she also agreed with his argument to DiFranza, that to someone like Ironwood, asking for evidence of UFOs to be released wasn't an impossible demand—not if he truly believed such evidence existed.

Nor had she understood, as Lyle hadn't, why the psychiatrist didn't take that into account. "Unless," she had added, "he wasn't really a psychiatrist. Maybe *he's* the guy with the key to the vault where they keep the alien babies."

Lyle had looked Roz right in her mischievous eyes and asked her point-blank if she honestly, *truly,* believed the government was capable of keeping such an incredible secret for so long.

She had smiled and said, "Just because I don't believe in government conspiracies doesn't mean I can't believe in—"

"Yes, it does," he'd interrupted. Then, quite wisely he thought, they'd both decided to leave everything alien well enough alone.

On Kingsburgh's computer screen, Lyle now saw that a schematic diagram was flashing on and off in all different orientations against a rough background of random smears of color.

"What now?" Kingsburgh asked.

"We keep the joint cool and we wait." Keisha swiveled in her chair, to face Lyle and Roz. "With such precise coordinates, it shouldn't take more than a few hours." She held up her handcuffs. "Deal done?"

"Not yet," Lyle said. Ironwood was still in Vanuatu, and still had to provide the names of everyone involved in getting him the database.

After that, the only mystery remaining to be answered was why the alien-loving billionaire was so interested in such a bleak, barren, snow-covered piece of rock.

In the end, Lyle decided, the answer to that mystery was unimportant.

He'd done his job. The case was closed or soon would be.

Nothing else mattered but returning to his ordinary life.

He sat back, closed his eyes, and thought again of Roz's eyes, wondering for the first time how old was too old. How young, too young.

In the shade of an umbrella woven from palm fronds, David lay back on the white-canvas-covered deck chair on the wood veranda and tried not to think of dying. The wounds on his chest had been cleansed and dressed and no longer throbbed. There was an ice bucket beside him—polystyrene, with a printed plastic sleeve that was supposed to look like wood, perhaps the cheapest ice bucket on the planet. Still, it was filled with cans of Red Bull, and there was a cupboard in the elaborate kitchen stocked with a never-ending supply of Doritos. A year ago, he might have thought it was a good thing to live like a billionaire—even a frugal one—but ever since his inadvertent genetic discovery, everything that surrounded him was simply a distraction to mask the sound of ticking, the clock of his life running down much too quickly.

Jess was facing troubles of her own, and proximity to Ironwood was still a problem for her. David had heard the man explain to her that he had always imagined their rivalry as a chess game. That the stakes they had vigorously played for were high, but were never life or death. That Nathaniel Merrit had acted on his own, and that he, Ironwood, accepted full responsibility for not realizing what his own security chief was doing. That it had never been his intention for anyone to come to harm.

"My aunt's still dead," Jess had said. That had been the end of Ironwood's first attempt at reconciliation.

In Australia, it hadn't been difficult for David to persuade Jess they needed Ironwood to help them search for the White Island, if that's where the coordinates led. Not after he'd pointed out that there were only three groups, as far as either of them knew, that had the required resources to help. Since the air force was only interested in arresting him for espionage, and her family wanted to "confine" her, at the very least, that left only Ironwood.

Besides, David had added, despite the long-standing animosity between the MacCleirigh Foundation and the billionaire, Ironwood *was* motivated to find the lost site and study it. If Su-Lin and Andrew, on the other hand, discovered it, there was no guarantee that they wouldn't dispatch another demolition crew.

Jess had agreed.

It hadn't been that difficult to reach Ironwood, either. Jess had called the CEO of Haldron Oil and given him a brief message for Ironwood. Haldron's CEO had called his counterpart at Royal Sovereign Oil—wholly owned by Ironwood Industries. Royal Sovereign Oil headquarters were only four blocks away from Haldron's in Aberdeen.

From there, the path taken by their message was unknown to David, but he knew studies had shown that any two people on earth could be linked by as few as seven intermediate connections between acquaintances. At the rarefied levels of connection Jess and Ironwood occupied, magnified by wealth and influence, he guessed it probably didn't even take seven.

Their message had been brief and to the point. *I know where to find the oldest outpost with your help. Jessica MacClary.* Then the number for a disposable phone.

That phone had rung six hours later. Message received and answered.

Now, two days later, he and Jess were guests in Vanuatu, and they were waiting for Jack Lyle to report that a temple had been found at the coordinates taken from the star and sun maps. Maybe that would change the dynamic between Jess and Ironwood.

There wasn't much chance it would change anything for him. Twenty-three days from now, he would reach the threshold age of twenty-six years, six months. Past that date, death would come at any moment. No one he'd yet found with his genetic anomalies had lived more than five and a half months past that. There was simply no more time left.

He felt numb, angry, frustrated. He burned with the desire to do something, anything—but he didn't know what.

The satphone rang.

David opened his eyes. The phone was on a small wooden table beside him. He sat up as he heard Ironwood's heavy footsteps thud through the kitchen and onto the wooden deck.

Ironwood read the caller ID, called out, "Jessica. This is it," then swung out the satphone's stubby antenna and accepted the call as Jess joined them.

He listened. He grinned. "As soon as I receive the file, I'll e-mail the full report." He listened again. Made a face. "If there's anything wrong with the report, Agent Lyle, you know where you can find me." He disconnected. Beaming.

"Keisha found it. Within a mile of the coordinates you two worked out. About fifty feet down inside a mountain, and she says that there look to be *miles* of tunnels and other chambers and who knows what else. It's not just an outpost, you two—it's a whole base! Maybe a whole city! In Antarctica! Now is that impossible or is that impossible!"

Ironwood looked ready to dance with excitement. David was struck by the improbability—no, make that impossibility—of the existence of a complex city constructed underground in Antarctica. Jess, though, was subdued.

"Jessica?" Ironwood asked. "Shouldn't this be about the happiest day of your life? We're on the brink of confirming a major—*major*—discovery!"

Rather than respond, Jess left the veranda.

David watched her go. "She's been through a lot the past few weeks. Her whole family's out to get her because of what she's doing with us."

"Family expectations. Not an easy burden." Ironwood paused, curious. "You're not a southern boy, are you, Dave? Where're your people from?"

"Here and there." David changed the topic. "So what happens now?"

"We plan an expedition. No way to get to Antarctica now—weather, they tell me, is too dangerous. In a couple more months, it'll be coming up on what passes for high summer. I'll hire an ice-rated tub, put together a team. Helicopters, generators . . . Heck, I'm tempted to call up National Geographic, see if we can make it a live television event!"

Ironwood threw his arms out as if to embrace the world. "What'd I tell you when we met? We're going to change everything! Two months' time, we're going to change the world!"

Caught up in his own delight, Ironwood had failed to notice that David was as unresponsive to his news as Jess MacClary.

Whatever was waiting in Antarctica, David knew he'd never see it. There'd be no discovery that could save him. Jess and Ironwood might still win what they were after, but David had lost everything.

FORTY-EIGHT

"How exactly did you obtain this?"

Andrew McCleary tapped a neatly shaped fingernail against the incomprehensibly colored printout on the mirror-polished surface of his desk.

Across from him, Merrit sat rigidly upright. His right ankle was still tightly bandaged, but his back had recovered and the wounds on his rib cage were healing as they should. None of those injuries interfered with his perception of danger, though. He knew the risk he had taken walking through the doors of this law firm, and into this man's office. These people were as experienced as he was in making the unwanted disappear.

"The government e-mailed that file to Ironwood as soon as they obtained it. I have access to his company's mail system. The encryption wasn't strong."

McCleary studied the yellow outline on the printout. It, at least, was recognizable, Merrit knew. Ironwood's alien outpost. Or a temple, as the Foundation referred to it. The rest of the background image was a jumble.

"How did you know the government would be sending it?"

"I didn't. I monitor everything going to and from Ironwood. That's how I know Jessica MacClary and David Weir are working with him. They probably have been from the beginning."

"No," McCleary said. "We've had another source within the Ironwood camp. This is the first there's been any contact with Jessica."

Another source? Merrit tried not to show his interest in what the man had just revealed. "Anyway," he said, "they're working together now."

The lawyer smoothed his already perfect tie, and looked over to the screen angled up from the side of his desk. "What say you?"

On the screen, Su-Lin Rodrigues y Machado pursed her lips in thought. Merrit had only seen a single photo of her in her file. It had been taken through an extreme telephoto lens at night, many years ago. She looked younger in person. Or what passed for in person these days. Ironwood's file said Rodrigues was based in Zurich, and, from the slight satellite delay in her video, Merrit thought it likely that was where she was transmitting from.

"What's your purpose in bringing this to us?" she asked.

"I need protection." That *was* the truth, and truth was required because, Merrit was certain, McCleary's inevitable voice-stress analyzers would be processing every word he said, probing for lies.

The woman's smile had an edge. "There are those in my family who could say the same: that they need protection from you."

"Miscalculations and wrong moves. I'm not the only one working for Ironwood."

"If you're so ready to betray your previous employer," McCleary asked, "how can we possibly trust you?"

"Ironwood betrayed *me*." That was the truth as well.

"If all this plays out as you hope," the woman said, "what form would our protection take?"

"Cross Executive Protection Services. I could be an asset."

"You'd work for us?"

"Same work I've been doing for Ironwood. Assembling teams and maintaining security at sites around the world."

Merrit watched as McCleary and Rodrigues regarded each other across the screen. There was some type of information being passed between them. *Subliminal?* If so, it betrayed a close association.

"Very well, Mr. Merrit," the lawyer said. "We'll take you on—provisionally. Until we see how this information checks out."

"How will you do that?" Merrit asked. Any time he spent waiting without the shield of the MacCleirigh Foundation was time he was at risk of arrest by the air force.

"You'll be doing it yourself," Rodrigues answered. "The Foundation has good friends in the Casa Rosada. You understand?"

Merrit didn't.

"Argentina, Mr. Merrit. There was trouble there a few years ago. The Foundation played a part in restoring their troubled economy and, as a result, we have the goodwill of many public officials."

"I don't get it." Merrit doubted he was supposed to. This felt like a test. "What's important about Argentina?"

On the screen, Rodrigues held up her own copy of the printout he had provided. "The location of this . . . underground complex is on territory Argentina claims as its own. Tierra de San Martín, they call it. There's an Argentine airbase and a settlement nearby, both within a hundred and fifty miles of this site. We won't have any difficulty enlisting our friends' assistance to locate it and confirm that structures, buried or otherwise, exist there. They will also assist us in taking the appropriate action."

Merrit realized McCleary and Rodrigues were expecting another response from him. An informed one this time.

"Appropriate action," he repeated, and saw their expectations rise. "Like in Cornwall."

His new employers shared the same smile.

"As in Cornwall," the lawyer agreed.

FORTY-NINE

Even worse than being ordered to make a deal with a criminal like Iron-wood was having to write a report of the sorry affair.

Jack Lyle had a stack of notepads to review.

Sealed in a plastic bag was the logbook used by Del Chang at the stake-out of Weir's warehouse lab. It was charred around its edges, blown clear of the hit by a shoulder-launched rocket. It was obscene to Lyle that no one would pay for that outrage.

The only consolation, if there could be one, was that it seemed the country, and the world, were safer today because the SARGE database was back under U.S. control. Even though the trigger to the deal was now classified at the highest compartmentalized level, General DiFranza had gotten word back to him that Ironwood's algorithm was everything they'd hoped for: Whatever the individual cost, the benefit to the country more than outweighed it. It was a trade-off only a warrior could understand—human life for a better world. Lyle understood the general's assessment, but that didn't mean he liked it.

Then there were the transcripts. Every conversation that had ever occurred between Weir and Ironwood.

Lyle sighed and rubbed his aching knee. It was going to take him longer to write his report than it had taken to close the case.

He looked out the door to Roz's desk. A few moments ago, she'd been there working on her parts of the report. He wondered where she'd gone. Lunch?

His phone buzzed.

He answered, wondering if she had read his mind. It was the sort of thing she'd believe in.

"Jack, it's Lou DiFranza."

It took a moment for Lyle to recognize the name without the rank. "General?"

"For this call, it's Lou."

"Two guys in a room?" It was the code for putting rank aside. He was about to hear something that the rules said he shouldn't, but that a three-star general thought he should.

"*Exactly. The Ironwood deal might not pan out.*"

"Lou" had his full attention.

"*Those coordinates he gave us. On the Antarctic Peninsula. It looks like there's a military connection after all.*"

"In the Antarctic?"

"*No one here knows what the connection is, but I got a heads-up from NSA that those coordinates are flagged in some back-and-forth traffic between assets of the Sixth Brigade of the Argentine Air Force.*"

"You lost me."

"*They're planning some kind of show of force, Jack. Analysts here are thinking it has to do with them maintaining their claim to the peninsula as their own territory. So they're going to conduct military operations there.*"

"What kind of operations?"

"*No word on that yet. They're moving their Mirage fighters and a refueling tanker to the Gallegos airbase, right at the tip of South America. And they're shipping supplies, thought to be munitions, to the Marambio airbase. That's on an island just off the peninsula, maybe two hundred klicks from the Ironwood site. ETA is four days, and they'll be good to go anytime after that.*"

Lyle was still at sea. "I don't know what to say. I've never picked up any sort of involvement with Argentina or Antarctica in any of our intercepts."

"*Well, things are getting fierce here, and I thought you should know. There's been a report floating around that the way Antarctica's been losing its ice cover, it's about to be a flash point for resource competition. Easy to sign a treaty promising not to mine or drill someplace where it's impossible to do it anyway, but if different countries are already starting to covertly establish commercial and industrial bases down there . . . I tell you, our big concern is that Ironwood duped us into using SARGE to reveal the location of a secret British base, and the Argentines are going to react as if their home soil's been invaded. It'll be the Falklands all over again, and if that's what's going down, they'll be looking for a fall guy, and I don't want it to be you. Watch your six, Jack.*" The general clicked off.

Lyle stared at the small phone in his hand until he realized he wasn't alone.

Roz was standing in his doorway, her concern evident.

"Interesting call?" she asked.

"How much did you hear?"

"Argentina and Antarctica. So I'm guessing this is something to do with our favorite pardoned felon."

"The pardon might not apply much longer."

Roz whistled. "Details?"

Lyle had her close the door, then told her everything.

When he had finished, Roz said, "That doesn't sound right."

Lyle tapped his fingers on his desk. "I know Ironwood's never given a sign of being in contact with a foreign agency, but—"

"I don't mean that," Roz interrupted. "I mean the Brits carving out a secret underground military base in Antarctica—without us and about twenty other countries happening to notice. I believe in a lot of crazy things, but that scenario's too far out. Even for me."

Lyle had his doubts as well, but if the Pentagon was investigating, there was some slim chance of possibility. Otherwise, what other answer could there be?

"Okay then, skeptic, this is what we do know. One: Ironwood's technique for finding underground structures with the SARGE database works. A little bird told me his algorithm's the real deal."

Roz shook her head pityingly. "A little bird? The real deal? You've been listening to Ironwood too long. I'd be happy to provide an upgrade."

Lyle continued, undeterred. "Two: Since the algorithm works, odds are good there is an actual underground structure at the site in Antarctica. Three: The Argentine air force is apparently planning to bomb the site. So given those facts, what conclusion do we draw?"

"A Nazi sub base?"

"Focus, Roz."

"No, I'm serious. There's always been talk about the Nazis building a base in Antarctica just before World War II. There was a German whaling industry, so they had a presence down there at the time. Whaling probably had some kind of strategic importance, so no surprise some country on a war footing would want to ensure supplies."

"How do you know this stuff?"

"Aliens beam it into my brain when I'm sleeping. I read, Jack."

"Okay, okay. So what else did you read about the Nazis?"

"Well, after the war, a couple of U-boats did turn up in Argentina. So maybe there's something buried in Antarctica that speaks to some long-ago involvement between the two governments. The Argentines today had nothing to do with it, but who needs the bad publicity, right? So they decide to obliterate a less than glorious bit of history in the name of public relations. Like we wouldn't do the same."

Lyle thought it over. In a crazy sort of way, Roz's scenario made more sense than thinking a modern installation had been built undetected during the era of satellite surveillance.

"Not bad," he said, "but there's still a problem."

"Only one? I'm improving."

"We used the SARGE database to find the underground structures. Sent the info to Ironwood. Forty-eight hours later, the Argentines know about it, too. How'd that happen?"

"Ironwood sold them the info is what you're suggesting?"

"Easier than believing the Argentines are listening in on our conversations with him."

"Okay. So here's what we do," Roz said. "Phone up Ironwood and tell him what you told me: In five days, his long-lost alien base is going to be a test range for the Argentine air force."

"What does that get us?"

"My read on Ironwood is that he'll freak."

"And if he doesn't?"

"Then he doesn't care. Which means we've been had. Which means he did sell the info to the bad guys. Which means his pardon is toast. Which means we get to go on a road trip to Vanuatu and slap the cuffs on him ourselves. Make sense?"

Lyle knew there was a reason he kept her around.

"I'll make the call," he said.

FIFTY

At night, the few lights of Port Vila subtracted some of the brilliant stars above but added to them below, their reflection glimmering in the slow rise and fall of the harbor's dark waters.

David found Jess on the veranda, hands on the thick wood railing, gazing down at the distorted mirror, or, perhaps, at nothing. He hadn't seen her since she and Ironwood had their run-in.

Her shoulders straightened as he approached, and he knew she'd heard him. He leaned against the railing, his back to the harbor.

"I called Cambridge," she said.

"The testing?" They'd been told the university's first attempt to sequence his DNA had been flawed. David could guess why the technicians had said that. He'd thought the same the first time he had made the attempt.

"Preliminary results."

"And?" David had almost forgotten about the DNA swabs they'd sent from Cornwall to Cambridge. No matter what those results were now, he had no way of using the information to save himself. No time.

"You've got the anomalies in your genes. I don't. They'd like to do a complete sequencing of your genome now."

That was it, then. He and Jess weren't what she called "cousins." *At least Jess is safe,* David thought with relief. Nor would he have to tell her what those anomalies might cost her, as they were costing him.

Jess's voice had betrayed more than disappointment, however, *Why?* A moment later, he had it. "You think that means *I'm* a MacCleirigh, and *you're* not."

She kept her back to him. "Finding your anomalies in other people is how you found our temples."

Maybe he couldn't help himself, but he could still help her. "Have you ever heard about genetic drift?"

She hadn't.

"It's something that can happen because of the way genes get divided through the generations." David turned to face the harbor, shoulder to shoulder beside her. "You know how a child is a fifty-fifty combination of her parents, right? Well, a lot of people think of a grandchild as twenty-five percent of each grandparent, but that's not quite right.

"You see, if the grandchild's a boy, there's a chance one of the grandmothers might not have made any genetic contribution. If it's a girl, one of the grandfathers might be out of the chain. So—and here's the important thing—after three or four generations, someone might still be able to definitely trace back their connection to a recent ancestor, say a great-great-great-grandmother or -grandfather by birth, but genetic drift means there might be absolutely no genetic connection."

He couldn't see Jess's face. It was hidden by her hair.

"Genetic drift happens all the time, Jess. In fact, it's probably the engine that speeds up evolution to make new species arise so quickly when small populations are isolated."

"So I'm a MacCleirigh by name. Just not genetically."

"Maybe think of it another way. Genetics is just how our bodies are put together. Names are what really define us. Our culture. Our beliefs. Our traditions." David was finding this part of his argument unusual for him. He'd never been one for family. Not even friends. He'd never thought of culture or beliefs or traditions defining him.

"You're still a MacCleirigh. You're still a defender. And you're only a few weeks from solving the Mystery of the Promise. In Australia, you told them you'd do everything you could."

"I'm doing that, all right. I'm working with the monster who's stolen our heritage and killed one of our own."

David took that statement to be a last echo of what Jess had been struggling with alone. "You know it's not as black and white as that."

"Maybe he didn't pull the trigger, but he gave the order, intentional or not. Not a lot of difference for my aunt."

Not a lot of difference for me, either, David thought. He took a breath. *No more secrets.* If she could accept the truth, so could he. Maybe he would tell her everything he knew about his genetic anomalies, about the death sentence they conferred. Who knew? It might even make her feel better that she didn't share those lethal markers with him. Maybe they'd both feel better equally unburdened.

Before he could begin, however, the kitchen door to the veranda flew open, and Crazy Mike rushed out.

"Mr. Woody needs to see you both, right now."

The quiet tastefulness of Ironwood's study was unexpected, especially after his casino, but, on second glance, David found it also had its oddities.

An antique globe at least three feet across, mounted in a polished wooden stand, was ornamented with what appeared to be a solid gold meridian, and Ironwood's gigantic desk was carved, it seemed, from a single block of wood, if such a feat were possible. Just getting it into this room would have required the removal and replacement of a wall.

"I've had a call from Jack Lyle. We need to talk." Ironwood gestured to a pair of wicker chairs, but his gaze was fixed on an oil portrait on a nearby wall. It was of himself, much younger, and a diminutive woman with light brown hair. In the background, David recognized Port Vila harbor as seen from this room's windows.

The down-feather cushions on the chairs were deeply comfortable. David settled back. "Something wrong with the database?"

"No." Ironwood's chair swiveled away from the portrait, a determined look on his face. "There's been some kind of . . . security breach. Don't know where. But . . . Jessica, it appears your people got hold of the SARGE printout of the outpost—the temple—on the peninsula."

David was about to ask how when Ironwood held up a hand to stop him. "Somehow, they have used their considerable influence on certain members of the Argentine government, or military, or . . . I don't know how they did it, but the Argentines are going to bombard that outpost with every weapon at their disposal."

"Su-Lin." Jess started to her feet. "I have to talk to her. She has to know how wrong this is."

"No, no, no." Ironwood motioned for her to sit down again. "Even if that woman takes your call, I guarantee that the only thing she'd do is play you along until bombs fall."

"You have a plan," David said.

"Already in motion. The Argentines are going to bomb in three days."

"From now?" Jess looked horrified.

Ironwood nodded. "So we'll be there in two."

Two days from now? David felt a jolt of hope, but still he asked, "What happened to 'It'll take months for the weather to clear'?"

"It's not my show. This is courtesy of the U.S. Air Force."

"Jack Lyle's sending us on the air force's dime?" Now David was confused.

"Oh, I'm picking up the tab." Ironwood grimaced. "Fuel, planes, crews. The air force lends its equipment and people for worthy civilian causes, provided the civilian covers the costs. About four million dollars, they figure. It's worth every penny if we find an alien outpost that hasn't been cleaned out by looters. Or one of your temples of the First Gods, Jessica. Maybe that White Island you told me about. Heck, I'd even settle for the first evidence of *human* habitation of Antarctica. Whatever it is down there, they're going to have to rewrite *all* the history books. Because of the three of us. Because we did not give up."

"Why's the air force helping us at all?" Jess asked.

David had the same question. He wasn't buying military civic-mindedness.

"Because"—the billionaire spread his arms to indicate the room, and by extension all that he possessed—"I gave up my pardon, all my guarantees, most of my company . . . so we could get there first.

"I've agreed that three days from now, they can take me away, make an example of me, and put me in prison for what will surely be the rest of my natural life.

"So let's make sure what we find is worth it."

CORNWALL 7,312 YEARS B.C.E.

CORNWALL 7,322 YEARS B.C.E.

HAVI ATOLL 7,418 YEARS B.C.E.

MALTA 7,567 YEARS B.C.E.

PATAGONIA 7,794 YEARS B.C.E.

ANTARCTICA 7,794 YEARS B.C.E.

In the innermost chambers of the Scholars' Peak, Tel'Chon swept down the spiral staircase, oil lamp held high, preparing his argument, incapable of believing he would not prevail.

At the spiral's end, he stepped through the narrow doorway and closed the vent of the lamp to extinguish its flame.

The path through the cavern was always lit. Tall braziers flanked the precisely worked stones that led from the stairway's narrow tower to the Hall of the Navigators. Flames roared from raised metal gratings, and smoke curled up to the distant ceiling, but the cavern was so large that the air was never harmful, even in the past when all the braziers had been lit along the pathway, instead of only one out of every three.

That was part of his argument. There was a time in living memory when all the fires of the cavern could burn continuously because there was ample fuel to be gathered in the lands surrounding the Scholars' Peak and the port of Carth below it.

Now, though, the forests seen in the murals painted throughout the corridors above were gone. The once green land supported only sparse bushes, useless clumps of blowing grass. Without vegetation to hold it in place, each year the winds blew more of the soil away.

And the snows, anyone with eyes could see, advanced down the mountains a little more each year. Sometimes not enough to notice from one winter to the next— but look at the murals, look at the landscape. In the centuries since the artists had done their work, the snows had advanced by stadii.

Tel'Chon walked quickly, fearing that Ganesh would change his mind and refuse the audience. But as he neared the end of the pathway, he saw the towering doors to the great Hall were open, and the braziers to either side, twice as tall as the ones marking the path, blazed as if there were no shortage of fuel, and never would be.

Tel'Chon paused for a moment before the golden model of the Navigators' cross, this one fashioned by the Navigators themselves. The supporting rod it sat upon, which served as a locking latch for the tall doors, was wrapped in bands of white and purple ribbons. Without them as protection, it was dangerous to handle the heavy cross. The underside of the rod was fitted with sharp edges that could cut unwary

315

palms and fingers. Why they were there, no one knew, though obviously the Navigators had placed them there for a purpose.

Tel'Chon cleared his mind, stepped through the doors that were more than twice his height, and announced his presence. His voice echoed in the Hall. It was circular, as wide across as fifteen khai *lying head to feet in a line.*

On its great, encompassing wall, Tel'Chon had heard, there was a diagram that explained the most complex known facts of the Earth's origin. Whether that rumor was true or not, the young scholar couldn't be sure. For now, the wall was covered by overlapping panels of woven purple cloth, to be removed only when the doors were closed and Gold Master scholars were assembled.

Tel'Chon had years of study to complete before he could even begin his ascension to that rank.

Ganesh looked over to him. The old scholar was by the central table, a circular structure of carved stone shelves, tiered to hold 1,321 of the Navigators' gold books. Each one was a collection of fifty-three thin squares of gold on which their numbers and charts and star paths were embossed.

There was other information in them, too, Tel'Chon knew. So far, however, despite generations of study, only the portions with numbers and star patterns had been translated.

"Your message said you have a study proposal." Ganesh looked back to the book he read in the light of the small braziers that ringed the tiered shelves. It was clear he didn't think this audience would last long.

Tel'Chon began with his carefully prepared preamble. "Gold Master, there is a need in the Fleet to prepare new charts of the Storm Sea passage from Carth to Nikenk."

Ganesh used a carved ivory rod to turn a gold leaf in the book he consulted. "The recent shipping losses have been caused by storms, not problems with the charts. You may go now."

Tel'Chon was prepared for that rapid dismissal. "Gold Master, the new charts I propose are not for revising navigation."

Ganesh looked up from his book. "What else would navigation charts be used for?"

"Records of the weather, of storm conditions."

"Can you read the Navigators' hand?"

"No, Gold Master, but the storm conditions can be inferred from the charts describing wave height and wind speed."

"What would be the purpose of that inference?"

"To better predict storms. To allow the Ship Masters to change course or delay a voyage in order to reduce the risk of loss."

Ganesh closed his book and tapped his leaf turner on the edge of a shelf, agitated.

"The same calculations could be used to support the contention of some that storm conditions are worse now than in the past."

Tel'Chon agreed. "Numbers show us the patterns of the world. Some patterns do change over time."

"But the world does not."

Tel'Chon had thought he would have prevailed with his argument for better storm prediction. Who could argue with the need? He realized there must be a hidden reason why Ganesh was being so obstinate.

"Gold Master, I share the contention that the storms are worse. And that the Navigators' charts show the landshapes are changing. And—"

"Enough!" Ganesh punctuated his command with a sharp rap of his ivory rod. "You may leave now."

Tel'Chon didn't know what else to do, except beg. "Please, Gold Master. We've lost too many ships this past year."

"Ships are always lost. The shipyards will build more."

"With what? Each ship lost on the return from Nikenk means a loss of cargo. Of fuel. Of food. What happens if we lose so many ships the people of Carth go hungry? Or freeze?"

"That will not happen. You may go."

"But it happened to the Navigators!"

Ganesh's dark face twisted in anger, a rare expression in any khai. "You should know better than that. The fate of the Navigators is not a known fact."

Tel'Chon felt reciprocal anger rise. "Their fate is in their books. Read them. They're only charts and observations. There's no sign they ever spread beyond these shores. They sailed the world, but like seabirds following the seasons, they kept returning to this one place. Never established a second home. They built this magnificent library of their knowledge. But they didn't act on it! And when this land changed, they vanished!"

Ganesh left the central table. With a trembling hand, he clutched the neck of Tel'Chon's tunic and pulled down, ripping the purple fabric of his scholar's colors.

"You're finished here," Ganesh said. "Leave now and never return."

Tel'Chon was stunned. To never see this hall again? To never read another book? To never know the secret that lay behind the fabric panels?

"I won't leave." It was unthinkable to give up the search for knowledge.

Ganesh raised his ivory rod and brought it down across Tel'Chon's face.

The young scholar rocked back in shock and pain. "Master, no!"

Ganesh struck again. And again. Until Tel'Chon could take no more and struck back, pushing the frail scholar with the force and the anger of youth denied.

Ganesh stumbled backward, fell, and the crack of his skull against the stone floor was like a lightning strike in the great Hall.

Panicked, Tel'Chon knelt by the scholar's side, but it was already too late. His eyes stared sightless, pupils dilated, and the blood that spread from the gash in his scalp flowed from gravity, no sign of a pulse.

With the knowledge that Ganesh was dead, Tel'Chon rose. There would be no gain in reporting what had happened. Calmly, he went to the shelves and found the book he required, listing the Navigators' voyages from the White Island to the near outposts, across the Storm Sea.

He would take this to his colleagues in Nikenk. It was the evidence they would need to finalize their plans.

Tel'Chon paused in the open doors, looking back at the body he had left where it had fallen. He wondered what their fate would be, the ones who denied the known facts of change and who would not prepare for it. There were some scholars, he decided, who would rather curl up and die with their old books than undertake the challenge of writing new ones.

He left the Hall of the Navigators, never to return. Never to know that in the ages to come, he would be proven right.

FIFTY-ONE

The noise was relentless. The vast cargo hold of the C-17 Globemaster cargo transport was a drum the size of a basketball court, constantly pounded by four roaring engines ramming through the Antarctic sky.

Less than an hour out, David had wadded up squares of toilet paper from the head and stuffed them into his ears. It helped, but not enough.

He'd tried leaning back, shutting his eyes, aiming for unconsciousness, and had almost succeeded. But the drop-down canvas seat on the outer wall seemed to magnify the engine roar, and the startling bang from the in-flight refueling maneuver wrenched him from a shallow sleep with a rush of adrenaline that left him wide-awake and haggard.

Air Commandos, however, apparently could sleep anywhere, even on top of the plastic-shrouded supply pallet at the far end of the hold. Some of them were snoring. Jess wasn't, but she was on the other side in another drop seat, eyes closed, asleep. David envied her.

Six hours into the flight from Christchurch International Airport in New Zealand, Jack Lyle pulled down a seat beside him. Like the others on this flight—including David, the twelve commandos, Ironwood, Jess, and Lyle's partner, Agent Marano—the AFOSI agent wore a white insulated parka with matching padded trousers. When the time came to deploy, there'd be about fifteen other articles of clothing and equipment to put on, but for now, the parka and trousers were enough to keep them warm in the cargo hold. Even too warm. Lyle's parka, like his, was open.

"How're you holding up?"

"Doing fine." David wished he had his iPod. It was a good conversation killer—and he could use one, especially with this man who'd threatened and lied to him. *Ambient recordings of the rain forest.* Just imagining that wash of natural sound made him relax. A bit.

"Look, kid, if you're pissed about the way things played out, I'm sorry you feel that way, but I had a job to do. And it turned out okay for you, at least, right?"

"Peachy," David said. He didn't like or trust Jack Lyle. He knew the only reason he wasn't facing charges for misuse of government resources, and wouldn't be in federal prison for the rest of his life—all five more months of it, if he was lucky—was that Ironwood had insisted that the original pardons he'd negotiated remain in force. His programmers—no surprise there—were already under contract to the National Reconnaissance Office to further develop the search algorithm they'd created. Now only Ironwood was left to carry the can.

David didn't understand why he was of any further interest to the air force. "You're only doing all this so Ironwood will give himself up. If he'd asked you to dress up like Mickey Mouse and sing opera in Times Square, you'd have done that, too."

"That would have been easier," Lyle said. "Anyway, just wanted to say I heard from your old boss a while ago. Colonel Kowinski. She was part of the investigation, you know."

Big surprise, David thought. "How's she doing?"

"I'm sure she'd say, 'Outstanding.'"

"Yeah, she would."

"She was very curious about that nonhuman DNA sample you tried to pass off as Neanderthal."

David tightened. *This* wasn't Lyle's business.

"Turns out it's yours. Care to comment?"

David's silence didn't deter the agent. "Me, I'm curious about how you and your 'anomalies' are at the heart of everything that's unexplained: Ironwood and his hunt for aliens. A young woman shot at in public by employees of her family. Argentines bent on blasting to oblivion whatever it is we're heading for. All of it's got something to do with you. You might as well tell me. I'm going to find out sometime."

Agent Marano joined them, swamped by her military cold-weather gear. Combat wear obviously didn't come in a size small enough for her.

She had a Thermos of coffee and some paper cups. "Caffeine?" she asked. Both David and Lyle said yes, so there was a momentary truce. *Predators at the watering hole,* David thought.

"Join you guys?" she asked.

David made no objection, neither did Lyle, so she poured coffee for herself, pulled a seat down, and sat beside her partner.

"So," she said, leaning forward to be in David's line of sight, "what do you think we're going to find?"

"No idea. Your turn."

"World War II Nazi sub base." Marano raised her coffee cup to Lyle. "The boss thinks it's a secret British research station. We've got ten bucks riding on it."

David couldn't tell if she was being serious. "What happens if it's a Nazi sub base that the British have turned into a secret research station?"

Her sudden grin looked genuine. "Good one. I guess that would be a draw." She took a sip of coffee. "Seriously, what do you think?"

"Not my area of expertise. Therefore, no opinion."

Marano wrinkled her nose at him. "C'mon, what do you *want* it to be?"

What David wanted it to be—not that he'd tell two AFOSI agents who were riding him for no reason he could deduce—was an answer. Something that no one had thought of, no one had considered, yet would somehow reconcile everything Ironwood believed, everything Jess believed, and everything that was locked in his own DNA.

That, he suspected, was not only improbable. It was impossible.

"Whatever it is," he said truthfully, "it's just going to raise more questions. Finding one of anything is never enough to change a scientist's mind. If you think about it, the experts say early humans couldn't have made the voyage to Antarctica, let alone build anything there. So if we do find an outpost—temple, whatever—like the one in Cornwall, Ironwood gets to say, 'I told you so,' but in the end, it'll be like finding those Viking settlements in Canada. People still say Columbus was the first European to reach North America because his voyage is what started the modern age of exploration and colonization. All the other Europeans who came earlier, they were all blind alleys, so who remembers them?"

"If it's not important what we find," Marano asked, "then why are you doing this?"

David caught the approving nod Lyle gave his junior agent. *In case there's the slightest chance there really is an answer there for me,* he thought. *Something that might make dying easier.* "Just seeing it through," he said. He sat back, holding his hands around the paper coffee cup, warming them.

Heavy bootsteps clanked on the metal floor of the cargo hold.

"Heard there was coffee," Ironwood said. He'd lost color; he wore a small scopolamine patch behind each ear and an acupressure band on each wrist, both measures failing to deal with his air sickness.

"More like tinted water," Lyle's partner warned him. She stood to pour from the Thermos as if Ironwood were one of her superiors.

The big man sipped the hot liquid, his expression signaling agreement with her. "What's the word?"

Marano led him through the competing theories of what was waiting to be discovered on the peninsula: sub base, secret station, a combination of both, a solitary outpost, or a temple.

"But I guess you know what's there," she concluded.

Ironwood stood in front of the three of them. Cold-weather combat gear did come in extra large, and, even weakened by motion sickness, he looked formidable, a walking glacier.

"Don't go putting words in my mouth, darlin'. I know what I *expect* to find, but I'm more like my friend Dave here than you think. I won't *know* what's there until I see it."

"Still," Lyle said, "you're thinking aliens." David was surprised at how reasonable Lyle made that question sound. As if he wasn't looking for an argument. Devious.

"I'm always thinking aliens, son. Ever hear of Occam's Razor?"

Marano's delighted smile transformed her face, making her even younger. "The simplest solution is the best."

Ironwood gave her a paper-cup salute. "So what's the simplest solution to the real historical conundrum? How is it that agriculture, written language, astronomy, and architectural engineering—in the form of pyramids— turn up around the world in unconnected human populations, all at the same time? Do we say it's a remarkable and highly unlikely chain of coincidences? Or did somebody with advanced capabilities simply drop off the instruction books?"

"Okay, but why aliens?" Lyle asked. "Why not an earlier civilization that figured those things out, spread them around the world, then disappeared?"

"Very good question," Ironwood said. "With an even better answer. No evidence. You'd think people like that would've left something behind. I mean, we've got scads of artifacts left over from the Romans, the Greeks, the Egyptians, the Babylonians—all the real, true early civilizations left their footprints in the sands of time. So, Occam's Razor again, what's the simplest solution? A mysterious civilization even more mysteriously disappeared off the face of the earth and took all the evidence with them? Or the spacecraft landed, handed out the knowledge we'd need to move from being hunter-gatherers to farmers—the beginnings of technological civilization—and then took off again?"

David couldn't resist offering a third possibility. "What if that early civilization told its followers, its students, to hide all the evidence of its existence? What if the evidence was selectively removed from the historical record, specifically to hide the fact that that civilization existed at all?"

"Conspiracy," Marano said. "I like it."

Lyle was no believer. "A conspiracy that holds together over thousands of years? How could anything remain a secret that long?"

"Yucca Mountain," David said.

"The nuclear waste facility that got mothballed?" Marano asked, intrigued.

David explained. "At the time it was being built, the authorities figured the waste they planned to bury in it would stay lethal for at least ten thousand years. So the government pulled together a group of scientists, historians, even science fiction writers, to come up with a way to mark the area as dangerous, to keep people from digging there for a *hundred* centuries. Because they expected entire civilizations to rise and fall, there'd be different languages and cultures. So their question for their experts was: How do we preserve and transmit a message through all those years?" David paused. "Any guesses what one of the solutions was?"

"Start a religion," Marano said promptly.

"The MacCleirigh Foundation." Ironwood snorted. "Wouldn't that be a hoot." Then he added, thoughtful, "I'd be more interested in *why* it's important to hide evidence of an early civilization."

David unbuckled his seat belt and stood up. "While you three figure that out, I'm going to check on Jess."

"One last thing, kid." Lyle reached into his parka's map pocket. "Just because this case is over. Almost over." He drew out a wallet-sized photograph that David recognized at once, and also knew had to be a copy. The original was in his fake passport with his belongings, in Christchurch.

"Back when this started, I was trying to get a line on you. This was the only personal item in your lab cubicle."

"Besides a Wolverine mug," Marano said.

Lyle conceded the point. "Photograph and mug."

"You thought they'd tell you something significant about me." David was incredulous.

"It's called profiling. Standard professional tool."

"The mug belonged to the guy who had my job before me. He left it in the staff kitchen. I inherited it."

"But the photograph," Lyle said. "That is yours. Taken on a family trip, at two twenty-four in the afternoon of July second, twenty-one years ago at Big Bear Lake."

David rolled his eyes. The air force had gone to a lot of trouble finding that out. For nothing. "January '94. California. Ring any bells?"

"The Northridge quake." Marano shot a glance at Lyle, who shrugged. "One of the biggest to hit L.A. at the time."

"My mother had all our stuff in storage there. The place was under a freeway overpass. The overpass collapsed. We couldn't get there till two days later. Whole place was roped off, and the bulldozers were already scooping everything up. It was all gone. Walking back to the bus stop, I saw that photo blowing around on the ground. It's the only thing we had that survived. Other than that, it doesn't mean a thing. Just random chance."

He left them to their unsubstantiated theories.

Nine hours out of Christchurch, the loadmaster dropped the cargo bay ramp, and Antarctica howled into the flying cavern, instantly devouring the last trace of warmth.

David gasped at the sudden change in temperature. The underlying snarl of wind and engines stayed muffled because of his balaclava, his combat helmet, and the white parka hood he'd pulled tightly over it.

"Everything's normal," Sergeant Dodd shouted into his ear. Dodd was the Air Commando David was strapped to for the jump. They stood together, well back from the pallet about to be deployed. Two other airmen wore tandem chutes to jump with the two AFOSI agents. Ironwood, to everyone's surprise, had extensive parachuting experience and had managed to convince the commandos' leader, Captain Lomas, of his expertise. The big man was jumping solo, as was Jess. She'd taken even less time than Ironwood to convince Lomas of her training.

A green light flashed, and the loadmaster pulled a lever on the side wall. Instantly, the pallet slid down the ramp and vanished from sight. The tandem jumpers walked forward slowly as the first nine solo jumpers ran for the ramp—Ironwood a head taller than the others—and then were swept away, into the blue void.

The tandem jumpers walked backward down the ramp, two pair to each side, holding on to guide ropes until they reached the edge.

David concentrated on breathing the freezing air. The wind tore at his gear. Every sensation was overpowering. He stared up at the wires and conduits of the cargo bay ceiling, saw the fabric insulation ripple in the swirling wind.

"Lean back!" Dodd shouted.

David felt himself falling. Catching sight of the enormous gray tail of the Globemaster. Seeing a quick flash of Agent Marano spinning beside him joined to Sergeant Childress, and faintly hearing her whoop of joy. Then he felt himself roll, and he was looking straight down at black rocks and white snow, icy wind tearing at his face. It was impossible to catch his breath.

Faintly, he heard Dodd shouting, "Look ahead!"

He tried. Saw the huge red umbrellas of the pallet's cargo chutes far below, but growing larger, larger . . .

David had just enough time to think they were about to collide with those chutes when the ground suddenly swung away and he was looking straight out to the horizon. Boundless snow, a frozen sea lapping against a jagged black shore, and a blue sky so pure it hurt his eyes to look at it, even through his tinted goggles.

Then the horizon rotated around him, and he dimly realized his chute must have opened. He looked up, and there it was, perfect. So silent, he only heard the vestigial hiss of the explosions in Cornwall. The air felt supremely still, and he knew it was because he was moving with the wind.

More shouted commands from Dodd. "Knees together! Bend your legs!"

The ground was suddenly hurtling toward him. David saw the pallet already down, a half mile away. Between it and the ground below, the other jumpers quickly gathered their chutes. There was a slight upward bounce and—

It was like stepping off a fast-moving escalator. He and his tandem partner took a few quick steps together, and then were still.

"Outstanding!" Dodd exclaimed. A few quick clicks and David was released. He stepped away as his partner shrugged off his chute and began rolling it up.

David looked around, shaking not from cold but from the experience. He closed his eyes for a moment, and was back stuck in traffic on the George Washington Parkway the night this had really begun, when he had gone to the Hay-Adams in D.C. and met Ironwood for the first time. Then he opened his eyes and he was still on the ice of Antarctica, and it felt as if everything that had happened in the past few weeks had happened in that same amount of time—a single blink of an eye.

Then everything changed again as Dodd ran to him and quickly disconnected his reserve chute and harness, pointing urgently to the sky. It was already darkening with the approaching sunset.

David looked up, hearing engines different from the Globemaster's, to see a black silhouette against blue and the dark specks tumbling from it, spreading apart as they fell, abruptly blossoming into pure white canopies.

They'd won their race by minutes, only to face a war.

FIFTY-TWO

"This training you had," Captain Lomas asked, "was it in the military?"

"Private security," Jess said. Side by side, they bundled their chutes, both moving quickly, economically. He was reassessing anything he might have been told about her, and she knew why. She'd leapt from the cargo plane like a soldier charging into battle because she knew that was what she was and what she faced. Dropping swiftly, she'd pulled her rip-cord with defiance, daring the parachute not to open, then guided it expertly to land six feet from the supply pallet, only two feet farther from it than Lomas.

"Seen action?"

Jess nodded, caught something from the corner of her eye, looked up, and saw another transport plane, other jumpers. So did Lomas. Without further talk, they broke out their knives, quickly slicing at the pallet's wrapping.

Less than ten minutes later, they were armed and equipped just as Corporal Rothstein—communication and positioning—confirmed they'd landed dead on their coordinates: a flat outcropping on a nameless mountain. However, while they were only eight hundred meters downslope from their planned point of entry, the roundabout path required to ferry their equipment up the rough and rocky incline was almost three klicks long.

Lomas tasked four of his men to take the fastest route, a direct uphill hike, to find and secure the crevasse flagged by the SARGE display. The captain estimated thirty minutes for the advance team's climb to the crevasse and almost an hour for the second group to reach the POE with the equipment. By then, it would be full-on night. Once all were in place, the demo specialists would plant the charges that should open up a shaft down to the structure. Then it was Mr. Ironwood's show until the helicopters from the USS *Roosevelt* arrived in two days' time.

Jess only had one problem with that plan. "Anyone see if the other jumpers had an equipment pallet? I didn't. They could have landed right on the POE."

"Then we'll know where to find them," Lomas said. He gave the order to move out, and they did.

▬▬ ▬▬▬▬ ▬▬

The commandos carried fifty-pound packs in addition to their basic weapons and survival gear. The agents and civilians had been given smaller thirty-pound packs, and in the –25°F air, that exertion was taking a toll. They'd stopped to rest.

The three-klick path to the point of entry didn't match Rothstein's topo maps or satellite photos. The tallest peaks were still useful as landmarks, but the exposed ground between them was all new.

"The maps are eight years old," the corporal explained to Jess. "The satellite photos are from last year. Terrain's changed already. There's barely half the snow that was here last year."

Ironwood looked at the maps and photos they were comparing. "We know where we have to end up." He tapped a gloved finger at the POE marked on the topo map. "And we know we're here." He tapped again. "So let's take a shortcut along that new ridge." He pointed ahead. "Should save a klick or so."

Corporal Rothstein used binoculars to check the end of the ridge and decided it was passable. Just as they all began to haul on their packs again to continue the trek, Jess heard the hollow pops of distant gunfire.

In seconds, the commandos had slipped out of their supply and survival packs and moved out on the run, ordering the civilians—her and David, and Ironwood, Lyle, and Marano—to stay put until someone came for them.

Five minutes later, before the second group of commandos could have reached the site, a cloud of black smoke rose up past a dark ridge, followed a moment later by an echoing rumble.

"I thought they were going to bomb it," David said.

Jess realized what was happening. Her stomach tightened. "They're blasting in." She felt powerless.

"They'll loot it first." Ironwood turned away, arms open in despair and frustration. "All this way, and for what?"

More distant gunfire. Another cloud of smoke and a long rumble.

"Our guys aren't stopping them, Jack." Marano turned to Lyle. "We gotta help."

Jess saw the senior agent struggle with the decision: Follow orders or his gut? She'd faced that, too. She turned to David, but he'd grabbed Ironwood.

"How old is the data in the SARGE database?"

"My version? From 2005. Oh . . . I get it . . ."

327

So did Jess. Of all of them, David had seen what no one else had. Years ago, when the SARGE database had been created, the ice and snowpack here were thicker by dozens of meters. So SARGE had identified an entry point high on the mountainside as the quickest way into the hidden structure, but with so much impassable ice removed, had another entry point been exposed?

"Right!" Ironwood awkwardly unfolded the printout. Jess had the others kneel to hold the three sheets of plasticized paper on the frozen ground for David to assess. He looked from map to photo to SARGE printout and back again, several times, as if aligning the three different views of the same terrain in his mind, until they came together.

"Here." David's finger stabbed the satellite image at a spot less than fifty meters down the steep slope of the ridge they'd been about to cross when the gunfire sounded. "There's something there. A side tunnel. A shaft. Only a few feet down."

"A few feet?" Jess said. "Does anyone know how to handle the demo charges?"

Jack Lyle stood up carefully, favoring one knee.

Roz Marano had already shed her mittens. Digging barehanded through the packs, she started pulling out the detonators.

Over the next twenty minutes, they heard gunfire and two more large explosions. Then nothing. No one came back for them. By then, Jess and Lyle had become a team working to keep their reduced unit moving and safe.

As Marano placed the charges at the point David identified, Jess, Lyle, and Ironwood hauled the supply packs down the ridge and hid them beneath a hasty cairn of rocks. If whoever had taken on Captain Lomas and his men came looking for stragglers, there'd be nothing here to see.

Less than half an hour after the final blast, the long dusk of the Antarctic night had begun. At this time of year, darkness would last only a few hours. But they were ready.

Jess moved over as Marano ran to join them behind a rock wall. Then, with hands white with cold, the agent plugged the last of the wires into the handheld firing control.

"Ready?" she asked.

"Go," Ironwood said.

Marano flipped the cover off the firing switch, toggled it. The rock wall appeared to bounce with the sharp crack of the explosion. Seconds later, a brief shower of gravel and dust rained down on them.

"They'll have heard that," Lyle warned. "Let's go!"

Jess was first to the blast site, where fine debris still cascaded into a dust-filled hole. "Yes! We've opened into something."

Then she was first again because she was the only one who'd know the story of the rock layers. Wrapping a rope around her waist and shoulder, she slid down the blast hole as the others kept her anchored. The tip of her boot touched bottom, detecting a small fissure. She kicked at it once, twice—

The ground gave way beneath her and she dropped, gasping as the rope around her suddenly tightened—

Swinging free, she looked down . . .

Black rock from the explosion . . . piled on honed square slabs of stone . . . *a floor.*

"This is it!"

She descended into history.

FIFTY-THREE

Nathaniel Merrit was a killer, and, falling from the sky, he saw his next victims arranged like pawns on a chessboard, waiting to be sacrificed.

Merrit counted seventeen of the enemy below, one in particular whose size and silhouette were unmistakable. Ironwood. Unexpected, but not unwanted.

Accompanying Merrit were twenty mercenaries he'd tasked with finding and documenting the underground structure before the bombing runs began tomorrow. First light would be in less than six hours.

Until yesterday, his team had been special forces operators in the Argentine air force's Grupo de Operaciones Especiales. If their mission achieved its goal, then they'd be reinstated, and this would be an official operation, but until mission success, they fought in white polar camouflage without identification or insignia. Failure, therefore, could not haunt the generals who'd obeyed the request of the MacCleirigh Foundation instead of the orders of their government.

At one thousand feet, Merrit pulled his ripcord, joining the rest of his team directly on the target site, a half mile from the other jumpers. There was more than enough time for his forces to prepare defensive positions and plant the first explosive charges for blasting their way into the structure before nightfall.

He was pleased the opposing force was Ironwood's. He knew he'd have to kill the MacClary girl eventually, if only because he'd killed her aunt and, as J.R. had correctly reasoned, she'd come after him. Still, he intended to kill his former employer here. Ideally, he'd do it with a knife up close and not a bullet at a distance. He wanted the man to know who was taking his life. Face-to-face. That had meaning . . . and what was life—or death—without that?

Twenty minutes later, the first of the other side's forces arrived on-site and started the attack. They took out one of Merrit's mercenaries posted in a sniper's position, but Merrit witnessed two other snipers he'd positioned catch the enemy in their crossfire, successfully dropping three: one killed outright with a head shot; two seriously wounded, writhing on the ground.

Issuing commands over the compact radio headset under his helmet and balaclava, Merrit instructed his snipers to hold position. He wanted to see how the other side would respond. He himself stayed back and out of the action. Not to avoid combat, but because his injured ankle would put him and any of the men with him at a disadvantage. He'd removed the bandages and given himself shots of Novocain before the jump. Tomorrow morning would be time enough to deal with any additional damage he incurred.

Five minutes passed, and when the enemy did nothing, he gave the signal to detonate the first charges.

The other side used the black cloud rising from the mountainside as cover to attack his snipers, costing Merrit two more men. Their polar camouflage, however, was ineffective crossing dark rock. Two more enemy were felled.

At this rate, Merrit knew he could win by attrition, but not quickly enough. He radioed his unit to prepare for another wave, then gave the order to detonate the second set of charges.

This time when the black cloud billowed up, the enemy attacked from two sides, even as Merrit's explosives specialist, *Teniente* Alvarez, reported good news—debris was falling in through an opening at the bottom of the blast crater.

The fighting was extended, and Merrit didn't like what he was hearing over his headset. He crawled from his position overlooking the entry point to see the enemy moving down from a higher position.

They were good—American military, he guessed—and there were at least two groups of them.

Then Alvarez radioed bad news: He and his team were being overwhelmed.

Merrit stayed low, moving quickly behind a stretch of jagged boulders to look down at the protected niche where he'd had the mercenaries unload their explosives. He could see that about half the charges had been used for the first two blasts. He also saw Alvarez and four more mercenaries cowering, on their knees, hands high, as six enemy commandos held weapons on them, searched them, and disarmed them.

Merrit considered his options—it was time. The *teniente* had reported debris falling *in*. That meant the first two blasts had succeeded in punching an opening into the structure.

Merrit tugged off one of his mitts, reached to his side, and unclipped the HK69 grenade launcher he carried. He extended the stock and flipped up the short sight for a range of less than fifty meters, an HE-FRAG round already in the breech. Alvarez and his team had completed their mission. They and their remaining explosives were expendable.

He checked the niche again and ducked back behind a boulder, with the image in his mind. He pictured the clear shot he had, then swung up and fired just as the enemy soldiers looked up and—

The high-explosive fragmentation grenade hit the stacked demolition charges as Merrit dropped back behind the boulder.

Small red flecks fell with the rocks from the enormous blast.

There was no more gunfire.

Merrit listened to the chatter on his radio. Of his twenty men, six survivors were unhurt. Three or four more—judging from the weak cries and pleas they were transmitting—were badly wounded. More significantly, there was no sign of enemy action, even though by his count when he'd parachuted in, of the seventeen he'd seen, not all enemy had been killed.

Ordering the six survivors to take up positions around the entry point, Merrit didn't wait for them before using a rope to drop into the opening SARGE had pinpointed, not stopping till he reached a mounded pile of rocks. Favoring his ankle, he let go of the rope and slid down the debris until he was on the floor of a corridor paved with squares of stone.

He paused to let his eyes adjust.

In the dim gloom, he judged that, while the passageway was not identical to the ones in Cornwall and the South Pacific, it was similar enough.

He pulled off his hood and his helmet, removed his ski mask, then opened his parka. Out of the wind, the air was warmer, and he had considerable ground to cover. If there was a treasure room here, the Rodrigues woman had promised $1 million for every artifact he recovered from the central table. Combine that payout with the look on Ironwood's face as he felt Merrit's knife slide into his chest, and this was going to be a good day.

As he took his first step forward, from somewhere ahead he heard the unmistakable whump of an explosion.

Whatever else was down here waiting to be found, he wasn't the only one looking for it.

Still, he intended to be the only one who claimed it.

Jessica Bronwyn Ruth Tamar Elizabeth Miriam Ann, child of MacCleirigh, Defender of Boston and the Line MacClary, stood where no member of her family had ever been before.

She felt the weight of centuries and of responsibility. Reflexively, she put her gloved hand to her chest, then remembered she'd given her cross to David when she'd thought he was a long-lost cousin.

Beside her, he exhaled noisily, his warm breath touching her cheek as he shook off the loop of rope he'd descended on. She was surprised by how tired he looked. "Do you think this is it?" he asked. He unzipped his parka, pulled off his hood and helmet. It was marginally warmer here.

The commandos' supply packs, survival gear, and radio hit the floor just behind them, dropped by the two AFOSI agents. Ironwood followed, slowly being lowered.

"I don't know," Jess answered honestly. She held up the SARGE print-out and shone her flashlight on it. "That round room looks like a Chamber of Heaven. It's larger, but it's the only circular area on this level."

"So we'll start there?"

"We'll start there!" Ironwood's voice boomed in the constricted space. Lyle and Marano climbed down ropes behind him. "How long do you think it's been since voices echoed off these walls?"

"Human voices?" Marano asked. She and Lyle worked together to cover the packs with black gravel and stones. The blast was going to attract attention, and it was wise to conceal their trail. "Or any kind?"

Ironwood cocked a finger at her, pulling an imaginary trigger. "We'll see what we see, young lady."

Lyle squinted at his watch. "They're going to start bombing in four and a half hours. We need to be a couple of miles away by then."

Jess checked the printout again. "It's not enough time. Not to see it all."

"Then there's no time to waste standing here," Ironwood said. "Let's move."

They started down the corridor, carefully skirting fallen stones and raw rock that had dropped from above. In a few places, floor stones were also missing, and they used their flashlights to see that there was another corridor running beneath theirs on a lower level. Not knowing what kind of supports were holding up the floor they were on, they began to place their feet more cautiously, first testing suspicious stones to ensure that they were solid.

Then they came to the first mural.

Ironwood clapped his hands as they all held their flashlights on it, the vapor of their breathing forming a cloud through which they looked into an unknown time, at an unknown people.

Parts of the plaster had fallen away, but the damage wasn't enough to erase the incredible scene that stretched for twenty feet. It showed a harbor, dark green sea below, and on the horizon, dark peaks crowned with snow. Between the sky and sea, there were piers and buildings, some of two and three stories. Banners waved from tall poles, most of them purple, some white. The most prominent element in the scene before them was the ships. They were angular, with a high prow and aft section, and each had two rows of oars, at least forty on each level.

"Look at them," Ironwood marveled. "They're not coast huggers. They're oceangoing."

"How can you tell?" David asked.

"Shape of their hulls," Ironwood answered. "Just trying to cross the Drake Passage between here and South America, a big ship can snap in two on the kind of waves she can face. So the hulls have to be engineered like span bridges—able to support their weight if there's suddenly no water under one end or the other." He nodded in admiration. "These folks were smart."

Jess didn't care about the ships' construction. She was transfixed by their large bright yellow mainsails; painted on each in cobalt blue was a simple, unornamented version of her family's cross.

"Tuareg," Ironwood said. He looked at her. "That's MacCleirigh, right?"

Jess didn't have to answer because, beside her, David had pulled aside his layers of insulating clothes, taken out her cross, and handed it back to her, before kneeling to take a camera from his bag. Her fingers tightened on its remembered weight.

"I knew it!" Ironwood said, triumphant. "Everything's coming together." He swept an arm toward the symbol on the mural, didn't touch it. "No one," he said, "no one knew how far back that symbol goes. Here's the proof it started here! Spread up to the Mediterranean, probably with a Phoenician connection—no one knows where *they* started out from. Then down into North Africa, kept alive by the Tuareg people. Those desert nomads are probably some offshoot of your people, Jessica. Matrilineal. The men wear the veils and the women are bare-faced! And they're right next door to the Dogon tribe. And the big library in Timbuktu. It all fits!"

"Something special about the Dogon?" Lyle asked.

"The Dogon are supposed to have received advanced astronomical knowledge from aliens," Marano helpfully explained.

"In case anyone hasn't noticed," Lyle said, "this picture doesn't show aliens. Just people."

Jess's flashlight joined the others moving back and forth along the mural. He was right. Stick figures, small and dark, were represented everywhere: on the ships, the piers, the pathways along the harbor side. All had two arms, two legs, one head.

"Of course," Ironwood said testily, "if they're enough like us to interbreed, I bet they don't look all that different at a distance."

Jess turned to David. "We need to keep going."

"I'll catch up." He began to take a panoramic series of flash photos. Before they reached the first turn, he was back at her side. "How much farther?"

Jess didn't need to look at the printout. "Next corner, twenty meters on the right."

That's where they found a second mural. Even though some sections were damaged, Jess could still make out the groups of animals, herded together, some in fenced areas. In what seemed to be a slaughterhouse, animals were being butchered, skins tanned, bones being ground up for something that was unclear.

"What are those?" David snapped picture after picture. "Llamas?"

"Quite possibly." Ironwood's flashlight settled on the animals in question. "Definitely cold-adapted. Look at those shaggy coats."

"No one's ever found mammal bones on Antarctica," Marano said.

Ironwood didn't think that was important. "Nobody ever found this outpost, either. If these folks were sailing around the world, who's to say they didn't bring back useful animals from South America?"

"Over here." Twenty meters along, Jess stood once again before a closed set of double doors set into the sidewall of the corridor. These, however, weren't made of wood. The others rushed to join her.

"Gold?" David raised the camera.

Ironwood shook his head. "They're tarnished. Brass, maybe? Bronze?"

"Bronze isn't quite the cutting-edge space-age alien metal." Jess regretted the words as soon as she'd said them. Without this man, she'd never have been here. He'd helped her when her own family had deserted her.

Ironwood took her comment with good humor. "It is if that's the recipe the aliens gave out, knowing it's all that could be accomplished with primitive technology." His flashlight beam played over the doors. "Anyone recognize these markings?"

Each door was roughly four feet across, eight feet high, with twelve inset panels. The panels themselves contained rows of tiny embossed figures.

"Some kind of writing?" David adjusted his camera lens for zoom.

"Not cuneiform," Ironwood said. He took his mitt off and ran a finger along the markings on the right-hand door. "There's enough repetition for this to be an alphabet, not pictograms. Could be the basis of the first written language."

Marano rubbed some of the markings herself. "Or it could be the pattern home designers of 9000 B.C. thought worked best with the drapes."

Jess closed her ears to their chatter and tried not to think of the other defenders' reactions to outsiders touching Family property. She pushed lightly against the left-hand door. It moved.

"That's astounding," Ironwood exclaimed. "The hinges still work."

Jess pushed with more force. The door was resistant but slowly gave way with a high-pitched squeal. She took a step forward, and the others pressed close behind her, their flashlights moving back and forth over the room inside.

Jess's heart sank.

"It's not the same," David said.

The chamber here was twice the size of the one in Cornwall, and there were no stars embedded on its low, curved ceiling. The mural painted on its encircling wall was of a harbor city, perhaps the same one as on the first mural they'd found.

Jess fought disappointment, struggling to even hear David's next words. "Jess, I wonder if it's what this place looked like." With his flashlight, he drew her attention to how, on the land side, the horizon showed jagged black mountains crested by snow. Across the room, opposite those peaks, the harbor gave way to open sea. His flashlight moved to the horizon line of the ocean. "Are those icebergs?"

Whatever they were, Jess thought, they were small, white, and irregular. Maybe distant sails. Maybe . . . snow and ice. Could that be why this continent was called the White Island? If the First Gods had temples all around the world, why was this the one they had to return to?

"Whenever this was painted," she said, "this place was cold." *Look closer,* she thought. This place was different, but it still belonged to the Family. *What makes it special?*

David shone his flashlight into the center of the chamber. "No table."

Jess walked to where the table should have been. Instead, there was a round metal disk, the diameter of a stone table but only an inch thick, embossed with symbols like those on the doors.

"Is it covering something?" David asked. Camera in hand, he stood beside her.

Jess's flashlight swept the area around the disk. In dust undisturbed for millennia, she saw *footprints.*

Fresh ones. Leading to the disk, then vanishing.

"We're not alone," Lyle said.

He drew his gun.

FIFTY-FOUR

Merrit had heard the voices, indistinct but coming closer, and, following his map, had moved quickly to the double doors guarding the circular treasure room. Slowly and quietly he opened one of the doors just enough to squeeze through, then headed for the center of the room.

No table—but the round trapdoor at the chamber's center more than made up for it. It was hollow and lifted easily. Underneath was a stone staircase spiraling down through a tower of closely fitted stone blocks.

He slipped into the opening. With one hand he slipped the disk back into place above him, then continued down, leaning against the curved stone wall to ease the stress on his injured ankle.

One hundred and forty-four steps later, he faced a narrow, open doorway in the curved wall of the tower. He paused before stepping through, onto a stone-block path that led into pitch-black depths. His flashlight beam revealed a natural cavern beyond, with unusual metal stands, twelve feet high, supporting wide and shallow metal bowls. The stands flanked the pathway, alternating every fifty feet as far as his flashlight reached.

Merrit moved into the cavern and made a new discovery. Around the base of the stone tower that enclosed the staircase to the room above, piles of charred wood were scattered randomly, as if many separate small fires had burned out. Among them were small mounds of cloth, as if this had once been a campground.

Then the scrape of metal made him freeze in place. Metal on stone. Whoever else was in this place was coming down the staircase—in the tower with only one way out, through the narrow doorway.

Merrit smiled.

A perfect choke point.

The perfect ambush.

He moved swiftly into position, twenty feet to the side of the tower doorway, and turned off his flashlight. The darkness was instant and total.

Merrit thought back to the last time he had been in the same situation, in the sunken chamber in the South Pacific.

This was going to work just fine.

▪▪▪▪ ▪▪▪▪▪▪▪ ▪▪▪

"I'll go first," Lyle said.

No one argued. Except for Marano.

Jess listened as the two agents negotiated, but she didn't intervene.

"Seriously, Jack, whoever went down there first is sitting at the bottom waiting to pick off whoever's dumb enough to follow."

"That would be me," Lyle said, "and I have a gun."

"Seriously," Marano repeated. "I'm small, I'm fast, let me draw fire, then you smoke 'em."

"I know what I'm doing, Roz."

"Boss . . ."

He reached out and took her hand. "Give me your flashlight. I don't care if it gets shot."

Marano handed over her flashlight, and Lyle stuffed it along with David's into a pocket of his parka.

Jess and Ironwood kept theirs.

Lyle took the first step onto the spiral, then said to his partner, "Stay close, stay quiet. The rest of you, don't come down till I give the all-clear."

"What if you don't?" Jess asked.

"Don't come down. Go back the way we came. Dig out the radio. And get as far away as you can by dawn."

David and Ironwood immediately exchanged glances with Jess, letting her know they felt as she did. There was no chance any of them were leaving before seeing what lay below.

Lyle started down, Marano behind him. After a few seconds, the spilled light from Lyle's flashlight was imperceptible. Jess stared into the darkness, wishing she were in the lead, but knowing they were right. At least about going first.

David turned to her. "Jess, what do you think the connection is? Between this place and your family's temples?"

Ironwood answered first. "This feels older to me, Jessica." He pointed out details with his flashlight. "See? The stones are larger, not as precisely cut as in India or Peru. And look at the top steps of the stairway. See how worn they are? Folks went up and down them for centuries. There's no wear like that in any of the other outposts. They were built ages ago but not used for long."

"You don't suppose this is where it started, do you?" David said. "That first civilization?"

"How does a civilization *start* in Antarctica?" Ironwood asked.

"What about the murals?" David added. "When they were painted, the land wasn't completely icebound the way it is now. In fact, the way the planet's heating up, it probably won't be icebound in another century."

"Don't start with that global warming crap," Ironwood warned.

"I'm not saying *why* it's warming up, just saying that it is. Natural or man-made, you can't argue that the ice *isn't* melting all over the place." He turned to Jess. "What about it? You know about ancient climates. Was Antarctica ever as warm as this painting makes it look?"

Jess wanted to shout that they were wasting time talking about intangibles, though she knew none of them could do anything until they got the all-clear from Lyle and Marano.

"No." She corrected herself. "Unless . . . there's no question central Antarctica's been icebound for millions of years, but the Antarctic Peninsula? It has the mildest conditions, and ten thousand years ago, coming out of an ice age . . . the sea level was so low, no one really knows how the deep ocean currents were affected—and those are what drive local climatic conditions. So maybe, with a different current pattern, this small part of the continent *could* have been habitable year-round back then. But not for long—a couple of hundred, a thousand years at most."

"From the Magna Carta to the moon landing," David said. "A lot can happen in a thousand years."

Lyle descended slowly, and with each step, he asked himself what he was doing here.

Arresting Ironwood had been the right thing to do. That did warrant the logistical nightmare of arranging this mission, made possible only because the condemned was picking up the tab for his own funeral. But there'd been gunfire aboveground. Men were dead. If he and Roz and the rest of them weren't out of here by first light, more would die.

And for what?

Archaeology?

He deeply regretted thinking this was a good idea. Mostly, he regretted having Roz here with him. Biggest road trip yet, she'd called it. Looked forward to it.

At step 138, Lyle's flashlight beam found the floor. At step 140, he could see the single opening in the curved wall that led out into darkness. There'd be no room for anyone to hide inside the stairwell. The shooter would be outside the doorway.

Lyle stood on the last step and shone his light through the opening.

The beam was swallowed up, ineffective. Whatever was out there, it was a huge space.

"You ready?" he whispered.

"For anything," Roz whispered back.

Lyle committed to memory the layout of the small space beyond the bottom step, then turned off his flashlight.

He took three paces with his hand extended and touched the stone wall exactly when he anticipated he would. Next he moved his hand slowly to the right until it reached the open doorway.

Then he listened, hearing nothing.

He whispered to Roz. "Sideways, against the wall."

She moved to stand behind him, left shoulder against the wall.

He slipped his gun inside his parka and, in one smooth motion flicked on a flashlight just as he threw it out the doorway to the right.

The flashlight spun through the air, painting the floor of the space beyond, but nothing else—no walls or ceiling. Hitting the floor, it rolled, then rocked back and forth until the movement stopped. Its beam followed suit, eventually settling so the cone of light shone steady at a ninety-degree angle to the doorway, off to the left.

Lyle didn't wait for any reaction from the shooter outside. He repeated the toss with a second flashlight, this time to the left.

The second flashlight struck the floor, its beam pointing away from the doorway.

Lyle pulled off his parka, zipped it up, then held it out just at the doorway's edge. Moved it slightly, angled it. Pulled it back a bit—

Crack!

The shoulder of the parka exploded in a puff of insulation made visible by the flash of ricochet sparks as the bullet caromed up the stairwell. Almost instantaneously, with the flash whiting out his vision, Lyle let the parka fall to the floor. The tossed flashlights had created just enough light for the shooter, whose eyes were by now dark-adapted, to pick out the white of the polar camouflage parka. Not in detail, but enough to know the shape was there.

Another *crack* and another flash of ricochet sparks as the parka jumped and—Roz gasped. "Leg." He heard the rustle of her parka as she slid to the floor. "Oh crap," she breathed.

A scrape beyond the doorway. "Shh . . ." Lyle warned, almost inaudible. Roz's breaths were coming in short gulps. She was in pain.

More footsteps. The shooter approaching to inspect his prey.

Lyle's hand sought Roz's face. His fingers pressed against her lips. Felt the vibration of a hum from her. *Please, Roz . . . please . . .* He couldn't speak.

Roz tensed, and Lyle felt the unvoiced scream of pain as it was building.

The footsteps were even closer now. Lyle knew the shooter had a gun in his hand. Knew they were vulnerable in the faint light from the fallen flashlights.

If Roz so much as breathed now, they'd both be dead.

The footsteps stopped. The shooter was right outside the doorway. Looking down at the parka, about to realize there was no one in it, that it was a trap and the enemy was just inside and—

Lyle felt Roz's mouth open against his hand as she tried to suck in breath to release her pain in the only way she could and—

With no other choice, no other hope, Lyle threw himself over his parka with a primal roar, firing his gun blindly, sighting the shooter with each strobing muzzle flash, rolling as he fired and as the shooter returned fire, and then—

It was over.

Lyle lay prone on the cold rock, arms outstretched, gun ready, breathing hard, scanning back and forth, blinded by the gunfire, knowing at least that the shooter was blinded as well, calling up each strobelike image, certain he'd hit the shooter with his third or fourth shot. He pictured the man doubling over. Running off. Or was he just ducking for cover?

Lyle's breathing slowed. Roz was in the stairwell bleeding out. He had to get back to her—but was the shooter waiting for him to do just that?

He blinked, eyes straining to pick up details in the dim light from the two tossed flashlights. Something beside him, a cloth-wrapped bundle? Cautious, he tugged at it. Froze as he saw a skull, skin shriveled tight and black, cheekbones oddly flat. *A body?* Beyond it, more cloth-wrapped mounds. More bodies? All around him? How many? What had happened here?

But this wasn't the time. Couldn't be the time. He was up and stumbling, running, diving through the tower doorway, and no one shot him. "*Roz!*"

She answered, weakly. "Sorry . . ."

Her right leg was soaked and limp.

In the darkness, Lyle scooped her up, nearly tripping over his shredded parka, found stairs and started hurtling up them, knee forgotten.

On step 54, descending flashlights found them.

Bounding down the spiral staircase, David was first to see Marano in Lyle's arms, her right leg crimson, her face dead white.

Jess pushed past him, her utility knife already out.

Working swiftly, she sliced open the padded trousers, cutting through every layer, one after the other with steady hands, no hesitation. She'd kept telling David she'd been trained. *For what?* he'd wondered. Now he knew.

Next Jess ordered Ironwood to hold his flashlight on the wound she found, a small dark circle weakly pulsing with blood. "No exit wound," she said, and, within seconds, from the trouser material and Marano's own knife, she rigged a tourniquet that she tightened around the agent's thigh, above the wound.

"Can you find your way back?" she asked Lyle.

He nodded, shaken. Jess was in charge now.

"Get the survival packs. You can use them? The meds? IV fluids?"

"Yeah," Lyle said. "I can do that."

"Then do it fast. She's in shock, but she'll make it if you do it fast."

Lyle lifted Marano, held her close, started up the stairs again.

"Did you get him?" David called up to him.

"I think so," Lyle called back

Jess had a different question. "Did you see what's down there?"

"I did," the answer floated down. "Bodies. Lots of them."

FIFTY-FIVE

Jess stepped out of the stone tower and swung her flashlight all around.

There was no sign of the assailant who had attacked Lyle and Marano, but the bodies were everywhere. Each one bound in a blanket, clutching a gold book.

Ironwood was in heaven. "The Mycenaeans had books like this," he said reverently. "Gold sheets with writing and illustrations hammered in. I think there are exactly two known to exist." He shone his flashlight over at Jess, kneeling by a body. "Unless your people have more squirreled away."

"Three or four," she said, "but nothing like this."

David knelt beside her, examining one of the books. "The symbols in it, they're like the ones on the door and the disk. And look at this . . ." He showed her a page with a distinctive pattern. "Recognize it?"

She did. "The Southern Cross."

"So they're star maps or astronomy texts."

"Or navigation charts." Ironwood sounded struck with wonder. "They sailed the world, and *this* is how they did it."

David retrieved the two flashlights Lyle had thrown, then began taking photographs, walking from one body to the next. "Jess, you think they were buried here?"

Other than the blankets, she saw no sign of funerary preparations.

"I think they died here, in place."

"All of them? At the same time?" Ironwood was intrigued.

Once again Jess wished her family's longtime rival weren't here. "I don't know. Maybe they all drank hemlock. Maybe volcanic fumes filled this cavern. Maybe they all just froze to death."

David directed one of the recovered flashlights at the stone path that ran through the center of the cavern. It was edged by braziers on either side. "I wonder if these people had anything to do with where this path goes."

Jess tapped her watch, making the display light up. "We've got two hours. Half an hour to get back to the surface with as many of these books as we can carry. An hour to get out of bombing range."

343

"That gives us thirty minutes down here," David said.

"Forty-five if we move it," Ironwood said.

They began to walk quickly along the path. It followed the curve of the cavern floor, but smoothly. Here the stones were set on the diagonal, though, in a diamond pattern, different from the style used in the corridors above them, and in the temples.

"They must have rolled something along here, a lot," David said. "Look at all the grooves."

Jess saw them. "Were there wheeled carts in any of the murals?"

"They're not wheel tracks," Ironwood said. "They're not contiguous. It's like they dragged something a bit, picked it up, dragged it again."

Jess thought of the worn paths in the floor stones of the Shrine of Turus. How many generations of defenders had followed that path? Of all those generations, how was it that she became the first defender to follow this path into . . . what?"

"Hold it." David stopped abruptly. "Lyle said he thought he got the guy."

Jess and Ironwood converged their flashlight beams on David's, and Jess saw the drops of fresh blood on the stones.

"Winged him, maybe," Ironwood said, "but he's still out there."

As one, they all switched off their flashlights, listened.

No sound, but ahead of them . . .

"Do you see that?" David whispered. "Something flashing . . ."

"A flashlight?" Ironwood said.

"It's like someone's swinging it."

David switched on his flashlight. "If he's busy, maybe he won't notice us."

Still bodies all around them, they pressed on.

― ―― ――

The cavern ended in a solid wall of blank rock, but in its center were set two tall gleaming metal panels, each twelve feet high, eight feet across, flanked by braziers larger than the ones that edged the stone path.

"Can you imagine what this looked like with those things lit?" David said.

Ironwood ran his flashlight over a brazier. "We should take wood or charcoal from them. For carbon dating."

Jess was searching for any sign of Lyle's shooter. They'd found more blood on the path, but not enough to think he'd be dropping soon. A few minutes earlier, the odd moving light that might have been a swinging flashlight had stopped.

"Is that what was flashing?" David asked.

Jess saw what he saw, felt her pulse race.

Ironwood recognized it, too. "Your cross again, Jessica."

Centered low on the two metal panels was the sign of her family, as in the murals in the halls above. Once again it was a simple Tuareg cross. This cross, though, was polished gold, at least a meter high and almost as wide, perfectly symmetrical, mounted on a golden rail that fit into brackets on the metal panels.

Jess felt the power of the moment, but she was tormented by new questions she couldn't answer. *Why was this built? What does that cross mean? Is this where the First Gods arose? Is this the White Island they left us for?* She turned from the sign of her family to David beside her. Looked up at his face, glowing gold on one side, deeply shadowed on the other.

Suddenly she saw another face.

The Shrine of Turus. The carved figure of the male. That eerie, skeletal face wasn't the product of uneven erosion. It was the face of the bodies on the floor here. Dark and narrow, the nose flat, the cheekbones . . .

"David . . ." She reached out to place her fingers lightly on his cheek, in wonder. "You're not descended from my family."

He looked at her, confused, but not shying from her touch. "We know that, Jess. You said you got the test results."

"You're—"

A harsh voice shouted from the shadows. *"Hands high!"*

———

"Perfect," Merrit said as he limped from behind a towering brazier, his bloodied left hand shoved under his right armpit, his bloodied right hand holding his Browning 9 mm. "You're *all* working together now?"

Ironwood stepped forward. "Merrit, you know this isn't necessary."

"Don't tempt me, old man. There's only one reason why I don't take care of you right now—that cross."

"What about it?" Jess said.

"You know how much McCleary and Rodrigues will pay for that? It's my retirement bonus."

Jess stared at him. The man who'd killed Florian in Polynesia was now working for Andrew and Su-Lin—for the Family.

"I'll double the price," Ironwood said.

"No sale. You cut me off, remember?"

"You left my son for dead."

"His own damn fault. The only reason the MacCleirighs were in Cornwall was because J.R. told them where to go!"

"That's a lie!" Ironwood jerked forward, and Merrit raised his gun to point directly at his head.

"Junior's been in their pocket since he let slip where the Indian temple was."

Ironwood turned to Jess, his cheeks high with color. "Is that true?"

"I know our security people tried to find sources. I don't know if your son was one of them."

"He was." Merrit's laugh was short and cruel. "First time was when he got drunk in the wrong bar. After that, he kept telling them whatever they wanted to know because he thought you'd kill him if you found out he was behind you losing control of the site in India."

"I'd never do that."

"No argument. That'd be my job."

Jess saw the look of anguish and betrayal that swept over Ironwood.

"He said you came close to it once," Merrit added. "After the accident when he killed your wife."

"It wasn't his fault! I love my son . . . I'd never kill anyone . . . I never told *you* to kill anyone!" Ironwood's voice shook with such indignation that, for the first time ever, Jess believed him. Though she wasn't sure she could ever forgive him.

"'Do whatever it takes' is what you said. So I did." Merrit wiped his hand across his face; the gesture left a smear of blood.

Jess's eyes went to his left side, above his waist. Merrit's white parka was stained there, and there was a bullet hole. Lyle *had* shot him.

"None of this is worth a life, Merrit."

"Keep thinking that," Merrit said. "So you'll do as I say, and no one will be hurt."

"What do you want us to do?" Jess heard David quietly ask. Her attention was fixed on Merrit's hands . . . both of them were bloody. *Injured?*

"Take down that cross, carry it up top for me, I let you all go."

"Okay." David shot a glance at Jess. She understood. If they cooperated, there was at least a chance to get aboveground before the bombing raid began.

Ironwood knew better. "He'll kill us when we're finished."

"I believe he'll kill us now, if we don't start," Jess said.

Hands held high, the three of them approached the cross.

As David and Ironwood began looking for some way to lift the golden sculpture, Jess blanched as a sudden memory flashed into her consciousness. "Don't touch it!"

They stopped, looked at her, surprised.

"That support beam it's on, it's got sharp blades underneath."

David crouched down, shone his flashlight up, whistled. "How'd you know?"

Jess made a fist, remembering the heavy iron latch on the doors to the shrine. "I've seen one just like it."

"Smart girl." Merrit was standing beside her, gun in hand.

"You already tried it," Jess said. "You wanted us to be hurt." His next words told her she was right.

"More than one way to do that." Then, before she could react, Merrit slammed his Browning against her face.

Jess had only a glimpse of David as he reacted at once, jumping at Merrit, only to be pistol-whipped himself, thrown back against the metal panels.

She saw Merrit edge back, limping, favoring one foot.

She struggled to regain her footing. *His ankle's sprained.* She filed the thought.

Now Ironwood confronted Merrit.

"Go ahead," Merrit said. "Try something."

"Not much of a loss for me, you know. I get out of this alive, tomorrow they send me to prison for life."

"You're breaking my heart."

"Just explaining I've got nothing to lose down here."

Merrit gestured with his gun. "Take down that cross or you won't even see jail."

David was on his feet again. He looked at Jess, who nodded back at him, her hand going to the cross she'd given him and he'd returned.

"I've got a better idea," David said. He stepped away from the metal panel, and Merrit swung his gun from Ironwood to cover him.

Jess dropped her knife into her hand and charged.

Merrit swung back to her too late. He fired, but his aim was high as she dove in low, slashing upward, her blade tangling in his open parka so her momentum twisted them around and they fell, without her knife making contact.

They rolled from the stone path and hit the side of a brazier. Merrit fought to bring his gun down to her as she fought in turn to raise her knife up to him. Each time David or Ironwood tried to come near, Merrit fired his weapon and they were forced to jump back.

Then . . . Merrit rocked one final time and wrenched her hand to make her drop the knife, and with one more roll he was on top of her shouting at David and Ironwood to stay back as he pressed his gun to her temple.

"Interfere and I'll shoot her now."

Jess gasped for breath as Merrit kneeled on top of her, the gun barrel painful, the thought of defeat unbearable.

Merrit grinned at her fiercely. "Give up."

"Never."

"Good." He pulled the trigger and—

Only one thing pierced Jess's pain and filled her vision: the antique silver Tuareg cross that dangled above her from the chain around Merrit's neck.

—the gun clicked empty.

Merrit hesitated. Jess didn't.

Seconds later, David and Ironwood pulled Merrit from Jess, but by then his throat had already yawned open, ripped by the blade she'd pulled from the cross *he'd* worn.

Florian's.

Merrit flailed like a swimmer dragged down into a dark and endless sea. He struggled to speak, but whatever words were to be his last were lost. Then he stilled, his hot blood steaming in the cold.

"Good," Jess said.

There was only one thing left to do.

FIFTY-SIX

Jess took Florian's cross and chain from Merrit's body, slipped the blade back into place, then wore it as she was meant to.

David touched her arm. "Jess . . ."

She tapped her watch. "We still don't know what this place is, why it was important."

Ironwood gave her a quick look of concerned assessment. "How would we even know where to start to look for answers?"

"We already do," Jess said. Nothing, and no one, could stop her now from learning what she'd come here for. She was a defender. She'd promised. "These metal panels—they aren't panels. They're doors. We need to see what's on the other side."

Together, Jess and David and Ironwood, using their parkas as pads, lifted the heavy golden cross from the latch brackets.

The metal doors were much heavier than the ones in the upper corridor. It took the three of them pushing as hard as they could to force one side open enough to squeeze through.

This time no one disputed who should go first.

Once beyond those doors, Jess stood still, letting her flashlight reveal all that was before her as understanding grew within her.

It was a Chamber of Heaven . . . and it was huge.

David eased through after Jess, his flashlight joining hers, and he saw what she saw.

The room was circular, but five times the size of the one in Cornwall, well over a hundred feet across. On the encircling wall was a sculpted relief map, so large it was hard for any of them to comprehend its details, given the small sections each flashlight beam could reveal.

In the center, in place of a table, rose a circular tier of carved stone shelves. Most were empty, but several were still filled with even more gold books, enough that all the people whose bodies lay outside could each have taken one and still left these behind.

Ironwood was awestruck. "It's some kind of library."

"David, it's like the Shop," Jess said. "A safe place. Perhaps the safest they could find to store all the knowledge they'd accumulated."

"We still have to get out before we're sealed in. Or we'll be like those bodies out there." David stopped. There was that look on Jess's face again. The one she'd had just before Merrit had surprised them, when she'd reached out to touch his face and . . . "What did you want to tell me out there, about my not being descended from your family?"

"You're descended from *them*," Jess said. She glanced around for Ironwood, but he'd walked far enough away that he wouldn't hear what she said next. "The people who died out there, holding books . . ." She shook her head. "Holding books instead of each other because knowledge was the most important thing they had."

David still didn't understand.

"Those people out there, *they're* the First Gods. They have to be. Their civilization started here. How, I don't know. Maybe we'll never know. But they're the ones who built the ships that crossed the oceans. They built the temples around the world. And wherever they went, they're the ones who taught the people they found all that they knew."

She stepped back from him. "*That's* how your genetic anomalies appeared in different populations all at the same time around the world. Just like agriculture, and writing, and astronomy." She shook her head at the thought. "Ironwood was right. There *was* interbreeding—but not between humans and aliens. Between humans and *your* family."

David was startled as Jess then bowed her head and knelt before him. "Child of the First Gods, I am your defender. As predicted by the *Traditions,* the Promise is fulfilled. You did come back. To me."

"No, Jess. We're just you and me." David took her hands and brought her to her feet, unnerved by the sudden irrational hope that she might be right. *Is this the answer to my mystery?*

Looking quickly to see if Ironwood had noticed—luckily the man was rapt before the shelves of books—David continued holding Jess's hands, trying to make her, and himself, see reason. "There's no way we can know anything like that yet. Even if you're right and those bodies share my anomalies, we won't know until we run tests, lots of tests."

Tests that take time, he thought. *Time I don't have.*

David forced himself to go on. "Even if I do have some trace of these people in me . . . it doesn't make me special. There's a price."

He knew it was time she knew the truth about him.

"Jess, in one way I am like those people out there. I'm dying, too. I don't know why or even how it'll happen, but I do know when. Those clusters I found, those people whose genes share my nonhuman markers—

maybe from the genes of the people out there—none of us has lived to reach twenty-seven. I'm going to hit the threshold age in a few more days and then . . . it's like a countdown. I won't make it more than five months."

Ironwood came back, and David reluctantly let go of Jess. "You two want to know where these books came from? Or where this *map* came from? This *map* that doesn't show any world I happen to know about."

"It's upside down," David said. He looked at Jess, and she was still staring at him. "North's at the bottom, south's at the top. Then it makes sense."

"It's more than that, Dave! They've put Antarctica in the center of the thing, with all the other continents stretched around it."

At that Jess, as well as David, trained a flashlight on the section of the map that baffled Ironwood.

"What do you call that?" he demanded.

"Antarctica," Jess said.

"But it's two islands."

David stated the obvious. "Antarctica without ice. But that would be . . . Jess? How long ago?"

She blinked. "A long time . . . Millions . . ."

"And lookit here!" Ironwood hooted with delight. "The artist signed his work!" His flashlight took aim at a section of the map beneath the ice-free Antarctic islands.

David's and Jess's flashlights followed suit to discover that the artist who had created the map had signed it as artists in ages past often did. By placing his hand, or her hand, against the wall and blowing pigment over it, creating a shadow of that hand—the hand of the maker.

A thumb and three long webbed fingers, all with talons, inhumanly splayed from top to bottom, forming a silhouette like that of a bladed cross . . .

Ironwood's joyful laughter filled the chamber.

Then the ground shook. The bombing had begun.

FIFTY-SEVEN

It was 4:00 A.M., and Jack Lyle was on the ground, Roz cradled at his side, in the lee of a rocky outcropping about a mile from the opening to the underground site. He was watching the thin line of low clouds on the far horizon that glowed with the approach of dawn. The sun would bring the bombers.

Lyle knew they'd have to leave the sheltering hollow soon, but he needed to rest a few minutes before carrying Roz again. For now, his partner was swaddled in thermal blankets, warmed by chemical heating packs. Her color was back. Her attention wasn't—muddled by morphine.

She opened a bleary eye, unfocused. "Let's never do that again, okay?"

"Do what?"

"Road trip."

Lyle squeezed her gloved hand lightly, reasoning it might not be so wrong to finally step out of the chain of command, wishing he'd done so long ago. "Never again," he promised. Then something in the air changed. A vibration?

Aircraft. The whine of approaching jets. From the north.

Lyle edged over the rise of loose black rocks to scan the night sky.

Deep indigo, stars still visible. No aircraft lights. The planes were running dark.

Then the whine of engines became a roar, and sudden, silent fireballs erupted across the rocky terrain. A moment later, the dull crack and the thundering rumble of the bombs' explosions shook the ground.

The Argentines . . .

They'd advanced their attack by at least an hour, but, since they were flying under night conditions, Lyle knew their targeting would not be precise. This far south, the Global Positioning Satellite system wasn't always reliable—fewer satellites were overhead at any one time. He thought of the narrow passageways of the underground site. The loose debris around its opening. The only chance MacClary, Weir, and Ironwood had of escaping was if they were already on their way. As the light improved, so would the bombers' aim. One direct hit on the point of entry would be enough to seal it. It could never be reopened in time to save anyone left below.

"Hey, boss . . . what's happening?"

Roz was fumbling at her thermal blankets, trying to unwrap them so she could stand. He slid back and pushed her down just as more flashes in the distance lit up dark skies. With more explosive concussions, new bombs struck the land around them.

"Roz, listen to me. I have to go back to where we landed. I have to find one of the radios, let Command know what's happening. The helos from the *Roosevelt* will be too late."

Roz tried to stand again. "I'll go—"

"No. You have to stay here." More explosions. A small stream of stones poured down the sloping rock to pile beside her. "And you have to stay down. I'll come back as soon as I can."

Roz's eyes met his and, for a moment, cleared. "Promise," she said.

Lyle wouldn't lie to her, said nothing. He ran as fast as he could into the strike zone.

＊＊＊＊　＊＊＊＊＊＊　＊＊＊＊

"Dave! We have to go! Those fools are bombing us!"

Ironwood was squeezing his bulk through the two huge metal doors guarding the enormous chamber, one arm carefully shielding five gold books he'd pulled at random from the tiered stand inside.

"Almost!" David called back. He was taking flash photo after flash photo of the encircling map. The ground shook again. Rocks fell from the chamber's ceiling to clatter on the floor. "Damn! Memory's full!" He whirled about and raced for the doors, shoving the camera into an inner pocket of his open parka.

"I got maybe half the map," he said to Jess.

Ironwood blinked rapidly as distant blasts echoed in the cavern beyond the doors. "What about the signature? You got that, right?"

"I think so. I—"

The harsh squeal of metal grinding on stone obliterated David's words as one of the entrance doors toppled inward, trapping Ironwood. He lost his breath explosively. "One of those braziers," he gasped, "fell over, hit the door . . ."

David and Jess were already straining to push the door away from him. Wedged in the opening, Ironwood leaned back against the heavy metal panel, using his broad shoulders for added leverage . . . pushing . . . pushing . . . then, suddenly, he was free as the door shifted to the side. He fell into the cavern on the other side, his hands stretched out to brace himself, the precious gold books scattering.

Jess and David were right behind him.

Breathing heavily, Ironwood was already scooping up his books, shooting apprehensive glances at the cavern's ceiling forty feet overhead as an enormous crash resounded from the chamber they'd just escaped—more of it was breaking apart.

"This cavern's a natural formation," Jess said. They ran for the only exit: the stone tower staircase leading up to the passageways above. "No stones to come loose."

Their bulky cold-weather gear made them awkward, and their pace was more like double-time marching than true running. Their flashlight beams lit the way.

Halfway to the tower, more explosive rumbles thundered and the ground trembled. Still, as Jess had told them, the cavern ceiling held.

The tower, though, was not a natural formation. When they neared it, less than fifty feet away, the first of its outer stones dislodged with a groan and tumbled heavily to the cavern floor, where the thud of their impact raised a cloud of dust.

The three runners stopped. Their flashlight beams probed the tower. It was still intact—but for how long?

Ironwood was wheezing, struggling to catch his breath.

"The explosions—they're coming in waves about every sixty seconds," David said.

Jess and Ironwood understood.

"Get ready . . ." David said. "Get ready . . ."

Four concussions, in the air and through the ground. The terrible, grating sound of more stone blocks being pushed out, cascading from the tower's side to strike the cavern's floor.

"Sixty seconds—go!" They rushed for the tower's doorway before the next bombs fell.

Even through the protective layers of his balaclava, his helmet, and the hood of his borrowed parka, Lyle's ears rang with the thunderclaps of each detonation.

Debris rained down as he pushed himself back to his feet, ready to continue his sprint until the next bombing run, back to the point of entry. He'd seen bodies near it when he'd brought Roz to the surface, even took a parka from one. He'd checked for survivors among the commandos, but there were none. No sign of the enemy combatants, either. He'd found a medic's pack and made the split-second decision to treat Roz and get her a safe distance away before searching for a radio. That was when he thought he still had more than an hour before the attack would begin.

The roar of engines grew again, and black shadows screamed across the sky. Lyle dropped for cover.

At least now the growing light of day was enough that he could identify the attackers. Lyle didn't need to see specific markings to know they were the Argentines' French-built Mirage 5s. Each could carry more than eight thousand pounds of ordnance, including two air-to-ground missiles and rapid-fire cannons. Even if anyone did escape the structure below, once the sun was up they'd be easy targets.

The next cluster of bombs was closer to the entry point.

Three more waves, and it would be over.

Lyle was on his feet and running.

Jess was faster and led the way. By the time she reached the upper third of the spiral staircase, she couldn't separate the thunder of their footsteps from the thunder of explosions.

Until she stopped abruptly and David slammed into her as the wall of the tower fell away, exposing the last few steps above her, leaving the staircase partially unsupported. A moment later, Ironwood reached them, puffing heavily. His flashlight beam joined theirs, shooting off into nothingness, catching only swirls of dust.

The final rumble of the explosions faded. "That's the last for this wave," David said. "Let's go!"

Ten steps to go. Jess put a foot on the next one, testing it before committing her full weight, then the next ones.

Five steps left. Jess slipped her flashlight into her parka and lifted both hands to grip the edge of the stone floor above her head. She pulled herself back into the round chamber they'd descended from. "Clear!" she called out.

Five steps from the top of the spiral staircase, David passed his flashlight to her, then took her outstretched hand and was up beside her.

Jess shone her flashlight into the opening as he called "Clear!" to Ironwood.

Five steps below, Ironwood handed up his books and flashlight, then placed both hands on the opening's edge to brace himself. He sighed, pulled back. "That's not going to work." He moved up another step. Then another. One more and he was able to put his hands on the edge again and hoist himself up until one knee was half on the chamber floor.

Then the next wave of explosions started and the staircase swayed, collapsing.

Ironwood's knee slipped, and he dropped with a grunt of shock, hands still gripping the cut stone of the opening.

Jess and David dropped their flashlights and each grabbed an arm and pulled on it to haul him back to safety. The big man's thick parka bunched against the opening's edge, making it even harder to draw him up. Caught in the crisscrossed beams of the flashlights on the upper floor, billows of dust from the fallen tower roiled up past Ironwood. Everyone began to cough.

"Swing your legs!" Jess strained to position her boots flat on the floor so they wouldn't slip. Ironwood swung himself side to side, but the closer his right boot came to hooking onto the edge of the floor, the more his arms slipped in Jess's and David's hands.

Another wave of bombs struck. The sound of falling stones from the passageways beyond the chamber escalated, the noise like a stampede of something wild about to overrun them.

David told Ironwood to start swinging his legs again, and this time do it as if he meant it!

Ironwood's answering grunt became a hacking cough, but he kicked his right leg higher, higher. David released his grip on Ironwood's arm and lunged, caught hold.

Ten seconds later, Ironwood was on the floor, wheezing, exhilarated by his close escape. "That was almost worth going to prison—almost."

Ten seconds more and Jess had them on their feet as the ripple of destruction spread and the underground site approached extinction.

As they rounded the corner by the first mural they'd discovered, David shone his flashlight ahead. Through a haze of dust he saw the rubble they'd landed on when they'd dropped down from the surface. The mound was larger now, and growing. More debris was falling from above.

Fifteen feet between the top of the mound and the crevasse opening overhead, thin rays of daylight spiked through. In that light, he saw—

"The rope's still there!"

They rushed for the pile of rocks and stones, scrambling up its sloping sides, sliding down two feet for every three gained. Just as they made the top and Jess grabbed the rope to pull on it, a blinding flash of light blazed down, accompanied by a deafening crash and a hail of rocks that struck them like a shotgun blast.

It was a minute, and another wave of bombs, farther off this time, before David's hearing recovered sufficiently that he heard Ironwood's labored coughing, his breath almost whistling. But David's first thought was for the rope. If it had been lost in that blast . . .

Jess had it. She'd wrapped it around her forearm and was testing it to see if it would hold her weight. It did.

David steadied the rope as Jess began to climb, hand over hand, up-ward, to the patch of sky.

"I surely can't make that climb, Dave." Ironwood stared up as they both watched Jess reach the surface, crawl out, and turn to shout for David to follow her.

"You don't have to." David released his grip on the rope and shucked off his gloves. "The agents lowered you down, we'll pull you up."

"Good man." Ironwood gripped his shoulder. "You remember what I told you we were going to do, the two of us, way back in that hotel?"

David did. "We're going to turn this world upside down."

"So what are you waiting for? Climb!"

David reached the top and swung his body out of the opening. His lungs had only an instant to register the burning change from cold to freezing air before he and Jess flattened to the ground as jets flashed by and the air shuddered with more explosions over a nearby ridge.

Jess's eyes were bright with unshed tears and despair. "They're bombing everything. There won't be a thing left down there. After all this time—"

David reached for her hand to comfort her. "We've got pictures, and Ironwood has books. This time there's evidence."

Jess was inconsolable. "It's not enough. It was the First Gods' temple." She twisted around to call down to Ironwood, jerked the rope to signal him. "Ready?"

His voice echoed back, unintelligible.

David peered down to see Ironwood kneeling on the mound of rocks, his parka off. "What're you doing?"

"The books go first." Ironwood stuffed the books into his parka and tied the makeshift bundle to the end of the rope. He gave Jess a thumbs-up. She hauled the parka to the surface and untied it quickly.

"Okay," David shouted down. "You're next."

He threw back the rope as the roar of approaching jets shook the sur-rounding rock. "Grab it!" David shouted.

But Ironwood cupped his hands to his mouth and called up as if he already knew what was about to happen.

Tell them, David! Change the world!

Then the next bomb hit and sound ceased to be sound and became something physical.

The impact slammed David and Jess back against the slope of hard rock and ice, and in a final, endless moment, David watched the ground around the opening shift, and then with terrifying speed it was sucked down, eras-ing all traces of the opening.

And all traces of Ironwood.

FIFTY-EIGHT

One after another, three jets streaked past, so low to the ground David could feel their wake, taste their fumes. Stung by flying rocks, he staggered across the unyielding terrain, disoriented by the blinding light and deafening noise, yet somehow beyond the hurt of cold or injury and the dreadful, senseless loss of Ironwood. All that mattered now was the camera's precious records. Ironwood's five gold books. And Jess.

She dragged him down one slope as bomb after bomb exploded close behind them. At the bottom of that slide, a large white rock stood up and ran for them.

It was Agent Lyle. He had a radio in one hand, and he dove at them both to force them down as a line of small explosions stitched the ground beside them.

"They've seen us!" he shouted. "Get to cover!" He pointed to a tall pile of rocks that offered protection on two sides, and they ran to it.

"Where's Ironwood?" Lyle asked. Jess shook her head. The agent's attention immediately turned back to the sky.

"Not good," he said.

Distant jets were banking, turning, coming back.

"This way." Lyle got to his feet and led them running past the rocks and—

Another jet. On approach from the opposite direction.

Lyle yelled, "Scatter!"

Then the *sky* exploded—not the ground.

What had once been a jet became a madly spinning fireball cartwheeling past them, spewing thick black smoke and flaming wreckage.

There was a second explosion. This time behind them. The death spiral of the second jet.

The air above them thundered as three more jets shot by.

This time, Lyle was on his feet and waving, shouting.

"Raptors! They're on our side!"

Later, in the protected hollow where Roz Marano dozed in thermal blankets, Lyle set up an emergency shelter from the commandos' supplies, cracked the chemical packs to heat their rations, and listened to the reassuring words of the captain of the *Roosevelt,* now less than a day away. Later, Jessica MacClary and David Weir showed him what had cost Ironwood his life.

Weir had carefully removed five small objects from his parka and set them on a blanket. They were books of gold. An embossed cross marked the top sheet of all but one book. That book bore the image of a face.

Lyle looked at Weir, then back to the book. "Huh," he said. "That almost looks like you." Then he looked at Jessica MacClary with even more interest, because his observation had caused her to put a hand on Weir's arm. A protective gesture.

"You're not going to believe what we found down there," David said.

Lyle looked again from David to the book.

"Probably not," he agreed, "but Roz will."

FIFTY-NINE

Deep in the cavern near the Colorado River, twelve women gathered, because that was the number the Talking God and the House God required to pray at the *tsenadjihih*. It was an ancient shrine, a table made of stone, three feet high, eight feet wide, and holding the Spider Woman's gifts. It had been moved many times for safety through the years, and now a wide, round kiva had been built around it, for protection. Coleman lamps lit the inside.

Each woman placed her hands on the object before her, each object cradled by a hollow indentation in the table, each object different, old and revered and many times repaired, and they chanted their prayer for good fortune on their journey.

Three of the objects were covered jars of fired clay. Their contents had been lost long ago, but the designs incised around them hinted at their purpose. One showed seeds planted in even furrows, and beside them tall grasslike plants growing in lines. Another showed a tree, a curl of bark, a figure on a litter holding the bark, and then a figure standing, robust. The third showed the jar itself, but as if it were transparent, so that inside the women could see it once held a central core and winglike filaments and was filled with liquid. Though none of them knew what that liquid was supposed to be.

Other objects were more easily recognizable. A model of a boat, with precise lines etched in it, as if to show its construction. A thin, hollow cylinder with inner ridges that once held disks of some type, and if the disks had been glass, then the cylinder was obviously a telescope. And a heavy stone of metal with one polished side on which a diagram of the sun and planets had been inscribed.

Then there were those simple objects whose purpose was unclear. A bundle of woven cord, a weight like a plumb bob, and a rod of metal marked with the same precise lines as were found on the boat. Another bundle of several small planks of wood joined by knotted cords, with the edges of the planks dotted with what could be, but might not be, random indentations, though each was identified by a carved figure, undecodable by the women. There was also a badly tarnished metal box, no larger than a hand, that held a collection of tiny gears.

Two objects were fired-clay cylinders in which stones and metal had been embedded, and which some women thought might be recipes. One cylinder had flint and a chunk of metal, so it seemed reasonable to conclude it was to show how fire could be made. The other cylinder was more puzzling. It held three stones with threads of metal ore, and a final small ingot of a different metal. The women assumed it took the first three ores to make the metal, but it was not their place to understand, only to preserve.

The final object was the most obvious in purpose, and the most precious: a collection of thin gold sheets, bound together like a book, on which the Spider Woman had written her words, though in symbols none today could read.

Someday, all the women knew, Spider Woman would come back to read those words to them again, and all would be understood. That she had promised.

Among the women who prayed today, Yazhi was the youngest, a new generation, and when the prayer was completed, she asked to speak.

Shimasani was eldest and gave her permission.

"Have you seen the news?" Yazhi was excited and nervous, all at the same time. "In Antarctica, they've found a *tsenadjihih*. Like this one!"

"I find that difficult to believe," Abequa said. "There are no people there."

"But there were, they say. They found bodies. Hundreds of them. Very old."

"You say the bodies were left there?" Chochmingwu asked.

Yazhi nodded urgently. This was so important. "All over the place."

"What people leave their dead like that?"

"Old-time people. They say they traveled across the whole world a long time ago and built *tsenadjihih* everywhere they went to teach the people that they met."

"What things did they teach?" Shimasani asked.

Yazhi gathered her courage. "The things we say the Spider Woman taught us."

"Yazhi, you are young. You know the White Man does a lot of confusing things to try to mix us up. I think this story is one of those things."

"But they had pictures. I saw them."

The older women spoke among themselves, and as far as they could tell, there was a simple explanation for what their youngest member had seen.

"Yazhi, there are people everywhere," Shimasani said. "Maybe different gods made them in different places. I don't know. But we were made here, and this is the land the Spider Woman gave us. And here on the *tsenadjihih* she made for us, these are the gifts she gave us, to protect and care for until she returns to us.

"We know this is true because this is what our mothers told us. And it's what their mothers told them. And their mothers and their mothers all the way back to when Spider Woman told the first mother. So that's what it is. And you shouldn't listen to what the White Man says."

Yazhi bowed her head, embarrassed for having questioned the truth. "I'm sorry. If . . . if you want me to leave the *Naakits'ladah*, then I will go."

Shimasani smiled for the young girl. "We all make mistakes. We're all the same. That's why the *tsenadjihih* is round."

Yazhi felt better. There was comfort in the place, knowing the secret things she knew, knowing the sacred trust she had accepted.

So for the rest of the day and into the night, the twelve women chanted all the verses of how the land was formed and the people made and all the other lessons taught by the Spider Woman.

In time, Yazhi would memorize the entire saga, and then add the stories of the twelve women gathered here today, so she could teach the verses to her daughter, who would teach them to her daughter, and on through the journey that would last until the Spider Woman returned to the people, as she had promised.

Still, Yazhi couldn't help wondering, why had the Spider Woman left in the first place?

And where had she come from?

SIXTY

"Homo antarcticensis," Colonel Kowinski said to David and Jess. "It's not official yet. Probably be a few more years and a lot more sequencing, but that's what they're calling them for now. It's an entirely new species, as different from modern humans as Neandertals."

They were standing in front of the glass wall that overlooked the sample preparation lab. In that sterile environment, two workers in masks and gowns delicately dissected one of the 432 bodies recovered from what the MacCleirigh Foundation had named the Ironwood-Palmer Site.

"The biggest anatomical difference so far?" Kowinski continued. "It's the brain. The Navy Medical Research Center's done MRIs. No corpus callosum. No cerebral hemispheres. It's just one undifferentiated lobe. Nothing like it in primates at all."

"Do they know what that would mean?" Jess asked.

"Not a clue. Other than there're a few more cubic inches of gray matter packed into their skulls, and communication between different areas of their brain was likely more direct, without hitting the bottleneck of the connecting tissue between hemispheres. Judging from what the archaeologists are pulling out of Palmer, the calculating machines with all their gears, the blueprints for their ships . . . I'd say the structure of their brains made them smart. Exceptionally smart."

"Couldn't be that smart," David said. "They're extinct."

"As a species, yes. Now that we've started examining their DNA, we can conclusively say they interbred with modern humans." She looked at David. "Maybe that's where we get our geniuses from."

"I hope not," David said. "Imagine being so smart you figure out how to thrive in Antarctica for the one brief window when it's actually possible. Then the climate swings back to normal and you're done. Maybe there's such a thing as being too smart."

Kowinski's eyebrows shot up. "So modern humans have managed to survive because we're stupid?"

Ironwood's missing all the fun, David thought. He'd have loved debating with the colonel. "There's got to be a reason, and that's as good as any."

David allowed a lab technician to take new cheek swabs and blood samples. It was the least he could do to make his apologies to the colonel, and to thank them for the medical protocols he was following.

Afterward, he and Jess waited in the entrance lobby of the building.

"You back to Zurich now?" he asked. He knew he would miss the intensity that had thrown them together and changed both their lives. He wondered if she felt the same. If so, she didn't say. It had taken her some time just to treat him as an ordinary person again. *Because of years of conditioning,* David thought. Beliefs that had to change now, even if human nature didn't.

"Zurich soon," Jess said. "There's a lot the Family has to talk about, and do. The Shop needs a new director. Su-Lin and Andrew are nowhere to be found. So that's three defenders who need to be replaced. Though, if the Promise has been fulfilled, it may be there's no need for the Twelve anymore." She broke off and frowned. "And there's still the mystery of whatever was on the tables in the temples."

David had been keeping up with that search. So far, based on the map he had photographed in Cornwall, five more outposts had been located in distant locations around the world, and confidence was high all the remaining ones would be found within the year. None so far had been found intact, though, even the most inaccessible ones. Which to David meant there could be another reason why the tables were empty and the artifacts gone.

"I don't think it is a mystery why the artifacts are missing," he said.

"Neither do I. Looters took them all."

"I agree they were taken, but not stolen."

Jess looked confused.

"I think the artifacts on the tables were *used,* Jess. The sun maps are like calendars, to save us from 'the confusion of days.' The maps showed our world and how to travel it. Who knows what other kinds of instruction books or manuals or models were on those tables? But I bet they showed people how to build things, how to plant crops, write . . . all those skills Ironwood told us about that . . . that kick-started civilization around the world all at the same time, even though . . ."

"Even though the First Gods had gone home to die?" Jess didn't look convinced.

David smiled. "Their knowledge survived. What more can any of us send on to the future?"

Jess wouldn't give in. "Our genes."

Neither would David. "With genetic drift, catastrophe, just plain bad luck, there're a lot of genetic dead ends, but knowledge survives. Your family and all that they've done through the generations is proof of that."

Jess was quiet for a moment. "You and I are going to be writing a new chapter of *Traditions*. New lessons for more than just the children." She banished whatever dark thought had momentarily clouded her features. "But, first things first. I'm off to Roswell, New Mexico."

She said "you and I." So she *was* planning to see him again—*but when?* Until he'd made her see reason, Jess believed she was his defender. Now David wished she still believed it. She wouldn't be leaving him two months before his twenty-seventh birthday. *So few days left.*

"Roswell?" he asked.

"Ironwood filed a new will his last day in Vanuatu. He left his entire collection of historical artifacts to me."

"The government isn't going to confiscate it?"

"Agent Lyle doesn't think so."

"What about the . . . other thing?"

"The other thing," Jess repeated. "The 'signature.' Right." The look on her face told him she was no happier about this part than he was.

"So you got the talk, too," he said. "Too many religious implications, which means political implications, so, until there's more evidence, *don't* mention the impossible ten-million-year-old map or the three-fingered inhuman hand."

"The map *is* imprecise, David. I've heard some experts say it's an artistic interpretation no more than ten thousand years old."

"Imprecise compared to what? Computer simulations of what the Earth looked like back then? Maybe the computers got it wrong."

"And there's only one of those handprints. No other sign of . . . whatever it might have been."

"No other sign, you mean, except for those grooves on the stone path in the cavern. Apparently, they match the size of the talons, fit the spaces between the sharp metal under that gold cross . . . You think maybe that's how my ancestors—your First Gods—jump-started their own civilization so quickly? They reached Antarctica, checked out the caves for shelter, found the library of golden books some other even earlier civilization had left, and then spread it around the world?"

"It's going to be a long time till Antarctica's ice-free again. We'll probably never know the answer." Jess fell silent, then looked up at him. "What about the treatments?"

"I'm not dead yet." Time slowed for David as he saw her pale.

"What do the doctors say?"

"I'm in perfect health, but some of my anomalies are in gene regions that may be involved in sudden cardiac death."

"Oh, David . . ."

"No. That's a good thing. It's what I hoped for. A direction. Something to try." He smiled. "It's knowledge."

"What can they do?"

David shrugged. "I'm on a raft of drugs. Sunday night I check into Walter Reed to get a pacemaker. If my heart acts up, I'll be okay. And if that is what kept everyone else from reaching twenty-seven, then I'm going to be fine."

"I don't like all those ifs," Jess said.

"Not knowing just makes me like everyone else."

A Maybach drove up to the main doors.

"Willem's here . . ." Jess looked at David, and time stopped for both of them.

She reached up, touched his face. "I've spent all my life waiting for you. You'd better wait for me."

"Twelve Winds of the world, Jess."

Jess understood. She touched the silver cross he always wore now. "No one ever knows . . ."

Yet in that moment, both did know one thing for a certainty: However long their journey would be, it wasn't over yet.

CORNWALL 7,312 YEARS B.C.E.

CORNWALL 7,322 YEARS B.C.E.

HAVI ATOLL 7,418 YEARS B.C.E.

MALTA 7,567 YEARS B.C.E.

PATAGONIA 7,794 YEARS B.C.E.

ANTARCTICA 7,794 YEARS B.C.E.

ANTARCTICA 10,800 YEARS B.C.E.

On the twenty-first day of their journey they saw it, just as the sun slipped into the terrible waves and darkness claimed the raft and the seventeen who clung to it. A shimmer of difference at the distant edge of the endless sea. Not the frothing white of the cresting waves that relentlessly attacked them, sweeping them up in huge surges, driving them down in blinding, stinging agonies. Instead, an arc of white that remained still and untroubled.

Land.

That glimpse gave them hope as they rode the waves and the night.

The wind sliced through the salt-spray-stiffened hides they wore, even as the seventeen huddled to conserve what little body warmth they had remaining.

The last of the fish had been eaten seven days ago. The gourds of water from the last icy downpour had been empty for three. The bright-eyed seabirds that glided so slowly and so tantalizingly near, their lace-feathered wingtips only a handsbreadth from the heaving surface of the waves, never came within reach.

The raft-riders fought the near-overwhelming urge to gnaw at the tendon and leather bindings that held together their mat of resin-sealed bamboo and woven vine. When the sun broke free from the sea again, only sixteen were alive to feel its warmth.

No one had seen Stonecutter slip from the raft. If he cried out in despair or release, no one had heard him. All on the raft were his kin, but none mourned. Death was the way of things.

Netweaver was youngest now. Fourteen years old. Both her children were lost in the first days, after the storm swept the raft from the shoreline of home. On the fourth day, her boy was thrown off by a wave and never resurfaced. On the sixth day, her girl, not yet a year old, didn't awaken, her once black skin ashen. The young mother held her daughter close for two more days before Firemaker slid the small, still body into the green depths.

But all the others on the raft were her kin as well, and now, for them, Netweaver used her young eyes to stare through the slowly brightening haze of dawn. The white was there, larger, closer. The random, capricious wind that had lifted them from one shore was taking them to another.

At her side, Carver, the oldest, almost twenty, stoically kept his apprehension to himself. He had journeyed up the mountains of home and understood what white meant. Making landfall on ice and snow was no better than remaining adrift on open ocean. Either alternative meant death within days.

The wind picked up as the morning passed, and, in the stark blue sky, thick clouds tumbled into billowing towers, darkening with rain above the new shore.

Netweaver forced her cracked, stiff hands from the palm-fiber rope that bound her to safety, and fought exhaustion to rise unsteadily to her feet. Others near her braced her legs on the slippery bamboo deck so she could see just that small bit farther as the raft creaked at the crest of the next wave.

She held her arms out for balance, gasping as the raft slid down the next trough, then leaned sharply forward as the raft careened up the next wave. There, at the top, for just a heartbeat, just a moment, she saw something more than white.

There was green as well, sweeping down from distant mountains to the nearing shore.

Carver listened to what Netweaver shouted to him over the roar of wind and water. With the help of the others, he stood beside her, to see for himself.

She was right. There was more than ice ahead, and the raft was closing quickly.

More hours later, as the twenty-second day of the journey ended, they were soaked anew in the plumes of spray from wild waves crashing against sharp black rocks. Past that barrier, they could see a crescent of dense trees framing wide stretches of waving grasses.

Green.

The raft held together almost long enough.

A hundred meters from the black stone beach, a corner of the raft snagged on a jagged boulder. The bindings tore, and the bamboo floats under the back half burst free like fish leaping into the air.

Netweaver and the rest scrambled and slid to the intact end of the raft as Trapper and two others were swept away. Before anything else could be done, another wave slammed down on the floundering raft and burst it apart completely.

Twelve of them made it to the black beach that day. Crawling, gasping, cut and gouged flesh stinging with salt. Twelve of twenty-three.

Firemaker and two others didn't pause but searched through the stones, collected driftwood, finding the raw materials of their trade, of survival.

Carver and Netweaver crawled to the top of a small rise to reach the first clumps of tall grass, chewing on the blades for moisture.

A growling sound stopped them. Fur seals crouched among the grassy hassocks. The pups snarled to defend their territory, aggressive though barely whelped. Carver bared his teeth in a smile. The sleek sea creatures were easy prey on land, and the beach rocks would make good projectiles. The twelve would eat tonight, with or without fire.

For tomorrow, though, Carver found a new reason to be apprehensive.

He saw a ruddy mass of antelope nearby, as many as the fingers on both hands. Netweaver was excited to see them. She knew that with a few days to hone rocks and fashion spears, the twelve could use the antelope for nourishment and tools and warmer skins.

But Carver, older and wiser, noted how the herd stopped its grazing to scent the air, then followed the wind to see the newcomers on the rise above the beach.

The antelope halted.

To Carver, their reaction could mean only one thing. He and his kin were not the first hunters to come to this land. There were new dangers ahead.

That night, around the fire that blazed on the beach, their stomachs full for the first time in weeks, the twelve formed a circle beneath the dazzling austral stars.

Carver scratched lines in a flat rock, showing that the twelve who had survived had made their circle here, and he told his kin what they already knew, because the truth of it was so deeply written in their genes, the truth that had compelled them to build their raft and see what lay beyond the horizon of their home.

They would rest here for now, Carver told them, to gather their strength and learn what they could about this new place. But they would not stay long. There was so much more to see. So much more to do.

All they could know with any certainty, was that however long their journey would be, it wasn't over yet.

ACKNOWLEDGMENTS

At Thomas Dunne, our heartfelt thanks go to our editor, Pete Wolverton, who was the first to hear this story, and who asked all the right questions at all the right times as we wrote it. Thanks, too, to Elizabeth Byrne, for so deftly keeping things organized and moving.

We are also grateful to the entire team that worked with such care and enthusiasm to transform our story from a stack of mundane pages into this handsome volume, including Jonathan Bennett, designer; Bob Berkel, production editor; and India Cooper, copy editor. Many thanks to all.

We're fortunate to have had the support of two fine agents for this book's journey from manuscript to printed page (physical and digital). Marty Shapiro has been with us since *Icefire,* and got this project started. Mel Berger has ably picked up the torch and brought the project home. Our thanks and deep appreciation to both.

Finally, thank you to John Ordover, who was the enthusiastic editor who opened new doors for our writing many books ago, and who remains a trusted first reader who always offers new insights that make our work richer.

Usually in our acknowledgments, we comment on some of the concepts and technologies that helped shape a particular story so those readers who wish to explore certain subjects in more depth have a place to start. For this story, though, those comments could fill a second book, so we invite those who are interested to visit us at www.reeves-stevens.com to read much lengthier comments.

J&G Reeves-Stevens
Los Angeles–Victoria, April 2010